HUNTER'S KISS

RUTHLESS GODS: WOLF GOD, BOOK 2

VERONICA DOUGLAS

DREAMSPIRE
ORACLE'S TEMPLE
THE FORT
REALM OF THE UNDYING COURT
SACRED GLADE
SARION'S PORTAL
SHIFTER VILLAGE
DEAD FOREST
FROSTFALL
DEAD FOREST
MIST SEAS
SHADOWSTONE
THE 3 PYLONS
SOUTHERN ROAD TO AUREN'S DOMAIN
THE WOLF GOD'S REALM IN THE DREAMLANDS

OUR STORY SO FAR...

In case you need a refresher...

The **Dark Wolf God** was a monster dwelling in the space between nightmare and legend. A thousand years ago, he raised an army of shifters to wipe out humanity and restore the world to wilderness—but before he could strike, the **Moon Goddess** trapped him in the Dreamlands within a shimmering prison of light. The Dark God raged against his prison walls but could not break through. Yet, as the centuries passed, the spells weakened and eventually a prophecy set him free.

To protect **Magic Side** from the Dark God's wrath, our heroine Samantha Bennet and her packmates took a desperate stand against him. Guided by the Moon Goddess, they entered the Dreamlands to renew the spells of his prison using her magic. The Dark God attacked, but Samantha drew on the Moon's power to curse and temporarily trap him. In retaliation, the Dark God seized control of Sam's best friend, and forced her to tear out Sam's throat.

Samantha died in that moment—but **the Fates** weren't done with her yet. They met her in the place between life and death and offered her a bargain. When the Moon Goddess brought

Sam back to life, she couldn't clearly remember what the Fates had said or the deal she'd made.

Although the Dark God destroyed much of Magic Side and killed many of her packmates, he was defeated and imprisoned again at last (*you can read more about these events in Wolf Bound, book 4: Shadow Kissed*).

At the beginning of *Wolf God*, Sam escaped the wreckage of her home and visited her sick mother in **Deerhaven**. While there, she was approached by **Sarion**, an emissary of the queen of the Fae who wanted Sam's help to defeat the Dark God once and for all. But before Sam could meet the queen, the Dark God captured and imprisoned her in his fortress at **Shadowstone**.

The Dark God believed she had the power to cure the curse that she'd given him, but to his frustration, she had no magical powers of her own and was determined to resist him. After days locked in a cave, Sam agreed to try healing him in exchange for her freedom.

Sam quickly discovered that she had magical talents and that little in the Dreamlands was as it seemed at first. The fae weren't innocent victims, but waging a war against the Dark God by killing shifters and infesting his realm with vines that leeched the life from his land. The queen even sent assassins to hunt Samantha down.

Sam also began to see another side of the Dark God: that of a ruthless protecter. She earned his gratitude by saving three werefoxes from **Frostfall**, and the Dark God saved her life in return. She began to think of him as *Cadean*, and they shared an intimate moment—but it was not to last.

Sam witnessed him destroying a fae village (after he shifted the walls of his prison with an artifact called the **moonshard**) and learned that she was half-fae herself. No longer trusting anything he said, she spied on him and learned he had no intention of ever letting her go, and that if she healed him, he would use the moonshard to annihilate all the fae villages along the border.

Determined to protect the innocent people on both sides of the border, Sam drugged the Dark God and stole the moonshard. She healed him, then fled with the help of **his brother, Auren.** The Dark God tried to stop her at the border, but she stabbed him in the chest with the moonshard and used her newfound magic to turn the shimmering walls of his prison to crystal.

They escaped to Auren's palace, but Sam could still feel Cadean watching her intently from the shadows. He was a beast capable of compassionless brutality, but she could also see the noble protector in him and wondered...was there a chance that he could be redeemed?

And that is where this story begins.

1

The Border of the Dark Wolf God's Realm

Samantha

I ducked beneath the drooping bough of an ancient tree as my horse picked its way along the hillside. Fiery orange leaves drifted downward as I brushed by, becoming bright explosions of color atop the silver moss that covered the rocky slope. The scents of maple and fir wafted around us, and my wolf stirred in my chest, eager to shift and explore the unfamiliar woods.

Tomorrow, I told her. *Today is about taming the wall.*

I'd been trapped in the Dreamlands for nearly six weeks, and yet, I still hadn't gotten used to the eerie way the trees and landscape changed slightly whenever I looked away. It was never anything significant, just an extra branch here and there, brighter leaves, or a tree that was a different species than I remembered.

They were subtle, but the changes were there. Nothing in the Dreamlands was ever quite what it seemed. Not even me.

Back in the waking world, I'd only ever been Sam the bartender. But in the Dreamlands, I'd discovered that I had hidden magic and that my past had been a lie. I wasn't just a shifter but half fae—a part of me I never knew existed, and that I barely understood.

My horse nickered and shied away from Auren as he brought his griffstrider alongside my mount. Half falcon, half horse, the griffstrider was a shoulder higher than my mare and had a razor-sharp beak that could crush skulls like millet. I didn't blame my poor mare for being skittish around the beast, especially since the strider eyed her like she was tomorrow's breakfast.

Auren kept looking at me the same way: hungrily.

A soft glow radiated from him as if he were siphoning the last rays of the sun. In contrast with Cadean's rugged looks, Auren had painfully elegant features and a flawless wave of blond hair that glinted in the fading light. He couldn't be more different than his brother, the Dark Wolf God.

But I wasn't fooled by his face or his apparent friendship. He'd helped me escape the Dark Wolf God's clutches, but he had his own inscrutable agenda, and I was certain he was just as perilous as his brother.

The corners of Auren's mouth twitched up, as if he were reading my thoughts. "Feeling nervous?"

"No," I lied.

He gave a soft, skeptical laugh and leaned back in the saddle. "Well, that makes one of us. Frankly, I don't like being this close to the barrier. My brother is out there somewhere, planning his revenge."

"Let's hope not."

I offered the Moon Mother a quick prayer of thanks for the wall of light that encircled the Dark Wolf God's realm. It was the only thing that kept the beast from charging across the border and taking me back.

The thought of the Dark God drew my gaze past the Moon's luminescent barrier to the murky forests beyond. Was he lurking in the shadows and the mist? Or was he pacing the halls of Shadowstone, his citadel? I could just make out the glint of its white, claw-like towers on the horizon, like Venus rising above the fog.

A shudder of trepidation shook me, and I tightened my grip on the reins. "I'm pretty sure I'd feel it if he were out there."

The golden god raised an eyebrow, and a glint of amusement returned to his face. "Would you, now?"

"I'm unlikely to forget what it feels like to be close to a monster like that."

The smile faded from his eyes. "I expect not."

The truth was, I'd escaped the Dark Wolf God, but I couldn't escape his presence. When Auren wasn't around, it often felt like there was a fragment of the Dark God hovering at the edges of sensation, pulling me back toward the wall. I'd felt him watching me from the shadows. He never revealed himself or spoke, but I knew he was there.

I'd started telling every shadow to *fuck off* out of habit, and I was sure my handmaids were beginning to wonder if I was deranged.

"Don't underestimate my brother. He knows you're with me, and there is nothing he won't do to get you back. He's a hunter, and he won't stop until he's caught you and dragged you to his lair."

A shiver of terror skated down my spine. It felt a little too close to delight for my own comfort.

"I know. That's why I need to find a way to lock him away for good." I spurred my horse toward the wall.

Before we'd made it ten strides, Auren pulled alongside me and seized the reins, drawing my mare to a halt. "On that note, this is close enough. Too close, in my estimation."

"*You* told me that if I could learn to control the wall, I could change the course of the war between your brother and the fae.

If I'm going to learn to manipulate it, then *I need to be near the wall*. This is important."

My throat tightened as I thought of Selene and Sigrun back in the Frostfall, and of all the decimated villages on both sides of the border, fae and shifter alike. I belonged to both people, and to none.

Auren dismounted. "Fine. But you'll start by practicing from a safe distance—from here."

I opened my mouth to object, but the signature of his magic swirled around me. It was like wind racing over a field of wheat and the echo of swords clanging against shields. I fought the press of his power, but my shoulders soon relaxed, and I compliantly slipped out of the saddle. "On second thought, you're probably right."

A doubt tugged at my mind, as if somewhere along the way, I'd lost my train of thought, but I shook it off.

The barrier drew my gaze upward. It was a masterpiece of magic, like a reversed waterfall of light streaming into the sky. Even at a distance, the raw power of the wall was overwhelming —cool and warm, foreign and familiar all at once.

I couldn't help feeling that its magic was calling to me.

A lump formed in my throat. I knew I didn't matter an ounce in the schemes of the Fates, yet I felt that if I could just reach out and touch a sliver of that power, if I could shape it, then maybe I could take control of my life.

Determination welling in my heart, I opened the satchel that held the moonshard, the bladelike fragment of the pylons that powered the Dark God's prison. He'd used the shard to manipulate the barrier, and somehow, I was able to do the same.

As soon as I wrapped my fingers around it, the moonshard's magic raced up my arm like a thousand tiny pinpricks—the tingly feeling you get when you've fallen asleep on an arm or leg right before it goes numb. A soft susurrus rose on the wind like the whispers of ghosts. *Release us, and we will release you. Heal us, and we will heal you.*

I sucked in a sharp breath. The voices shouldn't have surprised me. The ethereal whispers always came when I touched the Moon's magic, but I had no idea to whom they belonged or what they meant.

"Everything okay?" Auren asked.

"It's nothing." I raised the moonshard and glanced at him. "I'm just not entirely sure how to do this."

Golden light swirled around his fingers. "Magic is about willpower. See the shape of the wall in your mind and bend it to your will. Force it to harden and take the form you want, like you did before."

Reaching for the Moon's magic, I focused on the wall, trying to remember what it had felt like to control the barrier when I'd stopped the Dark God from crossing two weeks before. I pushed with every inch of my soul, straining until my muscles felt like jelly and my arms started shaking. Finally, I dropped my arm with a disappointed laugh. "I'm afraid I have no idea what I'm doing."

Auren's mouth turned down in disapproval. "I've seen you do it. You held back my brother, for fates' sake. You have it in you. Try *harder*."

His magic swirled around me, and some of my exhaustion faded away.

I tightened my grasp on the moonshard and thrust it like a knife at the wall, pouring all my frustration through it, trying to shape the barrier to my will. I pushed until my body quaked and aches reverberated through my limbs.

When I couldn't take it any longer, I threw my head back with a snarl. "Fuck this!"

The corner of the golden god's mouth ticked up. "Well, B-plus for effort, but I'm afraid you have a long way to go. Let's call it a day. I don't want to be this close to the wall longer than we need to."

I flexed my hand. Sure, I got pissed and lashed out at things, but I wasn't a quitter. Glaring at the wall, I raised the moonshard again. "I'm going to master this even if it kills me."

Auren stepped behind me and placed his hands on my shoulders. "Then focus."

Every muscle in my body tensed, and my heartbeat raced. His touch was light but intimate in a way it had never been before.

Too intimate. While my skin had welcomed the Dark God's touch even though I hated him, with Auren, it was the opposite. It made me feel like his dirty plaything.

I opened my mouth to protest but stopped. The taste of bitter chocolate formed on my tongue, and I caught the sudden scent of wildfire. The scar on my arm began to tingle, and my blood turned cold.

Cadean.

I didn't even have a chance to move.

A savage gust of wind ripped through the forest around us. The trees bent and twisted, then shuddered to life, animated by his magic. I shouted as the branches of a weathered maple lashed out, clawing at me like the hands of some great beast. Beyond the barrier, the sky went black, and shadows consumed the forest.

Auren wrenched his sword from its sheath and hacked through a thick limb with a single explosive stroke, sending shards of bark and wood flying. As branches lashed the air, he pivoted around me and cut through each as easily as if it was made of flesh and bone. "Get to your horse and ride!"

I turned to saddle up, but my horse had already bolted.

Two bright eyes appeared in the deep darkness beyond the

wall like twin flares in the dead of night. Then the Dark Wolf God emerged like a warrior stepping out of legend.

His hair was braided back, and his muscles shifted with every stride. I couldn't run or think or even breathe.

And then it was too late.

The ground shuddered, and roots burst up through the soil around me. I cried out and stumbled to my knees. A cruel smile traced across the Dark God's lips as the roots tightened around my ankles. My throat clenched, and I could imagine the cold metal of his collar about my neck once again.

I would not be taken.

Fury cascaded through me—fury, and something more. At first, it was fire racing through my veins, but then I was drowning in a sea of sunlight and icy water. I choked on a rush of wild power that I didn't understand and could barely control.

I ripped my hand free of the roots and thrust it toward the wall. Silver light streamed from my palm and spread like whirlpools, and everywhere the light touched, the luminescent barrier crystallized into glass.

In a single breath, the raging wind died, and the trees stilled.

The Dark God roared, and a wave of power shook the earth, but the wall stood in defiance. His magic couldn't pass through.

Elation filled me even as I dropped to the ground in exhaustion. *Holy fuck, Sam, you did it.*

Auren grasped my arm and hauled me to my feet. "Let's get out of here."

The Dark God's voice reverberated through the wall like deep drums in the distance. "I always knew you would betray me, Brother."

Auren sneered. "And I always knew you were a poor sport. She chose me, Cade. Get over it and move on."

The Dark God's fists tightened while his expression shifted

from anger to something deeper and even more primal. Shadows curled around his arms, and the trees behind him ripped themselves free of the earth one by one.

Was he jealous? Impossible.

I yanked my hand free of Auren's grasp. "I didn't choose either of you assholes."

The golden god nodded to his griffstrider. "We can debate the semantics of your situation another time. And while I'm impressed you can hold my feral excuse for a brother at bay, we should get out of here before his presence becomes even more taxing."

Auren's magic rose around me, tendrils of coercion pressing me to comply. But with the strength of the Moon's magic still raging in my chest, I pushed back against his power. "I'm not leaving before I have my say. I can hold him back."

The confidence in my own voice surprised me.

The corners of the Dark God's lips curled up in a smile that lit a fire low in my belly. "Can you, now?"

His power suddenly surged against mine. Beads of sweat chilled my brow, and every muscle burned as I strained to keep control of the barrier. I felt like a sapling holding up the weight of a giant falling oak.

My claws extended, my wolf railing to be released as I took three steps toward the barrier separating us. "Leave me alone," I snarled. "You will never take me again."

A tornado of branches and leaves churned the air behind the Dark God, blotting out the forest and the sky. He seemed impervious to the cataclysm whirling around him, but I knew from the deep lines on his face that it was agony for him to stand so close to the barrier and the Moon's magic.

I should've run, but his gaze drew me forward with a treacherous, magnetic pull. Although the barrier separated us, I could still feel him, still taste him on my lips, and it made that familiar, wicked heat pool at my center.

Anger and dread fought for control of my thoughts, but they were just a mask. Beneath them, I struggled against something far worse: need.

My fangs erupted as I struggled to restrain the wolf raging inside of me. "We had a deal: I heal you, and I go free. You're healed, and I'm free, and I'm going to stay that way. The deal's done."

The Dark God's fingertips grazed the new white scar on his chest where I'd stabbed him with the moonshard. "Not completely healed."

Then his gaze dropped to the moonshard in my hand. "And you still have something that belongs to me, little wolf. I'm not inclined to let that theft go."

"The moonshard doesn't belong to you. It belongs to the Moon and to your prison. You're not getting it back."

The Dark Wolf God's eyes flashed with rage, and he slammed his hands against the barrier. A wave of power thrust against me, and it was all I could do to maintain control.

I shoved back with every last ounce of strength I had. A burst of magic rippled through me, and lightning sparked around his hands. He leapt back, eyes wide with surprise for just an instant.

My satisfaction was short lived. Exhaustion tugged at me, and I knew that the flare of power had cost me almost all my reserves. I needed to get to safety before the barrier dropped for good.

2

Cadean

The Moon's magic was like a waterfall of fire, searing my skin and drowning my ability to think and reason with pain. Yet it was the wound Samantha had left in my chest that burned brightest, strangling me with every heartbeat.

I released a low growl as the infernal woman gave me one last look, and then walked away.

I couldn't help but notice how her dress hugged the curves of her body or how the dying wind played with the sun-kissed strands of hair that had torn free from her braid.

She was mesmerizing, the most beautiful creature I'd ever laid eyes on. I couldn't let her get away. Not into the arms of my brother, and not with the moonshard. I needed her even more than I needed it, but what would make her listen after everything I'd done?

I pushed myself another step closer to the burning barrier. "Samantha...please. Help me protect my people."

She stopped short but didn't turn around.

As much as the Moon's magic tormented my senses and filled me with rage, I forced myself to keep my voice calm and level. "The fae have increased their attacks, and my people are suffering. Return the moonshard to me. I can't defend my lands without it."

When she looked back, the disappointment in her eyes cut me to the core. "I wish I could believe that, but I've seen how you use the moonshard to kill and spread desolation beyond the wall. I'll never give it back."

"I *need* to retaliate," I snarled, my patience giving out. "If I don't, the fae will keep draining the life from my land and killing with impunity. There will only be dead forests and burned-out villages left when they're done. Retaliation is the *only* thing the fae understand."

The tornado I'd gathered around me intensified, breaking branches and even uprooting trees.

Auren shouted for Samantha to go, but she ignored him and started striding back toward me. "Is it? You've been fighting them for centuries. What's changed? What good did you do?"

The venom in her words was almost as painful as the truth. Battle after battle, village after village, they hadn't stopped, and neither had I.

"You need to find another way, Cadean."

Auren brought his griffstrider between us, cutting us off. White-hot hatred flared in my chest as the treacherous bastard reached down to pull her up. I slammed the storm against the wall, and Samantha stumbled as our magic collided.

She couldn't defy me much longer.

Auren seized her arm and yanked her into the saddle behind him, then swung the strider around and galloped into the woods.

As soon as Samantha moved beyond sight, the crystalline barrier began to crack. I roared in frustration and drove my shoulder into the wall, along with the full force of my storm. The barrier shattered and dissolved, returning to a wall of light.

The storm of my magic exploded into Auren's realm, tearing through the forest and yanking stones and trees from the earth.

As soft as moonlight or as hard as diamond, the state of the wall didn't matter—I couldn't cross. The little thief was out of my grasp and gone once again.

I stalked back through the woods to where I'd left Melanthe and our griffstriders. The pain of the Moon's magic faded with each step, but the relief didn't balance out losing her to *him*.

Mel was waiting in a clearing a quarter mile back, arms crossed and leaning against the trunk of an old leafless maple. The blood sorceress gave me a mournful smile. "That went well."

I glared at her.

Her purple dress and raven hair whipped in the dying wind as she pushed off the trunk. "I thought the plan was to watch and wait and *negotiate* if you had a chance. I don't remember discussing you calling down a *tornado*."

My shoulders tensed, and shadow magic coiled around my arms like vipers formed from smoke. "That asshole put his hands on her like he was planning to *fuck* her. I could see it in his eyes. If I ever get free, I'm going to ram my claws through his chest and rip out his heart, even if I have to tear the Dreamlands apart to do it."

"That seems a little bold, even for your brother."

"He's playing games with her, but the fool has no idea how valuable she is."

Mel raised her brows. "If he begins to suspect that she might be your mate—"

"She's not," I snapped, cutting that line of argument short. "The Fates are wicked, but they'd never cross that line again."

History had shown that the only thing that came from the bond between a god and a mortal was two shattered souls: one trapped for eternity in the land of the dead, the other condemned to eons of despair.

And yet, as impossible as it seemed, for a time, I'd almost believed Mel's theory.

The fucking power *that woman* held over me was staggering. Whenever she'd been in the same room with me, I hadn't been able take my eyes or mind off her. And now that she was gone, she haunted my waking thoughts. Sometimes, I imagined I could still feel the soft touch of her lips against mine or taste the sweet nectar of her body.

It was infatuation or madness, but it wasn't the mate bond.

Old-fashioned desire had led plenty of gods to ruin, and it seemed that I was no different. In the end, she'd drugged me, stolen my only means of freedom, and stabbed me in the heart with it.

No, Samantha Bennet was not my mate—she'd simply been sent by the Fates to drive me to the brink of insanity.

Mel brought our griffstriders over, and I patted Vega's neck. "It's not a mate bond, I'm certain of it. It has to be the Moon's magic. When the Moon brought her back from the dead, she must have infused Samantha with a fragment of her power. It's why the little vixen could cast the curse on me in the first place, and why she could heal it."

"That doesn't explain your bond—"

"That *wall* is the bond we share." I swung into the saddle. "It grants her power, just as it traps me here."

Mel mounted up on Elowyn, and I furrowed my brow. She always rode Dawnfire. Why had I selected Elowyn for this ride? Had there ever been a real chance that Samantha would return with me willingly?

I glanced back at the shimmering barrier of light behind us.

"You should've seen her today. She was breathtaking. She's getting more powerful every day, powerful enough to stand up to a god—that's divine magic, not fae. The Moon's magic."

Melanthe pursed her lips as her expression darkened. "If you're correct, she's in grave danger. Mortals aren't meant to wield that kind of magic."

Dread settled over me like a cloud blotting out the sun. "I know."

I spurred Vega to a canter, hoping the ride would clear my mind.

Vega charged into the trees, driving over fallen trunks and narrow streams. I tried to settle into the cadence of the ride, but instead, my thoughts kept returning to *her*. To the times we'd ridden together. I could almost feel the warmth of her back pressed up against me and catch the scent of her hair and skin. I couldn't forget the way her hips rose and fell and how, despite her attempts to resist, our movements had synchronized as we rode.

Now, she was riding alongside my brother in the same fucking way.

I tightened my fists around the reins and spurred Vega to run faster. He could no longer avoid the limbs and brush, so I thrust my magic ahead to bend the forest out of our way.

"Slow down!" Mel shouted over the thunder of hooves. As she pulled up alongside us, she demanded, "Are you trying to kill me or just our mounts?"

I reined in Vega until he slowed to a canter again, and Mel matched our pace.

"How the hell am I going to get her back?" I asked. "My bastard brother barely lets her out of his sight, and he sure as hell won't let her go near the wall after this."

"Easy, Cade," she cautioned. "We'll find a way. I don't like the idea of her being with him any more than you do."

"I'm out of solutions," I growled. "Auren will annihilate any wolves I send over the border. Kassian is locked up, too, so I don't have access to his spies. What am I supposed to do, summon a fucking Noctith demon?"

They were colossal living nightmares, capable of tearing holes in the fabric of the Dreamlands themselves. But if summoning went wrong, it would create an aberration that could destroy the heart of my realm.

"Don't be insane." Mel swung Elowyn around to cut me off, and I pulled Vega to a halt. "Abduction shouldn't be plan A. Samantha doesn't deserve that, and she'd fight you with every ounce of her will. You need to find another way."

That was what Samantha had said at the barrier.

I released a low rumble of frustration. "Auren has shielded his palace with spells that block my magic, so I can't shadow-cast to her, either. I'm blocked every which way I turn."

Normally, my ability to shadow-cast allowed me to peer through shadows as if they were windows. But it was different with Samantha, almost like I was with her—I couldn't touch anything because I wasn't physically there, but she could see me and speak with me.

It would have been the perfect way to communicate, to make my case without the maddening presence of the wall—except for Auren's wards.

Mel pursed her lips. "I thought you'd seen glimpses of her in the palace."

I spurred Vega forward once more, and we continued at a slow canter. "I've seen fragments. When Auren is nearby, it's impossible. And when he's gone, it's like peering through murky water."

Mel nodded. "That means there's hope. Auren's wards might be strong, but glimpses mean they're not impenetrable. I'll try to create a spell to boost your ability to shadow-cast. Perhaps your bond with her will help as well."

I ignored the mention of the bond. "I'll try anything at this point. What do I need to do?"

Mel had closed her eyes and rubbed her forehead, and I knew better than to disturb her.

We rode on in silence for a long while, until finally, she looked up. "Bring me the elements of your realm—earth, water, life, light, and blood. I'll prepare the spell, but *you* need to find the right words. You can't risk driving her further away."

My grip tightened on the reins. "Everything I do, everything I say, everything about me only makes her hate me more."

Mel gave me a stern look. "There was a time when it didn't. Find the right words, Cade. Fix this."

3

____

Samantha

The raging windstorm faded the further we rode from the wall, but the sound of the Dark God's roar stayed with me, twisting my heart. I pressed my eyes closed, but the vision of him was still there, lurking in the darkness of my mind—furious, relentless, and in pain. I could hardly bear it.

Why the hell did I feel anything other than hatred for him?

I let my gaze drift over the passing trees. In my heart, I knew he was more than a monster. I'd seen him lay waste to fae villages, but I'd also seen the protector who'd fought to defend his people, who'd fought to protect me.

That was the man I'd kissed. Not the Dark God, not the destroyer or my captor, but that sliver of him that was good—that was the god I'd healed. *Cadean.*

I glanced back at the abating storm and the ruined forest it had left in its wake. *Perhaps healing him was a mistake.*

Auren briefly looked over his shoulder at me. "Are you all right, my dear?"

"I feel like a wrung-out dishcloth."

"I'm not surprised. You stood up to a god today. To say that I am impressed would be an understatement."

I shifted uncomfortably behind him. "I got lucky and barely survived it."

"Perhaps, but you called your magic and held a divine being at bay—there aren't many who can do that, let alone shifters."

I sucked in a deep breath. I *had* faced down a god, and somehow, I'd won. It was the third time I'd challenged him and the third time I'd stood my ground. That was something.

We headed into a thick bank of mist, one of the seams that divided the separate patches of the Dreamlands. Even after months in that realm, I still wasn't used to traveling through them. The paths were unclear, and the features around us were always changing and shifting. I was never certain where we were going to emerge on the other side or what kind of landscape it would be.

"How do you find your way?" I asked, pitching my voice low so as not to disturb whatever creatures haunted the fog.

"Cadean and I forged these lands together. We both know the mistways by heart. Most of the people in our lands use guides and cross at known passes. To venture off the path is to step into madness."

The clinging mist thickened until the ground was nearly invisible, and I shivered as the damp chill bit through the long coat that Auren's handmaids had forced me to wear. It wasn't as warm as the one Cadean had given me, and for an instant, I regretted losing it, along with the earthy scent of *him* that had lingered on the fabric. Why had it given me such a feeling of comfort? I was far safer with Auren.

Safe, but never truly safe. He had his own agenda.

"You keep risking your brother's wrath to help me. Why?"

Auren released a strained laugh. "Well, you put me in a

tough position, and I had to make a choice: either hand you over to my brother or take you with me."

"So why not turn me over? Aren't you allies?"

"Only to a point. We've had millennia to fight and millennia to work together. Fighting comes more easily. It's what siblings do."

"You two are nothing alike," I muttered, frustrated at myself for allowing the Dark God to invade my thoughts yet again.

Auren scoffed. "We're not. Shifters take human and animal form, and as shifter gods, we each embody one aspect more strongly than the other. While I tend to live a civilized existence, Cadean indulges the feral, animalistic side of his nature. It's not really his fault. Millennia of beliefs have shaped who he is and what he is striving for."

A deep unease settled over me. "And what, exactly, is he striving for?"

"Desolation and regrowth. My brother would annihilate civilization and return the land to a feral, untamed state. Yet the truth is that the waking world has moved on—humans no longer fear nature, but rather master it. There's no place for the Dark Wolf God in the waking world anymore. The balance has changed forever, but he won't let go."

The all too familiar memories of Magic Side flickered through my mind. Corpses, broken buildings. The Dark God had tried to turn my pack into possessed killers and release them on the unsuspecting world. Hell, he'd nearly succeeded.

"The Moon understood that Cadean put humanity at risk, so she imprisoned him here. Although I didn't see it at the time, she was right. Cadean can never be unleashed." Auren shifted in the saddle and looked back. "That's why I need your help. I need to keep him at bay to preserve the balance. And after seeing what you can do with the wall, I know I made the right choice."

The truth was, Cadean had to be locked away for the sake of

Magic Side and the waking world. I *knew* that. But the vision of him stalking the barrier like a caged animal sickened me to my core.

I swallowed hard, trying to calm the nausea rising in my throat. "I still don't know how I controlled the barrier or if I can do it again."

Auren looked back at me over his shoulder. "You'll learn."

After the incident at the wall, Auren didn't let me leave the palace.

My brother will not stop until he gets his hands on you. He may not be able to cross the wall, but his agents are everywhere. If you don't do as I say, you'll find yourself locked away in his dungeon or dead—and this time, I won't be there to help.

And the Dark God wasn't the only threat. Ayanna, the queen of the fae, had sent assassins to kill me while I was in Shadowstone. She might try here as well.

Thus, I was under complete lockdown. I couldn't approach the wall, run in the woods, or go anywhere without Auren at my side. When he wasn't there, guards and attendants hovered around me, tracking my every move, reporting everything I did straight back to him.

I dug my claws into the frame of my bedroom window and closed my eyes. Outside, the mountain slopes with their shimmering aspens called to me, but it was not to be.

The reality was that Auren had me trapped as securely as the Dark God ever had. The only difference was that I didn't have to wear a collar, just whatever dresses Auren selected for me. I'd begged him for trousers time and time again, but he seemed to delight in seeing me flutter about the palace in flowing, overwrought outfits.

Gods damn, I miss my jacket and jeans.

Retracting my claws, I ran my hands through my hair. "How did you ever get yourself into this mess?"

I was over it. Despite the weeks in Auren's domain, I hadn't found the answers I sought, only more questions.

Something had to give. With an exasperated sigh, I wrenched open my door and headed out. My ever-present cadre of bodyguards came to attention.

"Morning, boys. Ready for a stroll?" I asked with a forced air of cheer. "I need to talk to Auren."

The captain simply nodded and walked at my side, hand on his blade.

I wasn't sure if they were just assholes or had very specific orders not to speak to me. I'd made it my daily mission to get something out of them—anything—a smile, an eye roll, or even a knife to my chest, but so far, I'd struck out. Rather than reassurance, they'd become a claustrophobic reminder that no matter where I was, I was in danger.

I half suspected that was Auren's intent.

I found him in his office, deep in a pile of correspondence. He slid a golden sheet of paper off his desk and into his drawer as he stood. "Samantha, what an unexpected delight. Our lesson isn't for several hours."

Everything was always on his schedule. It had to change. Either he gave me a little freedom, or he let me go.

"I'm going crazy cooped up in this palace," I said. "I need to return to Deerhaven and see my mother. She's sick, Auren. You've put it off long enough."

Auren clasped his hands behind his back and shook his head as he rounded the edge of the desk. "I'm afraid that's out of the question."

"You want me to practice my magic? Well, it's not working, and we both know it. I need to talk to her. She might know more about it, or at least know what type of fae I am. It could help."

"I know this is hard, Samantha, but you are in peril every second of every day. If my brother is desperate enough to ambush you at the barrier, then he'll have people waiting for you in Deerhaven. He knows you'll try to go home. The moment you show up, they'll strike." The corner of his mouth hitched up, revealing the same dimple that Cadean had. "It's what I would do."

"If that's true, then I can't leave my mother there unprotected."

He gave me a pained expression. "I'm afraid that's another problem. It seems that after you disappeared, she left town. But don't worry. I have people looking for her, and the moment they find her, they'll bring her here."

"What do you mean, she's gone?" My skin grew cold, dread building in my chest. "Why didn't you tell me? I need to go find her!"

"I didn't tell you because I didn't want you to worry. You have enough on your mind as it is."

He gently squeezed my upper arm, but I flinched and pulled away. "You said that you'd help me, but this isn't help—this is imprisonment."

"I'll find her," he snapped. "I'll bring her here and protect her, just as I protect you."

His signature flared and pressed in on me. I pushed back against his power with my own, but my skull began to throb as I was overcome with an avalanche of heat and sunlight. I found myself drowning and tumbling in his will, and suddenly, everything became calm as a warm sense of serenity washed over me.

"Put your mother out of your mind," Auren whispered. "I will protect you both as long as you obey me and stay within the walls of my palace."

I shook my head. I was worrying needlessly. Of course, Auren would take care of things. He always seemed one step ahead. He'd find my mother, and then I'd be able to leave.

Auren lifted my chin so that I was looking up at him, and I complied. "You need to focus on your goal, Samantha. What did you tell me you wanted?"

"To protect Selene and her people. I want to stop the war with the fae."

He smiled, and my chest swelled with an unexpected pleasure, though it didn't feel like mine.

"Stopping the war means stopping my brother. You need to focus on your magic. Discover how you cursed him and increase your control. Don't let worries about your mother keep you from your goal. Put her out of your mind. I'll take care of everything."

I nodded. "I know."

The sunlight of his magic released, and I blinked. Everything around me seemed brighter, clearer...except my mind.

"Now, why don't you take a walk in the gardens and join me again when it is time to practice?" Auren clapped his hands. "Captain?"

I followed the guards along the wide veranda that overlooked the palace gardens. The sunlight reflected off the leaves, creating a shimmering sea of light, and I savored the sudden sense of peace that had come over me.

I was lucky to be here. Auren was like a rock in a stormy sea.

Unfortunately, my throbbing head dampened my mood, and my thoughts felt sluggish and foggy, a sensation that had become all too familiar lately. It was nothing in particular, just the nagging feeling that I'd misplaced something or forgotten what I was looking for.

Was it just part of being in the Dreamlands? The place was always playing tricks on me.

I glanced back over my shoulder. Auren stood in his doorway, watching me like a hawk, and I had a sudden sense of déjà vu, a feeling of claustrophobia. I was a horse, running around the same racetrack again and again and again.

My heart beat faster as the faintest hint of panic blossomed in my chest. I quickly looked away and hurried down the hall.

What had I gotten myself into?

4

Cadean

The darkness of the great hall settled around me as I perched on my throne, twisting the point of my axe back and forth on the floor.

Find the right words, Melanthe had said. Well, I couldn't. Maybe they didn't exist.

I'd chained and collared Samantha. I'd lied to her and showed her the truth of what I was, a savage monster lurking in the darkness. I knew she hated me, and nothing I could say would change that.

But shouldn't I hate her, too?

She'd stolen from me and crippled my ability to protect my realm. She'd cursed me and stabbed me. And yet, rather than sending me into a rage, the thought brought a grudging smile to my lips. She was fierce and relentless, a true wolf through and through, despite her fae blood. A rival who was far too intriguing.

Light flared in the corner of the room, pulling me from my thoughts.

Melanthe.

She strode down the central aisle of the great hall with a little ball of flame hovering above her raised fingertips. Bemusement tugged at the corner of her lips. "Brooding again...or did I wake you from a nap?" she teased.

I leaned back on my throne. "As long as Samantha has the moonshard and is on the other side of that wall, my kingdom is in peril. So how do you convince a thief to give up the things they stole and return to prison? Because that's what this place was to her."

"You don't."

I dismissed my black axe into the ether in frustration, wishing I could make my problems vanish the same way. "Then what am I supposed to do?"

Mel crossed her arms. "Focus. What is the single most important thing you need to do?"

Closing my eyes, I rubbed my temples. Instead of blackness, all I could see was Samantha, like a mirage on the other side of the wall. Auren's hands rested on her, gently guiding her movements as he whispered in her ear.

I thrust myself off the throne with a curse. "I need to get her away from *him*. He's looking for a way to break me and this kingdom. If he finds out about the oracle..."

Mel raised her eyebrows as my words failed me. We both knew it was about more than that.

She shook her head. "Auren is the greatest threat to you both. You need to forget about the moonshard or even convincing Samantha to return. Just get her to safety."

"He's got her wrapped around his fingers. Even if I could break through Auren's wards and shadow-cast to her, she'd never trust anything I say."

"She's been betrayed so many times, I doubt she trusts anyone anymore, your brother included. She won't be any happier being under his control than under yours. What she needs most is an *ally*, so be one. Figure out what she needs and find a way to help her. Earn her trust."

"I wouldn't know where to begin."

"Maybe with an apology?"

My shoulders knotted, and I fixed the sorceress with a scouring glare.

She shrugged. "However you want to proceed, you need to figure it out soon. The spell is prepared, and my assistants are waiting."

"You want to try now? It's nearly midnight. She'll be sleeping." I stepped down off the dais and flicked my wrist. The roof of the great hall vanished, revealing the expanse of stars overhead. This was how I always saw it, but mortals preferred the illusion of safety created by wooden walls.

Mel looked up. "I'm well aware of the time. I don't know how much force it will take for you to break through your brother's wards, but your powers will be strongest when the shadows are deepest, and the moon just set..."

The fucking moon. It was a relentless symbol of my imprisonment, gleaming in mockery every single day.

"Fine. Let's do it now."

She lifted her brows. "Did you collect everything I asked?"

Earth, water, life, light, and blood.

I grabbed my pack from beside the throne. "Everything but the right words."

Melanthe led me up the stairs to a dimly lit room in the high tower. Flickering candles lined a massive sigil carved into the floor, and her robed apprentices waited at its corners.

She guided me to the glowing brazier at the center of the sigil. "Our spell will amplify your power while you shadow-cast.

It should let you break through Auren's wards, but I don't know how long you'll have."

"What do I need to do?"

Mel held out a slender blade, and I grimaced as I took it. Blood magic.

"Once we begin chanting, give your offerings to the flame. As soon as you feel your power swell, search Samantha out with your magic. Talk to her, but don't try to convince her to return. Just find a way to help her." She poured a thick black resin over the glowing coals, and pungent alkaline smoke billowed around me. Then she returned to the edge of the sigil, raised her hands, and began to chant.

Her apprentices followed in unison, their voices echoing unnaturally through the tower around me.

I offered each of the components I'd gathered in turn, dumping them into the flames. Earth from Frostfall and a vial of water from the edge of the lake. Blossoms from where I'd taken Samantha riding and phosphorescent fungus from her cell deep beneath Shadowstone. Earth, water, life, and light.

The last component was blood. I took Mel's blade and drew a crimson line across my palm. The sting focused my mind on the impossible task at hand, and I squeezed my fist, releasing my blood into the brazier below. The drops hissed and sizzled on the coals.

Offerings given, I closed my eyes and let the pungent smoke and drone of chanting voices lull me.

For a long time, I felt nothing. Then, as the chanting swelled, the room began to shift and bend in unnatural ways. My vision blurred, and I felt the floor rising into me—and with it, a surge of power.

Find the right words.

Summoning my magic, I projected my mind into Auren's realm. I let my awareness sweep out through the night, drifting over my misty lands, through the Moon's wall and over the rolling hills where my brother's palace lay. Even from behind the powerful wards that protected it, I felt her tugging at me with a magnetic force that I could not resist.

Although Auren's spells were invisible, I could discern them in my mind's eye—a spiderweb of sunlight that shielded his palace from intrusion and psychic infiltration. The wards were strong enough to thwart even the prying eyes of the Fates, and I knew if I attacked them outright, I would draw his attention instantly.

I would need to be surgical.

Slowly, I let my presence coalesce into the deep shadows of the trees. Though my corporeal form wasn't there, I still sensed the vibrations of the forest around me: the rustle of dry leaves, the scurrying of a mouse, the rich scent of moldering earth. Even as winter neared, there was more life here than at Shadowstone, and that only made my task more dire. My realm couldn't hold off Queen Ayanna's pestilence much longer.

Moving from shadow to shadow, I began circling the perimeter, searching for any point of weakness. Finally, I found what I was looking for: a single thread of magic weaker than the rest.

Breathing in, I drew upon the power of Mel's ritual. Two tendrils of inky smoke coalesced in the darkness, illuminated by countless explosions of Mel's light. At my command, they moved silently over the leaf litter, heading toward the chink in Auren's armor. Once I felt the weak point, I unleashed them, and with a single violent thrust, they struck against the spell like vipers.

Auren's wards lashed back with a searing burst of energy that lit up the forest and sent shockwaves through the ether. The harder I pushed against the wards, the more my mind burned. But I didn't stop. I took all that Melanthe had to give and more, devouring the power from the ritual.

With a flash of light, the thread shattered.

The moment the spell snapped, Samantha's pull on me amplified a dozen times over. I hurled my presence forward into the palace. I could sense other beings in the darkness, but her energy drowned them all out—even the powerful signature of my brother.

I let my awareness coalesce amid the shadows of her room.

She lay in a luxurious bed, contented and dreaming, with a thin sheet draped across her. My eyes traced the curves of her body as memories assaulted me.

How many times had I lurked in the shadows, watching her sleep? At first, I'd only caught glimpses of her when I'd shadow-cast into the waking world. But when she'd become my prisoner, I hadn't been able to resist checking in on her at night, or lingering when I brought her food at the break of dawn.

And now, she was impossibly far away, trapped beyond the wall and entwined with my brother's magic.

I opened my mouth to whisper her name but closed it without a breath. Breaking her peaceful rest felt like sacrilege. I could let her have another minute free of fear and anger, free of me and the darkness that always came with my presence.

5

My eyes snapped open as an unsettling dread tore me from sleep.

Someone's in my room.

Lying still, I scanned the chamber. The shadows were darker than usual, and though I couldn't see anyone, I felt a presence. I listened for breath or a heartbeat or a shoe scuffing on the floor.

Nothing.

Inching my hand beneath my feather pillow, I wrapped my fingers around the steak knife I'd snatched from dinner the other night. Then I flipped over and thrust the blade in front of me. "Don't come any closer!"

But the room was empty. I sat there, chest heaving, as I searched the darkness. Had it been a nightmare?

The wound on my arm had begun to itch, and my stomach dropped. The Dark God wasn't supposed to be able to reach me here, but it was him, all the same. I could smell the earthy scent of his body and taste the bitter chocolaty signature of his magic on my tongue. A low warmth built in my belly even as terror hardened in my chest.

I shoved myself upright, blade still raised. "I know it's you. Stop hiding in the dark."

For a moment, there was no response. Then, like a silk robe dropping to the floor, the deep shadows in the corners of the room slipped down the walls and pooled near the fireplace. The dying embers flickered and extinguished themselves as a midnight silhouette stepped forward—the striking form of the god who'd haunted my dreams.

My heart thrummed against my ribs as he stalked toward me, pausing less than an arm's length away.

I was overcome by the sharp and beautiful angles of his face, one that could have been carved only by the Fates themselves. I fought the sudden urge to reach out and touch him. Instead, I leveled the knife at his throat. It wasn't any kind of defense against a god, but it sent the message I wanted to convey. "Back off."

The corner of Cadean's mouth twitched up in silent mockery. "Did I frighten you, little wolf?"

Fuck, yes.

But my heartbeat had begun to slow. I knew there was no way for him to cross the wall or get into Auren's palace. He was shadow-casting. I'd seen him use the same trick when I'd been in Melanthe's workshop. He could see and hear me, but he couldn't touch me.

I forced my shoulders to relax even as I tightened my grip on the blade. "What are you doing? Watching me sleep?"

His smoldering gaze warmed my skin and sent a shiver along my spine. As his eyes slowly roved down my body, a slight, arrogant smile tugged on his lips, revealing that single dimple on his cheek. "I was, but this is much better."

I glanced down. My nipples were like diamonds, popping through my sheer linen nightgown. *Fuck me.*

I flung myself off the bed and snatched the soft golden robe that was draped over the chaise longue. "Do you do this every night? Sneak into women's bedrooms and stare at them like a perv?"

"No. I'm afraid my brother's spells have prevented me from watching over you as closely as I would like."

More like stalking me. Yet the way he casually said *watching over you* heated me in ways I didn't want to admit.

I tied the robe shut. "So, what changed? How did you get past them?"

"I have Mel's help tonight. I think she misses having you around."

The pang of loss pressed in on me, and my throat tightened. We'd never been on the same side, but Mel had almost been a friend. I didn't have anyone like that in Auren's palace.

I crossed my arms. "What do you want, besides haunting my dreams?"

"Have you been dreaming about me, then?" he asked as he slowly rounded the bed.

He was so different away from the wall. I knew it hurt and enraged him, but I couldn't help but think it was better that way. He was far more dangerous when his mind was clear...and focused on me.

I took a step back, but my thighs hit the teak writing desk. My heart pounded again—this time, not from fear, but from something far more dangerous.

He leaned down, close enough that if he were truly there, his lips might brush against my neck. "You've haunted my dreams as well," he said softly. "And consumed my every waking thought."

His words skated over my skin, leaving a delicious trail of goosebumps in their wake. Before I could gather my wits about me, he turned and strode to the window and peered out. "I needed to speak to you without a searing wall of magic or my bastard of a brother looming between us."

"So say your piece and leave me alone."

He hesitated for a moment, as if searching for the right words. "I want a truce."

My heart skipped a beat, and an ember of hope flickered in my heart. Had challenging him at the barrier changed something? Or was this a ploy?

Retrieving my knife from where I'd left it on the bed, I crossed to the center of the room. "Why should I trust anything you have to say?"

He glanced out the window as a solemn expression cloaked his face. "I'm fighting for the life of my realm, and you're trying to get home. We could both use one fewer enemy right now."

That was for sure.

I fought to keep my thoughts steady, even as the hope in my chest began to smolder. "What would a truce even look like?"

His eyes flicked to the blade in my hand. "Well, you could put that knife away, for starters. I'm in shadow form. I can't hurt you, and you can't hurt me. We might as well pretend to be civil."

Blood heated my cheeks, but I forced a smile and let the blade fall to the stone floor.

The real question was, could the moonshard hurt him in shadow form? It was in my satchel, inconveniently located just beside his left foot.

The Dark God leaned back against the windowsill. "I want you to leave my brother's domain and return to the waking world forever. In exchange, I'll stop hunting you."

Something about the way he said *forever* cut through me. He was offering exactly what I needed, so why did it suddenly feel like a slap in the face?

"Why propose this now? What's the catch?" I asked, keeping my voice steady.

His eyes darkened. "Because my brother is a treacherous bastard. As long as you're with him, you're in danger."

The intensity of his voice took me aback.

I'd seen that look on his face before, right after he'd butchered the deathwing that had attacked me at Frostfall, and again when he'd eviscerated Queen Ayanna's assassin. Did he actually care? Or was it that I'd been the key to healing him, a piece too valuable to lose?

I shook my head. He was playing games. This wasn't about my safety. It was about sibling rivalry.

She chose me, Cade. Get over it and move on.

I was a prize, and if the Dark God couldn't have me, no one could.

"You're jealous," I said.

The faintest hint of a smile ghosted his lips. "Would you like it if I were, little wolf?"

He shoved off the sill and approached through the darkness. There was something thrilling about the hunger in his eyes. Each step he took made the room feel smaller, and I slid back once more until I bumped into the cold stone wall.

He stopped inches away. And again, even though he was just a shadow, I could almost feel the heat of his body. My breath shuddered as a flurry of repressed emotions rippled through me.

It might be more than jealousy.

The possessive way he loomed over me stirred desires I'd fought hard to forget, but my body wouldn't—the way his lips had felt pressed against mine at Frostfall, or the shivers of ecstasy that had erupted through me when he'd had his way with me in the forest.

And the truth was, I wanted it. His desire, his jealousy, his protectiveness. I might have escaped him, but he still had me wrapped around his finger.

6

———

Samantha

As the rational part of my mind kicked into overdrive, I evaded the looming shadow of the Dark Wolf God and circled to the other side of the room.

I couldn't risk thinking about him *that way* again. Queen or pawn, I was just a trophy that Cadean and his brother were fighting over. But was there a way to use his jealousy to my advantage?

I inched closer to my satchel and the moonshard. "Since I've been here, no one has tried to attack me except you. Why should I leave? I'm safer with your brother."

It was a lie. Nothing felt safe about Auren, but I wanted details. What was Cadean so worried about?

A muscle in his jaw tightened, the way it always did when he was frustrated with me. "Auren will turn on you the instant it benefits him. He's not your friend, no matter what he pretends. His goals and alliances are always shifting. You can't trust him."

"But I can't trust you, can I?"

His fists knotted. "Auren is using his magic to manipulate you. I can see the traces of it clinging to you like strands of smoke. You were my prisoner once, but I never toyed with your mind like this."

My gut tightened. How did he know? Could he really see it? I couldn't count the number of times I'd walked away from a conversation with Auren feeling like I'd lost, but unsure why. I knew he was manipulating me, but was it more than that? Was it permanent?

Dread coated my throat. How much of a puppet had I become?

I glared back at the Dark God, using my anger to drown out the shame of helplessness. "You're not innocent, either. You used your magic to force me to betray Sarion the moment you captured me. You forced me to tell you about him and the Moon. How is that any different?"

"That was before—"

"Before what? Before you decided I was useful?"

"Before I knew you."

The softness of his voice was like a caress, and I shivered as he stepped forward. "I never compelled you to heal me or to fight at my side, and I never used my magic to change the way you thought about me. I let you hate me and fight me the whole way."

I lifted my chin. "As long as I wore your collar."

"I may have been your captor, but I gave you free will. That's something my brother will never let you have. He'll control your thoughts and shape you into the exact tool he needs."

My cheeks heated with shame. "Don't you think I see that? Don't you think I've tried to stop him? I *can't*."

Over a decade ago, I'd promised myself that I'd never let myself be powerless again, that I'd always be strong enough to fight off whatever bad guys came my way. Yet here I was, a caged wolf who couldn't see what was right in front of her. The powerlessness was poison, eating away at my soul.

The lines of the Dark God's face softened, and his hand rose as if he were going to touch my cheek. After a moment, he let it fall again. "My brother is powerful, but you're the most strong-willed creature I've ever met. You have the strength to resist him."

"I don't. Not even with the strength of the Moon's magic. I've tried."

"Fuck the Moon's magic," he growled.

I flinched, half expecting him to wheel around and hurl the bedside table across the room. But of course, he couldn't. He was no more than shadows.

Cadean paced away, frustration boiling off him like heat waves. "Your will is what allows you to shape the barrier, and it's what will allow you to resist Auren. That does not come from the *fucking* Moon. It comes from you."

Despite my doubts, his confidence gave me a spark of hope. "So how do I stop it? If you're serious about a truce, you can start by teaching me this."

He spun on me. "I'll train you whether you agree to a truce or not. Learn to resist me, and you'll be able to resist my bastard of a brother, or even a siren's call."

I raised my eyebrows. "Resist you? You can use your magic here?"

He shrugged. "I've never been able to speak or appear to anyone else while shadow-casting, so I haven't tried it."

Dread trickled through my veins. "What's to stop you from just compelling me to rush back to your kingdom?"

"I'm not my brother," he growled.

My heart leapt in my chest, but I shook my head and backed away. "That's not good enough."

He sighed, studying me with a dark, unreadable gaze. "Then I swear on my love for my people that I will not try to compel you to return."

Could I trust him?

No, my mind screamed. But in my soul, I knew that for this moment, at least, I could. The Dark God might be a bloodthirsty warlord, but unlike his brother, he was ruled by a deep-rooted sense of honor. That much about him I understood.

For a long moment, neither of us spoke, until at last, I sighed. "Fine. Let's do this."

I was so tired of Auren's manipulation and his iron control that I was ready to try anything.

Cadean reached out and let his fingers hover just above my pounding breast. "Mastery begins here. No matter what Auren's magic can do to your thoughts, nothing can change the truth in your heart. Cling to that truth. Forge it into a wall like the Moon's, a barrier that no one can cross. Not Auren, not me, and not the fucking queen of the fae."

My breath quickened. I knew that he was just shadows and that he couldn't touch me, but the electricity in the millimeters between us was so strong that I swore I could almost feel him. I swallowed hard. "What do I do?"

His hand dropped away. "I'll compel you, and you'll resist. And if you fail, we'll try again and again, for as long as I can stay."

I squared my stance to challenge him. "Okay, but you'd better not mess with me."

"I won't, but I will need to test you. The more reasonable the request, the harder it is to resist. That is how Auren manipulates you so easily: he asks you to do something you want to do. To give you the best chance to succeed, I'll need to ask you something I know you'll never agree to."

Sudden doubt coiled in my gut. "What?"

"Give me the moonshard." His command thrummed with a primal energy that vibrated down to my core. The power in his voice dragged across my skin like a caress, and I wanted to melt into it. I wanted to obey and to please him.

I was halfway to my bag before I realized what I was doing. My eyes rounded, and I spun around. "Fuck that!"

His magic and the urge to obey pressed in, but I pushed back, funneling the shock and surprise burning in my heart. Suddenly, I gasped as the magic binds around me burst and fell away.

"Well done," the Dark God purred.

"How dare you ask that!"

He grinned. "I'm just a shadow, so you don't have to worry. Now give me the shard."

The words drove his power back into me, twice as strong as before. My soul screamed in rebellion, and I pushed back, but every fiber in my body wanted to obey him. I fell to my knees and began fumbling through my bag.

Cadean gave a low growl of displeasure, and the wave of magic subsided, leaving me gasping for air. I glanced down at my hands. I was holding the moonshard. Another few seconds, and I would have handed it over.

Was I really this powerless before him? I gritted my teeth as bitterness raged. I'd held his magic back twice at the barrier. I'd do it again.

"Hand me the shard," he commanded.

I was on my feet and stumbling toward his outstretched hand before I knew what was happening. Frustration shot through me, and I tightened my grip around the moonshard. I reached for its magic and drew it in until I was nearly bursting.

"No," I snarled, and pushed back against the Dark God's will.

He stumbled forward, and the urge to obey vanished. I let a triumphant smile spread over my lips.

Frustration flashed in his eyes. "You're using the Moon's magic. Use your own will."

"You're a god, and I'm a wolf. I'll use anything and everything I can."

"Drop it," he snapped. The command lanced through my chest, and the moonshard clattered on the floor.

I bent to grab it.

"Stop."

This time, the command was gentler but still powerful enough to make me stand. I was a marionette in his hands, a fucking puppet for him and his brother.

Tears of frustration formed in the corners of my eyes. "If you can do this to me, why didn't you just make me heal you? You could've commanded me to do anything."

His eyes burned with an emotion I couldn't place, and he released his magic. "Because that's not who I am."

Jaw set, I glared back at him.

No, it wasn't. Some part of me knew that, but I didn't dare admit that he was anything more to me than the beast who'd killed my people and locked me away. "You could have forced me to hand the moonshard over or to stop fleeing. Wouldn't that have been justified in your eyes?"

Cadean released a soft laugh. "I don't think I would've had a chance to stop you. You're far stronger than you know when you put your will to it."

I smiled halfheartedly. "You mean when I have the moonshard to give me strength."

"Not at all," he said sharply. "You knew exactly what you wanted, and you weren't going to let it go. I didn't have a fucking chance to stop you. That's how you fight compulsion. Stop resisting me and focus on what it is that *you* want. That's where power comes from."

Something about the way he was looking down at me made my breath catch, but I pushed the feeling away and steeled my resolve. "Fine. Let's try again."

Cadean was my enemy. He might be helping me right now, but the one thing I could never do was give him the moonshard.

He extended his arm and locked my gaze. "Give me the shard."

The strength of his magic slammed into me, and I dropped to my knees beside it.

No.

Despair and helplessness poured through me, but I squeezed my eyes shut and fought back, bracing my will against his. I would never give him the moonshard. In his hands, it was death, but in mine, it could protect. It could save. It could change the Dreamlands.

It was meant for me.

My heart skipped a beat as the truth crashed into me like a wave of ice water. His power, his command, it was all meaningless. The moonshard wasn't his. It had been meant for me. It had *chosen* me.

I growled and hurled myself forward as his power over me shattered. He staggered backward a step, and I plunged the shard up to within an inch of his throat. "I will never give it to you."

For what felt like an eternity, there was silence. Then a slow grin spread across his face, revealing that dimple I could never forget. "That's certainly one way to not hand it over. Well done."

Cheeks heating, I stepped back and let my arm drop.

His praise lit a warm glow in my chest, but it turned to surprise when I realized his form seemed less substantial, like he was fading into the shadows. "Did I hurt you?"

He glanced to the window and the blue glow forming on the horizon. "Dawn is nearing, and I suspect Mel's spell is almost exhausted. Projecting my influence and compelling you consumes my power. You're stronger than you realize."

I swallowed, surprised by the sudden sense of disappointment rising up within me. "Do you think I'll be able resist Auren?"

Cadean hesitated, and my stomach sank. "Auren is sly. He will use your own desires against you, playing you against yourself to get what he wants."

"Oh." The hope that had built inside me came crashing down.

He stepped close and drew my eyes to his. "Don't worry, little wolf. If you can resist me, you can resist him. It will just take time and training."

I nodded, but I couldn't overcome the emptiness that had bloomed in me. How long would I be their puppet?

His eyes drifted to my lips. "Figure out what you truly want, Samantha. It will give you strength. I don't think he has any idea what you're capable of."

The shadows suddenly slipped away, and the Dark God vanished. Moments later, the sun broke the horizon and cast my room in soft morning light, yet rather than feeling relief at the dawn, I thought the palace felt a little colder.

I flopped back on the bed, exhausted and spent. The ceiling was decorated with women and men in various states of amorous rapture, some of them being carted off by angels into a baby blue sky. My thoughts followed them, whirling into the clouds.

Cadean had offered me a truce. He could help me resist his brother, and he'd vowed to stop hunting me. I was certain he was playing another game, but if I could leverage his jealousy against his brother, I might have a way out of this mess at last.

The Dark God might be my enemy, but apparently, he was the only ally I had in Auren's realm.

7

———

Samantha

The late morning sun woke me a few hours later. I pulled my pillow over my head, but when I couldn't sleep, I groaned and rolled away from the window.

Of course I'd dreamed of *him*.

He'd chased me through the woods like a wild animal. Fear had propelled me through the roots and vines faster than I'd ever run. And then it wasn't just him, but Auren as well—two massive wolves, cornering me at every turn. The forest was a labyrinth, choked in vines, and the only way forward was the one way I didn't dare to go.

With a grunt of frustration, I threw myself out of bed and stalked into the bathroom. I scowled at my reflection as I scrubbed my teeth. I'd gotten myself into a fates-damned mess once again.

The bastard who had rescued me was fucking with my head and wouldn't let me go, while the bastard who had imprisoned me was trying to help...and fucking with my head all the same.

I splashed icy water from the basin over my face. What the hell was I going to do?

Figure out what you truly want, Samantha. It will give you strength.

"I want to be free of you!" I shouted at the shadows—but of course, the target of my wrath wasn't there.

I wrapped my robe around me and flung open the window. Sunlight glinting through the fluttering aspen leaves had turned the hills into a sea of gold, and the crisp mountain air blowing in began to clear my thoughts.

What *did* I want?

It was simple, wasn't it? I wanted to be free of Auren's control as well as Cadean's. I wanted to go home and see my mom again. That was all.

But even as I held those hopes in my mind, my stomach tightened, and a bleaker truth pressed in on me. Those old wants weren't enough. Maybe it had been sufficient for that girl from Deerhaven, but I wasn't her anymore.

I'd died and been brought back to life, and as much as I wanted to deny it, I knew that my life was no longer my own. I'd made a bargain. I could run from Cadean and Auren, but I couldn't outrun the Fates.

The wind brushed over my skin, and with it, the rustling of the aspens. For a moment, they sounded like whispers calling my name, like the Dreamlands reaching out for me. My eyes drifted to the moonshard lying on the table. I picked it up and shivered as its magic tingled over my skin.

I'd been given the power and the responsibility to use it. Stopping the Dark Wolf God from attacking the fae wasn't enough: I had to protect his people as well. I had to stop the endless cycle of violence that was consuming his lands.

But how?

I closed my eyes and thought of the Dark God's realm. The people and villages, the deathwings, and the forests strangled with vines.

The vines. They were the key to everything. Destroying them would protect his land and people. It would change everything.

I put on the plainest dress I could find and swept out of my room in search of Auren. My guards had doubled, but the silent captain offered no explanation as to why.

I was done being a puppet. Even if he wouldn't let me go, I was going to find a way to force Auren to help me.

To my surprise, he was tending to the apple trees growing in the vast garden that occupied the center of the palace. His aura radiated around him, and the toasted wheat of his signature mixed with the scent of apples in the air.

I looked up into the tree above him. "What are you doing, pruning? Don't you have people for that?"

"I do, but there is something I love about taking a hands-on approach—nurturing each branch to flawless perfection. It makes the fruit taste all the sweeter." He plucked a green apple from the tree above me, then held it out. "Care for a bite?"

The fruit faded from green to bright crimson in his hand. I started to reach for it but paused. Auren didn't like no for an answer.

"No. That's not why I'm here."

He smiled, but it didn't reach his eyes. "You're not here about your mother again, are you?"

A dreadful chill pricked my skin. It felt like the lines of an old, familiar movie. How many times had he used his power to divert me? Was it stronger today than yesterday? Fragments of memory filtered through my mind, though they turned into mist when I tried to concentrate on them.

Fucking hell. How often had we played out the same damn conversation?

"No."

"Good. I'm glad you've come to your senses. Things are more dangerous for you than I feared. Last night, the Dark God breached my defenses with his magic. I spent all morning repairing them."

My gut tightened. How much did Auren know? Did he have any idea Cadean could communicate with me?

I swallowed. "The Dark God was here? But the border..."

Auren shook his head. "He was spying, which means he's trying to keep an eye on you. He's likely looking for another opportunity to strike."

"Here?" I asked, praying my voice didn't give me away.

"Don't worry, I doubled my wards. He won't break through again. However, out of caution, I'm switching you to a different room." He took a bite from the red apple in his hand. "Returning to the waking world is, of course, out of the question."

Of course it was.

"That's not why I'm here. I want to talk to you about the vines."

He raised his eyebrows. "The vines? Why?"

"They're draining the life from your brother's realm, and they feed the broodlings. Cadean attacks the vines to stop them from killing his land, and the fae retaliate."

Auren shrugged. "This is the way the Dreamlands have been for centuries. Cadean and the fae keep each other occupied."

"The fae don't care about conquering his land, just siphoning power from it. Destroy the vines, and there's no more deathwings, no reason for the fae to risk sending warriors over the border, and no reason for him to retaliate. Find a way to stop the vines, and the Dreamlands might have peace for a while."

Auren's jaw tightened with frustration. "The politics of the Dreamlands are not your problem. Focus on containing my brother and leave the fae to me."

"If we destroy the vines, he won't need the moonshard to raid across the border. Maybe he'll leave me alone."

Auren's expression darkened. "My brother will never stop hunting you, no matter what you do. Now, the captain will show you to your new room. Put the vines out of your mind."

His aura flared, and I was surrounded by a cascade of sunlight and power. It pummeled me, wave after wave, but I held my ground, clinging to the one thing in my life that made sense: that feeling of purpose building in my soul. It was bigger than Auren or Cadean or even my own desires, and the more he pushed with his magic, the stronger it grew.

Auren's power swelled, and then it broke like a wave flowing over the shore.

I straightened my spine and met his eyes. "I know what you're doing. Stop."

The wind whipped around him, and the trees of the orchard shuddered. Suddenly, he was no longer Auren, but a force of nature, no different than his brother: relentless, brutal, and long accustomed to getting his way. His power buffeted against my dress, but I held my ground. "Stop trying to control me and start helping me or throw me in a cell with Kassian. I will not be deferred any longer."

His eyes narrowed. "You're getting stronger. That's good."

I stepped as close to the golden god as I could. "I'm here for a reason, Auren, and it's not to be your plaything. Help me find a way to stop this conflict."

A sly grin twisted over his lips. "And you're assuming peace is what I want?"

"You'd fucking better, because once the Undying Court has drained your brother's land dry, they'll come for yours. What are you going to do to stop the vines then?"

His gaze flicked to my bodyguards, then back to me, evaluating. He bent his head close. "This isn't a discussion we should be having in public."

"Then send your goons away."

He studied my face for a moment, then released a burst of magic. It rolled outward through the orchard like a thunderclap, shaking the leaves of the trees, and the guards stiffened. "You will recall nothing you've heard this morning," Auren growled. "You will await Samantha outside of my office."

The captain and his men saluted and marched off.

Auren offered me his arm. "How about we start again?"

I clasped my hands behind my back. "Let's."

8

Samantha

I felt a sudden sense of lightness as I followed Auren out of the garden and up the stairs. How many times had I succumbed to his influence?

Cadean's training had changed everything—though the truth was, he hadn't quite been right. What I wanted didn't matter. I wanted to go home and see my mom and Magic Side. It was knowing that feeling of purpose that gave me strength. As long as I held to that, I'd be able to find my way.

I stepped into his office, and Auren shut the door behind me. "For future reference, I'd rather you not speak to me that way in front of my men."

"Then you shouldn't treat me like a doll in front of them."

His expression hardened, but not with anger. It was like he had removed a mask, revealing a face that was ancient and tired. "I see that you are not." He crossed to a small bar in the corner of the room. "We should discuss this over a bottle of wine."

Was it a peace offering or simply a way to lower my defenses and dampen my willpower? "It's not even noon."

He reached beneath the bar and pulled out a frosty bottle. "Then I'll make it champagne. This isn't a conversation for tea."

I lingered by the door as he filled two flutes with the sparkling wine. "I doubt you'll believe it, but I'm sorry for pushing you. I'm used to moving the pieces on the chess board as I see fit, whether they like it or not."

"You're right, I don't. Perhaps you have centuries to move your little chess pieces around, but I'm mortal, and so are the people I care about on the other side of the wall. Destroying the vines is the best way to protect them."

The air turned thick and dull, as if there was no resonance in the room—a spell to protect our conversation from prying ears.

He handed me one of the flutes. "Why is this so important to you? I created this realm. You, on the other hand, have lived here a few months. You don't know them. Why would you care so passionately about Cadean's shifters, let alone the fae?"

"I was brought here for a purpose. If it's not to protect the people here, then I don't know what it is."

Auren nodded, then set his glass on his desk as he studied the vast map adorning his wall. "You're right about the vines. I've thought of them often. I doubt the fae would risk attacking me outright, but I worry that once they've drained the magic from his land, it will destabilize the islands. Our magic is what holds this continent together."

My stomach lurched at the thought of his realm breaking up and Selene's village drifting off into the mists. "Then why don't you do something?"

He shrugged. "Don't you think I've tried? No one knows how to kill the vines, or Cadean would have done it centuries ago. If you cut through them, they come back twice as thick. Curses and poisons work for a time, but they heal quickly."

"There has to be a way. Nothing is immortal."

"Except the gods." Auren gave me a wink, then dropped into

the chair behind his desk with his hands folded behind his head. "The nature of the vines is a fiercely guarded secret, even within the Undying Court. I've tried sending spies, but the queen's palace is warded against anyone who isn't fae, just like the sacred groves. Moreover, her people ruthlessly vet anyone who wants to enter. It's impossible to get someone reliable on the inside."

I set my untouched wine down on the bar. "You're a god. There has to be something we can do."

As Auren slowly pivoted back and forth, scrutinizing me, I felt as if he were peeling the skin from my arms. Smoothing the creases of my dress, I glared at him. "Why are you looking at me like I'm a cut of steak?"

The corner of his mouth ticked up. "I might have a solution, but I'm trying to determine whether you're up to the task—rather, if you have the requisite determination and mental fortitude."

"I do."

"Perhaps." He pulled a slender golden scroll out of his desk drawer and twisted it between his fingers.

I took a step closer. "What is that?"

"An unparalleled opportunity to make a difference. Queen Ayanna wants to meet you. She's invited you to her court."

A chill crept down my back, and I tensed. "Are you insane? She sent assassins to kill me!"

He shrugged and swirled his wine. "What can I say? She's had a change of heart."

"I don't buy that for a second."

Auren waved his hand dismissively. "She's impressed that you found a way to stop my brother from crossing the wall, though I suspect her sudden realignment has more to do with the fact that you stabbed him in the chest. It was a rather *statement* move if I do say so myself."

My gut twisted, and I suddenly felt sick. I could see the scar I'd given Cadean in my mind's eye—a pale, jagged wound in the left-center of his chest. How close had I come to his heart?

Auren leaned forward. "The queen assumes you desperately want to kill my brother. She also knows you cursed him and can control the wall. She wants to train you. She thinks she can harness your talents."

Each breath became harder than the last. How did she know I could control the wall? How did she know about Cadean's wound? Had Auren told her? What else had he revealed?

I stepped back toward the door. "Have you been working with the queen this whole time?"

Auren laughed, and a foxlike grin crept over his lips. "Oh, sweet Samantha. Welcome to the game. If you are going to dabble in politics, you'd better learn to play all sides of the table."

"That doesn't answer my question."

"My brother is a monster and an asshole, but despite my best efforts, I'm rather fond of him. The truth is, I want to see Ayanna's kingdom crumble long before his, but I haven't had the right tool to deal with the problem—until the Fates dropped it straight into my lap." He pointed the golden scroll at me. "You."

"I'm not a tool."

He tucked the scroll in the drawer and slammed it shut. "But you are." Rising from his chair, he stalked around the end of his desk. "I can't get anyone inside the queen's court, but you have perfect credentials. You're part fae. You hate my brother; you stabbed him in the heart, you cursed him, and you possess the secret to locking him away behind the wall. Best of all, they're *begging for you*. You're the perfect little spy."

I shook my head. "I'm not going to spy on the queen of the fae—that's insane."

"If you really care about Cadean's people as much as you say, then this is your opportunity to help them. Learn the secret of the vines and how to destroy them."

The walls pressed in on me like the steel jaws of a trap. It *was* insane, but if there was even a glimmer of hope, shouldn't I at least hear him out? I'd been desperate for a way forward, and here he was, offering me one with an open hand.

"What would I have to do?"

Auren gave me a self-satisfied smile. "Accept her offer. She'll help you develop your magic, and all the while, you'll watch and listen. You'll find out where the vines grow and how they regenerate. You'll scour the palace for a way to destroy them. Most importantly, I want seeds or seedlings."

"Why?"

"To experiment with. Maybe we can breed a blight."

My mind whirled. One second, Auren had been standing in my way. Then the mask came off, and he was shoving me straight into the jaws of a dragon.

I shook my head. "It's suicidal. The queen will know something is up. When Cadean captured me, he forced me to confess. If she's as cunning as the stories suggest, she'll realize that I'm spying."

"Oh, Samantha, you have so little imagination."

Auren's magic flared, constricting around my throat like a noose. "You'll never speak of this plan or my intentions to anyone. You will never reveal that you are working for me. You will only be able to say hateful things about Cadean to the fae, and when you speak of me, you will imply that I am working against my brother and that I can be trusted."

I was drowning in sunlight. I grasped for my power, but Auren's magic brushed it away as if it were nothing but a fleck of dust caught in the wind. He'd been toying with me before, but this was real power, *divine* power. His voice reverberated through my soul, and his will became iron bands that bent around the truth, a truth that I could never speak.

"What the hell, Auren?" I snarled, as my wolf surged in my chest.

"It's for your own safety. If Queen Ayanna gets the slightest hint that you're working behind her back, she will not hesitate to kill you. Of that, I'm certain."

Anger heated my skin, and I bared my teeth. "I haven't agreed to anything."

"That doesn't matter. There was no way I'd let you leave this room without binding my secrets." Auren crossed his arms and fixed me with a chilling glare. "The question before you is a simple one, Samantha: do you want to help destroy the vines or do you want to leave this room with a gaping hole in your memory where this conversation had been?"

Rage and frustration shook through me. He'd boxed me in a corner. Had destroying the vines even been my idea, or had he planted it deep in the back of my mind?

Did it matter?

I closed my eyes and tried to calm my thoughts.

It would be dangerous, but I could do something neither Cadean nor Auren could do. If there was a chance to change things, didn't I have to take it?

I opened my eyes again and fixed him with a stony glare. "You said the queen wants to meet me—fine, I'll meet her here. Then I'll decide. But I'm not going without a guarantee of my safety and a way out."

Auren chuckled. "I doubt she has any expectation that you would come unconditionally. We can negotiate the terms, and I will personally provide you with a means of escape once your job is done."

Once your job is done.

Even contemplating it felt dangerous, but what mattered was

that I was doing something more than beautifying Auren's palace.

I took the abandoned flute of champagne off the bar and raised it. "Then I'll meet her. But you'd better not fuck me over."

Auren laughed and raised his own. "I wouldn't dream of it in a thousand years."

9

Samantha

I'd assumed I would have weeks to prepare, but it only took two days for Auren to arrange Queen Ayanna's visit. The imminent arrival set the palace into chaos. Every time I'd stepped into the halls, I had to dodge servants rushing in all directions, carrying linens and crystal, cases of wine and cleaning supplies.

The hubbub paled in comparison to the doubts and chaos in my own mind.

To prepare, I'd rummaged through the library, looking for anything I could find about the queen and her court. Unfortunately, there wasn't much, and Auren wasn't willing to share any inside intel in case it looked like I knew too much and made the queen suspicious.

Too quickly, I'd run out of time. The queen was expected at any minute, and I still wasn't finished getting ready.

I released an unladylike grunt as my handmaid tightened the lacing of my dress. She stepped aside. "What do you think?"

I turned and scrutinized myself in the mirror. This was not the Sam I was used to seeing. Somehow, my handmaids had returned the waves to my tired blonde hair and banished the circles beneath my eyes, remnants of too many restless nights and weeks of imprisonment. Auren had picked my dress, of course—just one more reminder that he was in complete control. Silken gold and lined with pearls, it clung to every curve, and when I turned side to side, it shimmered in the light. My calf peeked out of a side slit that revealed everything to my upper thigh when I took a step. While I could live with that, the plunging bustline exposed far more of my chest than I was comfortable exhibiting.

I pursed my lips apologetically at my handmaid. "Is there another option? This is a little...bold."

Absolutely gaudy is what I wanted to say. It was one hundred percent Auren's taste and zero percent mine. Give me boots and a leather jacket any day.

"This is the dress you are to wear tonight, milady," my handmaid said regretfully. She understood.

I sighed and checked it from another angle.

At least at Shadowstone, I'd had options. The dresses Mel and Cadean had selected were intimidating, but they'd felt like something I could live up to—that despite all my flaws, I could be graceful and pretty. Or maybe that had just been the way I felt when Cadean looked at me. For a moment, my skin flushed and began to feel rather sensitive to the weave of the fabric.

"Miss? Your breathing is strained. Is the back too tight? I can loosen it."

"No, it's fine."

Cadean hadn't visited me again. Either he felt no need to do so or Auren's efforts to strengthen the palace wards had been successful, and Cadean couldn't break through.

I wasn't sure whether I was relieved or disappointed.

I was desperate to train with him again, but I was certain the Dark Wolf God would be enraged if he discovered I was even talking to the queen, let alone contemplating entering her realm. There was no way to predict how he would retaliate once he found out.

It was all to help his people—well, in part—but I couldn't speak of that to him or anyone thanks to Auren's muzzling spell.

I adjusted my over-exposed chest and pulled on the pair of golden stilettos that went with the dress. They were gorgeous but vastly impractical. "Okay, I admit it, you two are miracle workers," I said to my maids. "I think you need to teach me some tricks next time. I'm lucky to have you around."

The maids blushed, and I felt a pang of guilt. I kept them at a distance because I knew they reported everything I said back to Auren, but perhaps I should have made a bit of an effort. We were all under his thumb.

I squared my shoulders and looked at myself in the mirror. Tonight, I wouldn't be under anyone's thumb. I lifted my chin. Maybe Auren had chosen the dress, but I could choose to wear it like armor.

The sound of trumpets echoed through the palace, and my heart skipped a beat. I was supposed to have met Auren before she arrived. *Shit.*

Thanking my maids again, I rushed through the door. As always, my bodyguards fell in line. "Your armor is looking shiny tonight, captain," I said. "Trying to impress the ladies?"

He gave me a blank stare, and I released a burdened sigh as I headed out onto the third-floor veranda that ringed the palace's central courtyard. It enclosed a vast garden containing Auren's orchard, walking paths, and flowerbeds. In the center, a polished stone carriageway circled an ornate fountain. Streams of water arced from a sculpture of maenads being ravished by werewolves in a wild, physically improbable orgy.

Auren definitely had a style.

Where was he?

As if in answer to my thoughts, the scent of wheat and the

sound of steel filled the air, and the sunlit warmth of his magic swirled around me.

I turned to find him grinning at me with a ravenous expression. "You look absolutely ravishing tonight, Samantha. Too bad that the queen is not a king—you could ask for whatever you wanted."

I pivoted back so I didn't have to watch his gaze drifting lower. "Unfortunately, you're asking me to play chess with a queen."

The trumpets blared again, and the giant golden doors of the front gate swung open. Six shimmering, winged horses trotted into view, drawing a gilded carriage behind them. The coach was shaped like a pearl-white swan with folded wings. The doors and trim were decorated with elaborate golden filigree. It was definitely straight out of a fairy tale.

Inside was the murderous queen of the fae.

I repressed a shiver. "Why do I have the feeling you're about to serve me up like a stuffed pig on a silver platter?"

He chuckled. "Really? That's the analogy you want to go with?"

My face flushed deeper with fury. "This isn't a joke. This is my life we're talking about."

His expression darkened as a cruel smile crossed his lips. "If I were going to betray you, I wouldn't put you in a dress and send you to dinner. I would've done it without your permission. I'd put you in chains and hand you over kicking and screaming, and there would be nothing you could do about it."

Just like that, the mask of civilization came off. Auren was just as feral and ruthless as his brother. More so, I suspected. The poise, the sophistication, the manners, it was all a game of appearances, rules he played to amuse himself. Like all the fucking rich bastards who ran the world, he felt entitled to do whatever he wanted because he owned everyone and everything.

I was certain that if it suited his purposes, he would have torn off my head right then and there and handed it to the queen.

With a flurry of motion and color, Auren's staff flooded the courtyard, forming lines of servants and soldiers.

"Don't gape." Auren chuckled. "Though I'll admit, she definitely knows how to make an entrance."

I snapped my jaw shut and glared at the conceited bastard. "Shouldn't you be down there to greet her as well?"

"Of course." He gave me a little bow. "Remember everything we talked about. You have to convince her that you hate my brother and you're desperate to learn more about your fae side. Make her believe you. She has to want you."

"And what if I choose not to go?"

His expression darkened. "The time for that decision is long past."

"But—"

"But nothing. You're committed now. You will convince the queen to take you on."

My fists knotted. "I'm not your property."

Fury flared in his eyes, and his expression darkened. "I'm a god, Samantha. I can do anything I want, with anyone, to anyone. So you might want to start showing a little appreciation that I'm on your side."

"Are you?" I whispered, as a shudder shook through me.

"That depends entirely on you." He looked back at the courtyard. "I'll send for you when the queen is ready to meet, so don't run off—and remember, don't fuck this up."

His aura flared as he stepped into the sunlight and dissolved. A moment later, he appeared on the grand stairwell that led into the courtyard.

For everything that Cadean had done, he'd never spoken to me like that. He'd never used his power to make me feel small and worthless. The truth was, Cadean had made me feel important and capable of more than I'd ever dreamed. How screwed up was that?

My thoughts were silenced as the most gorgeous woman I could envision stepped out of the carriage.

Although the wind was still, the ends of her silver hair flicked and flitted around her. She gracefully brushed it back, revealing an elegantly pointed ear. In that moment, I had no doubt of whom I was seeing: Ayanna, tyrant queen of the Undying Court.

Magic spiraled around her like streams of smoke, and many of the staff averted their eyes as she approached. Even on the third floor, I could feel the impact of her power buffeting against me like ocean waves. Her signature was wild and powerful. It smelled of sweet persimmons and tasted like tart berries. It sounded like water rushing beneath an icy river.

I knew that the fae were unnaturally beautiful, but in my imagination, the queen had been a twisted monster, draining the land like a vampire. Ayanna was the opposite, a goddess who moved with impossible poise, as if she'd invented the art of walking. Her long green gown shimmered with each step, reminding me of summer leaves rustling in the wind. She glowed with grace and confidence and was everything I could never be.

I started to back away, but the queen snapped her head up and looked straight at me, her gaze locking me in place. Her eyes were emeralds lit by the rays of the sun. It felt like she was looking into me, peeling away my skin and flesh, until there was nothing left but bones.

I had no doubt she knew exactly who I was.

Time seemed to slow. My chest clenched, and my breath

turned to stone in my lungs. She was a diving falcon, and I was mouse, caught and exposed in a barren waste. My instincts fought for control as a single thought formed in my mind: *run*.

But I would not.

My claws slipped out, and I dug them into the banister to anchor myself. I refused to fear her or submit before her withering gaze. I wasn't her equal, but somehow, I would find the strength to face her down as if I were.

Mercifully, she looked away as Auren descended the stairs and kissed her on both cheeks. They locked arms and strode up the steps together like old friends.

My doubts came roaring back, and I pressed my spine against a pillar as I took in deep, shuddering breaths.

What kind of nightmare had I gotten myself into?

10

Samantha

Auren sent his guards for me an hour later. The wait had been agonizing. What had they been discussing? Clandestine plots, or perhaps simply haggling over my price?

Each step down the corridor felt heavier than the last. I had no illusions about the danger I was walking into or how over-matched I was.

A pair of sentries swung the doors to Auren's private dining room open, and with a shaking breath, I strode in. Queen Ayanna looked up, and a million doubts crashed through my mind.

She was impossibly beautiful, with flawless skin and a languid elegance that was both poised and effortless. She lounged at the great table like she was in her bedroom, utterly relaxed, with her hand wrapped around a crystal goblet of wine. Her faint smile was disarmingly alluring, but I knew I was twenty feet away from the most dangerous woman in the Dreamlands.

Her green eyes scoured me with relentless precision, evaluating every flaw and failure. My palms grew sweaty despite the chill in the air, but I forced myself to meet her gaze as I walked forward.

A predator can smell fear.

Auren smiled and rose as I approached.

Neither of them had repressed their signatures, and their powerful auras crashed into each other like waves churning against the breakers.

An attendant rushed forward and pulled a chair out for me, and Auren made a dramatic flourish. "Samantha, this is Queen Ayanna of the Undying Court."

Was I expected to bow before her? To curtsy or kneel?

If she was anything like Auren, she'd be used to people treating her like she was a goddess, but she wouldn't respect it. For all the gold and glamour, the court was just another kind of fighting ring, and to show weakness was death.

To pass her test, I had to be strong.

I glanced down at the empty chair, then back at her. "You tried to have me killed."

The corners of her mouth turned up. "I did."

No denial. No charade. At least I could respect that.

The queen nonchalantly swirled her wine. "I thought you were trying to release the Dark Wolf God from his prison. If killing you could stop that, then it was my duty."

I gave her a patently false smile. "But I wasn't. I helped trap him there, and I nearly died in the process."

"So I heard. But then I received reports that you were attending to him and had even fought by his side. I gave my agents two options. If you were his prisoner, they were to help you escape. On the other hand, if you were trying to free him or were under his control, they had orders to kill you."

"I guess I'm lucky the assassin was shit at his job, then, because he sure didn't ask me any questions before trying to kill me."

Auren shot me a warning look. "I think we can put the knives away. Sit."

The queen didn't betray an ounce of concern. She placed her goblet on the table and leaned forward, looking me directly in the eyes. "The Dark Wolf God is a monster who is not just a threat to my realm, but to all of the Dreamlands. Even his cocky brother knows it, though he hates to admit the truth. If your intention had been to release him or help his cause, I wouldn't hesitate to kill you. We are at war, after all."

"Good to know."

"I'm not trying to intimidate you. The Dark Wolf God must be brought down at all costs. I don't want you to have any questions about my priorities." She leaned back and arched an eyebrow. "You do wish to defeat him, don't you, Samantha?"

Hadn't that been all I wanted once? To destroy the Dark God? To punish him for what he had done to Magic Side and me?

But that was before he was Cadean. For all the evil he'd done, there was a noble side to him. A protector of his people.

And of me.

I couldn't think of that way about him now, though, not in front of her. My pulse accelerated as dread crept up my spine. Would she see it on my face? Could she smell my lies like a werewolf could?

I glanced down and forced myself to recall the visions that once haunted my nights— werewolves possessed by his power, sprinting through the mists and tearing into the citizens of Magic Side. Their red eyes in the darkness. The look of hate on my friend Savannah's face when she'd ripped her claws through my throat.

I met the queen's icy gaze. "The Dark Wolf God forced my best friend to kill me. He turned our pack on itself and littered the streets of my home with the bodies of my friends and neighbors. With all my heart, I hate him for that."

She studied me with merciless attention, and I shivered under the tingle of her magic in the air, searching my soul. I replayed the violence and destruction over and over in my mind until my stomach was churning.

I buried the thoughts of the tragic king who'd been imprisoned for more years than I could count. I pushed away the visions of him relentlessly fighting to protect his people from the queen's monsters. Of him cutting through vine after vine in a desperate attempt to save his land, knowing the harder he fought, the worse they would become.

I forced myself to forget the way he'd fought to protect me and the way I'd felt when his magic had brought me back from the brink of death. And I banished the memory of his lips and of a kiss that made me feel seen for the first time.

I buried it all deep within my soul. It hadn't happened. That was some other girl. Another god. A dream. A delusion. The pain was the only thing that was real.

After an excruciatingly long minute, the queen released her icy scrutiny and relaxed her shoulders. "Good."

The tension in the air faded, and a wave of relief rushed through me. I wanted to collapse into a chair, but I forced myself to match her prying gaze another moment longer. "Any other questions?" I asked, trying to keep my voice steady.

"That was the important one," Ayanna said softly. "The rest can wait. I'm glad that you were unharmed and that we have a chance to finally talk in person. And you have my word, I do not wish to hurt you. I want to help."

"Samantha, please sit," Auren prodded. "We're all on the same side here."

The bastard was right. We were all on our *own* side.

I tucked my dress and sat as the attendant pushed my chair

in behind me. I sliced through the meat on my plate with a keen knife and forked a bite into my mouth.

Venison. It was tender and flavorful, but I couldn't savor it. I'd passed the queen's first test, but she would be watching every move I made and dissecting every word that came out of my mouth. I'd never be able to let my guard down around her.

I sipped my wine, relishing the warmth it lit in my belly, and met her eyes. "Since we've established that I'm not helping the Dark Wolf God and you're not intending to kill me, what is it that you want?"

After a beat, she spoke. "The same thing as when I sent Sarion to find you—your help."

"And what would that entail?"

"Initially, I'd simply hoped that you'd identified a weakness, but Auren tells me you've found a way to stop Cadean from crossing the barrier. That's extraordinary, far more than anything I expected."

I flicked my eyes to Auren, but his face betrayed nothing. Had he told her about the moonshard? I didn't want to give the queen anything I didn't have to.

I returned to eating, an excuse to break eye contact. "I don't really understand the barrier, but the Dark Wolf God won't be able to manipulate it anymore, at least not while I'm around."

"Our court owes you a great debt of gratitude. My people in the borderlands can finally rest easy at night knowing that the beast cannot reach them."

While Selene and her family lie awake waiting for deathwings to come.

"You look less than pleased," the queen said.

Was I that transparent? Apparently, there'd be no hiding my anger at what she had done, no more than I could repress my anger at the Dark God.

"You're not innocent," I said, setting my silverware down.

"I've seen the destruction on both sides of the border, and your forces are just as vicious as those of the Dark Wolf God. I watched your deathwings raid shifter villages. They weren't defending anything or even trying to take land. It was murder, an attempt to spread terror."

Her steel-hearted gaze cut through me. "War is murder and terror, and there's no getting around that."

"There is. Don't kill innocent people."

Her lips pinched in anger. "I admire that you're an idealist and that you have a compassionate heart. Unfortunately, as queen, that's a luxury I cannot grant myself. We're trapped in a war, and I will not stop fighting until the Dark Wolf God is powerless to harm my land."

I opened my mouth to protest, but she brought her fist down on the table, and the room went ice cold. "You have no idea what he's capable of. When the Dark Wolf God was strong, he ravaged our lands with storms that leveled cities and uprooted mountains. He doesn't need to cross the barrier to kill. The earthquake and the hurricane obey him. That is why there's not a single city within a hundred miles of the border. Because the Dark Wolf God is death incarnate."

My throat tightened. I'd seen that in him, too.

Auren rubbed his forehead and gave me an earnest look. "My brother has always had trouble controlling his anger. Before he was imprisoned, he upended the balance of the Dreamlands, leveling cities and returning them to wilderness. The queen and I want to restore the balance."

Folding her hands, she leaned forward and locked me with her impossibly green eyes. "I know you see yourself as a wolf, but you're also part fae. I believe that part of you has the power to change things for my people. *Your* people. That's why I want you to return with me to the Undying Court. I can help you discover the fae part of yourself that you've lost."

My chest tightened as my emotions twisted and turned within me. I desperately wanted to know more about that aspect of myself, to be able to seize the heritage my mother had hidden from me. And the queen also believed I had a purpose.

The temptation was real.

I wrung my hands beneath the table as I tried to keep my composure steady. It had been so much easier to imagine infiltrating her court before I met her—before she'd grilled me about Cadean and where my loyalties lay. Despite how much I wanted to go, there was no way it would work. The pressure would never let up. I'd make a mistake. I'd let something slip about Cadean, or she'd realize I had a covert agenda. Maybe I could fool her tonight, but I wouldn't be able to keep it up.

"I appreciate everything you're offering, but may I have some time to think?" I asked, praying she didn't detect the fear in my voice.

She smiled. "You belong with us, Samantha. You're bursting with power and potential, but you have no idea how to use it. Auren's not fae. He can't teach you that, but I can."

As I cast about for an answer, I noticed a slight tingle caressing over my skin, calming my emotions. I'd thought it was part of her aura, but it wasn't. The glamour was faint, but there was no ignoring that she was pushing me with her magic, making herself seem trustworthy and earnest.

Bending my will.

More kind words slipped from her mouth, but I didn't hear them as the horrid truth began to set in.

She'd do anything to stop the Dark God.

If she could compel me like Auren could, then she could force me to use my magic against the Dark God and his people —to shift the barrier back for her army as they sacked defenseless shifter villages like Selene's, perhaps to curse him like I had before.

I would be a deadly weapon in her hands. I tried to focus on eating, but my fork slipped.

Auren lifted his eyebrow. "Is everything all right?"

No, it's not all right. You're fucking feeding me to a dragon.

I had to get away.

I dropped my napkin on the table and rose. "I appreciate your offer to train me, Your Majesty, and I share your desire to make sure the Dark Wolf God never hurts anyone again. But I must decline. Perhaps we can discuss visiting another time."

Auren leaned forward. "I can vouch for the queen's good intentions, Samantha. We all want the same thing. Peace in the Dreamlands."

Although he was smiling, the fire in his eyes made his message clear: *If you sabotage this, I'll make you regret it.*

The queen smiled sweetly as the press of her magic around me intensified. "I know that we have a long way to go before we fully trust each other, but I promise you'll be perfectly safe."

Perfectly safe as long as I obey? Perfectly safe in a cell? Perfectly safe until you find out that Auren is trying to play you?

I backed toward the door. "I'm sorry. I've been through a lot. I just need some time."

The queen rose. "The Undying Court is the best place for you. Reconsider."

Although her voice was soft, the power beneath it rippled with iron-hard authority, bending my will.

I tried to push against it, but it only grew stronger.

She strode around the end of the table. "I want to help you master your magic, Samantha. And I want to help your mother, too."

The heat and light drained from the room in a single heartbeat.

"My mother?"

The queen gave me a compassionate look and brushed a

silver lock of hair from her cheek. "She's very sick with a fae curse, but our best doctors are looking after her. I want to do everything I can to help heal her."

The icy intent of her words rammed through my heart like a saber, and the room began to close in. The wolf inside of me woke.

"Are you telling me that you abducted my *mother*?" I didn't recognize my own voice, nor did I care that this woman was as lethal as a viper. If she'd harmed my mother, I'd rip the bitch's throat out.

"We *rescued* her." She paused at the end of the table, wisely keeping several arms' lengths between us. "Sarion told us about her predicament. We brought her to our court to see if there was anything we could do."

My wolf surged in my chest, and I knotted my muscles, straining to keep her under control.

The queen spread her hands apologetically. "I only wanted to help. We were worried that the Dark Wolf God would come for your family and that he'd use them to control you."

I dug my nails into my palms, letting the pain focus my mind. "And now you want to do the same? To force me to join you?"

"That is not my intent at all," the queen said, pressing with her magic.

"I thought only fae could enter your palace," I said, suspicion and anger burning at the tip of my tongue. "Where are you keeping her?"

The queen waved dismissively. "You needn't worry. She is in our diplomatic residence and is perfectly safe and under guard."

My claws slipped out. "You mean under house arrest."

Auren stepped forward and touched my arm as invisible sunlight washed over me, soothing magic to make me calm and pliable.

I jerked away from him. "What have you gotten me into?"

"Samantha. The queen is here to help. This is the best news possible. You were worried about your mother, and if there's a chance for her, it is with the Undying Court, and with you at her side."

His voice was calm and pleading, but I could see the calculation in his eyes. He couldn't have asked for better cover for his little spy.

The press of his magic flared as he tried to overwhelm me, but my wolf surged in resistance. My fangs erupted and hair bristled over my arms as my wolf fought its way free. I looked up in horror. "I...I have to go."

Wrenching open the door, I burst from the room. I had to escape before my wolf took complete control.

11

Cadean

I spread the maps of Auren's realm across the table. No matter how many times I looked at them, there were no answers.

"The best way is sending someone through the mistways," Wulfric muttered.

Melanthe shook her head. "There is no way for you to navigate—"

My body lurched forward as a tidal wave of emotion lanced through my chest: fear, desperation, and most of all, betrayal.

Samantha.

Mel backed away, and my other advisors followed. "Cadean, what's happening?"

"Samantha is in danger," I growled.

Closing my eyes, I hurled my presence through the darkness, shadow-casting to her. Glimpses of the Dreamlands flickered before me, then Auren's palace, shielded by his renewed wards.

I didn't bother looking for weaknesses. I threw my will directly against the wards, raging with every ounce of power the darkness gave me. I could feel her despair on the other side, and it gave me more strength than Mel's spells ever had—strength I didn't have alone.

The spells seared my mind and skin, but I shoved down the pain and roared as I shredded through. Suddenly, they collapsed, and I found myself in a dark garden ringed by high walls and illuminated by flickering torchlight.

Samantha's despair yanked me through the shadows to a group of apple trees. She braced herself against a trunk in the throes of a shift as she tried to hold back her wolf.

I cast my power toward her, wishing more than anything that I could comfort her, and whispered, "Be calm, little wolf."

Her body quaked, and the shift subsided. She dropped to her knees in the dirt, shoulders heaving from the exertion. My chest tightened. She looked so vulnerable and broken, completely unlike the woman I knew.

"What did my brother do?" I snarled, advancing through the trees toward her. "Did he hurt you?"

"Cadean?" She looked up with startled eyes, and then let her head drop. "How is it always you? When everything is crashing down around me, why are you always there in the darkness? Why is my life so fucked?"

The golden gown she wore was torn, revealing a swath of bare shoulder and the bewitching length of her leg. She was breathtaking even in her anguish, and yet, all I could think of was destroying whoever had made her feel this way. I wanted to fold her in my arms and take her away from there, but of course, that was beyond the limits of shadow-casting.

Instead, I dropped to one knee beside her. "Whatever's happened, I can help you escape."

She looked up at me, her expression torn between agony and fury. "Escape? What does escape even mean anymore? Escape you, escape Auren, escape the queen? It doesn't mean anything. I'm so entangled in this mess that I'll never be free."

"The queen?" Dread began building in my soul like a thunderhead climbing in the dark sky.

"She's here."

A deep, low growl rose in my throat, protectiveness vying with the rage that surged through my soul. Ayanna would only be there with Auren's permission. My chest felt as if it were splitting in two. Did my own brother's treachery truly run that deep?

That would be an unforgiveable betrayal.

Fury seeped into every crack in my heart, and I wanted nothing more than to unleash it on my brother's kingdom, but I fought it down. What mattered now was getting Samantha away from them both.

"Listen to me. You need to run, *right now*. Get out of the palace. I will send demons and shifters over the border to protect you. The queen is more dangerous than you can possibly imagine. She already sent assassins once. She'll kill you the first chance she gets."

Grasping the rough trunk, Samantha pulled herself to her feet. "I'm not going to run, Cadean. I have to go with her to the Undying Court. I don't have a choice."

"Are you insane?" I asked, leaping to my feet.

"The queen has my mother. She's sick with a fae curse, and Ayanna can heal her. I have to go."

Fucking hell.

Kassian had proposed we take her mother hostage, but I'd shot him down, and now, my weakness had bitten me in the ass.

"I know what she means to you, but you can't go after her. I'll send raiders over the border."

Samantha shook her head. "You'll get her killed. They have her under house arrest, and if the queen is as ruthless as you suggest, do you think they'll let you take her? Hell, it might even be impossible to get to her. Only fae can enter the queen's palace."

How did she know about that? Had Auren told her, or the queen herself? Everyone I'd sent to infiltrate the court had ended up with their throat slit. I couldn't let Samantha end up the same way.

I knotted my fists because there was nothing else I could do with my hands—I couldn't grab her or hold her or even attempt to shake sense into her. "It's too dangerous. I'll find a way to get her out."

Samantha's expression hardened, and she glanced over her shoulder. "It's more than just my mother. There's a chance to—"

Her voice caught abruptly, and her eyes flared with frustration. She fumbled for words, but nothing emerged.

Realization dawned. She'd been silenced. This was Auren's handywork.

"Whatever my brother's convinced you to do, it's not worth the risk," I said.

"It is." She raised her chin and met my gaze. "And so is my mother."

The torchlight reflected off the tears that gathered in her eyes, and yet she stood there with the courage of a lion. My chest felt like it was caving in. "The queen will kill you as soon as she has whatever she needs."

"She's not going to kill me, Cadean. She thinks I'm the key to stopping you. She thinks I hate you, that I would do anything to destroy you, including killing you with my own hands. That's what she wants to train me to do."

Was this their game? I circled her, scrutinizing every line of her face. "And do you hate me, little wolf? Do you want to kill me?"

Samantha's expression turned cold. "It's what I told her."

But it wasn't the truth. She could have unleashed the full force of her magic when she'd stabbed me in the heart, but she hadn't. She could have left me lying on my bedroom floor when she'd escaped, but she'd healed the curse.

If she felt anything for me, an inkling of what I'd come to feel for her, it put her in more danger than she could ever know.

"You can't lie to the queen of the fae."

"I wasn't lying," she snapped. "I hate you for what you did to me, to my friends, and to Magic Side, and I'll do anything to stop you from ever doing that again. *That's* the truth."

The look in her eyes was raw and unforgiving, and regret tore into me. I wanted to apologize, to beg her forgiveness, but I didn't dare say a thing to weaken her hatred. It was the only thing that could save her.

"Ayanna will manipulate you the same way Auren has. She doesn't want your help—she wants your magic. She'll take the moonshard from you and force you to use it to—"

"The moonshard? Is that why you care about this? About me?"

Too late, I realized I'd chosen the wrong words. I raised my hands "That's not—"

"I'm going, Cadean. I have a chance to save my mother and to make a difference in the world. It's what I have to do. What I *choose* to do."

She threw her hands up in front of her, and a wave of searing magic raced over my skin. The shadows around us exploded into smoke, and the vision of her dissolved.

The world spun around me, and suddenly, I was back in my tower with Mel and Wulfric, and a floor strewn with maps.

I let out a long, shaking breath. She'd shut me out. Could I break back through her will, as well as Auren's magic?

Mel grabbed my arm. "What's going on?"

When I shadow-casted, my physical body remained motionless just as if I were dreaming, so she had no idea what had happened.

"Samantha is on her way to the Undying Court, and I'm afraid I've fucked up any chance of convincing her to come back." I yanked my arm free of her grasp, and dark shadows coiled around me.

Mel's eyes rounded. "What are you talking about? What happened?"

"Auren set up a meeting with the queen, and Sam's going into the fae realm with her. Ayanna is holding her mother hostage."

"Oh, shit," she whispered.

Wulfric stepped out of the shadows and approached. "Kassian was right. We should have grabbed the old woman when we had the chance. Now the queen has the leverage to turn Samantha against you, and you can be damned sure she'll use it."

"How did Auren let this happen?" Mel asked.

The shadows drained from the corners of the room and poured into me as I imagined slowly dragging the blade of my axe across my brother's throat.

"I suspect he's been working with the queen for a very long time, and if he realizes how desperate I am to get Samantha back, he'll find a way to twist the knife further."

Wulfric extended his hand. "Give me your axe. I'll take my wolves and get her out."

I glanced down at the black axe in my hand, my father's axe. It was more than an ancient artifact—it was dark power made manifest. It would give Wulfric the destructive power of a god, but it would not make him invincible.

"I'm not going to blindly sacrifice you and your people. Auren would kill you the instant you crossed the border."

Wulfric's lips curled back in a snarl. "Then I'll be very fucking sneaky. We need to stop her before she gets to the queen's palace."

I tightened my grip on the handle of my axe and rammed it down into the stone floor. "Then I'll call up devils and demons and tear a hole in the Dreamlands if I have to. I'll find a way to stop this."

12

———

Samantha

Cadean disappeared in a cloud of shadow, leaving me alone again in the darkness. I sucked in a sharp breath, as if coming up from a deep dive.

The Dark Wolf God's scent lingered in the air, mixing with the aroma of the ripening apples. It wasn't just the scent of his magic, but the deep, earthy aroma of his body as well. He'd been so close to me that I'd almost felt him, but of course, he hadn't been there at all.

And you should be thankful he wasn't, I chided myself.

Yet his absence had left a hollowness in my chest. Maybe it was just the ache of being absolutely fucking alone.

Cadean, Auren, and Ayanna. Each was more powerful than I could imagine, and each wanted a piece of me. I felt like a rabbit cornered by a pack of wolves. No matter which direction I fled, I'd run straight into the jaws of death. They were going to tear me to pieces and fight over the scraps.

I could almost feel Sigrun's single good eye boring into me accusingly. *Stop hiding. Learn your magic and figure out where it came from. Once you master your power, no one will be able to control you. Not even the Dark Wolf God.*

Wasn't that what Ayanna was offering? To train me?

I hadn't realized I'd made the decision to go with Ayanna until the words had blurted out of my mouth, but it was the only choice. My magic, my freedom, the vines—it all came second to my mother.

Leaves crinkled. I spun and sniffed the air. "Auren?"

A gold-lit silhouette stepped from between the rows of trees and bowed his head. "Pardon my intrusion. I heard voices, and I needed ensure that you were safe."

Yeah, right. He'd deliberately suppressed his signature so that I wouldn't feel him coming. Had he heard me? Did he know Cadean could shadow-cast to me and that we could speak?

At this point, secrets were my only weapons, and that seemed like a big one.

I pulled my dress around my shoulders and stalked toward him. "I was just cursing the moment I ever stepped foot in the Dreamlands. I've got some pretty choice words for you as well if you'd like to hear them."

"I'm sure you do." Auren chuckled softly, and then he silently applauded. "That was a masterful performance at dinner. It will throw Queen Ayanna off our scent and make her want you all the more. Brava."

"Don't you dare try to compel me again, or I swear to the Fates, I'll ram the moonshard through your chest."

He held up his hands. "I apologize. Force of habit. I won't do it again."

Right.

His eyes played across the tears in my dress, but I ignored his heated gaze.

"Did you know she had my mother?" I snarled.

"I'm ashamed to admit that was a surprise. But if Ayanna is

telling the truth, it's a stroke of luck. Your mother can get the medical attention she desperately needs, and you'll be able to get her back."

I gaped at him. "Are you serious? The queen is using my mother as leverage already! The moment I step out of line, or she gets suspicious, she'll put a knife to my mom's throat. She knows she has me trapped, Auren."

"We'll make your mother's safety one of our conditions."

I raised my eyebrows. "Do you think the queen will honor any agreement after I'm over the border? If she needs me as badly as she claims, then she'll use her magic to compel me to do whatever she wants, just like *you* do."

Auren put his arm around my shoulders. "Ayanna is desperate to get her hands on you, and she knows that I won't let you leave unless *my* conditions are satisfied. We can force her to sign a pact that will protect you and your autonomy."

I shoved his arm away with disdain. "A pact?"

"A powerful magical contract. Do you think I would let Ayanna into my realm without some sort of guarantee? She pledged not to make any attempt to capture you, harm you, or even speak with you without my direct permission. We would draft a contract protecting you."

My thoughts began to turn. What stipulations could I set? Freedom from being compelled? Freedom of movement?

I had none of that here. A pact could finally set me free.

I studied his expression. "How does it work? What's to stop her from breaking it?"

A wicked smile spread over Auren's lips. "While blood oaths are easily manipulated, a pact is a binding contract, secured against the power of your own magic. They're extremely hard to circumvent."

My heart sank. "I'm not very good with fine print."

My firstborn could belong to Netflix, for all I knew.

"I have professionals for this sort of thing. We'll make sure that you and your mother are safe, that the queen won't use her magic to compel you, and that your efforts on my behalf are not impeded." He shrugged nonchalantly. "But the choice to go remains up to you."

As if.

I took a deep breath. I didn't trust Auren, or any of them. But I was so far in over my head that it almost didn't matter. All I could do was keep moving forward every chance they gave me.

I looked down at my hand and retracted my claws. "Okay. Let's do this."

My eyes snapped open the next morning at dawn. I threw off the covers and sat up in bed, heart pounding. I was about to jump into the deep end with only a devil's bargain to save me.

Maybe I should've felt a sense of dread or doubt, but instead, I was practically vibrating with energy. I always got amped on adrenaline before a roller derby match or fight, and this was no different. I was going head-to-head against the queen of the fae with my life on the line. The pact was another test, and if I got outmaneuvered, I could end up trapped or dead.

I splashed water on my face and checked myself in the mirror. *Let's do this.*

As soon as I stepped out of my room, Auren greeted me with a glistening smile. "I hope you slept well, my dear. You'll need your wits about you today."

I followed him down the hall. "Any last-minute advice? I don't want to shoot myself in the foot or end up a prisoner again."

"She's difficult to read, but I think she's more interested in securing your assistance than locking you up, and that should make our part of the bargain easier. Remember: our goal is to get the seedlings and get out, so make sure you insist on freedom of movement and the right to leave whenever you wish."

Ironic. Those were the two things I didn't have in his realm.

"What happens if one of us breaks our agreement?"

A devilish grin cut across Auren's face. "I wouldn't advise that, darling. You seal the pact with an investiture of magic. If you break it, your own powers will be turned against you, burning you from the inside out."

My eyes rounded. "Holy shit."

"Reflective magic minimizes the problem of forging contracts between powerful beings like me and lesser ones like you. It means the consequences of the queen breaking her word would be far more severe for her than they would be for you if you did...well, perhaps not relatively speaking." He paused before a set of large golden doors and turned to me. "Just don't give up anything you don't have to or compromise the plan."

If only it were that simple.

The doors swung open, revealing a room bathed in shadow and candlelight. The air smelled of blood and brimstone, and an ominous magical presence hung in the air. It felt like rusted nails dragging over my skin and tasted like kerosene.

The queen waited beside a heavy wooden table, but beyond her, I sensed something lurking in the deep shadows of the room—an alien presence I couldn't put my finger on.

Auren smiled broadly. "Don't worry, my darling. The pactfiends might seem a bit sinister, but they're the best in the business. They delight at creating and exploiting loopholes."

"This sounds like the opposite of what we need."

"The only thing that pactfiends hate more than their clients is each other. While it's a contract to us, it's a savage competition for them. Any time one tries to create a loophole, the others will move to strike it. Among the five of them, they'll create a watertight contract. I wouldn't trust anyone else."

With that, he swept into the room and delicately kissed the queen's hand.

I followed him across the threshold with a shuddering breath. Perhaps I would have found his reassurances comforting if I trusted him at all.

The door slammed shut behind me, and five dark shapes rose from the shadows. I ducked as they soared overhead on leathery wings, then landed on the far side of the table. The spindly creatures had sharp teeth and the twisted faces of gargoyles. Their bodies blurred slightly as they moved, and they glared back at me with coal black eyes and predatory expressions.

They're on your side, I reminded myself. The queen was the one I had to be careful of.

She dominated the room, despite Auren's glow and the lurking presence of the pactfiends. Ayanna inclined her head slightly in acknowledgment. "I'm elated that you've decided to join me, Samantha. I was concerned after you disappeared last night."

I forced a smile in return. "I'm sorry about that. I didn't anticipate you'd have news of my mother."

She waved her hand dismissively. "You're here now, and that's what matters. Please understand, I want only the best for you, and I'm excited to show you my realm."

Said the spider to the fly.

"I'm eager, but I'll need you to guarantee my safety and that of my mother."

"Of course. That is what our contract is for—so neither of us need worry about the intentions of the other." She motioned to the largest of the pactfiends. "For as long as Samantha remains in my realm, she and her mother will have my protection as well as that of the Undying Court."

The pactfiend summoned a quill and scroll from the ether, then began scrawling in microscopic black writing.

"I also need you to promise that you won't use your powers to control me or force me to take action against my will," I said.

Her gaze flicked to Auren, and a knowing smile formed at the corners of her mouth. "I wouldn't dare try to manipulate a guest. You, however, have powers of your own—you must agree not to use them against me or any of my subjects."

The pactfiends looked to me for confirmation, and I tensed. *Don't give anything away.* She had a whole kingdom at her disposal, but my claws and magic were all I had.

"What about self-defense? What if the Dark God sends assassins like you did?"

Her eyes narrowed. "Self-defense is acceptable, as is training. Anything else?"

"I need freedom of movement throughout your palace and realm, and the right to leave whenever I choose, with my mother."

She raised a finger. "You're free to leave whenever you wish. However, you must agree not to enter any room I forbid and not to spy, eavesdrop, or steal anything from the palace."

My heart skipped a beat.

Agreeing to that would upend everything Auren was planning. I was supposed to steal the seedlings and gather information. I glanced at him as nonchalantly as possible, but I felt like I was broadcasting my intentions on a megaphone.

Auren gave me a subtle nod: *agree.*

The queen's jaw hardened. "You hesitate?"

Fuck. She was on to me. My pulse raced as I searched for anything that would throw her off the scent.

"This sounds like a trap," I blurted.

She raised her eyebrows. "A trap? How could not stealing and snooping be a trap?"

"What if you bring me to a room with one exit, then forbid me to enter the hall? You won't technically have stopped me from leaving your kingdom, but there would be no way out."

"Clever little wolfling," the pactfiend next to me muttered, then snatched a pen from the ether and began scribbling in red as he released a slew of demonic curses at his brothers.

The queen gave me a scouring look. "It's my intent that Samantha has genuine freedom of movement, unrestrained by tricks, as long as she agrees to my terms. Take nothing not freely given to you."

I still had no idea how Auren's plan was going to work, but he'd given me the okay. "I agree, as long as you vow not take any of my possessions, either."

The queen released a malicious laugh. "Do you seriously consider me a thief?"

I had to protect the moonshard, and I was not going leave it with Auren, so I shrugged apologetically. "Of course not, but I'm a bit traumatized from my stay in the Dreamlands. The demand stands."

"Well, after what you've been through, I don't blame you. I agree to your terms." She crossed her arms. "Anything else, little lawyer?"

Auren subtly shook his head.

I sucked in a breath. "That suits me."

"Then let us sign and be on our way."

The largest fiend asked, tilting his head in a birdlike movement, "How long is the duration of the contract, Your Majesty?"

"For as long as she is in my lands."

Unease pulled at me. That meant the moment I stepped beyond the border, I'd be fair game.

Before I could object, all chaos broke out. The fiends

attacked the document like hyenas, correcting, adding to, and striking out each other's handwriting. They cackled maniacally as they shoved and fought, stealing the contract back and forth. Soon, it was filled with a rainbow of corrections, asterisks, footnotes, amendments, and strikethroughs.

"This actually works?" I whispered to Auren.

"Infallibly."

Slowly, the fiends transitioned from maniacal glee to focused attention until finally, they were all standing around the contract, flummoxed. The largest hesitantly reached out with his quill, but another slapped his hand away. "It's done."

The rest bobbed their heads in assent, and reluctantly, the largest waved his clawed hand.

The dense scribbles lit up with a white light, and the words began rearranging themselves until all that was left was a neat, clean document where absolute chaos had been. The smallest fiend held the scroll and a quill to me. "You must sign."

As I carefully read through the document, my eyes blurred, and my temples began to throb. The script wasn't English, but somehow, I could read it—sort of. Despite my best efforts, it was an incomprehensible sea of legalese stretching on, minute paragraph after paragraph.

Every instinct I had screamed for me to abandon my plan and flee. I was bargaining with a god and a queen and far outmatched.

My hand hesitated, and Auren muttered, "Trust the process."

I didn't, but what choice did I have? My mother's life and freedom were on the line—not to mention the fate of Cadean's people. Maybe I couldn't trust Auren or the contract or the queen, but I trusted the Fates. They had a plan for me, even if I had no idea what it was.

Fuck it, let's do this.

I scrawled my name. I'd gotten safety, freedom of movement, and an agreement not to compel me. Hopefully, it was enough.

With a violent burst of power, the contract sucked my magic in. I pitched forward over the table and dropped the quill like it was hot iron.

"What the hell was that?" I gasped. It had been like having my breath ripped from my body, and my limbs felt weak.

"The pact takes what it requires," Auren said.

Right. Just enough of my own magic to kill me.

Queen Ayanna pulled back the sleeve of her gown and gracefully signed in looping script. Her expression hardened as the contract stole her power as well.

The scroll began to glow, then split down the center. One half zipped toward her, while the other half wrapped around my wrist, becoming a thin golden bracelet. I turned my arm over. The bracelet was beautiful, but was it a mark of freedom or a new chain to bind me?

The queen raised her arm, revealing the bracelet's twin. "Now that we're bound by this pact, I hope that you can begin to trust me. I can feel your potential, and I can't wait to help you harness it."

She offered her hand, and I shook it. "I'm ready when you are."

I sure as hell wouldn't trust her, not after last night. I knew she was treacherous, and the pact only masked the danger, but I was committed. I had my mother to rescue, and beyond that, a whole realm of problems to solve.

13

Samantha

I rushed back to my room to pack. My maids had folded my clothes and left a small travel bag on my bed, as well as a bundle of necessaries. I grabbed my riding outfit and a few things and shoved them in, leaving all but two of the gowns that Auren had given me. Despite his apparent generosity, I knew he'd selected each for his own satisfaction, like I was doll to be dressed and played with.

Live or die, I wasn't going to be his toy anymore.

The only possession I truly cared about was the moonshard. I wanted it hidden and near me at all times so that I could draw on its magic if necessary. Unfortunately, if I was going to be wearing dresses at the fae court, there wasn't a great solution to carrying it around. I'd worked until late at night modifying a knife sheath so that I could strap the moonshard to my thigh. The dresses concealed it well enough, so if I was lucky, no one would even know I had it.

I pulled the gown up over my leg and strapped it on, then looked around my room one last time. The luxurious bed, the ornate dresser, the clothes—it had all been a beautiful cage.

While I was walking into danger, at least I'd be free of Auren and his mind control. Maybe that was enough.

Or maybe I was a dead woman.

"Let's do this." I pulled my bag shut and fastened the clasps, then headed to the veranda. Auren and the queen were arm and arm and speaking in low voices like old lovers. A glimmer of dread coiled in my stomach.

Who is conspiring against whom, here?

I followed them down the stairs and out into the courtyard, where the queen's carriage was waiting. Her movements were so graceful, it was almost impossible to take my eyes off her, like a siren calling me to my doom.

She paused and lightly kissed Auren on the cheek. "Thank you for facilitating this meeting, Auren. My kingdom is in your debt."

Regarding her with a ravenous look, he raised her hand to his lips. "It's always a pleasure, Ayanna. Please return soon."

She slipped out of his arm and glanced back at me. "Join me when you're ready."

Auren pulled a feather pendant from his pocket and fasted it around my neck. "A parting gift to remember me by. It will be sad to lose you."

I pretended to admire it for a moment, but as soon as the carriage door closed, I whispered, "The pact is a problem. Are we fucked?"

He raised his eyebrows, and the air grew heavy as he muffled our voices. "Nothing we can't work around. If you're unable to steal the seedlings, then perhaps we can sneak someone in."

"I also agreed not to spy."

"Palaces are full of whispers, and you have werewolf hearing. You can't be held accountable for what people will say." He tapped the pendant. "The necklace turns into a quill and paper.

Write to me what you hear, and I will write back. The words will erase themselves once they're read."

Hell, real espionage stuff. I glanced back at the waiting carriage. "Why do I have a feeling this could all end very badly?"

A knowing smile brushed across his lips, and the muffled aura around us dissipated. "Good luck, Samantha."

And with that, he turned his back and headed into his palace.

One of the queen's footmen took my bag, while the other helped me up into the swan-shaped carriage. I slipped into the seat opposite Queen Ayanna and examined my surroundings. The interior was just as luxurious at the exterior, with soft cushions, crystalline windows, and elaborate golden trim around everything.

"I'm glad you're coming, Samantha. I cannot wait to show you my kingdom." She tugged on a thin red string dangling from the ceiling, and the carriage lurched forward. The clop of hooves echoed off the walls as we rolled through the front gate. I glanced through the rear window as Auren's palace and its last illusions of safety fell away.

"Honestly, I can't believe Auren let me go."

"I can only imagine. Let's depart quickly in case he has a change of heart," the queen said slyly, and pulled the cord again. The pounding of hooves accelerated, and soon, we were flying down the winding mountain road, kicking up a spray of pebbles and dust in our wake.

Holy crap, I'm going to die before we even cross the border.

We tilted up on two wheels as we rounded a curve, and I clutched the seat to hold myself steady. There was a clanking sound, and I looked out the window just in time to see the carriage's giant wings unfold.

With a sudden jolt, we lurched into the air. Aspen-covered slopes whipped by below us. "Holy shit."

"Never flown before?" she asked.

"Not like this."

Eventually, I sat back as mist consumed the landscape below.

The queen smiled. "Can I offer you something to drink? Wine, perhaps?"

"Sure."

She tapped on the wall behind her. "Two glasses of summer wine."

Summer wine.

Cadean's favorite.

A moment later, the small hatch opened and someone passed out goblets of shimmering liquid. The queen handed me one. "I find it helps when the air gets bumpy."

The patchwork landscape rolled by beneath us—islands of forest and mountains, tundra and deserts, all separated by the mists.

The queen grilled me about living in Magic Side and what the waking world was like. At first, I thought she was genuinely interested, but I was soon certain of what game she was playing. She wanted to see how I answered questions when I was comfortable and had nothing to hide. She was establishing a baseline so that she'd know when I lied.

A glinting light on the horizon offered the perfect opportunity to deflect. "What's that?"

"More of Auren's hubris." She knocked on the carriage wall. "Take us past the gateway, but not too close to the city."

The carriage banked toward the glinting light, and it disappeared from view.

"What city?"

She sniffed. "Jewel. It belongs to Auren's realm. It has...a strained reputation as a den of splendor and vice."

"Are there many cities in the Dreamlands?"

"A few in the realms of the wolf brothers. There are more in ours, though they're all far from the border, as you might imagine. Did you ever visit the Dark Wolf God's capital?"

I shook my head. "I spent most of my time in chains."

Selene had mentioned it, but I knew nothing of the place.

The queen wrinkled her nose. "Unfortunate."

After another ten minutes, the carriage banked again, and two enormous statues came into view: a pair of rampant wolves fighting each other. They were impossibly tall and sheathed in gold.

The queen frowned. "This atrocity is the gateway to Auren's realm. Hideous, isn't it?"

I looked back at the sprawling white city ringed by mists in the distance. *Jewel.*

"Does this mean we're in your realm now?"

The queen smiled and folded her hands in her lap. "We entered just a moment ago. The border was the seam of mist. Welcome to the land of the Undying Court."

I swallowed. I was officially hers.

Leaning over, I looked down as we passed over a vast forest of red and yellow leaves. Purple vines snaked through the clearings, winding their way toward the Dark Wolf God's realm. I could see the shimmering barrier through the right-hand window, and beyond it, miles of skeletal forest and desolation.

"When Sarion first brought me here, he let me believe that the Dark Wolf God's magic had killed the forests beyond your border—but it was your vines, draining the life from the land," I said.

"He let you believe that because the truth was complicated. Everything would have been explained once you reached us." Her expression turned cold. "I have one mission in life: to save my people. Our court was cursed long ago. Instead of living for centuries, we die young. I created the vines to extend the lives of my people."

"By draining the life from the land?"

She glanced out the window toward the border. "We didn't take so much at first, but the war has stretched us thin. The Dark Wolf God's aggression has weakened our magic and thinned our numbers. We take what we must to survive."

The carriage suddenly lurched, and I was hurled against the wall. The coach began to dive, and I braced myself against the velvet roof. "What the hell is going on?"

The queen's hand flared with purple light as she crouched against the cushioned bench. "I don't know, but this must be the Dark Wolf God's work! Prepare yourself!"

My claws ripped out of my fingertips, and I bared my teeth. *We had a truce.*

I should've never trusted the bastard.

The carriage shook as something enormous slammed into the side. A black shape blotted out the window, and splinters of wood exploded around us as talons punched through the wall.

I leapt back and pressed myself against the other side of the carriage.

Streaks of purple light streamed from the queen's hand, cutting through the sides of the carriage like an acetylene torch. The black shape fell away, and an earsplitting shriek burst through the air.

I clapped my hands over my ears and buckled in pain, but another lurch hurled me to the floor.

There was a moment of stillness as the carriage leveled out.

"What was that?" I whispered, seeing nothing out my window besides the blue sky and endless forest below.

The queen moved to the window, her hand still engulfed in purple-pink magic. "I don't know. I can't see it or our escort of deathwings."

My stomach dropped as a thunderous impact drove the carriage downward, flinging us up and then to our knees. A monstrous clawed paw ripped through the roof, sending shattered fragments of wood raining down around us.

"Get back!" the queen shouted as a large chunk of the ceiling pulled away, revealing the beaked face of a monster. Its enormous owl-like eyes took me in, and then it opened its mouth and screeched.

14

Samantha

Pain exploded through my ears as the waves of sound rippled through me. I crumpled back against the carriage door and flung my hand up. The cool tingle of my magic flared to life, a bluish-white glow radiating from my palms. I released a halo of light, creating a domed shield between the thing and us.

It rammed its clawed arm through the gap but screeched when it ricocheted off the crackling shield.

"Well done!' the queen shouted, but I barely heard her words over the agonizing ringing in my ears.

A momentary glow of victory swelled in my chest.

Then the coach shook again and tilted sideways. I dug my claws into the couch as the righthand door ripped off its hinges and tumbled into the sky.

A woman appeared in the gap, hanging from a rope and braced against the side. She thrust out her hand. "Samantha! Come with me!"

I froze. Her eyes were a brilliant gold. She was a shifter.

The woman ducked out of the way as crackling purple light blasted through the doorway. I saw her leap, and then she was soaring skyward on the back of the giant beast—it had the hulking body of a bear, but with a beak and feathered wings.

A deafening crack erupted next to my head, and a storm of purple lightning burst through the door and into the creature's side. Rider and beast spiraled downward in a haze of gray smoke.

My throat leapt into my mouth, and I froze, braced against the open door.

The coach shook with a massive impact and tipped, and I flipped out into freefall.

Twisting in midair, I flailed, and my claws caught the footwell. My body jerked to a halt, and I hung dangling from the side of the carriage. Panic flooded me as I looked down at the vast expanse of trees rushing by below.

I was about to die.

One of the bear-like creatures swooped beneath me, its rider dressed like the first in greaves and scaled leather armor. She motioned to me. "Jump! I'll catch you!"

"Fuck that!" I snarled as I hauled my ass halfway into the carriage.

The queen grasped my wrist and pulled. "Get in!"

The creature banked and hurled straight toward us. Its bear-like paws spread wide, ready to drag me away.

Apparently, they weren't going to take no for an answer.

Panic pulsing in my veins, I hauled myself fully into the carriage and spun. The cool warmth of my magic cascaded down my arm, and a brilliant tendril of light burst from my fingers, exploding around the winged creature, and encapsulating it in a ball of energy.

My breath caught. I hadn't realized what I was doing when I cast it, but now I recognized it: it was the same thing I'd done to trap Cadean the first time we'd met.

The monster beat its wings against the shimmering ball of

light, but it couldn't spread them. Rider and beast spiraled downward in an uncontrolled descent.

My stomach twisted in horror as I watched them plummet toward the trees. I didn't want to kill them.

I fisted my palm, and my connection to the magic severed, like closing a faucet. The bluish-white orb surrounding the creature dissipated. Free of its binds, it righted itself and veered upward just before crashing into the forest—the rider still clinging to its back.

Relief flooded through me.

"What are you doing?" the queen shouted, as the roaring wind whipped through her silver hair. "Finish them!"

She rushed to the door, the air around us vibrating and cracking with her energy. Before I could speak, a torrent of dark gray light burst outward from her hand, shaking the carriage violently.

My heart stopped.

Her magic moved like a shock wave, bulldozing anything in its path. The canopies of the forest below whipped against the force, and the beast and rider I'd released tumbled backward through the air as if caught in the whitewash of a rogue wave.

"*That* is how you deal with your enemies," the queen said, turning to me. "You annihilate them and spare no time for remorse."

Speechless, I swallowed hard, my ears popping from the sudden pressure change.

Ayanna's power was profound and untamed. In a way, it reminded me of Cadean's magic. Was it the hint of a wildfire scent?

Whatever it was, the familiarity sent a chill of dread through me.

Clinging to the doorframe, the queen scanned the horizon.

"I think they're gone. Stay away from the open door but keep an eye on the sky."

She grasped an amulet around her neck and closed her eyes. "We were attacked by a wing of eulenbjorn and their riders, and they almost got the girl. There's no sign of our escort. Send anyone you can." Turning to me, she said, "I see you have talent, but never show mercy, not if you wish to survive. We got lucky."

"I know."

She scowled and turned her gaze back to the sky beyond the window. "I tried to keep our departure a secret, but the Dark Wolf God must have spies in Auren's kingdom."

He did: *me.*

By telling Cadean what had happened in the garden, I'd brought this on myself. On us...and on those poor shifters and their beasts.

I braced against the rush of the wind and scanned the forest below, queasiness building in my stomach. "Do you think the eulenbjorn will return?" My tongue tripped over the unfamiliar name.

"They've lost the element of surprise, so I think not. But now that the Dark Wolf God knows you're headed to my palace, you can be certain he'll make every attempt to get his hands on you. He will never stop hunting you."

I looked out across the trees toward the barrier beyond. "I know."

There was a long silence, and when I looked back at the queen, she was scouring me with an icy gaze, as if she were trying to peel my skin away and look into my soul.

"What?" I asked.

She pursed her lips, not taking her eyes from mine. "I don't think you understand the gravity of your situation."

My mood darkened. "Then why don't you enlighten me?"

She hesitated for a moment, then sat back. "There's an oracle about you. You're fated to end the Dark Wolf God—you have the power to bring him to his knees and bind him with bonds that cannot be broken. That's why he wants you so badly, and why I'll do anything I can to protect you, pact or no."

I was fated to *end* him?

A chill edged up my spine. "And the Dark God knows about this oracle?"

The queen folded her hands. "I desperately hope not, but I suspect he does. He interrogated Sarion savagely and destroyed the spells that protected his memories. Sarion may have revealed the oracle to him—I'm not sure. He came back to us broken and could not remember what he'd confessed."

"Is Sarion..." I hesitated, not knowing how to ask.

The queen shook her head. "He's not the man he once was, but he is fit enough for duty."

"Why didn't you tell me about this before now, back in Auren's realm?"

"I didn't want Auren to know. If he realized your true worth, he might never have agreed to let you go. He would have kept that power for himself. It was costly enough to pry you from his fingers as it was."

I was going to be sick.

Was this why Cadean wanted me so desperately? Not just the moonshard or my power over the wall, but because I could finish what the Moon had started? Because I could bind him once and for all?

Fear and suspicion colored my thoughts, and I suddenly didn't know who to believe anymore.

"Why didn't he kill me?" I asked. "I was there for weeks. Why keep me alive if I could potentially end him?"

The queen's mouth twitched. "That's an excellent question."

I regretted the words the instant they left my mouth, as I already knew the answer: he needed me to heal him.

Had he been planning to kill me the moment I succeeded? The terror and heartbreak of it flared in my chest, but something in my soul pushed back.

No.

No matter how much of a monster he'd been, Cadean had never intended to kill me. I knew it in my heart and by the way he'd looked at me. He'd had plenty of chances since I'd healed him, and he hadn't taken them.

But if the oracle *was* true and Cadean knew it, he should have.

My thoughts began to coalesce with certainty: something was off. There was a missing piece the queen wasn't telling me.

I looked up as casually as I could. "Where did this foretelling come from?"

Ayanna feigned a smile. "The oracle—an ancient creature that lives within my lands."

"Might I visit her?"

"The oracle rarely speaks to anyone and never repeats her foretellings." The queen's air of calm faltered—just slightly, but the hesitation was there.

My brows rose. "If her prophecy is about my powers, shouldn't we at least try to speak to her? Perhaps she could provide insight on how to use them."

Ayanna looked back to the window. "Perhaps. But for now, we need to keep watch. Our escort should join us soon, but we should stay vigilant."

I sat back against the cushioned seat and turned my gaze to the blue sky beyond the open door.

Twenty minutes later, a dozen dark specks appeared in the distance—an escort of deathwings. My palms itched as the nightmarish creatures descended on us, their iridescent moth-like wings shimmering in the sun. Their spiked legs were meant for rending flesh, and their poisoned stingers could kill in a single strike. I'd almost succumbed to one myself, but it was their eyes that I saw in my nightmares—hundreds of pink, soulless orbs staring back at me from the depths of madness.

These were the terrors that haunted Cadean's realm, and they were the spawn of the vines. Now, they were my escort into the heart of a hostile kingdom.

I shuddered as they swooped by and took formation around us. Fae soldiers in shining armor were mounted on the backs of some.

What kind of man did you have to be to form a bond with a creature like that?

The queen and I spoke little during the rest of the journey. The wind rushing through the gaping hole in the carriage and the open door made speaking in anything less than a shout nearly impossible—but I sensed there was more.

My questions about the oracle had drastically changed her mood. She was hiding something. Of that much, I was sure.

15

———

Samantha

The moment the fae capital came into view, the doubt lurking in my stomach was replaced with wonder. I'd never seen anything like it, even in my strangest dreams.

A sprawl of buildings was nestled amid a mass of purple vines. I couldn't tell which had been there first. The vines wound out from a massive palace at the center of the city, its spiked towers carved from a dark, crystalline stone.

"Welcome to Dreamspire," Ayanna said reverently.

"It's extraordinary...like the city is cradled above the landscape."

"When we first settled here, we used the vines to create a high refuge from the nightmarish creatures that stalked these lands—the Dark Wolf God's monstrosities. Eventually, the city and vines became one."

The center of the city appeared vibrant and wealthy, but at the edges, I glimpsed shanties and dilapidated buildings on the ground below. Had they been part of the original settlement?

"How long has this city been here?" I asked.

"Nearly three hundred years."

The stark contrast between the decadence of the inner city and the decay around the edges became clear as we swept over the opulent houses of the city center. There was something unsettling about it.

It reminded me of the border between Cadean's realm and the queen's territory.

Our escort of deathwings peeled off as the carriage looped around the crystalline spires of the palace and descended to a long, paved pathway. The carriage jolted as we touched down. The thundering hoofbeats of the horses slowed their cadence, and soon, we rolled to a stop.

Courtiers and servants crowded the edges of the path, along with a hundred warriors in shining armor, halberds raised.

I was stepping into the lioness's den.

A footman in a tailored coat appeared on the other side of the carriage, looking aghast at the opening where the door had been.

"Other side!" the queen hissed venomously at him. "I am not exiting through a *hole*."

The footman turned pale, and moments later, the door on the other side swung open. The queen took his hand and descended as I'd seen her do once before—as if she owned the world. As if she were a goddess descending to earth.

I self-consciously touched my hair, which felt tangled and ratty from the wind. How was Ayanna still immaculate after all that had happened?

Well, she didn't fall out the side of a carriage a mile above the earth.

After quickly finger-combing my hair and smoothing my dress, I stepped out. A second footmen helped me down, and a cadre of warriors fell in beside us. They wore silver and electrum scale mail, and their cloaks were emblazoned with a knot of vines—the symbol of the Undying Court.

I glanced back at our ride and sucked in a sharp breath as the sight confirmed the worst of my fears. The gilded coach had been torn to pieces. The roof and sides had been shredded, and little remained of the ornate beauty it had once held. Its swan-like wings began to fold up, but only one rose—the other kept grinding and vibrating.

The winged horses were frothing at their mouths, their eyes still wide with panic. But where were the driver or the footmen who had accompanied us?

Nausea twisted my gut.

"Come along, Samantha," the queen muttered, and I hurried to her side.

The palace soared above us, and I had to crane my neck to follow the spires all the way to their tips. I was now certain that the palace had not been built stone by stone but rather carved from pure crystal. It was impossible to imagine the magic or effort involved.

Dozens of open-air balconies and terraces decorated the levels, all supported by webs of purple vines that seemed to have grown into the rock itself. At least those would prove useful if Mom and I needed to escape quickly.

"What do you think?" the queen asked.

"It's the most gorgeous palace I've ever seen."

Her lips lengthened with a satisfied smile.

In yet another way, the sculpted spires and living vines reminded me of Shadowstone, with its claw-like towers and great hall formed from trees. But while Dreamspire was an ornate work of living art, Shadowstone was savage and primal. It felt like the earth itself had thrust the fortress straight up from the ground.

As we began to ascend the stairs, my gaze settled on the silhouette of a man draped in a flowing cloak. His hair was raven black, his face as hard as the stone palace. He wore a polished breastplate engraved with the symbol of the Undying Court and carried a blade in a gilded scabbard at his side. I knew instantly from his chiseled physique that the sword was nothing. *He* was the weapon.

His aura crackled with power and violence, and I was certain his magic was as lethal as his blade. His signature reminded me of the subtle perfume of lilies and the sting of a whip, alluring but deadly. Although he smiled as we approached, his eyes drilled into me with relentless suspicion.

The warrior bowed before the queen. "Your Majesty. I am glad that you have returned safely." The queen scoffed with displeasure, and he dipped lower. "I took the liberty of executing General Tarvad. Your escort should never have been so weak."

The queen's expression showed no reaction. "It was my intention to keep a low profile, not to be a sitting duck. Find someone competent to replace him."

My blood iced. These people were ruthless.

The man rose. "Of course."

The queen turned to me. "Samantha, this is General Slaine."

"Nice to meet you, General," I said coolly as I stepped up to the landing.

He dipped his head, but his eyes stayed on me, a glimmer in them. "I assure you, the pleasure is all mine."

It clearly seemed to be.

"General Slaine is the head of the palace guard and will ensure that you are safe during your time here," the queen continued.

The head of the palace guard? He'd just executed another general without asking the queen's permission. Whatever his role was, he had power.

The general's eyes didn't waver from mine. "You will have the best protection possible while you are here, Miss Bennet."

A shiver of unease zinged down my back as the general's

dark brown eyes scrutinized me to a degree that was far past appropriate. I crossed my arms. "Am I in danger here, General Slaine?"

"There are snakes everywhere." The way the words lazily curled off his tongue made it sound like a threat, and I caught a glimpse of the dangerous edge lurking beneath his charismatic façade. "I'll be certain to keep a close eye on you, milady."

Fuck. That was the last thing I wanted or needed.

"Thank you," I said, but I was certain the timbre of my voice betrayed my thoughts.

"And of course, I would love to discuss your experiences at Shadowstone. I'm certain that you will have a very"—he paused as his smile widened into a predatory grin—"*unique* perspective on the Dark Wolf God."

Double fuck. That was actually the last thing I needed.

"You will have plenty of time to speak with our *guest* after she's settled, General. The threshold of my palace is not that place, however." The queen took my arm and led me through the ornate wooden doors as they slowly swung open.

We entered a grand hall that was breathtaking in its expanse and beauty. The sides were lined with long, open galleries, supported by thin, gracile pillars of stone. Light streamed in through high windows, casting glinting reflections that made the dark stone glow with a purplish light.

The galleries were lined with murmuring faces, and all eyes were locked on me. My feet faltered as the signatures and voices of the crowd threatened to overwhelm my senses, but the queen tugged me forward. "Don't gawk, Samantha. They are here to gawk at you."

"Me?"

"Of course. You're quite famous. A prize plucked from the grasp of the Dark Wolf God and his insidious brother."

A prize. Was that what I was?

Heat crept up my neck as their gazes burned into me. The fae whispered and scrutinized me as we passed, some appearing curious, while others shot me downright nasty looks. They were adorned in wild costumes and finery. The women wore extravagant dresses of all colors, while the men wore suits with embroidered cuffs and jeweled brooches. It was overwhelming at first, but soon, I realized that each of the levels dressed differently.

"Are these all part of your court?" I murmured.

"Most are simple nobles wanting to be seen, but those belong to the fourth order." She indicated a group of men and women near the dais dressed in feathered finery and wearing polished, unflappable expressions. "Most have been with this court since the founding of the city," she continued.

While the majority were adults, there were a few children in the crowd, and as we moved deeper into the palace, a young boy stepped forward and touched my arm. I smiled.

A shadow fell over him, and his look of wonder turned to fear. With a loud crack, the general backhanded him. The crowd gasped and surged backward as the boy collapsed.

The general stepped toward the boy, but I seized his arm. "Don't! He didn't mean anything!"

The general spun and captured my wrist painfully. His skin was cold to the touch, but the sting of his magic burned my palm.

A low growl curled from his lips. "The boy needs to learn his place. As do you."

I wrenched my hand free of his iron grasp. "Touch me again and—"

"Slaine," the queen said sharply, stepping between us. "Samantha isn't used to our customs."

She took my arm, wrapping it through hers, and towed me away. "You have much to learn about court life here. I should like to introduce you to several members of the third order..."

She glanced at my dress and hair, as if noting my appearance for the first time. "If you aren't too tired after your journey, that is."

I tightened my fists, the tips of my claws digging into my palm. "I want to see my mother."

She was the only person here I cared to see, and a part of me feared that this was all a trick, a lie spun to lure me into a trap.

"Of course," the queen said, obviously relieved that she wouldn't have to parade me around in my current disheveled state. She turned to Slaine. "I'm sure there is much for you to attend to, General, considering what happened on the way here. You can speak with Samantha later."

"Of course, Your Majesty." He bowed and met my eyes as he stood. "I look forward to it."

I couldn't help releasing a sigh of relief as he walked away.

The queen waved her hand toward the silver-clad soldiers lining the hall. One broke rank and began striding in our direction.

"While you're in my domain, you will have freedom of movement—as we agreed—but you'll also have a bodyguard at all times. If you leave your quarters, he is to be at your side. I made a pact to protect you, and I intend to fulfill my end of the bargain."

A bodyguard? More like a babysitter and spy. At least it would only be one. Auren had stifled me with a cadre of soldiers.

The fae warrior removed his sleek, silver helm, revealing a handsome face with auburn hair and ethereal features. My chest tightened. "Sarion?"

He bowed low. "Samantha. I am glad to see you are well."

I turned back to the queen. "He was supposed to *assassinate* me. Why would you appoint him to look after me?"

The queen lifted her chin, her face an emotionless mask. "I

ordered the hit, and now you're working with me. I hope that you will show Sarion the same courtesy and forgiveness, as he was acting on my orders."

He clanked his gauntlet against his breastplate. "I have orders to protect you with my life, whether from wolf, demon, or fae. I will carry out my duty to you, to the queen, and to this kingdom. My life is entwined with yours."

I raised my eyebrows. Sarion in armor was a lot more formal than Sarion at the bar. Then again, he'd disguised himself as a werewolf with a glamour. Who was the real Sarion? A potential ally? A smooth talker? An assassin? Or my protector?

"Why him?" I asked, suspiciously.

The queen shrugged. "You may have your differences, but Sarion is the only person that you know here. I thought a familiar face would help with the transition—but of course, if you would prefer someone else, it can be arranged."

Sarion stood to attention. "Whatever you prefer, Miss Bennet."

His expression was hard and unyielding, yet I was certain that for the briefest moment, I'd seen fear flash across his face. I could smell it. If I rejected him, would they hurt him? They'd executed a general for not sending enough outriders for our journey.

My life is entwined with yours.

Was this Sarion's penance? He'd failed to kill me, now he had to keep me alive?

I dipped my head in acknowledgement. "The queen is right. I don't know anybody else, but you and I will have a *lot* to discuss."

The tension in his body eased ever so slightly. "Thank you for this opportunity, Miss Bennet."

The queen took my arm, and we headed down a side hall.

"Sarion is skilled with magic and is one of the best swordmen in our kingdom. You'll be safe with him at your side."

I had no doubt that I would—as long as the queen wished it. While anyone she assigned would be obeying her orders, my assassin-turned-protector was an unforgettable reminder that the Queen of the Fae held my fate in her hands.

16

———

Samantha

The queen led me through the mazelike corridors of the palace while Sarion and her squad of bodyguards trailed behind. Given what I'd see her do with her magic, they were only there as body shields.

"After we visit your mother, Sarion will show you to your room. You will have a lady's maid, just ask her for"—the queen paused and waved her hand at my disheveled dress—"whatever it is that you wear."

My face flushed, but I couldn't help feeling a spark of relief. At least I wasn't going to be subject to Auren's gaudy whims of style any longer. "Thanks for your generosity."

"It is not generosity. You're here to develop your powers and help find a way to defeat the Dark Wolf God—or at least bind him permanently. That is our bargain."

My shoulders tensed, and the queen's eyebrows peaked. "Is that not what we agreed to?"

"I hope you're not expecting instant results. I'm afraid I know as little about my powers as I do about my heritage. I can't control them, and I have no idea of their extent."

The queen glanced at me in displeasure. "From what I witnessed in the carriage, you're well on your way—though your judgement and instincts need to be improved."

"I've only ever been able to summon my powers when there's danger. I was almost never able to do it when working with Auren."

Her lip curled up. "Auren is a god. He didn't have to learn to master his power. He came into being able to move the heavens. It's like asking a rock to teach you to sit still—he knows nothing else."

I had to stifle a laugh. She might be a murderous tyrant, but I liked her dry sense of humor.

"Will you teach me?"

She sniffed with disdain. "Despite what you may assume, I have a kingdom to run, and we're at war, as you may recall. I'll assign you a tutor for history and magic, though I'll still summon you from day to day, and we can evaluate your progress."

"Thank you, Your Majesty."

"I'm sure General Slaine will want to speak to you as well, but I will put him off until you're more settled."

The budding sensation of potential disintegrated into dust. The last thing in the world I wanted was to be trapped in a room with that bastard.

The diplomatic residence was in a small tower attached to the main palace by a short covered skybridge, guarded by sentries. At least my mother would have a beautiful view if she wasn't allowed to leave. Lush flower gardens and orchards ringed the tower, and beyond were rolling hills.

As we passed the sentries, my skin tingled like I was stepping through a band of starlight. The magic had to be part of the wards that prevented anyone but fae from entering the palace, and conversely, kept my mother trapped within.

We paused beside a pale door, and a lightness filled my chest as I caught the honeysuckle scent of my mother. Nothing had ever smelled so good.

She's really here.

My stomach fluttered with warring emotions. A part of me had hoped that it was all a ruse and that my mother was still in the waking world somewhere. The other part was relieved to see her and for a chance at a cure.

One of the queen's guards stepped forward to open the door, but Ayanna subtly raised her finger, and he paused. "You mother is very sick, Samantha. I don't know what state you last saw her in, but you should prepare yourself. Some days she seems fine, others..."

She didn't finish the thought, and my chest tightened like all the air had been sucked from the room. Had she run out of the medicine I'd brought her from Magic Side? She'd been frail in Deerhaven but still full of life.

Ayanna nodded at the guard, and he opened the door. My mother's signature and scent washed over me, and my heart leapt...until I saw her. Pale and thin, she sat motionless in a lofted chair, her gaze fixed at the wall like she was in a trance. Once as alert as a fox, she didn't even glance our way.

"Mom?" My voice trembled.

Her heavy gaze shifted to me, and a soft smile broke across her face. "Baby. I was wondering when you were going to get here."

She struggled to rise, and I rushed to her side, falling to my knees as I wrapped her in my arms. "I missed you so much. I'm so sorry I left that night."

"Left?" she asked, confusion hovering at the edges of her voice.

I took her hands in mine. "We had an argument that night

about Wyland. I left and didn't come back. I'm so sorry, I didn't mean to."

She looked down at me and nodded. "Yes. Of course. How are you, sugar?"

My stomach sank. She didn't remember at all. Had she been glamoured, or was her sickness accelerating?

I forced a smile and brushed a strand of hair from her face. "I'm okay, but I'm more concerned about you. How are you feeling?"

"Very tired these days. To think I used to be able to outrun all the boys. It hasn't been that way for years, but now, I'm just...tired."

My throat was in knots. It was like she was withering right before my eyes—that she'd had the very life and brightness sucked out of her.

"How did you get here?" I asked.

She gave me a wan smile. "I'm very sick, Samantha. These nice people are helping me."

That wasn't an answer.

"What about the pack?" I asked, my suspicion deepening.

"The pack is fine. I had to leave them to get better, so that I could find you."

No matter how many times I'd begged her, my mom had always refused to leave the pack—even for me. I'd pleaded with her to move to Magic Side so that I could take care of her, but she'd shut me down. That was the day I'd been abducted.

I knew my mother. She never would have agreed to go with the fae. Not willingly. They must have glamoured her out of her mind. Was that where the fogginess came from?

My wolf rose with my fury, and I had to force her back down. This was all part of a game, a trap, and confronting the queen would do nothing. I had to find a cure.

I had a dozen burning questions I desperately wanted to ask

her, but not with the queen and Sarion looming by the door. Instead, I tried coaxing her memory forward with small talk of Deerhaven, but her head began to nod.

Eventually, she squeezed my hand. "I'm so glad you're here, Samantha, but I think I'll take a rest. Will you visit me again soon?"

I stood and dug my fingers into my palms to keep myself from shaking. "Of course, Mom. I'll visit you after your nap." Lifting her from the chair, I helped her to the large canopy bed and kissed her lightly on the forehead. "I love you."

I was trembling on the inside as I stepped from the room. "I can visit her whenever I wish?"

"Of course," the queen said sympathetically.

I followed Ayanna down the hall. "She's much worse. What are you doing for her?"

"Our healers are doing what they can, but I'm afraid she has the withering curse, like we all do."

The floor felt like it was falling away as my mind struggled to understand. "The withering curse that afflicts your court?"

"It is surprising, but yes."

Ayanna's scent wasn't compassionate, but it didn't have any sign of dishonesty. I shook my head. "But...but she's a werewolf, not fae. Why would she have the curse?" The queen looked at me with a diamond-hard gaze, and my skin crawled. "What is it?"

"We suspect she contracted it long ago—from bearing a fae child."

The world around me became ash, and it felt like I was falling backward into myself—an endless drop into desolation. My mother was dying because she gave birth to me.

I was the one killing her.

The queen gave me a soft smile and placed her hand on my

arm. "Now you see why your mother needs our help, and why we had to bring her here. It's the only place she has a chance."

A range of emotions churned inside me as I silently followed Sarion back through the halls of the crystal palace. I tried to memorize our path, but my mind couldn't let go of my mother. My pact with the queen permitted us to leave whenever we chose, but there was no way I could take my mom, not with her so ill and glamoured.

I had to find a way to help her.

We wound up a set of spiral stairs and finally emerged into a curving corridor. Sarion paused at a large wooden door set between a pair of smaller ones, then unlocked it and swung it wide. "All the tower rooms have a view, but you should like this one."

I stepped inside.

The hexagonal room was illuminated by light pouring in through a pair of large windows that flanked an open balcony. A canopy bed sat in the center of the room, surrounded by six spiraling marble pillars that supported a domed ceiling.

"Is everything to your liking?" he asked.

"It's magical." I exhaled as I slowly circled the bed. The colors of the crystal walls seemed to shift and change as I moved, as if the stone itself was alive. And like everywhere else in the palace, the vines crept over and around the stonework—an unmistakable reminder that nowhere was free from the queen's power.

It *was* magical, but I was boiling inside and at the knife edge of my restraint. The moment the door clicked shut behind me, I turned to him. "No matter how elegant this room is, my mother and I are captive to the queen's intentions. I'm in this mess because of *you.*"

I was trembling with rage—because of the attack on the carriage, because I was trapped once again, and because of everything that had happened to my mother. I was overwhelmed, and I had an axe to grind.

Sarion paled. "Wulfric was the one who tried to abduct you, I just—"

"Abducted me instead. You lied about the nature of the war and let me believe the desolation along the border was the Dark God's fault."

Sarion backed up as I rounded the end of the bed. "All of it is forgivable, except you told the queen about my mother and her sickness. She's here and *glamoured* because of you."

His features tightened with regret. "She was sick, and I was afraid the Dark Wolf God would use her as leverage."

"So now the queen can use her instead. You never should have brought her into this."

He raised his hands in protest. "I only had the best intentions."

My fangs and claws slipped out. "Best intentions? You were going to kill me."

"I was ordered to help you escape. If I discovered that you were helping the Dark Wolf God, then I was to kill you. But I wouldn't have done it. I couldn't have."

I clenched my fists, my claws digging into my palms. "What are your orders now? Report everything that I say? Lock me in the moment I step out of line?"

Sarion looked away, his features hardening. "The queen has already ordered my execution, contingent on your safety. If anything happens to you, my life is forfeit. Instantly."

The moment he met my eyes, I knew it was true. My

stomach twisted, and I scratched my scar as it began to itch. "I guess that's a pretty good reason to keep me alive."

Sarion crossed to the balcony and looked out. "This is my fault. Let me redeem myself. Let me be your friend in the court. It's full of vipers and no one you can trust."

"Can I trust you?"

He placed his hand on the side of his scabbard. "Whether you forgive me or not, I'll serve you here above all others."

I paused at the foot of the bed, stunned by the implication. "You realize that's technically treason against your queen."

"Your safety is my only concern." He held my stare for several breaths, then tapped on the ornate balcony door. "If the Dark Wolf God was willing to attack your carriage, he'll try again. Close these doors at night. They're enchanted to turn to stone. No one will be able to enter while you sleep."

I nodded. "Good to know."

Except the truth was the Dark God could visit any time he wanted, stone doors or not. I scratched my scar again and froze.

Hell. He was watching me right now.

I'd grown so used to the subtle press of his magic that I'd started to ignore it. But the thrum of his presence was unmistakable, tracing over my skin like a soft whisper. A shiver rippled down my spine, and I looked toward the dark corners of the room.

I didn't see the soft glow of his eyes or the silhouette of his form, but I knew he was there, lurking in the shadows. *Hunting me.*

"Is everything all right?" Sarion asked as his fingers slowly wrapped around the hilt of his blade.

I sat on the end of the bed. "Nothing you need your sword for. It's been a long day. I just think I need to rest and process."

"Of course." He bowed and headed to the door, then paused beside a pair of dangling ropes. "Should you need anything, the left summons me, while the right summons your maid. Our quarters are on either side of yours."

"Convenient." *For spying on me.*

"It's for your safety," Sarion said, as if reading my mind. He pulled a large key from his belt and tossed it to me. "Your maid will bring dinner, and if you wish to leave your room, I'll escort you wherever you need to go."

I turned the key over in my hand. "Thank you...and I mean it. It will be good to have a friend in the court."

He might be a spy, but I wasn't going to wall myself off like I had in Auren's realm.

Sarion nodded and stepped out. I locked the bolt behind him and pressed my ear to the door, following his footsteps.

When the door of the adjacent room clicked shut, I turned to the unnaturally deep shadows in the corner of the room. "I know you're there, Cadean. We had a *truce*. What the hell were you trying to do?"

17

———

Cadean

I stepped into the shadows of the sunlit stone room. "I had to try. Our truce was that I'd stop hunting you if you returned to the waking world—and as Sarion so aptly put it, you've walked into a pit of vipers instead."

The little wolf's eyes were alive with anger, and her stance told me that if I'd truly been in the room with her, she would've thrown herself forward, claws out, and driven them into my neck.

Fates, she was beautiful when she fought me.

I breathed in her scent and signature, exalting in the way it intoxicated my mind. I wanted to drag my fingers through her windswept hair and across her tanned shoulders, but of course, I couldn't. I was only a shadow—and the futility of it infuriated me.

"I killed some of your warriors today, Cadean. I didn't want to, but they died all the same."

Remorse pulled at me, and I set my jaw against it.

The eulenbjorn and their riders had accepted their fate when they'd volunteered to cross the border, though that made their loss cut all the deeper. I would speak to their families and try as best as I could to honor their memories.

"You could have gone with them," I growled. "They would have taken you anywhere you wished to go. Out of the Dreamlands, away from my brother, and away from the fae."

"Dreamspire is where I wanted to go. My mother is here."

"Then get her and leave. Do it tonight before the queen gets her talons any deeper into you, or you will never leave here alive."

"She and I made a pact," she said, holding her chin high. "It guarantees my protection and freedom of movement—things I never had with you."

I relaxed slightly. A pact was something, but she was still in extreme danger.

"If the queen was willing to make a pact, then she has a way to circumvent it. She'll keep you as long as you're of use to her and kill you the moment she has a doubt."

"She won't kill me," Samantha said, her voice low and vibrating with warning. "She believes in an oracle that I have the power to bring you to your knees. There is no way she'll harm me with that at stake."

I sucked in a sharp breath. Ayanna had told her? How much?

Samantha's eyes narrowed to knife slits. "You knew about it, didn't you? Fuck. She suspected as much. Is that why you're so desperate to control me? To not let me fall into her hands or develop my magic?"

"I knew, but—"

"But nothing. You lied about me being fae, and you lied about this. What else aren't you telling me?"

So many things.

That the thought of her there, trapped in the queen's domain, was driving me to the edge of madness. I wanted her back, not just because of some kind of prophecy or even because of the moonshard alone, but because I was a better man when she was near.

My frustration ignited, and I wanted to bury my fist in the wall. "Yes, I knew, but while I didn't tell you about the oracle, the queen is keeping half of it from you to give you a false sense of security."

Outrage flashed across her face. "What other half?"

"The one she will kill you over." I leaned against the wall, crossing my arms. "According to the oracle, you're a coin, spinning on edge. If you fall one way, you will have the power to bring me to my knees and bind me. If you fall the other way, you will have the power to free me."

Her eyes widened. "This is why you want me so desperately?"

"I have wanted freedom for a thousand years, but I would rather see you spin forever, like a nymph dancing at the river's edge. The queen, however, would rather kill you than risk the slightest chance you would choose to free me. Sarion told me as much. That's why she sent assassins."

"Fuck."

I launched myself off the wall and strode forward until we were inches apart. "If the queen ever discovered that you willingly chose to heal me, or that we could speak like this, she'd find a way to break your pact and behead you in an instant. The oracle isn't your shield—it's your death sentence."

A little of the color drained from her face. "What am I going to do?"

"Flee. I will find a way to help you out of the Dreamlands. I'll even make a pact never to pursue you. Just *run*."

"No," she snarled, and I stepped back. The conviction in her voice was like a hammer breaking through stone.

"I'm done running. I will..." Her voice seized up, bound by Auren's spell. "I will do what I came to do."

"Samantha—"

"This is bigger than me." She looked up, determined and relentless. "I'm living on borrowed time, Cadean. If the queen kills me, you're safe from me as well, so you shouldn't object."

"I won't let that happen!" I growled as the wolf within me came near the surface. My body shook, and the shadows billowed around me like the flames of wildfire. "What is so important that you would risk yourself this way?"

Fuck my brother and his muzzling spell. I was working in the dark.

"I'm here to protect the Dreamlands, Cadean. All of it. You should understand what that means. If there's anything you love here, then help me. Trust me. *Stop fighting me.*"

Her voice rang with passion that twisted my soul, and the room pressed in with an impossible, inevitable weight. Could she be doing this for my people?

I'd seen the truth of her long ago in Deerhaven. At heart, she was a ferocious protector—of her mother, of her people, and even of my shifters.

Just not of herself.

I would have to be her protector.

Even if I didn't yet understand her purpose, I'd be her ally, just as Mel had told me that I needed to be.

I began pacing the room like a caged animal. The powerlessness of my position raged through me, a cruel jest played by the Fates. But I'd find a way to help. I'd be a watcher in the shadows. A voice of counsel. "The fae are ruthless. They'll watch everything you do and measure everything you say. At least the attack on the carriage will have convinced them I'm trying to kill or capture you again."

"I know. I'll be careful."

My gaze snapped to her. "You called me Cadean. Maybe this room is safe, maybe it's not. Either way, you must never use my name again, even in private. The moment you do, you will betray a closeness that the fae will not ignore. They'll wonder why we're on a first name basis, because no one but Auren and my court calls me that."

She closed her eyes and rubbed her temples. "Shit. You're right."

"Although I'm helping you, you must never think of me as an ally. Never think of the kiss we shared or the time you spent healing me. You need to prove to them that you hate me with every fiber of your being, which means you have to live that hatred. Dwell on everything cruel and horrible thing I've done to you—imprisonment, Magic Side, attacking you—until you can no longer think of me without loathing. Make that your shield."

She looked away, and eventually she nodded, though there was a sense of remorse to it. "Does this mean we have a new truce then? That you're going to help me?"

"I'll do everything I can to help you achieve your goal and get you and your mother out of the queen's realm alive."

"In exchange for?"

"Your trust." I crossed my arms and leaned back against the wall. "You need to listen to my advice, and you need to be careful."

"As far as trust, we'll see. But I *will* be careful."

It was as much as I could hope for. Trust had to be earned, and I knew where to start.

"Does the queen know about the moonstone?" I asked. "Its presence puts you in danger."

She narrowed her eyes. "I didn't tell her about it. Maybe Auren did. Why?"

I stepped close. "You must find a way to protect it. Don't let anyone in the palace know of its existence. Ayanna could steal it and use it to shift the wall and bring devastation on my people."

"I know. That's why I built it into the pact. She cannot steal from me or compel me for any reason."

"It's not enough," I growled, as my protectiveness surged. "If she finds out what the moonshard can do to the wall, she may decide she doesn't need you—that might be reason enough to break the pact."

She drew in a shaky breath. "You really think she'd betray me over it?"

"She sent assassins once. She's playing nice because she needs you, but if she realizes she can take the power for herself..."

Samantha rubbed the bridge of her nose. "Then what the hell am I supposed to do? Hide it under my mattress? I couldn't just leave it with Auren."

I held out my hand and summoned my black axe from the ether, then dismissed it back into the shadows with a snap of my wrist. "My axe is bonded to me. I can summon it at will from the ether. You might be able to bond the moonshard considering your connection to it and the Moon's magic. I'll help you do it, just as I taught you to resist compulsion. Get the shard, and we'll begin."

She hesitated. "Right now?"

"Yes."

She rested her foot on the chair, then pulled up the hem of her gown, revealing an indecent length of her leg. My pulse quickened as my mouth went dry. The moonshard was strapped in a sheath around her thigh, but as much as I craved the stone, it was her milky skin that captivated my gaze. I'd explored the depths of those thighs once, and it had tormented my dreams ever since.

Fucking hell. I can't think about her this way.

I quickly glanced away as she met my gaze.

"You must really want to get your hands on this for you to

look at it like that." She unsheathed the moonshard and set it on the table.

I met her eyes. "I don't want any hands on it except mine. I'm *very* possessive."

"So I've come to understand." She let her gown fall back in place and sat. "So am I."

Her look didn't waver, and I cleared my throat. "Which is why you must bond the moonshard. Once you do, no one will be able to take it from you. Not even me."

She raised her eyebrows. "Is that so?"

It wasn't like I had a fucking choice. I had to keep it away from the queen.

"Everything I'm teaching you makes you a greater threat to me," I said, frustration lining my voice. "The fact that I'm willing to risk it should give you a good idea of how much danger you're in."

She looked down and began flipping the moonshard over and over in her hand. "I'm pretty screwed, aren't I?"

All her feigned confidence melted away in a moment, and I saw the truth. She was not foolhardy or foolish but trapped and terrified and fighting on despite it.

I slowly sat on the bed across from her. "No, you're not. You found a way to escape me and steal my most valuable weapon. You can overcome the queen. I believe that without a shadow of a doubt."

She looked up and gave me a pained smile. "But all you are is shadows."

It tormented me, but I wouldn't let it stop me from helping her. "Yes, I'm nothing but shadow, but that means I can be wherever they are. I can be your scout, your watcher, or simply your advisor. The queen's presence blocks my ability to shadowcast, but as long as there is darkness, you won't be on your own."

She nodded subtly, and after a moment, her smile brightened slightly. "Thank you. I mean it."

A flicker of hope sparked in my chest. Was it working? Had Mel been right?

Making sure I didn't betray an ounce of emotion, I summoned my axe from the ether and laid it across my lap. "Then let us begin."

18

____

Samantha

Cadean spent hours training with me—first teaching me to bond and summon the moonshard, and then we practiced mental shielding again. He pushed me hard, and when I finally collapsed into bed long after midnight, exhaustion had rooted deep in my bones.

Unfortunately, the next day descended on me without mercy and pulled me headfirst into the frenetic pace of court life.

My new handmaid arrived early. By the clumsy nature of her idle questions, I suspected she was an agent for the queen, but I decided not to treat her as distantly as I had Auren's maids. Whatever her mission, she was warm and welcoming, and I immediately felt affection for her.

She grilled me about everything I could possibly have an opinion on: clothes, bedsheets, breakfast, bath products, makeup, and much more. "I know you came here with next to nothing," she said. "The queen insists that you will have everything."

What I didn't have was a moment of peace.

As soon as she was done taming my wild hair, I was passed off to my new tutor, Kindell.

He was an ass, and I disliked him the moment I laid eyes on his pointy ears. He expressed only disdain for me and wasn't shy about it. Every glance he gave me was judgement, and he carried himself with a deep, ceaseless air of arrogance that made me want to shove him out a window.

When I found myself unable to summon my magic around him, he kept asking things like, *Are you sure you're part fae?* and suggesting, *Perhaps magic isn't your gift after all.* Finally, he thrust himself up out of his chair and clapped his hands over his ears. "It's hopeless."

When I didn't bother to respond, he began quickly pacing the room. "It's not your fault, of course, it's just that I'm not used to..." He waved his hands at me.

"What?" I asked flatly, bracing myself for the inevitable back-handed comment.

He sighed and shook his head. "A complete lack of talent. Please understand that prior to this, I was tutoring the most magnificent young man. Absolute talent from birth. At seven, he could turn a handful of seeds into a bouquet that never wilted. He was going to be my greatest triumph, and now there's just...you."

Our relationship wasn't much better when it came to understanding my fae heritage. He offered me the direst history book you could imagine.

I asked him a dozen questions about where the Undying Court had come from and why they had been expelled from the Feylands, but he brushed them off as unimportant. "That was before. Our history begins with the Dreamlands. All the records of our time in the Feyland were destroyed, and our elders refuse to speak of it."

Instead, I learned about the dreary etiquette of the court.

There were five orders. Kindell said, "The queen has seen fit—though I do not know why—to bestow you the honor of being of the first order."

The way he said it made it sound as if I couldn't be more unworthy. However, as far as I could tell, it was also the lowest order—which meant I was lucky to be swill.

"Are there people below the first order?" I asked.

He sniffed. "Would it matter if there were?"

I began visiting my mother in the afternoons as an antidote to my lessons.

She wasn't the woman I remembered, but each time I visited, she seemed a little more lucid, like the glamour was fading away around the edges and she was a little more of her old self. When I could make her laugh, my heart began to sing.

On the second day, when I was certain no one was listening, I took her hand. "I know I'm part fae. Why didn't you ever tell me?"

Her lips pursed, and she squeezed my hand back. "You're all wolf to me, sugar. Don't get confused by things. Only a few things matter. Your honor, your pack, your mate, and your children."

She looked out the window, and I knew she didn't want to discuss it anymore, but I had to know. "Do you remember anything about my father? Was he fae? Where did he come from?"

She didn't meet my eyes. "Yes, your father was fae. I don't know where he was from or where he went."

I swallowed. "You must remember something."

Even though her memory of the last few months was hazy, our talks had established that she could recall the past pretty well.

"There's nothing to tell, Samantha. He was in and out of my life in a fortnight. I didn't keep pictures. Hell, I don't even remember his face." She clasped my hands and held them close to her lips. "He was nothing to me. You're everything. You'll always be the only thing that mattered."

I looked down and nodded, not wanting her to see my face.

Growing up, a lot of things had seemed like they'd mattered more. The pack. Drinking and gambling at the Barn. The strange men she'd disappear with on moonlit runs. All of them had felt like they were more important to her than me.

But those days were long gone, and so was the woman she'd been. She wasn't even the woman I'd known two months ago. If I ever found a cure, would I get her back?

I was finally able to meet with the queen again on my fourth full day in the palace. Rather than give me any sort of greeting, she simply motioned me to her side.

"Do your accommodations and servants suit you?" she asked as we walked through an enormous gallery lined with paintings.

"Yes, you've been most generous. Is there a private garden where I could run my wolf? I haven't had the chance to shift for a few days."

She scowled. "Shifting in public spaces is completely out of the question. Shifters are the enemy here, and there are many in this court that have lost loved ones to the Dark Wolf God's animals. Do not give them a reminder of what you are. Prove that you can control your baser instincts and perhaps they will start to accept you."

My baser instincts? Was that how they saw us?

My stomach curdled with disgust. "You can't be serious. It's not a choice—I *have to shift*, it's biological."

"I suggest you shift in the privacy of your own room."

I opened my mouth to protest, but her warning look told me this would not be negotiable. I gritted my teeth and looked away. I'd just have to find a way to sneak out.

The queen clasped her hands behind her back. "I know this

might be difficult, but you are also half-fae, Samantha. Your purpose here is to learn about that part and master your magic, and I hear your studies are not going well. I'm very concerned that your heart is not in this."

Her voice was pregnant with warning, and my stomach dipped. I couldn't get on her bad side.

"My heart is in it, I promise. I'm trying as hard as I can. It's just...I don't think I mesh with Kindell's education techniques."

"Kindell is a renowned tutor, and he has trained many of the best fae sorcerers."

"Maybe, but I'm not a fae sorcerer. I don't even know if my magic comes from being part fae, or if it's something else. Perhaps if I could speak to the oracle, I might understand—"

"I will consider it once you've shown some progress." Her tone screamed *out of the question.*

Why such resistance? Was it because she didn't want me to learn about the second half of the prophecy? That meant she didn't trust that I'd choose to destroy the Dark God if given the chance—and that was a major problem. Reminding her about my wolf certainly hadn't helped.

The oracle was my best shot at understanding anything about my situation *and* my magic, so I had to find a way to change the queen's mind.

"If you truly expect me to master my magic and face the Dark Wolf God, then I must speak with the oracle. It's my best chance to learn about my magic and how to defeat him—and we need to defeat him. Every night, I'm haunted by dreams of him, and what he did to my home. Please, help me make sure that never happens again to my people or yours."

She scoured me with her eyes, then finally nodded. "I will consider it."

Relief welled in my chest. Her words hadn't changed, but her tone had. I'd made a crack in her iron-hard stance.

I dined in my room that night, as had become custom.

Sarion had a stack of invitations, and I knew that I should peruse them, but not yet. I couldn't shake the feeling of all those eyes judging me on arrival, inspecting me like I was a bizarre curiosity or a piece of meat. Everywhere I went, people stared, and I always had Sarion hovering nearby. Dinner had become a sweet, silent moment alone.

I stepped out onto the balcony as the sun started to dip below the misty horizon, the clouds shifting through a rainbow of colors: red and yellow highlights like autumn leaves, and the deep blue shadows of night. Lights flickered on in the houses and shops below me, though the commotion and bustle of the streets didn't slow. Did the city have a thriving nightlife? Bars like those back in Magic Side? At that moment, I would have given anything to have the Dreamlands and its problems behind me and to just be Sam again.

Just a wolf—no magic, no curse, no gods or queen toying with my life.

"It's a beautiful sunset," Cadean murmured.

My heart nearly jumped out of my chest, and I glanced over my shoulder.

There he was, a shadow within the shadows. And he was smirking. Clearly, he'd seen me jump.

I looked back toward the city. "Are you planning on haunting me every evening or just on weekdays?"

"Night is best," he said softly. "Shadow-casting is easier in the dark when the shadows are deepest. It allows me to stay longer, perceive more—though it still consumes much of my power."

"Why isn't the queen's palace protected like Auren's?"

"It is, but the spells aren't as strong. Auren knows my magic better than I do myself, and he designed his wards specifically to keep me out. I still have to break through, though it wouldn't be possible without you."

I looked back. "How so?"

"Something about you draws me in and grounds me here. You're like a spotlight, illuminating the world around you."

His velvety voice sent tingles across my skin, and the way his eyes took me in made me feel like I was glowing.

A smile tugged at the corner of his mouth, and he nodded. "Don't miss the sunset."

I tore my gaze from that sinful smile just in time to see the last of the light dissipate into the mist. A few stray rays rose above the clouds.

"You've been staring at the city for a long time," he said, but this time, he was close.

I leaned on the balcony, trying to ignore the thrumming in my chest. "I saw my mother again today. The queen's glamoured her, I'm sure of it, and her underlying condition has gotten much worse since Deerhaven."

"Can anything be done?"

I turned toward him and braced my hip against the railing. He was an arm's length away, close enough that I could've touched him if he weren't a shadow. "She's got the withering curse like everyone in the court. Like me."

His jaw tensed. "That's impossible. She's a wolf."

"She bore a fae child. Apparently, that's enough."

He reached out to comfort me, but his fingers dissipated into wisps of smoke. Flashes of frustration and helplessness played across his face, and he dropped his arm. "I'm sorry, little wolf."

"I don't know what to do." I bit my lip to keep it from trembling.

"There must be a way. The Undying Court has found a way to stave off the withering curse. If they can do it for themselves, they could do it for her. Keep searching for answers. I will help you any way I can."

I nodded, unsure what to say. Finally, I murmured, "Maybe just sit with me while the light fades."

I wanted to remember the way my mother was, but I didn't want to do it alone.

19

———————

Samantha

Ayanna summoned me to the central tower of the palace the next day.

As seemed to be her way, she immediately launched into conversation. "You asked many questions about the vines and the withering curse on our flight here, so there is something I want you to see."

We emerged onto a high balcony overlooking a sprawling garden. There were no flowerbeds or trees or walking paths, just a series of terraces covered in a wild jumble of giant purple vines, some of which were ten to fifteen feet in diameter. Leafy creepers created a delicate spiderweb over the top of the massive vines, and flashes of red among their leaves hinted at clusters of dangling fruit.

The spires of her palace flanked the garden on three sides, but on the fourth, the vines cascaded over the edge like a waterfall of purple and green leaves. My gaze followed them as they snaked through the city and then on toward the horizon.

The queen raised her eyebrows expectantly.

"It's beautiful," I said.

It was also horrific.

I knew that beyond the mists, they were devouring the Dark God's lands, spawning deathwings and leaving desolation everywhere they spread. Somehow, I had to find a way to destroy them. It was what I was here to do.

I glanced over at her. "May we go down and walk through it?"

"Entry is forbidden to anyone below the third order. You are first, and Sarion is second, so you must enjoy the view from afar."

Forbidden, which meant that I couldn't enter without violating our pact.

"Why keep it locked away?" I asked.

She rested her hands on the stone railing and regarded the vines with reverence. "Because the garden is the beating heart of our kingdom. Eating the fruit staves off the withering curse and prolongs our life. Without it, we would not be the Undying Court—hence, it is protected with spells, and entrance is forbidden to all but the upper echelons of society."

A deep unease settled over me as I looked out toward the rooftops of the vibrant city beyond. "Then everyone living here must eat of the fruit or they'll die?"

"Unfortunately, the vines cannot produce enough fruit to feed a whole kingdom. So, no." Her hands tightened on the railing. "It is tragic but unavoidable."

"Then the city is dying? What will happen to them?" There had to be hundreds of thousands of fae dwelling in the city alone, not to mention the rest of her domain.

"Our curse is fatal, but it's also slow. Those who do not eat still live for seventy or eighty years—what humans would think of as normal lives, short, bitter, and futile. Eventually, they grow sick and frail, and the withering curse takes them in the end."

Bitter and futile? I pressed my lips together to stop the scowl.

The lines of her face creased, and she turned back to her garden. "Perhaps you've lived long enough among wolves and humans to think seventy years is normal, but for fae who live centuries, it is anathema."

What would someone who was my mother's age be in their eyes? A child?

Doubts wove through my mind as we stared out over the expanse of purple and green. Her people needed the fruit to live. If I followed through with my plan and found a way to destroy the vines, I'd be condemning them to the withering curse.

Could I really do that?

"If there's not enough fruit, then who gets to eat?" I asked hesitantly.

"Those who have earned it," she responded in a voice like iron. "Great warriors, sorcerers, and scholars, the high court and the administrators our kingdom depends on."

"So the common people just wither away?"

I felt sick. Dreamspire was no different than anywhere, it seemed—the rich and powerful enjoyed the fat of the land while the poor suffered.

Her lip curled in disgust. "Perhaps you think us cruel or coldhearted, but the truth is our civilization is fighting for its life. Not everyone has the same value. Sacrifices must be made, but we do not make them gladly."

"That's terrible."

"Maybe one day there will be enough fruit for all, but not while the Dark Wolf God lives. So much of the strength of the vines is wasted fighting him. But that's what you're here for, is it not? To free my people from his grasp?"

"Yes. I want your people to live in peace without fear of him." It was the truth, even if only half of it.

"Good. Don't forget your purpose here." She turned, and I

followed her along a columned veranda that connected the overhanging balconies as my mind spun.

What was I going to do? Keep looking for a way to destroy the vines? Her people needed the life the vines gave, but it was stolen from others. From Cadean's lands, from his people.

Did they feel no guilt over that?

I needed to learn more, like what exactly the fruit could do.

My heart quickened. "Would the fruit of the vines heal my mother if she also has the curse?"

The queen shrugged. "Perhaps, perhaps not. She's only a wolf, so it's hard to know how it would affect her. It doesn't heal anyone completely, just staves off death for a time."

"Could doctors try to use it?"

"Giving fruit to outsiders is expressly forbidden by our laws. Only those who have proven themselves worthy to ascend to the third order and higher may eat. The laws protect our greatest treasure, the inheritance of our future generations, so even I cannot violate them."

I didn't buy that for a second.

"There must be a way that we could try it with my mother," I pressed.

"The council will never allow the fruit to be given to a wolf," she snapped. For a moment, she hesitated, and her expression softened. "But you are part fae. If you're able to prove yourself worthy, then perhaps an official exception could be made for your wolf mother. But it would have to be earned."

"How?"

"Bind the Dark Wolf God. If you fulfill your destiny, you can save your mother's life."

My mouth soured.

Finally, the trap she'd laid was fully revealed. She had my mother and the cure at hand, but there was only one way I could earn it: bind Cadean forever.

I had no doubt that if she wanted, she would have the authority to pluck the fruit and cure my mother this very moment. Instead, she hid behind a mask of laws, laughing as she pulled my strings.

Although it took every ounce of restraint I had, I forced myself to remain calm. Somehow, I had to beat her at her own game.

"Is there a problem?" the queen asked.

"No. I understand what I need to do."

Although her expression remained as firm as stone, there was a flicker of victory in her eyes. "Good."

She knew she had me.

"Of course, if you expect me to bind the Dark Wolf God, then I need to understand my powers. The tutor will not be enough. I need to see the oracle—she's the one who foretold of my gift, so she'd be the best one to teach me how the binding can be done."

That glint of victory vanished, and she glared at me. "We've discussed this before."

"I should meet with her soon. Time is running out for my mother and me just as much as it is for your people. If you're serious about protecting them, then there's no reason to hesitate —otherwise, there's no point in me staying in your realm any longer."

She wasn't the only one with leverage.

The queen looked like she wanted to push me over the edge of the balcony, but slowly, her posture relaxed, and her characteristic calm returned. "Your point is well made. I will consider it. Good day, Samantha."

With that, Ayanna and her entourage of soldiers walked away, leaving me doubting everything in her wake.

They were the same words she always said, but this time, I knew they meant, *I refuse to admit that you won.*

I released a long, shuddering breath the moment she was out of earshot.

The victory of the moment was dulled by the truth: in my heart, I knew I would never be able to bind Cadean forever. I would never meet the queen's requirements, and therefore, my mother would never get the cure she needed—not unless I found another way.

Unfortunately, my pact prevented me from entering the garden, let alone stealing from it. I turned and grasped the stone banister and leaned out. If Sarion or the palace sentries weren't around, it would be so easy just to slip over the edge and climb down.

If I didn't have to obey the pact, what answers would I discover inside?

"I don't like the way you're studying the walls," Sarion muttered. "I hope you're not planning on finding a way in."

Fuck, was I that transparent?

"I wasn't—" I stepped back. "I was just thinking of how exposed the garden is, for something so important."

Sarion gave me a wry smile. "Don't worry, we've all thought about it—everyone who is of the first or second order. The garden is displayed for all to see for a reason: to cultivate desire." He nodded to the garden. "Throw a glove over."

I raised my eyebrows, then yanked off one of the leather gloves I wore and flung it into the garden. Halfway down, it hit an invisible barrier, and with a flash of light, it burst into flames. The leather fingers blackened and curled in on themselves, and a plume of smoke spiraled upward.

"You could have just told me what would happen. Now I've wasted a glove."

He shrugged. "I wanted you to see for yourself, so I don't have to watch the same thing happen to you."

I looked down at my bare fingers. "My pact prevents me from going anywhere I'm not allowed, so it's not an issue."

He gestured back the way we'd come. "Considering how relentlessly you interrogate the queen every time you two talk, I have a sense that everything will be an issue with you."

Fair.

I followed him through the long, winding halls toward my room. I couldn't stop thinking about the bustling city below my window—the noisy merchants and the well-dressed women, the drunken soldiers and the kids running in the streets.

"What is it?" Sarion asked after a long stretch of silence.

"This place looks like a fairytale kingdom, but it's just like every fucked-up society I know—the rich and powerful hold everything, while the rest suffer without any hope of rising."

Sarion lifted a brow. "There's hope for some of us. The queen holds trials—competitions in which commoners and nobles alike can prove themselves to ascend to the next level."

That piqued my interest. "What happens in the trials?" I asked.

Sarion paused and gave me a knowing smile. "A lot of people die vying for a chance to taste immortality." Shaking his head, he continued, "I see where your mind is going, and don't even think about it. You are neither strong enough nor skilled enough with magic to survive."

My neck flushed. "I've held off the Dark Wolf God and shot a eulenbjorn out of the sky. I'm not as weak as you think."

"I know your résumé quite well, but you'd be competing against other fae—people who have practiced for years, or even their whole lives. They're cutthroat."

I cracked my knuckles. "You watched me fight in the pits at Deerhaven. Are you certain I wouldn't have a chance?"

He looked down. "I know you well enough to know the

mistake you'll make. The trials aren't about holding back gods and monsters—they're about avoiding the knife in your back and putting your own blade in the neck of your friends. The person fighting at your side is the one you have to fear the most."

His expression was grim and tinged with remorse, and I saw the tension in his body, the desperation with which he wanted to dissuade me.

"You competed in the trials, didn't you?"

"Twice. And I regret it every day."

20

———————

Cadean

The evening shadows parted, and Samantha's room appeared before me, lit in faint, flickering candlelight. The balcony door hung open, admitting a cold but gentle breeze that stirred the golden ends of her hair.

My little wolf was hunched over her desk, scrawling away with a golden feather. Her hair was swept to the side, exposing a long, graceful neck that was almost begging me to softly kiss along it...if only I were more than shadow.

She touched her scar, but she was so focused on the paper that she hadn't noticed my arrival. My curiosity awakened, I stole closer, shifting from shadow to shadow.

Samantha set her quill down beside the paper, and then, to my surprise, everything she'd just written began to fade away. It was an enchanted correspondence set—but who was she writing to?

I was pretty sure I fucking knew.

New words appeared in gold along the top of the page, and though it was difficult to read from a distance, I instantly recognized my brother's handwriting.

My hands balled into tight fists as I imagined driving them into Auren's face. The bastard was still manipulating her, even here. What was his plan? Had he convinced her to spy for him?

The golden words began to fade.

Fuck. I needed to know what was on that paper. I stepped fully out of the shadows and glanced over her shoulder.

—and fuck the fae. You need to find a way into that garden to have any hope of stealing a seedling or destroying the vines. Whatever magic protects them will be rooted there. Find a way IN.

She picked up the quill and leaned forward.

But the—

Samantha's hand froze mid-stroke, then she burst out of the chair and swept the page behind her back. "How dare you spy on me!"

I grinned. "Isn't that what you're doing here? Reporting everything you see to my *treacherous* brother?

"I have a plan, and I will use every resource at my disposal. Him and you."

"Whatever you think you're doing, Auren is not helping you. He's helping himself, and as soon as you are no longer useful, he'll hang you out to dry."

She started to protest, but I held up my hand. "You broke off writing mid-sentence. Finish it, or he'll be suspicious."

She dropped back into her chair. "Jerk."

Golden letters appeared on the paper as soon as she set the quill down by it.

Why the delay?

Samantha glared at me as she snatched up the feather. "Privacy, please?"

"No."

She growled and began to write: *Had a problem with the quill. Was saying: the pact is a problem.*

"You're a royal asshole," she said to me as she set the quill back beside the paper. As soon as Auren's response began to come through, she turned to shield the words from sight, but I just rematerialized in the shadows on her other side.

Don't worry about the pact. There's a way around it. I'll tell you when it's time.

My blood chilled. If Auren had figured out a way around the pact, the queen would as well.

The quill sparkled, then slowly transformed into a feather pendant. Auren had signed off.

"Burn that paper," I advised. "The ink disappears, but you were pressing hard. It will leave impressions."

Samantha narrowed her eyes at me, then set the sheet on fire with her candle. "You can't keep sneaking up on me like this. We need to lay some ground rules."

"I can sense your presence, and I know you can sense mine. You need to be more alert. I'm the only thing you want sneaking up on you here."

She crossed her arms. "What do you want?"

"I want to know what you're doing with Auren. Does he have a plan to destroy the vines? Is that why you're here? It will never work. I've tried for centuries."

She opened her mouth, but Auren's spell stopped her voice. She cursed beneath her breath and fished about for something she could say. "If I had a chance to do something to protect your people, wouldn't you want that? Wouldn't it be worth trying?"

The vines haunted both my nightmares and waking hours. They were an endless grasping death that was choking the life out of my land. Of course I wanted it. But her?

"Is that why you're doing this? To protect my people?"

She gave me a look that said, *What do you think?*

The room felt heavy around me, and I rubbed my chest. I

imagined her that day in Frostfall, crouched behind a brilliant shield of light, protecting the fox kits. A protector was who she was at her core, and that instinct was going to get her killed.

I knew it was useless to try to dissuade her. Fates, I'd tried. But for her to take on this burden...my heart felt like it was being strangled.

"You haven't answered my question," Samantha said.

I paced to the open balcony door and looked out at the wretched city below. "If destroying the vines were possible, I'd seek it desperately. It could change everything."

She rose and joined my side. "Then help me do this."

"How?"

She started to speak, then pressed her lips together. She rubbed her forehead and gave me a look of strained patience. "I'm not sure what all I can say without having my damn tongue tied but let me tell you about my day. The queen brought me to the garden where the vines converge. I learned three things that make me nervous."

I'd heard rumors that there was a place where the vines met, but I'd never been able to project into the queen's realm before. If Samantha could get inside, could she find some way to poison them or sever them at their root? Was this what Auren expected her to do?

I put my calculations aside and focused on her. "And what were those three problems?"

"First, the garden is warded, and I'm forbidden to enter by my pact."

Apparently, Auren already had a plan, and if I could get close enough through Samantha, I might be able to find a way to break the wards. "We can work on that. What about the second?" I asked.

She swallowed. "The fruit of the vines protects the fae from the withering curse. If the vines die, the people—"

"Let them die," I whispered, trying to keep the hate from twisting my voice.

Shock and anger flashed across her beautiful face. "How can you say that?"

My lips curled back in a snarl, and I began to pace the room. "The city below you was built on the misery of my people, and the vines have devastated my lands for centuries. The queen and her court are vampires, bleeding the life from my people so that they can enjoy immortality."

"I'm not blind. I see Ayanna and her court for the self-serving monsters they are. They hoard the fruit and give commoners false hope through deadly competitions. But still, if the magic of the vines could cure them..."

"The court takes life that is not theirs to take, and while Ayanna rules, she will hoard that power for herself. Whether they taste immortality or not, her people are just as culpable for what is happening to my land. They deserve no mercy."

Samantha's jaw set, and she stared me down with a withering, accusatory gaze. On this, we would never see eye to eye.

Eventually, I looked away. "What's your third problem?"

She gave an unsatisfied grunt, then extended a claw and ripped through one of the tiny vines that covered the walls of her room. Almost immediately, it began to grow back, twice as thick as before.

I nodded. "Even if you get in, you don't know how to kill the vines."

That had always been the problem. Attacking only made them stronger. There was some form of magic giving the power of regrowth.

I rubbed the stubble forming along my jaw. "Perhaps there's a way to stop the magic that regenerates them if we attack the source. However, we won't know until we get in, so we should concentrate on that."

It was what Auren had also advised, though I was certain he had an ulterior motive.

Samantha stepped close enough that I could smell the citrus scent of her hair. "You'll help me?"

"I promised I would."

"Good. Then I have an idea." She crossed to the other side of the room, leaving me unexpectedly wanting. "You said that I was your anchor here. How far can you move from me? Can you pass through walls? I'm up for a little espionage."

A wolfish grin cut across my lips. "I've been wondering about the same thing. Let's test the limits."

I shifted through the shadows, first into Sarion's room and then the maid's quarters. From there, I went as far as I could down the hall before it dimmed to nothingness.

She raised her eyebrows expectantly when I returned.

"Sarion is currently finishing his dinner, while your maid is engrossed in a steamy novel. I could only get about a dozen paces down the hall before the connection weakened—so it would be a short leash."

"At least you're the one wearing it this time." She wrinkled her nose and gave me a playful smile that made my pulse beat faster. Fates, she was always stunning, but there was something about seeing her carefree that made all the shadows and suffering around me seem to fade away.

"What's your plan?" I asked.

"Tonight, while everyone is asleep, you and I sneak down to the garden. We check for alternate ways in, and we see if you can project inside. Maybe there's something you can discover about the vines."

"There will still be guards. If you get caught—"

"I won't, because you'll scout ahead."

I hated taking any risks with her, but the potential and the payoff were both too great, so eventually, I agreed. I was certain she would attempt something with or without my help, so it was time to let her lead, and I would be her shield.

21

———

Cadean

I returned three hours before dawn.

Samantha was wound up in silken sheets, her comforter cast aside. Her sensuous lips were slightly parted, and she was breathing slowly and softly. All I wanted to do was linger and watch her sleep, but we had work to do. I knelt by her side. "Samantha."

She stirred, and her eyes fluttered open. "Cadean?"

The sleepy way she said my name made my heart stir, and I didn't correct her. "It's time."

She nodded, and I backed away as she swung her legs over the side of the bed, then stood and stretched.

A wicked part of me was disappointed that she was already dressed.

She splashed water on her face from the basin, then slipped on her shoes. "I was so worked up, I had to drink a bottle of wine to get to sleep. Regretting that now."

The corner of my mouth ticked up. She was a wolf. She'd shake it off.

Samantha quietly unbolted the door of her chambers and

slipped out. I followed. Dim spheres hanging from wrought iron hooks cast light in patches, leaving most of the hall in shadow. It was perfect.

Sam locked the door.

"Try to speak as little as possible," I said quietly, though I knew no one could hear my side of our conversation. "Point which way."

She nodded.

I moved down the corridor, stepping from shadow to shadow, and motioned her forward as I reached the limits of my perception. Working in tandem, we slunk through the dim halls of the residence wing, then dropped two flights and entered the palace proper.

The potential of it all had my mind spinning. If Samantha could find out where high-ranking officers met, I could slip through the walls while she waited outside. I could watch their meetings, see their maps, and learn to read their tendencies.

I could get Samantha killed.

Guilt pommeled me, and I shoved the distractions from my mind. The thought of her being harmed made me physically ill.

She came to my side and gave me a questioning look.

"Just be careful," I growled.

She narrowed her eyes, which I interpreted as, *I am.*

"Not careful enough."

A few minutes later, we encountered our first patrol. I had Samantha duck down a side corridor as they passed, and we pushed on as soon as they were out of sight. At last, she led me onto a balcony that overlooked a sprawling garden of starlit vines.

The place was a nexus of death. If I'd had the power to call meteors from the heavens, I wouldn't have hesitated to reduce Dreamspire, both the city and its garden, to a molten pile of rock.

Fuck the Undying Court and their people.

"Are you all right?" Samantha asked softly now that we were outside and free of potential prying ears.

I looked down. Shadows were streaming from my hands.

"This place...it's evil."

"Or a source of life," she countered. "The fruit could heal my mother—but they won't give it to wolves, or anyone below the third order. The queen is going to hold it over my head until I help her bind you."

"And will you?" I rumbled low in challenge.

Her fangs slowly slid out, and she smiled. "Don't make me."

The limits of my shadow-casting were a problem. I could only perceive a small portion of the garden, but it was enough to give me some kind of idea of the defense. "The whole place is protected by layers of wards. Some bar entrance, others kill, and yet more are triggers if you attempt to dispel either of the first two. They're all woven together. We need to get closer and look for another way in."

Samantha nodded, and we made our way down two levels. Pausing, she put her hand up, lifting her nose as if to catch a scent. "There are more guards below—I can smell them."

"I'll scout ahead."

I descended the stairs and emerged into a vast room. Three-story pillars supported a ceiling of small domes, but the centerpiece was a fifteen-foot-high pair of doors on the far wall. They were inlaid with silver vines and flanked by half a dozen sentries.

Unfortunately, I'd reached the limits of my perception. I quickly surveyed the room, then returned to Samantha.

"I found the main entrance to the garden, but you'll need to get closer for me to shadow-cast to the other side. Unfortunately, there are six guards, but there's a large, planted urn you could hide behind at the base of the stairs. It might be close enough."

She nodded, then crept toward the stairs.

My heart thundered in my chest as she reached the bottom and slipped behind the urn. The guards hadn't noticed.

I crouched beside her. "If you hear any movement, get out of here."

She gave me a thumbs-up, and I stepped into the shadows at the far side of the room, then through the wall.

I emerged into the shadows of the garden. Vines clung to the walls, dangling with bright red fruit—the cure for Samantha's mother, and the curse of my people.

What was the secret to destroying it all?

To my frustration, the limits of my perception didn't permit me to see any deeper than the edges. Samantha would have to get closer—and with the guards, there was no way to do that. I could barely make out a pair of sentries posted on this side—

I felt our bond stretch and break, and shadows consumed me. Mel's workshop began to reappear.

Fuck, Samantha must have had to move.

I hurtled back through the darkness, searching for our bond. She was moving quickly.

The halls of the palace appeared, and I stepped from the shadows ahead of her.

She jerked back with fright, then quickly glanced behind her. "They spotted me."

"Go left," I snarled as the beams from a pair of lights swept into the hall.

Samantha bolted down the corridor as two guards rounded the corner. As a shifter, she was far faster and could see in the dark, but they knew the palace.

I leapt from one patch of shadow to the next, trying to keep an eye on the fae warriors and guide her at the same time, but the fucking palace was a warren. There was no grid system, only organic halls that twisted and turned when you least expected it.

One moment, I was certain we'd thrown them off our path, and then the next, I heard the clanking of steel boots moving back in our direction.

Suddenly, our corridor terminated in an open, circular room ringed with columns. There was no way out.

Fuck, Samantha mouthed as she turned around.

I pointed to a pillar wreathed in a dense knot of vines. "Get back there, and don't make a sound."

She crouched, and I drove my magic toward her, calling the darkness to form a veil. It took all my strength to affect even a wisp of darkness in the room, but my fear provided a deep reserve of strength. Slowly, the shadows began to rise and weave around her, and by the time the sentries burst in, I'd wrapped her in darkness.

The pair of warriors shone the bright beams of their hand lamps around the room. I held my breath as the light swept across her hiding place, but the magical shadows did not yield. Thank fates they didn't have a shifter's heightened hearing or sense of smell.

The captain cursed, and then they turned and headed back the way they'd come.

My shoulders sagged with relief when they departed. I stepped from the shadows and held up my hand, and we waited five more minutes. Once I was certain the footsteps had died away, I released the spell, and Samantha emerged from her cocoon of shadow.

Thanks, she said silently.

I nodded as a wave of exhaustion fell over me. I hadn't ever summoned my powers while shadow-casting like this—hell, it shouldn't have been possible, but then again, everything was different with her. It was like she'd been a focal point for my magic.

Unfortunately, what would normally have been the simplest

spell had taken most of my strength to perform. The limits of my perception were dimming, and I knew I wouldn't be able to remain with her much longer.

"Do you think they saw your face when they spotted you?" I asked.

She shook her head.

"Good. I'm starting to fade. I want to get you back to your room as quickly as possible."

Moving swiftly and quietly, we made our way around another patrol and up into the residential tower.

Samantha exhaled deeply as she shut the door behind her. "Holy shit, that was close." Her cheeks were flushed from running, and her eyes glimmered with excitement. "I think it was the most fun I've had in the Dreamlands."

The glow of joy about her was mesmerizing, and it pulled me in. If I'd been anything more than shadows, I would have greedily dragged my lips across hers. Instead, all I could do was give her a wicked grin. "I can think of things I've seen you enjoy more."

Her glistening chest began to rise and fall a little faster, and I could smell the scent of her building desire, heightened by the thrill of the chase.

She stepped close, and for a moment, I was certain she was going to try to kiss me—phantom or not—but then she slipped away like she was a shadow herself.

"I appreciate your help tonight. As much as I hate to admit it, we work together pretty well." There was a look of victory in her wry smile.

"It's not the only thing we do well together," I murmured. I couldn't help myself.

She blushed, but there was hunger in her eyes. She remembered.

Samantha strode to the bathroom door, then looked back

over her shoulder. "After all that, I need to cool off. Good night, Cadean."

The way my name slipped off her tongue set a fire in me that I wasn't going to be able to extinguish. It was dangerous on so many levels.

"I told you not to call me that," I said, my tone pure gravel and frustration. "Not even in private."

She gave me a demure smile. "Just this once. I like what it does to you."

That look. Her voice. Her lips. They would push me over the brink into madness.

Her magic pressed in like a feather's touch against my skin. "Now, if you don't mind, I need to sleep. Sweet dreams."

I let her push me away. The world became shadows around me, but I was filled with a lightness that I hadn't felt for a long time.

22

<hr>

Samantha

I didn't hear from the queen for several days, so I simply fell into a routine. I grilled my tutor in the morning about the vines and the court, visited my mother in the afternoons, avoided as many other gawking fae courtiers as possible, and went to bed early.

Then, at three in the morning, I'd sneak out with Cadean and carefully explore the palace, dodging guards and sentries all the while. We didn't dare go back to the garden so soon, but I wanted to map out the areas of the palace I couldn't see with Sarion hanging over my shoulder.

Finally, Ayanna summoned me on the third day—this time, for an excursion. I met her and her entourage on the steps of the palace.

She gestured to a wingless carriage waiting for us on the road below. "The oracle is willing to meet."

A surge of excitement welled up in me.

"Thank you, Your Majesty," I said, bowing deeply to hide the expression of victory that was most certainly plastered over my face.

Anticipation kept my thoughts spinning as we departed the city. It was my first chance to see it from the ground—or technically, from above the ground, as the entire place was constructed atop a nest of vines.

The wheels of the carriage clacked over the cobblestones, which had been embedded into the flesh of the vines. Villagers pressed back against the houses as we passed, clearing the way for the armored honor guard that rode alongside. There were shops and restaurants and multi-story homes, and I longed to be out there. What would it be like to be in a real bar again? To be away from the finery and pretense of the court? The more I saw, the more constricting the cage around me felt.

"Don't gawk at the window," the queen chided.

My cheeks heated. I was looking and daydreaming a little, to be sure—but I wasn't *gawking*.

I sat back. "The city is beautiful. I should like to see it."

Ayanna scoffed. "The city is full of pretentious shop owners and greedy merchants. You should keep your attentions on the palace and the court, the things that matter."

"Am I forbidden to go there?"

Her mouth drew into a thin line. "You don't need to mingle with their kind. Anyway, it would be more difficult to ensure your security in the city. I'm not sure how the commoners would react to a half-wolf in their midst. Our war with the Dark Wolf God has left many families scarred and resentful. I would not want you to find yourself the subject of an angry mob. Their reaction could be...unpredictable."

That wasn't an explicit no, but I couldn't shake the sudden unease that rose in my stomach. I might be part fae, but to them, I looked like nothing more than a human or a shifter.

I looked like their enemy—hell, I *was* their enemy.

We descended a long, slender bridge that led down to the

surrounding forest. Our riders stayed close at hand, and I saw the shadows of deathwings circling close overhead.

We passed through the mists twice, shifting from patches of pine forest to marsh, to an island of ancient trees with red and gold leaves.

The queen ordered Sarion and our guards to stay behind, and she led me down a narrow, winding path. Green and gray moss clung to the edges of the heavily worn trail, and I wondered how many had come this way, seeking wisdom and answers. How many had found what they were looking for?

The queen glanced back and gave me a look like she could read my mind. "Don't get your hopes up. She only appears when she is willing to speak. In the centuries since we arrived in this land, she has only answered my questions three times—one of which was about you."

"How long has the oracle resided here?" I asked as my feet crunched over the dry fallen leaves.

The queen gave a cold half-laugh. "She was here before the Dark Wolf God himself. This little patch of the Dreamlands is her realm if it is anyone's."

The possibilities began to weave in and out of my mind. Had Cadean ever sought her counsel while he still controlled this land? Could she tell me anything of him? Could she tell me if he was redeemable, or would he always be a destroyer at heart? My feelings for him flipped every time we met. Sometimes he filled me with light; at other times, the mask fell away, and I saw the ruthless destroyer he concealed.

Of course, I couldn't ask the oracle those questions in front of the queen.

The forest thickened. The path wound around the trunk of a fallen tree, and a stone archway came into view, set against a curtain of maples—a temple sculpted from living trees. They stood as pillars, and their roots knit together as steps. In a way, it reminded me of Cadean's great hall, but far more primal, if that was possible—a living building that had remained the same for millennia while the forest had risen and died and been reborn around it.

I glanced around the deserted glade. "Can anyone come here?"

"If you find your way to the temple, you were meant to arrive. I've tried many times but failed to find it. Today, we're lucky. She wants to speak."

The queen lifted the skirt of her dress and ascended the rootbound steps into the temple. She disappeared so completely into the darkness that for a second, I wondered if the archway was a portal. However, I could still smell her and feel the low vibration of her magic, so it was only some sort of magical veil.

I closed my eyes and sniffed the air, catching the scent of three women and another signature—the aroma of damp earth and fractured stone, and the low thrum of an approaching storm.

It was a fae presence, but far, far beyond what *fae* meant to me.

I had the uncanny feeling that it was waiting, and impatient. With a resolute breath, I bunched up my ungainly dress and climbed the stairs.

Dim light swallowed me as I crossed the threshold, like stepping through a curtain. Inside, there were no walls, only a ring of massive trees. Their trunks rose high above me like the columns of a Greek temple, and their branches entwined overhead, creating an intricate domed roof. Thin rays of light flitted down through the smoke rising from the brazier in the center of the room. Three hooded attendants in soft, gray robes waited beside it, each holding a slender silver pitcher.

"We've come to speak with the oracle," Ayanna said.

"She knows," the attendants murmured, though none of their lips seemed to move. "She's been waiting for you."

Their voices were like the rustling of leaves, and for a moment, I was uncertain whether the three women were even there.

They circled the brazier in a wild dance and upended their pitchers, dousing the flames with a wine-dark liquid. Steam boiled over the edges of the brazier and swirled upward along the columns until the chamber of trees was wreathed in a thick fog.

I looked around for the attendants, but they were gone.

The slowly circulating steam folded in on itself, and a tall shadow took shape behind the curtain of gray. The air went cold as the oracle emerged, and she was nothing like I could have ever imagined.

The oracle loomed over us. She was draped in dark robes, and a rack of antlers protruded from beneath her hood. Her feet were hooves, and her hands were not quite human, with long, grasping fingers and sharp nails. She was something halfway between fae and beast, but much, much more. Her ancient magic vibrated around me like the buzz of bees or the tension in the air before a storm.

"What are you?" I whispered, before realizing my lips were moving.

The creature turned to me, and I instantly understood the inadequacy of my question. She transcended categorization or understanding, a being formed from mystery and doubt. If she could see the future or know the secrets of the gods, I was certain it was because she'd been there when they'd been created, stalking in the shadows of the formless earth.

She reached out and lifted my chin with a crooked finger, and I shivered at her touch. "All beings sleep, dear child, even the Fates. I'm one of their dreams. I was here before the Dark

Wolf God brought these lands together, and I will be here still when they fall apart. The question is, what are *you*, Samantha?"

"A wolf and part fae," I stammered. The oracle knew my name, and no doubt knew exactly what I was, but I didn't know what else to say.

She pulled her hand away sharply, as if I was icy to the touch. "You're a wolf without a pack. A fae who does not understand her blood. You're both and neither—identities you wear like you don a gown or dress but do not accept as part of you."

"Then what am I?" I whispered, as if somehow speaking aloud would shatter the dreamlike vision around me.

The oracle chuckled softly. "Before you came here, what did they tell you I was?"

"An oracle."

"That's right, child. I'm an oracle. Whatever our appearance, in the end, we are only our purpose. It shapes us and makes us who we are. Yet you come here, not knowing your own purpose or who you are."

I glanced at the queen, who nodded.

"You told the queen that I had the power to bring the Dark Wolf God to his knees and bind him with bonds that cannot be broken. Is that my purpose?"

"That was an answer to a different question for a different person," the oracle murmured. With unnatural speed, she turned and brushed her hand down Ayanna's face, closing her eyes. When she pulled her hand away, the queen stood motionless, gently breathing.

My heart quickened. "What did you do?"

"Her answers are not for you, just as your answers are not for her. She brought you to me, and now, her role is done. We will leave her to her dreams, and she can leave us to our conversation."

But I wasn't going to let the question go that easily. "There was another part to your prophecy—that I could save the Dark Wolf God..."

"He must save himself," the oracle said softly, but with the strength of steel.

The finality of her words landed like lead in my stomach, and I felt a deep sadness creep into my bones. Was there nothing I could do for him? To change him?

I glanced at the queen, frozen in sleep. A perfect statue, she had a strength of will that I could only dream of.

"Is her purpose to save her people?" I asked.

"Our purposes are our own," the oracle hissed, turning her back to me and stirring the steam rising from the brazier with her hand. The fog began to spiral faster around the chamber of trees. "For some, they change or are forgotten, or they're consumed by new desires along the way. You must focus on yours alone."

"Then is it my purpose to save them? She and her people are cursed, and—"

The oracle whirled around and seized my wrist. "Do not seek your purpose within others—not the queen or her people or the Dark Wolf God. It is within *you*, waiting for you to grasp it. It's not an act or a mask you wear, but the thing that drives you forward—the thing that will not let you stop when every part of you wants to die."

I shuddered beneath her touch. "How do I find it?"

"The way all truths are found—through suffering." She released my hand and backed away. "The queen will test you, the Dark Wolf God will test you, and your own weakness will test you. They will try to break you, but do not turn away from the challenges they present. Face them and find yourself—that is how you'll learn what you are and what you are *not*."

Her words foretold pain and darkness and failure. Trembling, I forced myself to look up into the shadows where her face should have been. "Can you see the future?"

"I see the future, and the future sees me."

I swallowed. "Will I find my true purpose?"

The horned woman stepped backward into the mist. "If you do, it will destroy everything you are. Now, it is time for you to go."

She disappeared, and the room was suddenly three shades brighter. The steam wasn't nearly as thick as I remembered, and the three attendants stood on the far side of the room, waiting patiently.

"What happened?" the queen asked.

Her eyes shimmered like emeralds, and the power of her magic wrapped around me, desperate to force the words from my mouth—but of course, she couldn't compel me without breaking the pact.

Information was power, but she might understand much of what I didn't.

"The oracle appeared. She said I didn't know who I was or what my purpose was. She said that you and the Dark Wolf God would test me."

The lines of her face hardened. "The Dark Wolf God already has, but I have not. Come. Let us leave, and I will think on it."

I gave the three attendants one last look, and then stepped through the archway and out of the temple of the trees.

As we made our way along the forest path, I asked, "The oracle claimed that you would test me—what about the trials? Could I join them?"

I wasn't certain that was what the oracle had meant, but it could be a way to get access to the garden.

"The trials are dangerous. They are a way for my people to prove their loyalty to the court and to prove who is worthy of eating the fruit. Many fail, and many die."

"Would that not be testing me? My magic only manifests in the face of danger, so perhaps this is what is needed to bring it out."

The queen frowned. "This isn't about testing your power. You're vying for a way to save your mother. Plus, it isn't just one trial you would face, but many. Each grows harder, and the trials can take years to complete. You must ascend to the third order just for access to the garden and to eat once."

Multiple trials? Fuck.

But it didn't matter. Finally, I had a way forward that didn't involve breaking the pact. It was a way in—and I could tell that despite her hesitation, she was considering it.

"It's about the fruit, yes, but also about discovering what I am meant to be. Let me compete, test me, like anyone else from your kingdom."

The queen studied my face for a long time, and then turned and began walking back to the carriage. "I will think on it."

23

Samantha

Sarion pounded on my door early the next morning. "The queen wants you at the training ground as soon as possible."

My heart leapt in my chest. Had she decided to let me compete, or was this simply a different way to practice my magic?

Not knowing what to expect, I threw on a loose shirt and comfortable trousers and followed Sarion down.

Ayanna made me wait half an hour but finally arrived with her honor guard. The queen's expression seemed troubled, but she masked it the moment she saw me, and motioned for me to fall in line. "Do you still wish to compete in the trials?"

My pulse quickened. "Yes."

"I don't think you know what you're asking. For now, you will train with some of the other candidates. You said your magic only emerges when you're under duress, and they'll push you hard. In a few weeks, you'll know whether you're ready."

This was more like it. No more condescending tutors. *Real* practice. I grinned. "I'm looking forward to it."

The queen clasped her hands and gave me a side eye. "These fae are not going to be your friends. They're your rivals and competitors, though if my understanding of your rather checkered past is right, you should be on familiar ground."

My mouth went sour. Pit fights.

Sarion had watched me beat the hell out of a couple of werewolves the first day we met, and I was certain the fae had asked my mother where those skills came from. For a long time, making money in the ring had been the only life I'd known.

We paused before a grand archway ringed in vines. One of her guards opened the door, and I followed her in.

My breath stilled as we entered the cavernous room. It was like stepping inside a colossal geode. Crystalline spikes and ledges protruded from the walls, and vines wrapped around everything. Far above me, fae glided from amethyst spike to amethyst spike, their wings spread wide and magic flaring. I was in, far, far over my head.

"You're gawking again," the queen said beneath her breath, and I flushed.

The moment they saw us, the combatants stopped practicing and began to glide gracefully to the ground around us. A pang of jealousy shot through me, though my wolf rose in protest.

They can't shift, and they don't have a pack.

There were seven: four women and three men. All but one seemed about my age, but it was frankly impossible to tell with fae. They bowed before the queen, but their eyes kept darting suspiciously toward me.

The apparent oldest of the bunch, a battle-scarred man, stepped forward and briefly took a knee. "To what do we owe the honor, Your Majesty?"

The queen waved her hand at me. "This is Samantha. She's going to compete in the trial."

A blonde girl with a pixie cut snickered quietly to one of her friends. "As bait?"

My neck heated, and I dug my fingers into my palm. Although it had barely been above a whisper, the queen had caught it, too. She pursed her lips in displeasure and stepped toward the girl like a cat stalking its prey. "What was that, Astra?"

Pixie Cut quickly dropped to a knee. "I'm sorry, Your Majesty, I spoke out of turn. I didn't realize wolves could compete in the trials."

"She's half fae, as I'm sure you're all well aware."

The girl kept her eyes locked on the ground. "Of course, Your Majesty. My mistake."

I wanted to melt back in the shadows like Cadean could. This was exactly how you made enemies on your first day. Of course, none of that was a concern of the queen's.

Ayanna's lips curled in distaste. "I'd consider holding your tongue, seeing as Miss Bennet has already proven herself to be an asset to the court. That is more than can be said for you thus far."

Fuck it all to hell. Whatever chance I'd had here, I'd just earned an enemy for life.

Still down on one knee, the grizzled man looked up. "The trials are less than two weeks away, and this cadre has been training together for months. Is she anywhere near ready to join them?"

The queen gave a fake laugh that made me want to shrink down inside my boots. "Hardly. I've seen her hold off eulenbjorn, but she doesn't have full control of her powers. Get her up to speed as quickly as possible."

"Yes, Your Majesty."

The queen turned and gave me a look I couldn't interpret. "This will be good for you."

Doubtful.

As soon as she and her bodyguard stepped out of the chamber, the instructor rose and snapped his fingers at Pixie Cut. "Astra, seeing as you're confused about our new student's nature, you're with her. See what she can do."

A wicked smile crossed her face. "Gladly."

I'd grown up being tossed into rings and training pits with wolves who were far more skilled than I was, and I knew when I was about to get fucked, and I was about to get *fucked*. The queen had singled Astra out for a reprimand and doubled down on it. Worse, I could already tell this girl was the alpha student. She was going to make an example of me, for sure. My wolf readied itself, and I could feel my claws itching at the ends of my fingertips, but I pushed them away. *I'm sorry, not this time. Not for a while.*

As much as I wanted to sink my claws into something, for better or worse, this was about developing my magic.

As the other students returned to the training grounds, Astra circled me. "Can you fly?"

"No."

She released an incredulous huff. "What sort of offensive magic have you learned? Strangling lights? Prismatic bolts?"

I'm going to die today.

I gave her a pained, apologetic smile. "None?"

She raised her chin. "Defensive, then?"

I pressed my eyes closed as I begged the Fates for mercy. "Sometimes, I've been able to summon a shield. I don't have much experience. Usually, it comes out when—"

"A shield is a start." She pivoted and stepped back six paces. "Let's see how strong it is."

"I—"

A kaleidoscope of color burst from her outstretched fingers. I reached for my magic, but before I felt so much as a wisp, the bolts of light slammed into me. Pain exploded across my body, and I hurtled backward. My teeth slammed together as I hit the ground, and I rolled over with a groan.

Astra tisked. "Oh, okay. You're a little slow, then."

I squeezed my eyes shut as the memories of youth came flooding back. I'd spent a lot of time on my back, covered in my own blood. This was nothing.

Yet.

I thrust myself up onto my palms, and then my feet. "Look, I know you're far more talented than I am. I'm still working on—"

Spiraling bolts of light collided into me, and I flipped sideways. My arms and face ricocheted off the ground, and I rolled to a stop by the wall.

Okay, old lesson relearned. Don't get up until you're ready.

I closed my eyes and reached out for the power that I knew was buried deep within me. I could almost feel it, barely beyond my grasp.

"Are you just going to lie there?" she asked.

Still focusing on my power, I summoned it, like coaxing one of the fox kits to trust me. A shimmering shield flickered around me. I'd done it!

Just as I leapt to my feet, bolts of light exploded into the shield and drove me back against the wall. The halo of light protecting me fizzled and dissipated into mist—but it had worked for a moment.

I stood there, chest heaving, and couldn't stop the grin from spreading across my face.

Astra snapped her hand up, and a single jet of light blasted into my chest. My head and shoulders flew back and cracked against the amethyst wall, my vision exploding into a dance of lights that blurred around the edges.

Searing heat raced over my skin. I crumpled to the ground in agony, patting my chest as I rolled, trying to put out the flames—but when I glanced down, there were no flames, just burned skin that felt like someone had put a blowtorch to it.

I flopped onto my back, and a shadow appeared above me.

"Fates, you're fucking remedial. Have you been drinking roowine all morning? How the hell do you think you could compete with us, wolf-bait?"

Aaaaaand this was the time to submit. I'd been through this moment time and time again. Astra was pissed. The alpha had singled her out, and I was the cause. I could understand all of that. All I had to do was just nose down and grovel, and she might let me walk away, or even make my life a little less miserable. She just needed to show dominance. At the heart of things, the fae weren't much different from the pack.

I coughed and wiped a little bloody spittle from my mouth.

Unfortunately for everyone involved, submission wasn't really my strong suit. I'd been subjected to the Dark Wolf God, to his fucking scheming brother, and to the queen of the fae herself. This little winged bitch wasn't good enough to get the best of me.

I thrust myself up onto my forearms, and then to my feet, though I had to grab the wall to keep myself balanced. "So, we go again, then?"

"Look at yourself—you're pathetic. There's no way you fought off even a baby eulenbjorn."

I brushed the back of my wrist over my lips. "I did. I just have a problem summoning my powers when there's not a threat around."

"You don't think I'm a threat?"

The world was still slightly spinning, and I braced my hands on my knees and coughed. "Yeah, not really."

"Then you're dumber than you look. I put you on your ass in

a second, and that's me holding back. Maybe you should show a little respect."

I closed my eyes and savored the familiarity of the moment. I knew her type: petty, mean, and insecure.

Straightening up, I looked around. Everyone was watching, which made this all the worse. Either I was going to be Astra's little bitch or was I someone who had enough guts to get their ass kicked.

A couple of the girls looked away when my gaze swept over them, though most of the cadre kept their expressions steady, compassionless, and cruel.

"Again?" I asked.

"You're barely worth the effort." Astra snorted. "You know what we're training to be, don't you, half-breed?"

"Florists?"

"Enforcers. We hunt down wolves that wind up on the wrong side of the border and fucking kill them. I could end you in a second. You wouldn't be my first pelt."

My wolf stirred, and I jammed my nails into my palm to stop my claws from coming out. These were pelt-takers, and that changed everything.

Astra glanced down at my hand. "Having trouble keeping your wolf in, half-breed? Maybe you should let it out. Most of the girls haven't had the chance to hear a wolf squeal in pain. It's fucking delightful."

Images of the soldiers ransacking Selene's village leapt to my mind. Shifters running and screaming and being cut down by deathwings and fae alike...

I knew she was simply baiting me into doing something stupid so she could put me in my place with everyone watching. I also didn't give a flying fuck. No one talked about my people like that.

I closed my eyes and let my head fall back. "You really want to fight a wolf, huh?"

Astra stepped a little closer. "No. I want to kill one."

That was like music to my ears. I smiled and let my fangs pop out, and then I rammed my fist straight into her jaw.

24

———

Samantha

Astra's teeth cracked together, and she stumbled back into the wall with a sharp cry of outrage. She touched her mouth and cursed when her hand came away covered in blood. "You bitch!"

"Magic only!" the instructor shouted as I shook out my aching hand.

Now the bastard decided to step in, after watching me nearly get murdered? I shrugged at him. "Sorry. I accidentally cast *fist*."

Astra screamed in rage as she released a crackling bolt of pink lightning.

Not even bothering to call my magic, I sprang sideways and tumbled back to my feet. There was a smoldering fissure in the grass where I'd been standing. My eyes rounded.

Okay, fine. She'd been holding back *a lot*.

Astra snapped her arm out, and six bolts of light spiraled toward me.

I ran and rebounded off the wall as crystal exploded into dust in my wake. I rolled as I landed and launched myself forward. My fist rammed into her nose with enough force that her head rebounded off the ground when she hit.

I dropped to one knee and pressed the tips of my claws against her throat. "I get it. You have some pretty sick life ambitions, but you should keep in mind that wolves are faster, stronger, and can hear your heartbeat a hundred yards away. When you're out there, you're not the hunter. You're the hunted."

Her eyes burned with rage, but she didn't move.

The instructor pulled me back. "I said, *Magic only*."

I didn't take my eyes off Astra. The rage had taken over, and I barely had my wolf under control. "Don't you fucking talk about taking pelts again, or I swear, I will take yours."

She started to rise, but the instructor held up his hand. "This is over."

My pulse raced, and I flexed my hand. *Let her try.*

"Get a grip," Cadean snarled.

My heart skipped a beat, and I looked up. The Dark God was watching from the shadows of the wall. His arms were crossed, and cold rage emanated off him like gusts of winter wind. "Don't look at me, look at them. You're going to blow your cover."

I turned to face the rest of the cadre. Some were angry, others stunned. One or two repressed smiles.

My gut twisted. Twenty minutes on the scene, and I'd nearly outed myself. I had to remember what he'd told me—use my anger as a shield. Make them believe I hated him.

I pulled my arm from the instructor's grasp. "I'm not here to fight you or to take insults about what I am. I hate the fucking Dark God, but not his people. Don't talk about skinning shifters again. I take it personally."

I turned and stalked toward the wall where Cadean stood but couldn't shake the memory of dozens of werefoxes lying motionless in the dirt at Frostfall, or the sound of their kits and families crying. The scent of the pyre sending them into the dark night.

If I could just be near him, maybe his presence could drive

the memories away.

I was a foot from the wall when Cadean's eyes widened, and a surge of electricity in the air raised the hair on my neck. "Watch out!"

I spun as purple lightning lashed toward me and raised my arm out of instinct. My magic roared to life, and a shield of white light exploded outward. Astra's lightning crackled across the surface and dissipated in a shower of sparks.

She grunted in frustration and threw her hand back to cast again.

I moved without thinking.

My hand sprang forward, and a sphere of white light burst from my fingers. It crashed into Astra's chest and slammed her back into the opposite wall. Her body slumped to the ground, motionless.

Oh, fuck.

My stomach lurched, and I darted forward. The instructor dropped by her side and checked her pulse.

I sank to my knees beside him. "Is she okay?"

"Get back!" he snapped. "She needs space."

I put my hand over my mouth. What had I done?

The others gathered around, and the instructor looked up. "She'll be fine. She's just knocked out." He turned to glare at me. "You're banned from the practice field."

My gut knotted as my mouth turned sour. The first time the fae had prodded me, I'd lost my temper and blown my chance at training and making allies. Fucking hell.

"Astra was bullying her," a girl with mousy brown hair blurted. "You know what she's like."

"Astra used a killing curse!" a second said. "We're not supposed to practice those. The new girl had every right to put Astra down hard."

The instructor looked at the girl sprawled out on the ground beside him and scowled. "Killing curses *are* forbidden. Astra will not be returning to practice for a week." He glared at me. "As for you—"

"I'll train with her," Mousy interjected.

He sighed in exasperation. "Fine. Considering Astra was out of line, you can stay and train with Kirin. But one more dust up like this, and you're out—permanently. No hand-to-hand combat, and you're forbidden from using that spell in sparring until you learn to control it. Got it?"

I nodded. "Thanks."

"As for the rest of you, stop gawking and pack up your gear. Practice is over."

Several of the girls cast venomous looks in my direction, but Kirin gave me a soft smile, and the other who'd spoken nodded approvingly before she walked off.

"Are you sure Astra's going to be okay?" I asked the instructor.

He rubbed his forehead. "Yes, I'll take care of her. It's you I'm worried about. A sharp temper is a bad thing to pair with magic. You need to learn to control both. However hard it is, you need to learn to summon your magic when you're not in danger so that you can control it when you are."

I nodded. "I know. I'll try harder. Thanks for a second chance."

He glanced back at Astra. "You're here because it's what the queen wants. Not me. I don't care what you learn as long as my other students are safe."

"Got it," I said, then backed away.

His magic flared, and he placed his hand on Astra's cheek.

I turned and hurried away. I could feel Cadean's presence still lurking in the shadows, but I headed straight for the door. I didn't want to be around when Astra learned I'd gotten her kicked out of training, even temporarily.

As I pushed open the door, Kirin caught my arm. "Hey, don't worry about what happened. Tomorrow will be better, okay? I'm going to help you."

"I appreciate that. But while I'm grateful for everything you said back there, you might not want to make friends with the new pariah, particularly when she's part wolf."

She shrugged. "I was the old pariah, and Josephine before me. Astra has made all our lives miserable for months. You're the only one so far to take her out. I appreciate that."

My throat tightened. Kirin seemed like the first genuine fae I'd met, and I really, really needed a friend, but the last thing I wanted to do was fuck anyone else over.

I checked over my shoulder to make sure no one was watching us talk, then lowered my voice. "Look, I know Astra's type—*vengeful*. I almost married a guy like that. I guarantee she's going to find a way to get even, and I don't want you hurt in the process."

Kirin squeezed my arm and backed away. "You're right, she'll try. We won't let her." With that, she turned and headed down the corridor.

I raised my eyebrows as she rounded the corner. I was part wolf, the queen's favorite new toy, and a loose cannon—all things that screamed *stay away* to anyone with sense. If she was still willing to be friends, she had to hate Astra a whole lot.

Sarion strode down the corridor toward me. "How was practice?" He took one look at the blood and burns on my clothes and stopped short. "Oh."

I shook my head as we headed back toward my quarters. "I don't want to talk about it. Let's just say no one died, and they're expecting me back tomorrow."

He nodded and gave me a wink. "Good. Then it went better than expected."

25

Cadean

I paced the shadows of Samantha's room as I tried to seize control of my anger. The fucking fae were worse than animals.

I'd slaughter every enforcer in a hundred miles of the border if I was free.

The door cracked, and I melted into the shadows as Samantha slipped in. She shut it behind her and locked it, then leaned against the wall and let her head drop back. "I know you're there."

The patch of blood clinging to the corner of her mouth made me want to pull her into my arms. I wanted to hold her, praise her, ravage her.

But of course, I couldn't.

I let myself manifest from the darkness and prowled into the room. "That was too close. That fae snake could have killed you."

"She didn't," Sam said as she met my gaze.

"Your bastard trainer is right—you need to learn to control your emotions as well as your magic. You made an enemy today, and they'll have you pegged as a shifter sympathizer now."

She looked away and shrugged. "They were going to think that anyway. I'm half shifter. I just have to make them believe that I hate you so much, I'm willing to work with anyone, even pelt-takers."

The bitterness in her voice cut through me like a knife. No shifter should have to let someone talk to them like that. A part of me had wanted to see Samantha rip the enforcer's jugular out.

I couldn't help the smile that formed at the edge of my lips.

"What?" she said flatly.

"I think I like it when you get angry. You did well today."

"I got lucky."

I shook my head as I drew a little closer. "You called your magic and used it offensively. You're getting stronger."

Samantha released a bitter laugh and wrapped her arms around herself. "I'm nothing compared to the others, and I can't even seem to call my magic unless I'm really in danger, or..."

"Or what?"

Her eyes flicked to mine. "Or you're around. I couldn't fully summon it until I was standing right next to you."

I held her gaze a moment too long, then looked away. "I have nothing to do with it. You summoned it because you sensed danger. I'm nothing more than a vision. An illusion of light and shadow."

She held out her hand, and moments later, it began to glow with soft moonlight. "It normally takes me forever to do this for my tutor, but my magic always flows when you're around."

I stepped closer. "Then perhaps I still scare you, little wolf."

She inhaled slowly as she measured the vanished distance between us. Her intoxicating scent told me she was thinking of things other than fear, and my eyes drifted to her full lips.

"You will always scare me," she said, then stepped straight through me, like I was nothing.

Her magic brushed against mine, and I had to grit my teeth to prevent a growl of pleasure. It was like a warm caress across cold skin, an electric tingle racing through every part of me.

I turned around as she braced herself against the far windowsill. Her posture told me she'd felt it, too. Delight lingered on her face.

What was this connection we shared?

The moment faded as I watched, and her shoulders sank. "I don't think I have a shot at the trials. I have no idea what they will be, but I know I'm not ready."

She'd told me about it the night before, that the queen was to test her. It was a good plan, a way to prove her worth and get access to the garden.

"I'll be there. I'll help you, just like scouting the castle."

Samantha shook her head. "The others have been training for months and using their gifts since they were children. I saw the truth today: I can't count on my power."

"You can. I will help you."

"Auren couldn't help me. Neither could the tutor."

I gave her a warning growl. "And you would compare me to them?"

She turned and gave me a thorough once-over with her eyes, and finally, a smile broke across her intoxicating lips. "Never."

"Good."

I stepped back and paced to the far side of the room. "Eventually, you'll have to learn to summon your magic at will, but since it's easier for you to draw your magic around me, I'll stay with you every night while you practice. It will give you a chance to focus on mastering each of your gifts without a struggle to summon them first."

"I'm not sure what my gifts even are—my tutor suggests that I have none, just bursts of wild magic that can't be controlled."

My blood boiled with fury. I stalked forward until we were only a foot apart. "I want you to listen. You need to forget anything that your tutor or Auren told you. They're complete assholes."

Her nose twitched as she grinned. "I kind of suspected that."

"It's not wild magic, but the Moon's. I've fought against it for a thousand years and know it almost as well as my own. I also knew her before..." I hesitated as my throat tightened.

Before betrayal. Before imprisonment. Before she'd thrown our friendship into the flames of hell.

I shook the dark memories from my mind. "You've manifested seven gifts. I suspect you have more, but we'll concentrate on the ones that have emerged first."

Samantha raised her eyebrows in surprise. "Seven? Are you certain?"

I nodded, and her brow furrowed.

"I can control the wall. That's one," she said.

"Unfortunately, we can't practice that unless you'd like to sneak out and try releasing me."

She ignored the suggestion. "I can also create a shield, like I did today. The blast of moonlight I used on Astra, that was new. I'd never done anything like it before, but it makes three."

I nodded. "The fourth is the ball of burning moonlight you used to trap me the first time we met. It's quite unpleasant."

She gave me an apologetic look. "I'm not sorry."

"Fifth, you do the simplest without thinking about it." I gestured toward the moonlight that emanated from her palm. "You're doing it now."

"And the sixth?"

"The curse you gave me." I stepped to the shadows by the window and looked out. "That was the worst."

She hesitated. "I'm sorry about the curse."

I looked back at her and smiled softly. "But you healed me in the end—and that makes seven. Seven gifts you can use to beat this trial. Seven you can use to get your mother out of the queen's clutches. I think you'd better start practicing, don't you?"

Her expression hardened, and the moonlight around her brightened like pale fury.

26

───────

After a few days of nonstop practice, I began to miss my old tutor. Kirin was a good sparring partner, but she didn't hesitate to put me on my back. Cadean pushed me just as hard at night. We gave up exploring, and I practiced my magic until I was too tired to go on.

When the queen sent for me on the third day, I was ready for a break. I rushed back to my room, took a quick rinse in the bath, then threw on a fresh gown and followed Sarion to the upper floor of an adjacent tower.

By the time we exited the stairs, my outfit was riding up, and the muscles in my quads were trembling, but I forgot my exhaustion the moment I looked around. This portion of the palace was unlike anywhere else I'd been permitted to explore, with high, gilded archways and tall, crystalline ceilings. Vines sprouted from pots ringing the room, and hanging chandeliers cast flickering light across the polished amethyst walls.

"Where are we?" I asked.

"Council chambers. Only fourth and fifth orders are allowed in these areas," Sarion answered.

A pair of sentries waylaid us, and the queen arrived twenty minutes later, flanked by her ever-present honor guard. I bowed, then fell in at her side while the warriors trailed behind.

"How goes training?" the queen asked, as I followed her through the curving hall.

I smiled weakly. "They say that what doesn't kill you makes you stronger."

She sniffed. "Then I'm pleased to hear you haven't managed to kill yourself."

"I appreciate the opportunity to try."

She folded her hands. "Helping you develop your powers was part of our bargain, but we also agreed that you'd provide us with insights into your time with the Dark Wolf God."

Shit. I was swimming in very dangerous waters.

A chill crept over my skin, and I glanced down at my clasped hands. "It was a nightmare that I'd honestly rather not relive."

The queen stopped short and fixed me with a penetrating stare. "I'm sure. Unfortunately, it's necessary. We're in this together, are we not?"

"Of course," I said, trying to keep my voice light. "What would you like to know?"

"General Slaine would like to discuss your time at Shadowstone." The queen motioned to one of her guards, who stepped forward and knocked on a black door set in a large, gilded archway.

Slaine. My stomach lurched as my mouth went sour. "Am I being interrogated?"

"Of course not, you're a guest. Slaine is only interested in having a conversation and hearing what you have to say."

"I'd much rather speak with you. I thought—"

"That I would have the time?" Her lips pursed. "You presume too much."

The door swung wide, revealing the general, dressed in a

stiff black uniform with entwined silver vines. He wore a cocked smile, but everything about him broadcast unabashed power and malice.

The general bowed to the queen, but he kept his predatory eyes on me.

"General Slaine is much better acquainted with the ins and outs of the Dark Wolf God's realm and will be able to identify the fragments of information most useful to our collective interests."

The general stood to the side and motioned to the interior of the room. "Come, join me for a glass of wine."

My mind went blank, and I hesitated.

"Is there a problem, Samantha?" the queen asked, her voice pregnant with warning.

"Of course not, I'm delighted to help. Thank you, Your Majesty." I gave a quick bow, then stepped across the threshold into what I was certain was a wrought iron trap.

Sarion started to follow, but Slaine stepped between us. "This is fifth order business. You'll stand watch down the hall."

Doubt flickered over Sarion's face as Slaine shut the door, and the knot of dread in my belly tightened.

The room wasn't an interrogation chamber, but rather an office dominated by large windows and an ornate oaken desk. Hundreds of savage-looking weapons hung on the walls.

Slaine followed my gaze, and his lips twisted up with a cruel smile as he offered me a chair at his desk. "I'm a collector."

Of weapons or body parts?

I sat as he opened a bottle of wine and placed two glasses on his desk. He filled them, then reclined against the edge of the desk as he offered one to me. "I want you to tell me everything you know about the Dark Wolf God and his powers, as well as his forces and Shadowstone. Given that you spent nearly a month there, you should be quite familiar with its layout."

I cautiously took the glass. Had he laced it with something?

Shifting uncomfortably, I set the wine down untouched. "I'm happy to help, but I'm afraid I don't really know much about his realm."

The general's eyes flicked to my glass, and he laughed. Then, in a single motion, he scooped it up and drained the contents. "Let's not be so suspicious of each other." Slaine refilled it, then dropped into a massive chair opposite me. "And let's not play games, either. I know you were his little bitch, and you had access to most of the palace. So, you'll tell me everything you remember, starting with the moment you arrived."

Slaine's words slammed into my gut like a bullet, and my unsettled feeling turned into a spreading dread. *How much did he know?*

My lip curled back as I tried to keep my composure steady. "I was *not* his little bitch. I was a fucking captive, and it was a nightmare."

"And I can't wait to hear every detail." He rapped his heavy signet ring on the desk, then spread his hands wide. "Start talking, or I'll tell the queen that you're hiding something, and she will have to reconsider your position here."

I glanced at the door. "I thought this was going to be a polite conversation over a glass of wine. Not an interrogation."

Slaine's expression strained, like he was doing everything he could to stop himself from breaking the wineglass and ramming it into my throat. "It only stops being polite when you stop talking. As long as you give me what I want, we'll get along just fine."

My mind raced. How much could I tell him? I had to protect Cadean and his people, but I had to prove my use. I knew I was going to have to give up information, but I'd always imagined it was going to the queen.

My heart kept beating faster and faster, and my palms began to sweat. What was I going to tell this monster?

A sudden wave of power washed over me, and I froze as a low voice rumbled in my ear. "Don't worry, little wolf, I'm here."

The terror that had been choking my throat drained away, replaced by a sudden calm and a deep feeling of strength. I no longer had to face Slaine alone.

"Don't give him any indication I'm here," Cadean whispered. "Just keep your eyes on Slaine and do as I say. I'll help you navigate this."

The general's eyes narrowed, and he set down his glass. "Is something the matter?"

I had to force down the smile threatening to break at the corner of my lips. Slaine couldn't see the Dark Wolf God looming over me, and that knowledge filled me with an intoxicating thrill. What had seemed at one moment a death sentence had become a game of cat and mouse.

"Nothing's the matter." I snatched the glass of wine and took a large drink. "I just would have preferred to speak with the queen. I have a lot of bad memories from that place and the Dark Wolf God, so let's make this quick."

The general's gaze lingered on me for a few too many breaths, but at last, he leaned back and lifted his wine. "Very well. Let's start at the beginning. What happened after the Dark Wolf God captured you?"

"Tell him what a beast I was," Cadean said. "I bound you and interrogated you."

I scratched my scar. "The Dark Wolf God taught me I was powerless. His goons—Wulfric and Kassian—threw me in chains and paraded me through the great hall. The Dark Wolf God literally yanked me up off the ground with his magic and forced me to repeat everything Sarion had said." I glanced down at my hand. "It's not something I want to remember."

"Did he torture you?" the general rasped. "How did he tear the words from your tongue?"

I glanced up. I didn't like the glint of excitement in his eyes or his eager scent. My blood chilled as my suspicions turned to certainty. Slaine was a fucking sadist. He was hoping I'd been beaten within an inch of my life, and he wanted to hear the pain in my voice. He wanted to watch me relive it.

"Give him what he wants. Feed his hatred of me," Cadean said.

But I couldn't. Slaine would be hanging on every word, delighting in my pain. He'd know if I was faking. I'd have to embellish the truth and hope that it satisfied.

"The Dark Wolf God used his magic to force me to confess. I've never felt anything like it—it was like being torn apart. His power was like an earthquake shaking through me. I couldn't resist it."

Slaine's eyes dilated in frustration, and he sneered at me in contempt. "And after you stopped crying, what did he do with you then?"

I stiffened, and my fists knotted, but Cadean's voice traced over the skin of my neck. "Let him believe what he wants. Let him underestimate you—you know the value in that."

"His men dragged me to a cave and left me there, shackled and battered in the dark. Some days, they brought me food, and some days, they didn't. There was a pool of cave water and a corner to piss in."

"More," Cadean growled.

My shoulders stiffened as the memories came flooding back. "I have no idea how long I was down there. A week at least, maybe more. I was constantly cold, damp, and haunted by nightmares, and they never took off my shackles. Sometimes, I heard screaming, and I wasn't sure if it was my own."

Slaine smirked. Apparently, the wolf girl had gotten just the kind of accommodation she deserved. And the truth was, it *had* been fucking awful and terrifying—at first.

I looked down at my hands again, but Cadean's presence brushed against me. "I don't expect you to forgive me, but for everything I put you through, I'm sorry. And I'm sorry you must relive it."

The regret in his voice made my chest ache, but I pushed the rising emotions down and took another drink of the general's wine.

"Eventually, he let you out. Why?"

"Careful," Cadean whispered. "We have to assume he knows most of it."

I set the glass back down. "Because I agreed to obey and wear a collar."

"A collar?" Slaine mused with visible excitement.

"The Dark Wolf God was a fucking brute," I snapped. "I did what I had to in order to get what little freedom I could."

"Indeed," Slaine muttered, and I could almost taste his arousal. "And how much freedom did you...earn?"

I couldn't stop my lips from pulling back in disgust.

"Tell him everything you remember about the castle, but don't tell him your room was near mine," Cadean murmured in my ear. "If the bastard gets nosy, tell him that you heard the sound of water while leaving the dungeon, and that you think it might have an exit to the lake. He may not know about that entrance."

I hesitated. Could I really reveal all I knew? Was I putting Mel and the others at risk?

"Slaine has an army of spies and sent assassins after you," Cadean said. "He probably knows the ins and outs of Shadowstone better than I do. He's testing to see if you harbor any loyalty toward me, so give him everything you can."

I swallowed and began walking the general through everything I could remember: Mel's workshop, the great hall, the aviary, and the dungeons. I told him about Wulfric and Kassian, and the way Cadean's guards patrolled the grounds.

The more I said, the hungrier he grew. Dread began building in my chest as Cadean kept feeding me more and more. Did Slaine really know all of this already, or was Cadean putting his people at risk to help me pass the general's test?

My heart began beating faster.

The general drained a third glass of wine and set it down. "You seem agitated, Samantha. Is something wrong?"

Fuck yes, it was.

27

Samantha

Slaine smirked at me. He didn't care what I told him—he was looking for lies. He wouldn't be satisfied until he found a reason to strap me to a bench and pull my fingernails off.

I smoothed my gown and looked up. "You've been grilling me for hours. I've given you more than any spy could. I'm done. I don't want to think about that place anymore. Not ever."

Slaine leaned forward and gave me an absolutely predatory grin. "I'm sorry, Samantha, but that just won't do. I have so many questions left."

"Well, I'm out of answers."

I started to rise, but he rammed his fist into the table, his heavy signet ring cracking the wood . "You'll leave when I say you can leave—or shall I tell the queen you're harboring secrets from us?"

"All I'm harboring is a distaste for you."

"I couldn't care less how you feel about me," he snarled. "What I want to know is how you feel about the Dark Wolf God. What it was like being his little bitch?"

"Feed his hatred," Cadean growled.

My jaw tightened. "The Dark Wolf God is a fucking monster. He killed my pack and nearly killed me. I watched him burn fae villages to the ground. I desire nothing more than to stop him from doing it again."

It was the truth, but Slaine shook his head. "My sources say you went riding with him, and that you started visiting his chambers at night. What were the two of you doing together?"

The heat rushed from my body as my thoughts spiraled in. *How much did he already know?*

Cadean's voice traced over my skin. "Tell the bastard that I interrogated you ceaselessly, and without mercy, and that I beat you when you lied and just as hard when you told the truth. Tell him that you had to go to my sorceress every day for potions to heal your cuts and bruises. Tell him I'm a monster. Make him *believe* it."

I opened my mouth to speak, but the words wouldn't come.

My chest began to ache. Maybe the words wouldn't mean anything to Cadean, but they mattered to me.

He'd made me feel like no other man ever had. Sometimes, it felt like he was the only one who saw me for who I was. He trained me every night and watched me sleep, and now, he was here protecting me when no one else could.

The general leaned forward and rested his elbows on the table as he pressed his fingertips together. "Your hesitation makes me all the more curious. What exactly happened in that room?"

My magic came alive for the first time. I felt a connection with someone, like I'd never experienced in my whole life.

"Tell him that I ruined you!" Cadean growled. "Tell him I'm a monster!"

A quake of despair shook through me.

Slaine would know. He'd hear the lie in my voice, and it

would betray me just as well as if I shouted out the truth: I cared for Cadean.

"Condemn me!" Cadean said sharply, his words biting as he stepped into my line of sight. Dark plumes of magic swirled around him, and he looked every bit the monster I'd once thought him to be. Perhaps it was a mask he chose to wear, but it was a lie I could no longer tell myself.

I fixed the general with an icy stare. "We're done here."

The general rapped his ring on the table. "What are you trying to hide, Samantha? You'd better tell me, or I'll get angry. And you don't want to see me angry."

I shoved back from the table and rose. "My time at Shadowstone was a nightmare. I've given you everything I know about the palace, but I am not going to discuss what the Dark Wolf God did to me. Not with you, not with anyone."

Let him imagine the worst. I would not say it.

Slaine's face twisted in rage as he stood. "You're not going anywhere!"

"Fuck that and fuck you. I have a pact with the queen, so you don't get to dictate anything." I flung him the finger and strode to the door. I was done being the bastard's docile little plaything.

I pulled the door open, but the general slammed it shut with his hand.

Fates, he'd moved quickly.

"Why is it that you want to leave so badly, Samantha?" he asked, his voice thick with malice. "What don't you want to say? Perhaps you still have some affection for Shadowstone and its lord."

It was all I could do to stop my claws from coming out. "Take your hand off the gods-damned door."

Slaine bent close, and the heat of his breath raked over the skin of my neck. "Did he fuck you? Did he pull your nails off or break your fingers? You little wolf bitches heal so quickly—I find it an almost endless form of entertainment."

My stomach lurched into my mouth, bile burning my throat. How did he know? Had he done those things to shifter girls?

"Get away from her!" Cadean growled, as his black axe leapt into his hand. Streams of smoke billowed from the blade, but it only revealed how powerless he was to help me here. He was nothing more than a shadow, condemned to watch.

Well, I wasn't going to make him watch me submit. Not to Slaine, not to anyone.

I gave the general a smile, then rammed my palm into his chest. "Fuck off!"

He dodged back and seized my wrist with an iron grip that betrayed the lethal build beneath his uniform. My claws and fangs burst forth, and Slaine grinned. "Now the truth of what you are comes out: you're just another animal. It's time I started treating you as one."

The scent of his violent desire made me want to retch. He wanted to fight; he craved it. He wanted an excuse to hurt me and feel my fear.

I would give him nothing. I slowly retracted my claws. "Let go."

"Not until you beg."

Long-buried memories forced their way to the surface. I'd been here before, pushed up against a wall, with a man begging for any excuse to make me scream. Slaine was just another Wyland, just another Brent.

How many girls had the general made beg him for mercy? Had he stopped, or had the delight of it just driven him on?

A helpless urge to protect them surged in my chest, and a jolt of energy exploded through me. My hand flared with a halo of light.

A cruel smile spread over Slaine's lips. "And what do you

think you're going to do with that? I hear that you can barely control your powers. Not surprising for an animal. Perhaps you need a more forceful tutor. I can fuck and beat you far better than the Dark Wolf God ever did. Then maybe you'd learn."

Waves of magic hammered into me as the shadows exploded around Cadean. "Get the fuck out of there!" he yelled.

But I shook my head.

I knew who the general was now and how to handle him. This was a script I'd rehearsed time and time again.

He would never have control.

I yanked him close, so our faces were inches apart. "I faced the Dark God twice, and I won. You're nothing compared to him. How am I supposed to respect someone like you? A pathetic, mortal, weakling."

Slaine's face contorted with rage, and I jammed my knee into his thigh. The moment his balance changed, I shoved against him with all my strength until he staggered backward. My magic released in a wave of light and crashed into him like a battering ram.

He grunted, but I didn't stay to see the damage. I wrenched the door open and fled, slamming it behind me.

I hurried down the hall, my heart pounding and hands shaking.

Sarion's face dropped when he saw me.

"Let's get out here, *now*," I said.

My bodyguard opened his mouth, but before he could speak, Slaine charged into the hall. "You and I aren't finished."

I turned to face him. "We are. I'm not answering another question until I talk to the queen—and I won't be answering to you."

Sarion stepped in front of me and unsheathed his blade. "What the hell is going on here?"

"Put your sword away, soldier," Slaine snapped. "Remember who you take orders from."

"I do: Her Majesty, the queen—not you. Samantha has royal protection." Sarion glanced down at me. "Did he touch you?"

I lifted my chin, refusing to let the bastard see any weakness. "I think General Slaine is confused about the difference between a guest and prisoner. Her Majesty should be able to clear up that distinction for him."

Slaine sneered, making no attempt to hide his contempt.

Strangely, it was a relief. The venom in his eyes hadn't been born from a single conversation or what I'd done. It was a deeply nurtured hatred of everything that I was: a wolf, a half-breed, and a woman with the power to resist him.

It would have been there no matter what I said.

I still needed to play this right. The bastard would expect me to run straight to the queen with my tail between my legs. I had to show him I wasn't afraid.

I put my hand on Sarion's arm. "You can sheath your sword. Slaine's no danger to me. He understands the pact and what violating it would mean. He's impotent."

The general's face turned red. "You will get what's coming to you, dog."

I dipped low. "Good day, General. I hope you found our conversation useful. I found it very enlightening, and I expect the queen will, too."

With that, I turned and strode down the hall.

Sarion hesitated for a moment, then hurried behind me. "You've just made a very, very powerful enemy. What the hell happened in there?"

I checked over my shoulder to make sure the general wasn't following. "The fucker started asking inappropriate questions. Then he got handsy."

"Slaine is a snake," Sarion muttered. "Whatever he did, I'm sorry. I should never have left you alone with him."

I squeezed his arm. "It's not your fault. I'm just glad you were on the other side of that door."

"Do you want to go to Her Majesty? She doesn't like being disturbed, but this is important."

It would make me look weak in her eyes, and in Slaine's—like a schoolchild running to the teacher. I shook my head. "No. I know you report to her. Just send word that Slaine crossed a line. If she has any questions, I can wait to speak with her tomorrow."

When we reached my room, Sarion lingered. "Are sure you're going to be okay?"

I paused with the door open a crack. "I just need some time to think. It was a lot. Maybe you could send the maid away. I need to shift."

"The walls are solid stone. We can't hear."

"I appreciate that. I just need a moment where it feels like I'm not constantly under inspection."

Sarion hesitated, then nodded. "I'll send her away with your message, and I'll take up a post down the hall to make sure you're not disturbed."

I gave him a weak smile. "Thanks. And thanks for having my back."

Sarion pressed his hand to his left breast. "My duty."

With that, he turned away, and I stepped inside.

28

———

Cadean

Samantha slipped into the room and locked the door behind her. She leaned against it, and I could almost feel the exhaustion pulling her down.

I emerged from the shadows. "Little wolf…"

Her shoulders tightened for a moment, then relaxed—but she didn't turn around.

"You're here?" She shook her head. "Of course you are—you're always here."

Her voice was flat, and I couldn't read the emotion. Was she angry that I was waiting for her? Relieved? Ambivalent?

I circled through the shadows clinging to the edge of the room. "I'm sorry for everything that happened, and I'm sorry I couldn't help."

Samantha took up a position deeper in the room and leaned against the wall. Her eyes were golden yellow, and she was hovering at the edge of a shift. With a heavy sigh, she pressed her hands to her temples. "It's not your fault. It would have gone worse if you hadn't been there, so thank you."

My fists tightened as murderous thoughts raced through my

heart. "I would have killed Slaine if I could. Watching that unfold was fucking torture."

She gave me a weak smile. "How did you even know to be there?"

"I felt your anger. And fear." My blood boiled just to remember it.

"How?"

I hesitated. Mel would claim it was a mate bond, but that wasn't possible. It had to be something else. "The Moon's barrier separates us. Maybe it ties us together as well."

A long silence stretched between us. She didn't meet my eyes but turned to look out at the sunlit balcony instead. "Did I say too much?"

I took a step closer, wishing I could hold her. "No. Of course not."

She shook her head. "I know you're trying to protect me, but I don't want to put your people in danger."

A knot formed in my chest, tightening its grip. Even now, with vipers swarming around her, she was thinking of them. "The general has many spies. What you said probably confirmed information he already has, and as long as I know what Slaine knows, I can anticipate him."

It wasn't entirely the truth. Although he'd tried to mask his reactions, Slaine's eyes had dilated from time to time. Some information had been new to him.

Good. That worked in my favor. He'd risk assets to confirm the lakeside entrance, as well as other secrets I'd planted. In doing so, he'd expose who the spies in my citadel were.

Our game of chess was easier when he didn't know I was moving his pieces.

Yet the piece that mattered most was my queen, and she was in far greater danger now than she'd been a few hours ago. "You should have told him I beat you. That you will hate me for all eternity for it."

Samantha shook her head. "He would've known I was lying. It's better this way. I can claim that his questions were indecent and that I was appalled."

"He's going to come for you. He won't let this go."

Samantha crossed to the other side of the room and pulled the balcony doors shut. "He's a brutal, insecure bully. I know how to handle men like that. Hell, I almost married one."

I looked away as I tried to control the flames of rage that licked my heart. "I'm glad you didn't."

Samantha released a bitter laugh. "Well, you saw how that turned out."

I'd watched her pummel the douchebag into the dirt at that filthy barn in Deerhaven. Unfortunately, we both knew the general wouldn't go down so easily.

She put her hands on her hips. "Tomorrow, I'll talk to the queen. I gave up a lot of information, thanks to you, so maybe she'll grant me some kind of restraining order."

My temples throbbed.

Or maybe she'll hand you right back to him—it was a fear I didn't dare voice aloud. She'd been through enough already.

Samantha sighed with exhaustion and turned her back to me. "Either way, it's a problem for another day."

My words left me when she began unlacing her gown. She slipped one sleeve off her shoulder and then the next, revealing an alluring expanse of skin that froze me in place. My pulse quickened and a sudden heat clouded my thoughts. "What are you doing?"

Even though I was a beast at heart, I turned away. After her interrogation, I didn't want to make her more uncomfortable.

When she said nothing, I stole a glance at her.

"Really?" she said mockingly. Her honey-gold eyes revealed

the wolf that lurked just beneath the surface. "I never took the big bad Dark Wolf God to be ruffled by a little nudity."

Heat radiated through me. "You think I haven't seen this before, little wolf? Are you trying to tease me?"

She giggled softly. "I need to shift. It's been too long."

I let my gaze linger for a moment as she shimmied the gown down past her hips.

"Fates, woman. You're tormenting me."

The alluring siren glanced over her shoulder and gave me a playful smile. "Thank you for being there today, Cadean."

The way she murmured my name sent a shiver of heat down my spine and left me paralyzed with desire.

She turned back and unclasped her bra, and let it fall to her feet, revealing the full expanse of her back—and then, as if to torture me to my very soul, she hooked her fingers around her underwear and bent over as she slowly slid them down her long, mesmerizing legs.

Fates almighty, she was going to make me a madman.

With a sudden gasp, she let her back arch, and fur erupted from her skin. Her bones popped and broke as her arms became legs and her hands became paws. She dropped to all fours as the last throes of the shift shook through her. In their wake, a beautiful brown wolf remained.

Her fur was like flowing wheat, her eyes like midsummer honey. She was the most beautiful beast I'd ever seen, and I doubted I could ever take my eyes off her. She stretched, then hopped up on the bed and laid her head between her paws, watching me warily.

I nodded in acknowledgement.

Each time I took the form of a different animal, I assumed some of its nature, but with the wolfborn like Samantha, they took on much more of their wolf's personality—it was almost as if they had another being living within them. They thought differently in their wolf form, and I knew that while I'd earned some degree of trust from Samantha, I hadn't yet tamed her beast.

The toll of shadow-casting during the day was quickly draining my strength, but perhaps now was a chance to take the first steps to earning that trust.

I closed my eyes and let my mind drift back to the core of my being, to the savage wolf that dwelt deep inside. My original form—the ancient wolf lurking in the darkness. I seized its shape and shifted in a blur of shadow and smoke. My spine arched like hers had, and I dropped to all fours. Samantha rose halfway on her paws, and I could smell her sudden fear. I didn't blame her. I wasn't just a wolf, but a primal monster five times her size. My jaws were meant to crush the bones of men and beasts.

I averted my eyes in a sign of submission, then shook out my fur and padded to the door as she watched. Dropping down in front of it, I placed my head between my paws as hers had been.

I will keep watch while you rest, little wolf.

It was little more than a gesture. I was only illusion, and I couldn't stop someone from barging through, but I hoped it would mean something.

Cautiously, she laid back down on the bed. She didn't take her eyes off of me, but eventually, her lids drooped, and she fell asleep.

Samantha tossed and turned as the night slipped by. Deep into the small hours, she whined in the grip of a nightmare. Instantly alert, I sent my magic to soothe her, and she slowly relaxed back to slumber.

Had I been the monster that haunted her dreams?

She stirred as dawn broke through the window. She'd shifted back to human form several hours ago and was bundled under the blankets. With a groan, she rolled over and pulled the pillow over her head, but I knew she would not return to slumber. Once awakened, she never did.

As she yawned, I shifted and slipped back into the shadows, and the darkness closed around me.

My vision cleared, revealing a candlelit room: Mel's tower workshop. Although I no longer needed her ritual and acolytes to help me project through Auren's barriers, I still relied on her arcane circle and blood magic to shadow-cast overnight.

Mel's voice rose behind me. "Cadean? Are you back?"

I turned as she sloughed a blanket off her shoulders and rose. She'd slept on the floor, just beyond the edge of the circle.

"Thank you," I said. "But you needn't watch over me."

She yawned. "Someone needs to."

I headed toward the door but stumbled at the edge of a circle as a wave of exhaustion flooded through me.

Mel was at my side in a moment, hand on my arm. "This is what I'm talking about. You're spending too much time shadow-casting. You need to rest."

I knew she was right, though it galled me to admit it.

Shadow-casting had always drained my strength quickly, and when I appeared fully to Samantha, it took even more energy. I'd never pushed it for so long, so many days in a row. Even with the assistance of blood magic, I was running on fumes.

It didn't matter.

I pulled my arm away and stood. I shouldn't have to rely on my sorceress for strength, but with the Moon's barrier and the queen draining the life from my realm, I wasn't as strong as before.

"Samantha needs to rest, and Dreamspire is a nest of vipers.

There could be assassins, or Slaine might decide to pay her a visit. He has his eye on her now. As long as Samantha is sleeping, I'll keep watch. I should return to her—"

"You need sleep as well."

"I was asleep for a thousand years before she arrived. I can go without."

Mel shook her head. "You cannot. This is the Dreamlands. All beings must sleep in the Dreamlands, even gods."

"You're not my minder."

"I'm your advisor and sorceress, Cadean. I see you when you cannot see yourself." She pulled her slender knife out of her belt and held it up for me. "Look."

I examined the reflection in the blade. My eyes were tired, and stubble adorned my weary face. I looked less substantial, as if somehow, the shadows were becoming a part of me, the more I became a part of them.

Was this how Samantha saw me?

I pushed the blade away. "It doesn't matter."

"It does. You've given too much blood as well. You cannot keep bleeding yourself to amplify the ritual."

"Blood regenerates."

"Only if you eat and sleep."

My lips started to curl back in a snarl, but I forced myself to look away. She was right, of course. I sighed and held out my hand. "Give me another one of your potions. That will stave off the weariness for a time."

She crossed her arms and shook her head. "Those aren't meant to be taken every day. They'll do you more harm than good in the end."

I didn't drop my hand. "I'll hunt, and after I've fed, I'll sleep. But I need a potion to fight off the fatigue."

Mel pursed her lips, then walked to a small chest in the corner of the room. She slipped a little silver vial out and brought it to me. "Everything has a cost, Cade, these as much as shadow-casting. They take more than they give."

I took the vial and popped the cork. "Until we get her free, I will do what I have to."

I kicked it back. The bitter potion burned my tongue and throat as it slipped down. My stomach twisted in revolt, but soon, energy began flowing back into my tired limbs.

I handed the vial back. "Thank you."

"It's the potion telling you that you can't keep doing this, indefinitely."

I rubbed the bridge of my nose to soothe my raging headache. "With Slaine harassing Samantha, I need Kassian back more than ever. Find Wulfric and come up with a plan. Auren may not be watching the border as closely now that Samantha's gone, so we might be able to slip an owl shifter across. Also, backchannel with my brother's people again. He might be willing to negotiate."

She crossed her arms. "How much are you willing to give up? Auren is a swindler."

"Anything but my people or my axe. Push back on the price, but I'll pay it, whatever it is. You three are beyond value to me."

It was the truth. Auren had refused to negotiate before, but there was no longer any reason for him to hold on to Kassian, other than to infuriate me.

I headed for the door.

"Where are you going?" Melanthe asked, as I was halfway out.

"To hunt." With that, I headed down the spiral stairs.

As soon as my full strength had returned, I exited onto a tower balcony and leapt off the edge. Wind rushed around me as I fell, and I closed my eyes, searching through the thousand forms of the wilderness that I knew.

Shadows exploded around me as I seized the form of a

hawk, and I soared out over the lake that surrounded Shadowstone. The sunlit water gave way to mountains, and beyond it, pristine forest yet untouched by the queen's vines.

I spiraled downward, and just before I landed, I took my original form—the great wolf. Feathers became fur as I swelled in size. My claws could cut a bear open with a single swipe, and my jaws could bite through the trunk of a tree.

I was fear and death made manifest. Those were the beliefs that had given rise to me—the Dark Wolf lurking in the woods. Unseen, unheard. Death in the darkness, waiting to strike.

I prowled the forest until I caught the scent of a stag, and the compulsion to hunt rose within me until it consumed all other thoughts. I hungered for the chase. For the scent of sweat and fear. The stag's flesh would nourish my body, but its terror would nourish the god within me.

I pawed the earth in anticipation and let out a low growl.

If I ever got free, if I ever could cross the border, I would teach the fae to *believe*. I would feast on their fear and terror until my lands were pristine once again.

29

———————

Samantha

The queen was livid the next morning. Outpacing her honor guard, she barreled down on me with an accusatory look that could have skinned a werebear alive.

"What do you think Slaine told her about our meeting?" I asked Sarion.

"Nothing good," Sarion muttered, "but the queen is shrewd. Just explain what happened and she'll see reason as long as you watch your tongue and temper with her."

Easier said than done. My tongue was sharpened on both ends. Somehow, I was going to have to play the docile pet, throwing myself on the queen's mercy.

I curtseyed low in greeting as she approached, but the queen didn't slow her pace. "I heard you're refusing to answer General Slaine's questions. He claims you're hiding something about your relationship with the Dark Wolf God. What is it?"

The reek of Slaine's breath and the feel of him pressing me against the door shot through my mind, shattering any pretense of patience I had. "Your general is an animal. Put him on a leash."

Her face flushed with anger. "He's a tool for rooting out traitors and spies."

Although the power of her presence was withering, I held my ground. "I refuse to be treated like either. Did Slaine mention I walked him through every corner of Shadowstone? Or that I gave endless details on the Dark Wolf God's inner council and his forces?"

"He said you provided some information that will need to be corroborated."

"Some information? He held me captive for three hours, grilling me nonstop like I was a prisoner of war."

The queen frowned, but I sensed the faintest softening of her position. "Slaine said you were holding back about the nature of your relationship with the Dark Wolf God."

I couldn't hide the disgust that crossed my face, and I lowered my voice to a deadly whisper. "You mean when he asked how it felt to have the Dark God beat me? Whether or not he pinned me down and fucked me? I'm no longer a captive, and I will not relive that nightmare."

The queen hesitated a fraction of a second. "Whatever Slaine asked, he had reason."

I could almost smell the scent of his arousal again, and it made my stomach churn. "The reason is that suffering *gets him off*."

"Watch yourself, girl," the queen snapped. "General Slaine is of the fifth order and my trusted advisor."

I knotted my fists as my wolf surged in my chest. "Then you should know *exactly* who he is."

Her expression didn't waver, but her scent told me what I needed to know: she knew he was a sadist, and it revolted her. That was all I needed, a fragment of sympathy. I just had to widen the fracture into a crack.

I dropped my eyes. "Your Majesty, I've told you that I'm here to help, and the information I shared I gave gladly. But the general pinned the door shut and told me he could fuck and beat me better than the Dark God could himself. That kind of treatment is not what I agreed to when you invited me here."

Ayanna flinched almost imperceptibly, then glanced at her guards. "We shouldn't talk about this in public."

"I'm sorry, Your Majesty, but I don't feel safe with him, particularly when we're alone and behind closed doors. You offered me your protection, but I had to use my magic to shield myself from him. Please, do not let him near me again. I was afraid he would violate our pact."

Her aura flared, and her eyes flashed with fury, but this time, it was not directed at me. "I'll speak with the general and issue clear orders to him and his men. They will not bother you after this."

We held each other's gaze for what felt like hours, but slowly, I pushed my temper down. This was pack politics, and the alpha needed to win.

Taking a shaking breath, I curtseyed low in submission. "I know I've asked much of Your Majesty. Thank you for listening to me, even though I don't belong to your court. I gave General Slaine everything I know, but I'm happy to answer any questions you still have as long as he's not there."

She nodded. "The crown and council appreciate your candor, and I'm certain the information you've provided shall be of great service to the realm."

With that, Ayanna turned and walked away, flanked by her bodyguard once more.

I released a long, low breath.

"Well, hopefully, that should keep the bastard away," Sarion muttered.

But would it?

Whether he directly violated the queen's orders or not, I

knew Slaine and his men would be keeping a very close eye on me. I'd have to have Cadean scout the vicinity anytime we spoke, and it almost certainly meant an end to sneaking around the palace.

Ayanna had granted me as much as I could have possibly hoped for, but I knew that I'd turned the general into a dangerous adversary. No matter what orders she gave, he would be hunting me and looking for a way to make me pay.

The days became a blur of practice and preparations. I trained all day with my cadre, and then again with Cadean in the evening. Each night, I went to bed sorer than I'd been the day before, but with a swelling sense of triumph.

I visited my mother whenever I found a moment of downtime. She was happier than I'd seen in years, but she was so deeply under the queen's sway, I wasn't even sure if my real mother was still there. Some days she seemed almost normal and lucid, then the next she was foggy and confused. Was it part of the withering curse, or was she simply drowning beneath Ayanna's spell?

She remembered the old days, but not yesterday. When she asked me about my life, I couldn't shake the feeling that everything I said would be repeated later to the queen. The afternoon my mother asked about my time living beyond the barrier, it confirmed my worst fears: Ayanna was an evil bitch, glamouring my own mother into spying on me.

She had to suspect I could see what was happening. That meant either the queen was simply hoping I'd slip, or I was so deeply trapped that it wasn't worth creating more than the thinnest façade anymore.

Returning to check on my mother every day and pretending

nothing was wrong was the hardest thing I'd ever had to do. Every smile was bittersweet, and every laugh made me want to cry.

Over it all, the general loomed, an unseen presence that haunted every moment of my day. He never came near me again, yet he was everywhere. He had every guard, steward, and hand-maid wrapped around his fingers, and wherever I went, I felt their eyes glued to me. I knew they would repeat whatever I said.

My training cadre was no different.

"Were you really a captive of the Dark Wolf God?" one of them asked while we were all sitting in a sauna after a particu-larly painful practice.

"Yes," I said, not looking up. They knew it, so why ask?

"What was it like?"

My stomach twisted. Was she genuinely curious, or had she been ordered to mine me for information? I wasn't sure it even mattered. Anything I said would make it back to the general or the queen, one way or another.

I shrugged and put my towel over my head. "He kept me locked in a cave. There wasn't a bathroom or furniture. Just a pool of water."

"What was he like?" another asked. I could hear the fear in her voice—but was she afraid of Cadean or General Slaine?

I flipped the towel back and met her eyes. "The Dark God was death incarnate. He was stronger than any male I've ever met. I watched him kill deathwings with a single blow and cut through fae warriors like they weren't wearing armor."

The girl looked down, and I felt a little bad. But after the trials, most would be headed to the front lines. They should know the truth. They should fear him.

I leaned back. "I saw his true form right before I escaped—an enormous dire wolf, probably ten feet high at the shoulder, with fangs the length of my forearm and fur formed out of pure shadow. He could have torn me apart with a single bite. I don't know what they've told you, but if you cross the border, you will die. There is no escaping him."

"You escaped him," Kirin said.

"I had help, and he underestimated me." I glanced at Astra, who was scowling back at me from the corner of the sauna. "Most people do."

Astra had returned to practice a few days before, and so far, she hadn't given me more than glares and baseline snark. *That* scared the crap out of me. She wasn't someone to let things slide. Either she was acting on very strict orders or she was biding her time and had a plan to take care of me. The casual air with which she ignored me meant one thing: she was certain I was going to suffer, one way or another.

I kept answering their questions cagily until the first girl asked, "I heard you got close enough to stab the Dark Wolf God in the chest. How did you survive?"

My stomach knotted. No one knew about that but Slaine and the queen. My so-called teammates were definitely working me for information.

I rose and wrapped my towel around me. "Blind fucking luck —not to mention his brother was there, fighting at my side. Had it only been me...I never would've made it out alive."

I left, thanking the Fates that fae couldn't smell lies.

The truth of it all was that I wasn't safe if the sun was up. I didn't let my guard down until I locked my door each night and turned to search for Cadean in the shadows.

I was never disappointed. He was always there.

30

The day of the trials arrived like a hammer, crashing through everything that had become normal. I wasn't even certain I'd be allowed to participate until that morning, when Sarion passed me a note from the queen.

Your candidacy to the trials has been accepted by the council.

That was it. No congratulations or words of advice.

"I wish you weren't doing this," Sarion muttered as he stepped back out.

I shrugged as I laced up my light armor. "I have to."

The oracle claimed I needed to be tested, so I would be tested. My mother needed a cure, and I needed access to the garden, so I would beat this challenge and the next and earn the rank of third order.

It just had to be done.

But somewhere along the way, the trials had become about more than those needs. The prejudice, the looks, and the constant whispers behind my back—I wanted to prove them wrong. I wanted to prove to *myself* that I was good enough, that I was capable of wielding the gift of magic that had been given me.

The part of me that was a wolf had an entirely different outlook on the matter. She didn't give a rat's ass about magic or two-legged schemes and oracles. She wanted to put the rest of the pups in their rightful place.

It was alpha bitch time.

I made a few final adjustments to the unfamiliar armor I'd be wearing. The supple leather tunic that protected my torso was tailored for flexibility and allowed me to move unencumbered. It matched the leather vambraces and greaves that encased my forearms and legs.

"You look like one of the queen's soldiers," Cadean said from the shadows. His voice grated slightly, and I understood why—the sight of me like this set him on edge. Most of those who survived the trials would become enforcers. They'd be there to raid across the wall and murder shifters in their sleep.

"I'm not one of them."

"I know that, little wolf. Just don't forget that out there today. You owe them nothing."

"I won't forget." I moved toward the door, but he intercepted me. I could have walked straight through him like he wasn't there, but I took a step back.

He crossed his arms and gave me an iron-hard stare. "You're ready for this."

"We'll see."

"I know you are," he growled. "You have more magic in you than anyone you've practiced with. You're practically glowing. And you're also a wolf—faster, stronger, and smarter. Show them what you're made of."

I shifted uncomfortably. "Thanks."

"I'll be there with you, the whole way." He leaned forward

and whispered in my ear, "And I expect to see you kick some serious ass."

I grinned. "See you soon."

My cadre, along with several others, gathered at the outskirts of the city on the edge of a rocky cliff. It overlooked a twisted mass of vines that seemed to spill out of the earth like some strange alien creature.

I shivered. The air was bitterly cold, the sky a dull gray, but it was the anticipation of the moment that had sent the chill racing across my skin. None of us had any idea of what to expect. Apparently, every trial was different with one thing in common —we had to prove that we were worthy to serve the kingdom.

My cold fingers twitched with a mix of anticipation and nerves as I looked over the crowd. A throng of high nobles had clustered on the side of the cliff, while hundreds of commoners were gathered below. Both groups were animated and trading papers back and forth.

"They're betting on us," Kirin said as she nervously fiddled with the yellow ribbon in her hair.

I scoffed. "I don't think I want to know the odds."

"I think they're better for you than me. You have the queen's favor, and as a wolf, you're a wild card, so potentially worth a risk. I'm nobody, just fodder for their games."

I turned to her and crossed my arms. "Cool it. I've had people betting against me my whole life. It's a good place to be. Just because they don't know who you are doesn't make you a nobody. *Show* them. Break their wallets and make them regret their choices when the bills at the end of the month come up. I know you can do this."

"I don't even know *what* we're supposed to do."

"Whatever it is, you're ready for it," I said, giving her arm a squeeze.

Sarion's warning flashed back to me. *The trials aren't about holding back gods and monsters—they're about avoiding the knife in your back and putting your own blade into the neck of your friends. The person fighting at your side is the one you have to fear the most.*

I glanced at Kirin. Screw Sarion and his advice. Maybe fae couldn't tell friend from foe, but I was a wolf. Whatever happened out there, Kirin was not sticking a knife in my back.

Astra, on the other hand, probably couldn't wait. I glanced at her. She was gazing at me with a satisfied expression. *Vengeance day.*

Hell.

The crowd murmured and parted for Queen Ayanna, cheering as she made her way through the sea of bodies. General Slaine followed close in her wake. His dark eyes raked over me with unrestrained vitriol. He was here to watch me fail—preferably, to die.

Fucking bastard.

Ayanna raised her hands, and a hush fell over the crowd. "The trials are not a game. This is a sacred rite. Those who participate dedicate themselves to protecting our kingdom—our way of life."

Magic swirled around her, and she rose higher without wings. "Each year, the chosen trial is different, as there are many threats to our realm. This year, the high council asks you to remember that the vines are the beating heart of our kingdom—that being part of the Undying Court means protecting them with your life."

She waved her hand toward the mass of vines below, and they began to move and grow. "The threats to the vines arise everywhere—across the border, in this realm, and even within the city itself."

My skin turned cold as an irrational fear took me.

Did she mean me?

Had she somehow discovered my true intentions? That I was a danger to the vines?

I glanced around again at the faces of my cadre. Would they be asked to hunt me down as sport?

The queen motioned to the general, and he stepped forward to the edge of the platform with a menacing glance at me. Then he yanked something out of a large burlap bag and threw it in my direction.

The severed head of a monster hit the dirt with a wet thunk. Gasps escaped the crowd above, and I stepped back as yellow blood leaked onto the ground.

I'd never seen anything like it. Chitinous plates protected six pairs of lidless eyes, and it had three sets of vertical jaws. They were like nested bear traps, and I had no doubt the thing could shred skin and bones in a second.

"The krai'tan are a scourge to our kingdom," the general shouted. "They feed on the blood of the vines and our broodlings, and in doing so, they weaken us. Failures of vigilance have allowed them to establish a colony in an abandoned sector of the undercity, and they're spreading."

Murmurs spread through the crowd.

"We sent a squad of soldiers, but only one returned," the general continued. "The soldier reported that at least twelve krai'tan remain. It is your duty to exact vengeance for our people, to protect the vines that give us life, and to root out and exterminate every last krai'tan you find. To pass this rite, each of you must slay one and bring the head to Her Majesty." The general looked directly at me. "Those who do not return with one will fail and be barred from any future trials."

Shit. One shot only.

I looked around at the others; they were doing the same

arithmetic. There were at least three dozen competitors, so there weren't enough heads to go around. The queen was essentially pitting us against one another.

Of course she was.

All around, faces hardened. We all knew what needed to be done. Defeat your rivals, then the krai'tan.

Light flared around the queen's hands as she spread them wide. "Magic will be your best defense, but you are each allowed one weapon..."

We all leapt back as bolts of lightning leapt from her outstretched fingers and blasted into the earth at our feet. Where they struck, an assortment of weapons appeared, levitating in midair, one for each competitor. While they all had cruel edges and barbs, each was unique: swords, axes, throwing daggers, bladed flails, and more.

Kirin grasped a long silver-tipped spear, while Astra had gotten a crossbow. She grinned at me as I plucked a sickle-bladed knife out of the air. It wasn't the worst weapon, but it was far from the best.

How the hell was I going to cut through the two-foot-thick neck of a krai'tan with a nine-inch blade?

I tested its weight in my hand, my stomach twisting. I'd seen the same blade before, hanging on the general's wall. I'd seen all the weapons there. I looked up and met his eyes, and he grinned.

He didn't collect weapons—he collected death. How many combatants had my knife killed before? How many times had its bearer been stabbed by another? I had no doubt he knew the story of each and relished their bloody history every time he looked up.

A thunderclap split the air as the queen raised her hands. "The Fates have determined which weapon each of you will bear, but from this point, you will determine your own fate."

A current of magic swirled around us, and the mass of purple vines shifted, creaking and groaning as they unknotted themselves to reveal a dark passage.

"Good luck," Ayanna said, her gaze burning into me.

There was a momentary silence as we all stared at the black maw before us. Then the great mass of challengers charged forward into the darkness with weapons raised.

31

———

Samantha

I hung back, avoiding the initial stampede.

Everyone knew who I was, and plenty of my opponents probably thought like Astra: the best kind of wolf was a pelt hanging on the wall. The queen's favor put an even bigger target on my back.

No matter how important winning was, my first goal had to be staying alive.

I wasn't the only one with the same plan, and I tentatively followed a few of the more cautious fae into the darkness.

As soon as I stepped into the passage between the vines, a wave of magic surged around me, and the portal swept me forward like a riptide.

I stumbled out into a sprawling cavern. Dim light filtered down from a passage above—perhaps a way out?

The place was breathtaking and unnerving all at once. Vines spread across the walls and ceiling like spiderwebs and hung down in great bundles like the trunks of trees or living stalactites.

The portal had dropped me on top of a small wooden building that had been integrated into the vines. It was old and rotting and didn't feel particularly stable. The fae who had passed through the dark entrance were scattered about atop similar long-abandoned structures. Down below, I saw many of the others already on the ground rushing into the darkness. Some moved in squads, while others were lone operators.

I didn't see Kirin, but she had to be in here somewhere.

I crouched down as I took stock of my situation. So far, things boded well for me—as a werewolf, I had better sight in darkness, plus better hearing. I'd be able to navigate more easily as well as identify threats approaching in the dark. I also had claws to climb, and it looked like I might be doing a lot of that.

I began moving across the top of the platforms like some of the other fae were doing but froze as a harsh, grating noise reverberated from below—like metal scraping stone. Suddenly, the adjacent platform shifted. Several of the fae atop it began climbing down the vines in a hurry, while others leapt into the air, wings bursting from their backs.

That was one thing I didn't have.

A nearby tower that had been built among the vines twisted and crashed to the ground with a cacophony of echoes. Screams pierced the air, and I prayed that Kirin hadn't been among the injured.

As the dust cleared, I spotted two of the climbers lying among the splintered boards and rubble, not moving. Would anyone return for their bodies?

It was definitely time for me to get to the ground.

My own platform hung at an angle, and several of its boards were rotted and cracked. I tucked the curved blade through my belt and carefully inched to the edge.

The whole thing shifted under my weight and tipped sideways.

My feet slipped as the structure collapsed beneath me. Frantically twisting in midair, I snagged one of the vines and hung on with my claws as gravity curdled my stomach. Pumping my legs, I swung sideways onto a thicker pillar of vines, then scrambled to the ground using my claws. One look at the twisted wreckage told me I'd been very lucky.

"That was too close, little wolf," Cadean murmured from behind me.

My heart stuttered, and I spun around. "Damn it! A little warning next time."

"Where the hell is this place?" he asked, looking around the cavern.

"No fucking idea. I think the queen called it the undercity, so perhaps it's the remains of an early settlement here?" That particular bit of information was something else the fae might have going for them. Where was Kirin when I needed her?

I looked around to make sure we were alone. I didn't want it getting back to Slaine or the queen that I'd been seen chatting to the shadows. They might start putting two and two together.

Once I was certain the coast was clear, I motioned Cadean forward over the remains of a rickety bridge. "I need to hunt down some kind of thing that feeds on the vines. Fun fact: there're aren't enough for everyone, and I'm all the way in the rear."

"That's not a bad thing," Cadean muttered as he followed. "The moment those in the lead find one, they'll take each other out, vying for the kill."

"My thoughts exactly, but I don't want to get left in the dust, either."

"Do you know what you're hunting?" he asked.

"Krai'tan—whatever those are."

He released a low growl. "They're a problem—savage strength, big pincers, and ugly as sin. They're ambush predators and hunt by heat and sound, so staying still will get you killed, but so will running."

I pulled my knife out. "You're making me wish I'd taken my luck with the group."

He shook his head. "Want to attract a bunch of krai'tan? Make a lot of sound."

"Yeah, never mind." I dropped in through the roof of a fallen building.

"What's your plan?"

I glanced back. "Sarion said the fae will be the real enemy, so I'll keep my distance and do everything they can't. You can scout ahead, and we'll hunt by scent. The general threw the putrid head of one of the things right at my feet, so I got a whiff, and it won't be leaving my memory any time soon.

"Clever girl." He grinned. "Let's hunt."

I sniffed the air. The scents of the place were overwhelming —dozens of fae mixed with the aromas of panic and adrenaline. Decaying wood. Rotting vines. And very distinctly, krai'tan. Lots of them.

The remaining walkways had all collapsed, leaving only a tangle of vines as my option of getting around. It was a damn good thing I didn't mind heights.

As I made my way across, the sound of scratching echoed up from below.

"Stop," Cadean said.

I froze and glanced down. My breath caught as a massive shadow sprinted beneath us, running on four legs like a gorilla. It was bigger than a grizzly but moving impossibly quickly for its size.

At least it hadn't seen me.

"Krai'tan," Cadean whispered. "And it's on the hunt. The scent of fresh blood likely has them in a frenzy."

"So let's hunt the hunter," I said, then swung down.

We were away from the main group, and hopefully, the krai'tan would be too focused on whoever it was pursuing to notice me. I could get the kill and get out.

I dropped to the ground. The base of the cavern floor was a dark maze of vines and ruins. I sniffed the air and nodded left. "This way."

Padding forward, I kept to the shadows. I could hear the krai'tan's claws skittering over the ground again.

"What's the best way to kill one of these things?" I whispered, pausing to sniff the air again.

"Stab it in the heart." Cadean crouched down, then shot me a pointed look. "You should have no problem with that."

"Seriously? You're making jokes now?"

He rubbed his chest with a pained expression. "It's not a joke. Not entirely."

Grumbling, I glanced at my blade. It suddenly felt very small and very useless.

A scream echoed from up ahead, but I couldn't tell where it came from. Gods, I hoped Kirin was okay.

Cadean surged forward through the shadows, returning a moment later. "It's cornered a few fae, and a female is dead. Move now while it's distracted with the kill."

This might be my best shot.

I raced forward, knife out, and flew around the corner.

The monster had pinned two contestants in a nearby cluster of vines. Its talons ripped into the thigh of a female, and she collapsed. Her partner screamed and tried to climb away, but the creature leapt and plucked him off the vines like a piece of ripe fruit. There was a wet, gurgling noise as the krai'tan tore the fae's throat open with its nested jaws, then flung him into the void.

The thing was made for hunting in the dark. Its muscular body was encased in rocklike armor, and the leathery skin on its arms and legs blended seamlessly with the shadows. With a single blow, it decapitated the woman.

Then everything when silent. Fates, it was over so quickly.

My foot scuffed as I stepped back, and the thing whipped around with an almost alien speed. Its piercing amber eyes locked onto mine.

I turned and ran.

Its footsteps thundered behind, and I pushed forward with all the strength and speed I had.

Stowing my useless knife, I threw myself against a column of vines and began climbing. The thing had to weigh half a ton. If I could Tarzan to some smaller vines, it might not be able to follow.

"Climb faster if you want to keep your legs!" Cadean shouted from behind me.

I pulled myself hand over hand as rapidly as I could. Below me, the column of vines shuddered beneath a heavy weight. I looked down. The krai'tan was racing up the vines with the deftness of a gods-damned spider monkey.

With nowhere to go, I leapt to a smaller cluster, hoping it wouldn't bear its weight. The rough bark burned my palms before I managed to get a hold. With the vine swinging, I jumped onto another column and looked back.

The krai'tan sped toward the ceiling. Had it not seen me leap?

"It's going to try to drop on you!" Cadean growled from the shadows. "There's another cavern to the left. Go now!"

Heart pounding, I raced over a bridge of vines that stretched across a rift in the rock below. The hole was infinite blackness, and I didn't dare imagine what lived down there. The moment I got across, the platform shuddered, and I looked up.

Amber eyes glared back at me.

Magic flared to life in my palm as the krai'tan leapt, and then everything slowed.

I spun and wrapped my legs around a large bundle of vines, then whipped my hand forward, releasing my magic in a shimmering ball of light. It burst against the krai'tan's chest, and the thing roared. The sound drove through my skull, and I screamed, but I cast again and again, driving the creature back with my magic. It stumbled at the edge of the platform, then tumbled back into the darkness to gods-knew-where.

Chest heaving, I staggered to the edge of the ruin, searching the chasm below for my kill—but all I saw was darkness. "Gods damn it!"

"There she is," Cadean purred from behind me.

Chest heaving, I glared back at him. "Who?"

"My savage little wolf."

His eyes were burning with pride, and a flush of heat spread across my skin. Grinning at him, I leapt off the top of the building.

Cold air buffeted my body as I dropped like a stone through the darkness. I extended my claws and sank them into the thick trunk of a vine, then scaled the rest of the way to the floor.

"Are you trying to give me a heart attack?" Cadean said roughly when we reached the bottom.

A broad smile tugged on my lips as I searched the ground. "Were you worried about me?"

"Always."

His gravelly voice sent shivers down my neck. "Good."

Unfortunately, there was no sign of my kill. I sniffed the air and slipped through the ruins, tracking its scent. I found a sticky patch of yellow blood that smelled like krai'tan, but my kill was gone.

So…not a kill, then. "Is stabbing them in the heart the only way?"

"You could try beheading them, but I'm not sure how much luck you'll have with that knife."

"I wish I had your axe," I muttered.

"You don't," he said softly, and something about the stony weight of his voice made my heart ache.

I followed the thing's scent to an opening in the cavern wall. Its trail led off through a narrow crevasse, but the sharp, tangy scent of fae blood came from a larger opening a few yards further down.

My chest clenched as I walked forward and knelt beside a bloodstained yellow ribbon lying on the ground.

Kirin.

I clenched my fingers around the silk ribbon, and then a woman's scream echoed out of the tunnel ahead. Not Kirin, but one of my cadre.

Taking one glance back at the crevasse where my quarry had disappeared, I tucked Kirin's ribbon into my pocket, and took off in the direction of the screams.

I quickly rounded a curve and burst into a smaller cavern. The sounds of weapons and magic echoed through the cramped space, deafening and disorienting me.

The dismembered bodies of fae were strewn around the cavern, and I would've retched if I hadn't been consumed with terror.

Kirin was nowhere in sight, but three of my cadre were battling an enraged krai'tan. It darted to the side as Astra's magic ripped through the air.

A male leapt forward with sword drawn, but the creature batted him away like he was a tin can. His body cracked and crumpled against the wall.

I called my magic, but there was a sudden blur at my side.

"Behind you!" Cadean said.

I leapt forward, barely missing the pair of brutal talons that whipped through the air inches from my face. I spun as the krai'tan's muscled forearm crashed into the floor, sending chips of rocks flying.

Okay, there were more of them.

The creature stood on its hind legs, towering a good four feet above me. Glowing patches beneath its chitinous armor pulsed, and it let out a blood-chilling roar.

Then the krai'tan pounced.

My magic flared, and my shield blossomed in front of me. The creature's impact drove me back as it slammed into the shield. My magic held, and the creature thundered with fury, hammering against my shield with its talons. It was all I could do to hold on to my power as the blows vibrated through my bones.

Then Cadean was there, next to me, and I felt a swell of strength. "Get rid of that thing."

I screamed and thrust forward with my magic. The shield pulsed outward, and the thousand-pound beast staggered back.

It took one look at me, then turned and leapt toward Astra.

I lifted my arms, and streams of light flooded from my palms, striking the beast square in the back. It bellowed and crashed into the wall with a thunderous crack.

Darting forward, I scooped a spear off the ground and charged. The thing spun around, and I rammed the point straight into its chest, the tip slipping between a gap in the carapace. As soon as I felt it sink into flesh, I shoved the spear in with all the strength of my wolf.

Cadean's magic billowed behind me, and I felt more powerful than I ever had.

The creature flailed and drove me back into the wall. I

gasped and stumbled sideways as it dropped to the ground, dead.

"Not a little wolf any longer," Cadean rumbled with pleasure.

The sounds of battle had stopped, and I looked around. Only Astra and another fae were still standing. He was hacking the head off a dead krai'tan with an axe, while she was staring straight at mine.

I staggered forward and wrapped my hand around the spear. "Don't even think about it."

Then bile rose in my throat. I recognized that spear.

I looked up, wide-eyed and pulse racing. "Where's Kirin?"

Astra removed the sword from the hand of her friend—her very dead friend, who lay in an expanding pool of blood. "Kirin doesn't matter, and neither do you," she said, and stalked forward.

I extended my claws. "Stay back."

"You won't ruin this chance for me!" She flung her hand forward and unleashed a torrent of searing orange flames unlike anything I'd seen from her before.

I raised my hands, and the bluish tendrils of my magic formed a shield around me, but the inferno was overwhelming. It was consuming my power like a wildfire sweeping over dry hills.

I dropped to one knee as the moonlight around me began to dissolve. Flames licked over my skin, and Cadean roared.

In a boiling wave of darkness, the shadows in the cavern converged, and a shield of black fire wrapped around mine. The brilliant flames of Astra's spell vanished as Cadean's magic entwined me, and I lost control. The maelstrom of moonlight and shadow twisted and curled, battering against one another, and it felt like the cells of my body were being ripped apart.

Our magic detonated like an imploding star. Shockwaves

ripped through the cavern, tearing vines from the walls, and sending shards of rock flying. Astra and the other fae stumbled and ran for cover as stone rained down from the ceiling.

The walls of the cavern split open in an earthquake.

And then it collapsed.

32

Cadean

The cavern shook as if the gods of the underworld had been offended—and perhaps they had. Samantha's magic and mine were the antitheses of one another and had never meant to merge.

Torrents of earth poured down like waterfalls as massive boulders slammed into the ground. Though they passed through my shadow form without harm, I had never known such fear.

"Run, Samantha!" I roared, helpless to stop the rain of death.

She stumbled toward the exit, but a cascade of dirt brought her to her knees.

Suffocating fear clawed at my chest. "Get up, woman!"

A huge slab of stone above her broke free, and my heart froze.

This was my fault. I had done this trying to protect her.

In desperation, I unleashed my magic. Power quaked through me, and a tidal wave of spiraling shadows slammed into her, sending her tumbling across the ground into an adjacent tunnel.

The slab crashed to the earth, and rubble consumed it. My magic had affected nothing but her.

I shadow-stepped forward into the tunnel and dropped to my knees beside the little wolf, calling a flame to my hand as I inspected her. She was alive, and that was all that mattered. The cuts and bruises would heal quickly. She was a wolf.

The darkness seemed to shift away as my strength faltered, following the sudden expenditure of power. Visions of Mel's workshop flickered in the corner of my eyes, but I fought to maintain focus. Samantha was my anchor. I wouldn't leave her.

Groaning, she rolled over and pushed herself up. "What just happened?"

Regret clawed at me, and my jaw set. "I nearly got you killed."

She shook her head. "No. You saved my life twice. Three times, it seems."

"I tried to shield you from Astra's spell, but our magic isn't meant to work together. It triggered the collapse. It *is* my fault."

"If you hadn't, Astra would have killed me. Whatever her spell was, it was stronger than I was." She coughed, then wiped blood from her luscious lip.

"You're wrong, little wolf. I know you. You're stronger than she will *ever* be."

Pausing, she looked up at me and frowned. "How were you able to use your magic? I thought you could only watch."

I stood. "Normally, I can't, but...but being near you has allowed me to do many things I can't normally do—in this case, shoving you with my magic."

She looked back up at me with an expression that stoked a fire within me. "Thanks for that."

Relief and something else I couldn't discern overwhelmed me, and I felt each heartbeat like an earthquake in my chest. I wanted to pull the darkness around her so that she was the only thing in the world—the only thing I saw upon waking, and the only thing in my dreams.

I turned away. The truth was, I was falling for her, and it had to stop. She was mortal, and I was a god. Love would only break both of us. I knew it in my soul, and yet the darker, savage side of me wanted to say fuck the Fates and claim this woman as mine.

Mine to worship. Mine to desire. Mine to protect.

The shadows deepened around me, and I could no longer tell the difference between my need for her and my rage at the world.

For as much as she might hate me, her scent told me she felt the same.

Maybe we were like our magic, doomed to rage against each other and destroy the world around us, but I wanted it anyway. I welcomed it.

Coughing again, Samantha stood and summoned moonlight to her palm. It illuminated the collapsed tunnel around us. The huge slabs of rock that had nearly killed her blocked the entrance to the cavern, and the opposite direction didn't look any more promising.

She gave a bitter laugh. "I'm afraid your efforts to save my life may have been wasted. This looks like it might be my tomb. At least if it is, I'll have company for a time."

The sad smile she gave melted my soul.

"It's no tomb," I growled. "Wait here."

I shadow-stepped further down the tunnel. A huge wedge of the ceiling had collapsed, blocking the exit. However, high above, it had exposed a cleft—perhaps part of a higher tunnel. I raised my hand and felt the slightest movement of air.

I returned to the little wolf. "I think there's another tunnel above us, if you can climb."

She smirked. "Yeah. I can climb."

"Then let's get out of here."

But she hesitated and looked back at the rockfall. "Can you project back to the cavern where we fought? I want to know if the others..."

I nodded and shadow-stepped through the wall. The cavern beyond was riddled with bodies and stones. It had been sealed off on the same side that trapped Samantha. No one would be coming to collect the dead.

She looked up when I returned, dread in her eyes. "Was Kirin there?"

"Many were buried, but I didn't see Kirin."

She breathed a sigh of relief. "What about the others?"

"Astra seems to have escaped with that other bastard—and both heads of the khai'tan are gone."

Samantha's fangs dropped. "That bitch stole my kill."

"That's what you're worried about?" I laughed, suddenly overcome by the insane horror of it all. "She tried to kill you."

The little wolf grunted. "I knew she was going to do that. Stealing my kill hurts a little worse right now. Let's get out of here."

I shook my head as we headed to the cleft.

"Think you can get up?" I asked as she paused beneath the collapse. It was a several-story climb.

She snorted and rubbed her palms together, then jumped, her fingers curling into a thin crack in the wall. With a powerful thrust, she pulled herself up, her other hand finding purchase on a small protrusion in the cliff. She navigated the cliff face like she was built to do it, her body tensing and relaxing with each upward thrust.

"Piece of cake," Samantha grunted as she heaved herself onto the outcrop, unaware of the wicked thoughts in my mind. "I used to do this all the time near Red River Gorge."

"I guess this explains how you escaped from my tower at Shadowstone."

"Well, not exactly. That was a combination of freefall and the Moon's magic." She peered into the narrow space between the rock. "This, however, looks more like a good way to get stuck than a way out."

Her tone held a hint of amusement, but I sensed her heightened pulse.

"You're afraid of small spaces?"

She didn't answer for a while, and when she spoke, she didn't look at me. "I had a bad experience in a cave on the Washington coast." Her tone was sharp, accusatory even.

I lifted my brows, but she gestured toward the opening. "After you, Cadean."

I shadow-stepped up and through. The crevice would have been too small for my body, but Samantha was able to squeeze through on her belly.

The crevice opened into a narrow tunnel that wasn't large enough for her to stand, so she crawled forward cautiously and summoned moonlight to her palm. She examined the walls, tracing her fingers over the deep, jagged grooves. "These tunnels aren't natural, are they? They're burrows."

I nodded. "The krai'tan can burrow through solid rock. They're normally solitary hunters that dig up through the ground and ambush prey living in caverns or on the surface. I'm surprised to see them congregating like this."

"The queen said they were feeding on the vines. But why would a predator eat plants? The blood of the vines—it's not actual blood, is it?"

A shiver of unease rippled through me. "I don't know."

The vines fed off life—mine, and that of my land. Was that close enough to blood that it would draw predators?

I cleared my throat. "Maybe they're just eating the broodlings that spawn from the vines. Though why there would be chrysalises down here, I don't know."

"Well, hopefully, we don't meet one in here."

Scouting ahead, I led Samantha through the tunnel. I didn't need light to see in the darkness, and as a projection, I didn't make sound or heat. I wouldn't draw the krai'tan if they were waiting in ambush.

We came to a fork. I checked both ways but couldn't move far enough ahead to determine which path to take.

When I returned, Samantha was kneeling with her eyes closed. "We go right. I hear sounds, and the air is different."

After a few minutes, the tunnel began to expand, and she stood. We moved faster.

The distant sounds became shouts of distress.

"Damn it. I smell krai'tan." She began to run.

"Wait! Don't go rushing in! This isn't our battle," I snarled, as I followed in the darkness.

She didn't respond but started running faster.

I cursed and shadow-stepped as far ahead as I could get.

The tunnel exited into a large cavern, like the one to which she'd teleported, except this one was inhabited. Dozens of hastily assembled structures hung suspended in the vast network of vines, and diminutive people ran around. Erdelfen. I'd thought they were all dead.

Maybe they should've been. It seemed they served the queen completely now.

Screams pulled my attention to the far wall, followed by the wail of a child. A krai'tan was bounding over the vines that covered the walls. With a swift movement, it vaulted off the wall and clambered up to a dwelling.

Fuck, was *this* what they were feeding on?

Samantha burst from the tunnel.

I pointed. "Krai'tan just entered that house. There's only one."

"Thanks." She grunted as she leapt for a column of vines. "Watch for its fucking friends."

She scrambled hand over hand up the vines almost as quickly as the damn thing had. She was one hell of a climber. Despite the frustration raging in my heart, I couldn't stop the pride that swelled in me.

I shadow-stepped to a nearby platform, making sure I kept within thirty yards of her—I didn't want to risk our connection getting broken.

The creature burst through the wall of a house. Several male erdelfen rushed across a bridge, spears in hand, ready to fight it off.

They were only hastening their own deaths.

The krai'tan leapt over the spearmen and crashed onto the adjacent roof. Samantha kept climbing, and my throat clenched as I realized what she was about to do.

"Stop!" I yelled, but she didn't listen.

She pulled out her dagger, and then she jumped.

33

Samantha

The wind rushed around me, and for a moment, it felt like I was flying. My magic swelled like a raging fire, fueled by a relentless desire to protect.

Pain exploded through my palms and knees as I landed on the back of the beast, but I sank my claws into the exposed skin beneath its plates and rammed my blade into its back.

It roared, but I roared back as I released the boiling reservoir of magic within me. "This is for Kirin!"

Power cascaded through my arm and out the blade. The thing's chest exploded, and it collapsed beneath me in a pool of blood, going limp.

I released the knife and rolled free as the thing slipped onto the platform below.

A pack of little elfin men descended on it, poking the corpse with tiny spears. They were about three feet tall and pale, with large eyes.

My pants and vambraces were smeared with dark blood that smelled pungent, like the vines.

Cadean appeared in the shadows of the house. He glared up at me with a furious expression. "You're insane."

I wiped the blood from my hands on my gore-covered pants. "You're still worried about me then?"

"Of course," he growled, his lips curled back in frustration.

I turned away to hide the smile threatening to break across my lips and crouched down at the edge of the roof. The little men pointed their spears up at me, backing away.

"Easy, now," I said, raising my hands. "I just took care of that thing."

One of them pushed the other's spears down. "She wears the queen's insignia. She will kill us where we stand. Show respect."

The little men cowered, and those who had emerged into the doorways of the surrounding houses retreated inside.

My stomach twisted. Moments before, these men were fearlessly facing death with stone-tipped spears, but just the mention of the queen had them terrified. I understood the scent of their fear as clearly as their actions. It was the scent of a beaten animal, dreading the next blow.

"Look, I don't want to hurt anyone," I said as bile rose in my throat. "I'm not one of her warriors. I'm just wearing her armor. I got trapped here in a cave-in. I don't even know where I am or how to get out."

The speaker looked up. "You fight like one of her warriors, flying down from above."

"No wings or pointy ears." I showed them my back. "I'm a half-breed. I don't really belong up there."

I was taking a calculated risk, but the scent of their fear faded, and they stood, nodding with seriousness.

I moved cautiously toward the edge of the roof and hopped down to their level. Their speaker stepped forward and extended his hand. "My name is Rin."

I shook it. "Samantha."

He stepped back, folding his hands in thanks. "Thank you for killing the krai'tan. It was very brave to do so without wings."

That was the part of my stunt that stood out? I glanced down at the body. "Do they attack often?"

"No," Rin said, pointing to the ground below. "There was an earthquake, and it came up one of the fissures."

I looked up and found Cadean lurking in the shadows of a nearby building. The look in his eyes confirmed my fears. *Our magic did this.*

My throat felt tight. "I'm sorry, Rin."

He shrugged. "No one else would have thought to save us, but you did. Not the queen or her soldiers. We're nothing. How can we repay you?"

Guilt tore at me. How could I ask for anything after unleashing this monster on them?

"Don't feel guilty, not for this," Cadean said from the shadows. "The queen should have sent an army to remove the creatures. Instead, she made it a fucking game. This is her fault, or Astra's fault, or the Fates' doing—not yours."

I dropped to one knee. "I'm hopelessly lost, and I need to get back to the palace. Do you know how to get there?"

"I will lead you, but there must be more we can offer. Will you eat with us?" He looked at the creature in a way that made me very certain I didn't want to stay for dinner.

"No, thank you. A guide is all we need."

"We?" Rin looked around.

"I—just I."

Cursing inwardly, I tried to sift back through prior conversations. Was this my first slip? Or had I used "we" to refer to me and Cadean before?

Some of the men began tying ropes around the creature, and I bit my lip. "Actually, could I have the head?"

Rin beamed. "Of course. The best part."

An hour later, my legs and back were aching, and I was regretting my foolhardy leap onto the krai'tan's back—not to mention the hundred stairs I'd had to climb up to the entrance to the tunnels.

At least the tunnels were level.

Cadean had faded into the darkness. I only caught glimpses of him here and there. As it was, I couldn't speak with him in the presence of our entourage—erdelfen, according to Cadean. A dozen or so had insisted on following along, ostensibly serving as my bodyguards, though two were carrying the creature's severed head. I was grateful for that.

They'd also cut it off for me with a saw, for which I was also very, very thankful.

As I followed Rin through the dark labyrinth of tunnels, he pointed out a two-foot-thick vine that had been shredded. There was a dried puddle of purple-black blood beneath, which had seeped from the wounds. "The krai'tan have been feeding here. They drink the blood of the vines when they cannot find meat."

"How long does it take for the vines to heal after they've been attacked?" I asked Rin, my breath heavy.

"It depends on the queen," Rin answered. "They do not heal on their own, but by the queen's magic."

I glanced back at him. "Those along the border—where I'm from—heal quickly."

"When the reservoir is full, they heal. When it is empty, they must wait for her to feed them again."

"Feed them?"

"She feeds the vines, and they feed her."

I nodded. "The fruit."

Rin scoffed. "The fruit is nothing to her."

My mind raced. I opened my mouth, but one of the women

whispered something to him, and his face turned pale. "My wife says my tongue will get my head cut off. It is not something we are to discuss. Please, I should say no more."

I shook my head. "I promise I won't repeat a thing."

Rin's chest began to rise and fall more quickly, and there was a sudden sheen to his brow. "Please. Give no hint of what you heard. The queen is a goddess. She can make anyone speak."

His wife clasped his hand and squeezed it, giving him a forlorn look.

"You have my promise. I'll keep your secrets." I showed them the bracelet on my arm. "I made a pact with the queen. She's never allowed to force me to say anything I don't want to."

They nodded, though they didn't seem convinced.

As we continued, I traced my fingers along one of the vines. They wound their way through the tunnel like an electrical conduit that always branched in the same direction. Could that pattern point me to their source?

"Do all the vines originate from the queen's garden?" I asked. Perhaps I could follow them upstream and maybe find another way in.

Rin shook his head. "No, the garden is only a display, they meet in the Well—"

His wife hissed to cut him off, and he went ashen. "Please, do not ask anything more. I run my mouth and will ruin my family. We are stewards of the vines, and we must also be stewards of their secrets."

Fuck. I needed those secrets.

We continued in silence, winding higher and higher. The vines grew thicker, and the number of branches thinned.

We must be getting closer to the garden.

Finally, when I was certain my feet couldn't take it any longer, Rin paused at the base of a set of stairs hewn into the rock. He pointed to the mess of vines that covered the ceiling where they stopped. "This is the exit. When you touch the vines, they will part."

I took his hand in mine. "Thank you, Rin. Thank you all. I'm in your debt."

He gave me a weak smile. "Guiding you back was the least we could do. Many of us would have died today if not for you."

The pair of erdelfen carrying the head offered it over. It must have weighed a hundred pounds, and even with my wolf strength, it was a struggle to carry after the long day.

"Do not mention us," Rin's wife said before looking away.

I tried to give her a reassuring smile. "I stumbled around in the undercity and followed the vines back here. What else is there to tell?"

"Thank you. We are grateful."

Reaching up, I touched the vines, and a prickle of magic enveloped me as they slowly unwound and wrapped around me, pulling me through as gently as if I were moving through feathers.

I emerged into the bitter cold air of late fall. It burned my cheeks, but I gulped in the freshness of it after being stuck in the stuffy tunnels. It was night, and the gray clouds from the morning had passed, revealing a star-speckled sky.

Dreamspire rose above me, its glassy towers blending in with the darkness.

Thank the Fates.

I was pretty sure that the blood of the krai'tin had seeped down the back of my pants, and I cringed at the stickiness that coated every inch of me. Gods, I needed a bath.

The Dark God emerged from the shadows. "You have your victory, little wolf. I had no idea how impressive you'd be, but I should have known."

I blushed as a cascade of flutters filled my belly. "You left me for a while, back there. You missed some interesting information."

He stepped closer. "I'm never far away. Just look to where the shadows lie."

As he moved out into the palace courtyard, stars twinkled through his form, and I glanced up in concern. "You're fading."

"Staying with you this long and using my magic...there's a cost. I'll need to recover, but it shouldn't be long."

I smiled softly at the starlit god, wishing that even for a moment, I could reach out and touch him again. "Thank you for everything you did today. I'd be dead if it weren't for you."

Despite the starlight in his eyes, his expression darkened. "You wouldn't be here if not for me."

"That's not true. Not entirely."

"I know what I've done." He stepped back toward the shadows. "Take your prize to the queen. The sooner you are finished here and away from this place, the better."

With that, he turned and faded into starlight.

34

───────

As soon as I reached the palace steps, I was stopped by a dozen guards in silver armor that glinted under the glowing lanterns.

"Identify yourself."

I called the moonlight to my palm, illuminating my face. "The queen's fae-wolf. I just passed her test and want to give her her due."

They held me there until their captain was satisfied, then marched me through the palace. As we approached the great hall, the sound of music and the scent of food intensified.

My stomach growled, and I suddenly felt queasy.

They stopped me again outside the massive wooden doors that led into the hall. It was torture standing there, smelling the scents of meat, steamed apples, cinnamon, and wine. Fresh bread, venison, roasted winter roots—it was practically tearing my soul out.

While I was salivating, the guards were looking at me like I was an old carcass. It was probably a fair assessment. I was covered head to toe in dirt and blood, and the Fates only knew what else had dripped on me from the krai'tan. I was also carrying the monster's severed head, and probably smelled as bad—if not worse—than I looked.

There was an argument at the door, and Sarion emerged. "Samantha? I thought—"

The relief on his face turned to shock as his jaw dropped.

"Hi. Guess what? I'm not dead. Is the queen willing to see me?"

"I..." Sarion stammered. "She is, but I don't think she's expecting—"

"You heard him, boys," I said to the guards, then pushed past them and into the hall.

The room was filled with fae nobles adorned in opulent gowns and suits. Some were dining at high tables, while others mingled, glasses in hand. At first, most were too absorbed in their gossip and food to notice me, but as I moved through the room, the crowd began to part like the sea. Their faces twisted in outrage and disgust, but I paid them no heed.

I was focused on the queen. She was perched on a silver throne, her lips curled in amusement as she whispered something to the fae male at her side. She wore a crown of bloodred rubies that glittered in the flickering light of the chandeliers. She hadn't noticed me.

Neither had the general. He stood with his back to me, focused entirely on the fae woman he'd cornered. I envisioned stabbing him the same way I'd killed the krai'tan and felt a pang of remorse at leaving my sickle-shaped blade in the undercity. He made such a wonderful target.

A sea of murmurs swelled behind me, quieting to a hush as the queen's gaze landed on me.

I dropped to one knee before the great dais. "Your Majesty. I've done my part to protect your vines and your kingdom."

She leaned forward as if she were going to leap from her

throne and behead me herself. "What is the meaning of this? You are anathema to this court."

The harmony of flutes came to a grinding halt.

I rose and dropped the severed head at the general's feet with a squishy thunk, and gasps erupted around the room. The general's nostrils flared, and he looked down at me with an expression of pure rage.

"The conditions of the trial set by General Slaine were that I slay a krai'tan and bring the head directly to Your Royal Majesty. I apologize for my tardiness, but I'm afraid that I've only just emerged from the tunnels."

The general's hand lifted to his sword, but the queen raised her finger, and he eased back with a vindictive glare.

"I was told that you were crushed in a rockfall. Where were you?" Ayanna's lips curled into a subtle snarl, and her eyes flicked across the room to Astra, who stood among the lowest members of the court. The treacherous bitch wore silver laurels around her head, as did eight others.

The victors—now of the second order.

My throat tightened. There was no sign of Kirin. I extended a single claw and dug it into my palm as I fought to rein in my emotions. Triumph. Despair. Hate.

"Yes. I was trapped in a rockfall," I said, holding Astra's bitter glare as long as I dared. Then I turned back to the queen. "I squeezed through a crevice that led into a network of tunnels." I pointed to the head at the general's feet. "And I slew that thing on my way out."

The queen's eyes narrowed, and a glimmer of distrust flickered in them. "You are resourceful."

I bowed. "I hope that you'll accept the trophy even if it took me longer to present it to you. There were no stipulations on time or manner, I believe."

The lines of the general's face hardened, but Ayanna simply

pursed her lips and studied my face. The agonizing silence stretched, and my heart began to race. I'd made a huge gamble bringing the head here.

A knowing smile formed on her lips, and she stood, addressing the hushed room. "We are all too comfortable with what we have here in this court. We do not see what it takes to defend it. We are insulated from the blood and the gore and the true cost."

With a wicked look in her eye that I couldn't quite read, she turned back to me. "Thank you, Samantha, for reminding us that we cannot take our position for granted. All resistance must be stamped out, without mercy. We must all get our hands dirty. I accept your offering. Congratulations on passing your first test. You are now admitted to the second order of the Undying Court."

With that, she turned and took her throne, paying me no more heed.

There was no applause, no cheering, just shocked murmurs and horrified stares.

Stepping toward me, the general folded his hands behind his back and smiled. "I will find out how you did this and who helped. I will wring the truth out of them, one by one, as it seems I cannot wring it out of you."

I returned his liar's smile. "The only help I had was getting trapped in the cave. You might ask Astra what really happened. Also, sorry I lost your dagger. I hope it wasn't a favorite."

I left the head at his feet and walked away, feeling shaky.

Sarion was instantly at my side. "That wasn't the wisest of your decisions."

"I killed three of those things today and nearly died as many times. I'm feeling a bit edgy. I'm also famished."

I looked covetously at the banquet tables, which were mounded with trays of casseroles, roasted meats, and everything you could imagine. It was excessive and wasteful, considering most of it would likely go uneaten and there were plenty of hungry mouths in the city.

I decided it was my duty to eat as much as possible if they would let me anywhere near it. Before I got a chance to find out, however, a familiar voice cut through the crowd. "Samantha!"

My heart leapt, and I turned to see Kirin pushing her way through the drunken crowd.

I went to embrace her but stopped short and put my hands over my mouth. "I'm sorry. I'm covered in death."

She laughed. "You should have seen me."

I choked up. "I was so worried about you."

Kirin brushed a tear from her eye. "They said you were dead."

"Nah." I leaned close to her ear. "I'm a werewolf. We're hard to kill."

She wasn't wearing the silver laurel or embroidered tunic like the other contestants here.

She caught my gaze and gave me a weak smile. "I didn't get far. Barely made it out alive."

"I'm sorry, Kirin. I just...I'm glad you made it."

Her eyes glistened with tears, but she nodded. "So am I. The Fates must have different plans for me."

I squeezed her hands in mine. "I'm sure of it."

I felt her loss and hated that for her, but it was probably better this way. After everything I had learned about the queen and her court, I was thankful that Kirin wouldn't be a part of it. She had too much kindness.

An uneasy feeling burned down by spine, and I stiffened.

"The queen is headed your way," Kirin whispered.

"You should go. After everything, it's probably safer if you're not seen talking with me."

Kirin shot me a nervous glance and slipped away, and I

turned to face the queen. She glided through the crowd, her dress moving like a summer breeze. There was a radiant glow to her perfect skin.

"A friend?" the queen asked.

Fuck. I didn't want to put Kirin in danger, but the queen had to have seen us talking.

"She helps me train, and I put her spear in the back of a krai'tan. I was saying thanks." I shrugged. "She was also the only contender who wasn't trying to murder or backstab me."

The words came out harsher than I'd intended. Astra and the others—they hadn't triumphed through valor or skill, but from doing whatever was necessary to win. Backstabbing, stealing, cheating—that was how you passed the trials.

That was how you built a kingdom that accepted stealing power from others to feed themselves.

She gave me another knowing smile. "The competition is always fierce. Everyone wants a taste of immortality. You're one step closer to that after today."

"When is the next trial?" I asked, my voice sharper than I'd intended.

"I see you are eager to taste the fruits of your labors."

"I want it for my mother."

She swirled the wine in her cup. "The second trial occurs when and where I choose. And while it would be good to have such a powerful and...cunning young talent on our side, you are far from ready. Some train for years before they attempt to ascend to the third order."

"I don't have years," I replied, but of course, she knew that.

She shrugged and gazed over the room. "Then train harder. You will need to be many times stronger to pass the next trial, let alone bind the Dark Wolf God—and make no mistake, that is what you are here to do."

35

Samantha

They didn't let me eat in the great hall, or even let me linger. It was fair—I was covered in krai'tan bits and probably had put half the gathered nobles off their dinners.

As soon as the initial commotion around my entrance died down, I was brusquely escorted back to my room. At least they allowed Sarion to bring me a heaping plate of food.

Once we reached my door, I thanked Sarion and took the plate, but I paused when two of the soldiers took up stations on the far wall, across from the door.

"What are you doing?" I asked.

"The general ordered us to bring you to your room and to make sure that you stay there tonight," the largest of the two said in a deep baritone voice.

"I have freedom of movement, and I don't need additional bodyguards."

"We'll be keeping watch—for your *protection* of course."

I exchanged glances with Sarion. My leash had just grown tighter.

"I expect you to be gone by morning, so don't fall asleep with your spears in your hands, boys." I slammed the door shut.

Fuck the general, fuck Astra, and fuck all the others.

I'd just beaten their game. I was going to enjoy my damn dinner, and then a glorious, bubbly, steamy bath.

I washed my hands, and then, without bothering to change, I dropped down at the table and dug into the plate of food like a ravenous beast. I was halfway tempted to shift just to eat it faster, but I didn't have the strength.

The venison, the bread, and the roots drenched in heavy cream made my soul sing, but partway through, I froze with a chunk of rabbit halfway to my mouth. I turned around, horrified.

"You're watching me eat?" I glared at Cadean. He was perched on my bed, with his arms idly propped on his legs.

"I think I've seen a wolfpack tear apart a deer with more decorum."

"Screw you." I shoved the rabbit in my mouth and almost threw my fork at him, but of course, it would've just sailed through and made a mess on the bed.

He leaned back. "Honestly, I find it fascinating—a reminder that there's a savage beast still in there beneath the woman."

"And the bloodstained clothes weren't clue enough?" I whispered, my thoughts heating with irritation.

He shrugged. "I like it when your wolf comes out."

I finished my dinner and glanced over at him. He was staring at me with a charmed expression. Keeping my voice low, I said, "I thought you had to recover."

"I did."

Fates, I wished I had his healing abilities. I'd need a whole night to recover from today.

My muscles ached as I strode into the bathroom and ran hot

water into the large silver tub, creating a little extra noise to mask my voice from the guards outside.

When I glanced in the mirror, my stomach lurched. I looked like a madwoman—a psycho killer fresh from the Battle of Gettysburg. Blood was streaked across my face and matted in my hair. I had pink scratches on my cheeks and chest, and my clothes were almost black with soot, earth, and blood.

"Fates," I said, absolutely stunned. "I'm..." My voice caught as I touched a large gash across my cheek.

Cadean appeared in the mirror behind me. "You are beautiful. A warrior, a Valkyrie, soaked in the blood of her enemies. The wounds are a testament to the truth: you were magnificent today. A beautiful goddess of war."

His praise did things to me that I didn't want to admit, and my cheeks flushed.

"You're insane," I said, and splashed water on my face from the basin. "I'm nothing."

"You're not nothing," Cadean growled, and the power of his magic shook through me like an earthquake. I could feel his anger filling the space, consuming the room like an inferno.

"You are the most stunning creature I've ever laid my eyes on. You have more strength and compassion than any woman I have ever known. I will hunt down any man who has led you to question that."

The raw intensity and honesty in his words stirred something in me that I couldn't understand. My pulse began to beat faster.

"I watched you hurl yourself from the sky without wings to save people you'd never met," he continued. "Not even the angels do that."

The more he said, the more my chest hurt. I couldn't take it —the praise that had to be lies.

I turned away and dumped half a bottle of citrus soap into the bath.

"Look at me," he commanded, and I turned to face him.

He moved toward me, and my breath quickened. His eyes were unyielding, uncompromising. "I see you. I see the old wounds. I see the injustices done to you, and I see the marks they've left. The doubt. The inability to see yourself. But those scars don't need to define you, little wolf. Choose the ones that make you stronger and cast the others away."

My breath caught. It was as if he'd peeled back my skin and seen the darkest recesses of my soul.

The scar he'd given me burned with a fire that was close to pleasure. Even though I was a werewolf and could heal, that one had never faded. It was always with me—a reminder that he was never far away.

Had I chosen that scar, somehow? Was it one of the ones that made me stronger?

Yes.

He stepped closer, and I reached up to touch his chest.

My hand passed through. He was nothing more than shadow and magic. A dream. An illusion. The disappointment on his face told me he understood it, too, and it broke my heart.

I turned my back, yanked the blood-caked vambraces from my forearms, and threw them on the ground. "I'm tired of illusions. I feel like I don't even know what's real anymore."

Taking a seat on the wicker stool in the far corner, I unlaced my boots and slipped them off. Steam was beginning to fill the room, carrying the lemon scent of the soap. "I can hear you and see you and even smell the scent of your body, but when I reach out, when I *need* to touch you, nothing is there. It's like I'm going mad."

"You're not going mad. I *am* here, even if I cannot touch you."

"Maybe." I unlatched my greaves and ripped them off. "But sometimes, it's almost as if it's worse than being alone."

"When I'm here, you're never alone."

A subtle tingling traced over my shoulders like the soft caress of hands. I sucked in a sharp breath and looked up.

Cadean was still standing across the room, but his hand was raised, wreathed in shadow.

"What did you just do?" I asked, getting to my feet.

"When we were in the caves, I flung you away from danger with my magic. I can touch you in a way, little wolf—if only with shadow."

I held his gaze for a long moment, then I pulled off my leather vest and threw it down with the rest of my armor. The bloodstained tunic beneath was damp with sweat, but it was a relief to have the armor gone. "Do it again."

He stepped a little closer, and the shadows flowed around me. They drifted along my sides and spine, and my tunic fluttered like it was caught in a gentle breeze.

I closed my eyes, savoring every sensation, remembering what it was like to be touched—not attacked or shoved or hauled around, but to simply be touched with affection.

Grabbing my tunic by the edges, I slipped it over my head and dropped it to the ground. To my surprise and relief, my skin wasn't stained with krai'tan blood, just dried sweat.

Cadean stiffened, his gaze intense yet respectful. "Do you want me to leave so you can take your bath?"

Maybe I should've told him to leave. Things were complicated as it was, and it would've been the smart thing to do—but I didn't want him to go.

His eyes followed my fingers as I unbuttoned my trousers, sliding them down my thighs. "No. I want you to stay."

Plenty of men had seen me take my clothes off. I was wolfborn, so I did it every time I shifted. I'd even done it in front of Cadean. It didn't mean anything.

Yet for some reason, this time, it felt like it did.

I didn't understand the tapestry of conflicting emotions that he'd awoken in me, that left me feeling vulnerable and exposed. And yet maybe, with him, that could be okay.

Hesitating for a moment, I removed my bra, dropping it to the damp stone floor, and then, with a glance over my shoulders, I slipped my underwear down my thighs.

He exhaled sharply, his eyes lingering on my every movement as if he were committing the details to memory. "Gods, you're beautiful."

He was watching me with a mix of awe and reverence that felt deeply intimate. Too intimate. Heat flushed my cheeks, and I suddenly felt awkward under his scrutiny. I wasn't self-conscious about my curves or imperfections, but it was easy to feel undeserving under the gaze of a god like him.

"You know goddesses, Cadean," I said as I slipped into the water. "I know I don't compare."

"*They* do not compare," he whispered with an intensity that took my breath away. "You are a goddess, and I will teach you what it is to be one."

Reaching forward, I fumbled with the faucet and turned off the water.

"How will you do that?" I whispered, the steam curling under my breath.

Shadows pooled around his feet and began to slowly move toward the tub like spilled ink. The closer they got, the faster my heart beat. They rose from the floor, weaving slowly up the side of the tub like smoke. I could almost feel the rustle of wind moving through the forest, and the rich scent of wildfires caressed my exposed skin.

As the shadows drew over the lip of the tub, sliding over my arm, a wave of warmth spread. My breath hitched at the delicate and raw sensation, like tiny feathers caressing my skin.

It shouldn't have been possible, but it was like his magic was really here.

The corner of his lips pulled up in slight grin. "First, I will worship you so that you understand that you are special—that you are unlike any other woman in the Dreamlands or in the heavens."

I shivered out a soft moan as the darkness spread over my shoulders and collarbone, moving slowly and deliberately, and leaving a trail of new sensations I couldn't describe.

"Will you let me worship you?" he asked, his voice thick with desire.

Any inhibitions I'd had earlier were gone. I liked the way his eyes felt on me. Hungry. Full of desire. Like I was the sexiest woman alive.

I nodded breathlessly. "Touch me, please."

"I want more than to touch you. Say it."

"Worship me."

His magic gently crept over my naked skin, curling around my breast and teasing my nipple like he might with his mouth. Pain and pleasure surged, and my back arched.

"After I've worshipped you," he continued. "I will slay the demons that hold you back so that you can explore your deepest passions and desires."

His magic was suddenly everywhere, all at once. I bit my lip to stop myself from crying out.

Though I craved his touch, his skin against mine, the sensations of his magic heightened my awareness, awakening desires I didn't know existed. I wanted Cadean to ravish me, to take me the way he wanted.

"Show me," I whispered, as my other hand dipped beneath the water, moving to the apex of my legs.

A disapproving rumble escaped Cadean's throat, drawing my attention back to him. His gaze was fierce and possessive and filled with longing. "Take your hand away, little wolf. I want to be the only one who brings you pleasure. I want you to feel me when you come. Do you understand?"

I dropped my hand and nodded, my eyes closing.

His magic moved down my body, teasing and exploring, tracing invisible patterns on my skin, and lingering in my most sensitive places like he was giving them extra reverence. My core ached, and I felt an unrestrained need between my thighs.

"I bet you're slick and ready," Cadean said, his voice pure gravel. "Shall I see?"

I shuddered, delighted in the way his words caused my core to pulse with need. I could hear the guards outside my bedroom talking, which only made what we were doing even more wrong. Fates, if the queen knew…

Gripping the sides of the tub, I opened my legs, inviting him to delve lower, to ease the tension that was building. "Worship me."

The bubbles were gone, and Cadean could see every inch of my parted flesh. Possessiveness and tenderness smoldered in his pale eyes, and they locked on mine as the tendrils of his magic swirled below my navel, eliciting a cascade of delightful tremors through my body.

"Do you feel me, Samantha?"

I nodded. I could almost taste his arousal, and a primal need burned through me. I wanted to feel him on top of me, inside of me.

More, I begged with my eyes.

"Imagine that it is my fingers touching you."

I gasped as his magic wound around my thighs, moving higher, as it caressed my sensitive flesh. My hips jerked up, needing more.

The faint tingle of my own power rose under my sensitive skin as if it, too, wanted more of him.

Cadean groaned. "That's right, little wolf. Take what you want."

As if on command, my magic surged, rising like tendrils of ethereal mist. It swirled around Cadean's shadows, flickering and sparking with each touch as if our magics were exploring and testing each other.

"So fucking perfect," Cadean purred.

His shadows intertwined with my light, creating an electrifying connection. My back pressed into the hard silver tub as ecstasy resonated through my body. Flashes of light sparked in the shadows like lightning in a storm, my magic pressing against his and his against mine in the most exquisite way.

His eyes held an insatiable hunger, and he drank in the sight of our magic mingling as if my pleasure was his own. Our magic had become a bridge between us, a conduit for our desire. I guided his, showing him exactly what I needed. Taking everything I wanted.

Beads of perspiration gathered along Cadean's brow, and his lips parted as another deep groan escaped him. "I feel you."

The unbearable tension in me built when I saw how close he was to coming. I wanted it to be me, to be my power that brought him over the edge. I pushed my magic forward and wrapped it around him, caressing clumsily in comparison to his deft touch.

It didn't matter. He growled with desire, and it launched me past the brink. My center wept under his touch, and unable to last a second longer, I pressed my palm to my mouth, stifling the scream that tore from my throat as the explosion of warmth spread, my muscles clenching as wave after wave of pleasure rippled through my body.

Cadean's release followed mine, pleasure engulfing him in spasms.

"Holy shit," I whispered as we both drifted back to reality.

The faint glow of my magic dissipated, and the shadows slowly retreated, gently caressing my sensitive skin as they did.

"Yeah." Cadean crossed the room and knelt beside the tub. His lips pulled in a sensuous curve. "That was…"

"Incredible?" I whispered.

His eyes glimmered with something unreadable. He smiled softly. "Yes. You are incredible."

36

─────────

Samantha

For a while, I relaxed in bliss as we made idle conversation, but soon I grew drowsy, and the water cooled. I stepped out and dried off. I felt Cadean's heated gaze, and I welcomed it.

"You never told me how the queen liked your prize. I'm sorry that I had to miss your victory lap. I would have loved to have seen the look on her face, and on Astra's." Cadean's voice skated over my skin as I grabbed my sleeping shift from its hook.

I pulled the shift down over my head as I tried to repress a grin. "I marched into the banquet and tossed the head at the general's feet. I wish you could have seen him."

A low, throaty chuckle rumbled up from deep within Cadean's chest, and his typically stoic demeanor cracked. "You're absolutely unbelievable. I don't think even I would've had the stones to pull that off."

I found myself smiling, captivated by this rare side of him. "I like it when you do that."

He lifted his eyebrow. "Do what?"

"Smile. Laugh. Show emotions other than brooding and

anger," I whispered playfully, mindful again of the guards outside.

A wisp of his magic curled my hair away from my shoulder. "I haven't had much to smile or laugh about for a long time."

I was happy that I could bring that out in him, even if it was just for a moment.

He followed me into the bedroom and watched as I drew the blankets back. I met his eyes, and whispered, "Would you stay with me for a while, just until I fall asleep?"

He smiled, and it sent my heart fluttering. "I would like that, little wolf."

I crawled under the covers and faced him as he lay down beside me. The mattress did not bend, and there was no heat from his body, an unsettling reminder that he was a ghost, unable to truly interact with anything in the world without his magic. Yet if I closed my eyes, I could feel his presence prickling my skin—the impossible power of a god, just inches away.

It should have terrified me, but I was far, far past that. It calmed me and made me feel safe, and soon my breathing slowed. For a long time, we laid in silence, neither of us feeling the need to speak, just comfortable being together.

Finally, I rolled onto my back and stared at the ceiling. "Tomorrow, I'd like to go scouting and see if we can get back into the tunnels. If I follow the vines, they might lead us to the Well —or wherever Rin said the vines meet. There might be a way into the garden. Then I wouldn't have to do another trial."

"You'll never sleep thinking about things like that," he murmured.

I smiled softly at him. "I can't shut it off. Every day, it feels like I'm making progress, but when I lie down at night, it's like I'm one step further away."

A shadow snaked from his hand and traced over my side— not in a sexual way like before, but a soothing caress. "Today was a victory, little wolf, and you should leave it at that. Tomorrow can wait for dawn. For now, just close your eyes and rest knowing that today, you won."

I closed my eyes and focused on the sensations of his magic. It was hypnotic, and soon, my breath deepened, and my limbs grew heavy. "Good night, Cadean," I mumbled as I drifted into sleep.

~

Mercifully, Sarion was able to get rid of the general's goons in the morning. There was a lightness in my step as I crossed the skybridge to my mother's quarters. When she wasn't in her room, I descended the narrow stairs that led to the gardens below.

I inhaled deeply as I stepped outside, savoring the crisp morning air. It made me feel alive, like I was part of the world in a way I hadn't been before. The bruises and cuts of yesterday were a distant memory, and I'd slept in later than I'd intended. I'd needed it—I hadn't had such a good sleep in a while.

I could thank Cadean for that. For all of it.

Warmth spread through my chest, and I smiled. The way his magic had mingled with mine last night had been otherworldly and deeply intimate. Had it been the same for him?

Sarion hung back by the door. There was, of course, nowhere I could go. The garden had a high wall, and I wondered if my mother could feel the spell around it that locked her in, preventing anyone but fae from crossing.

I found my mother picking fruit from an overburdened apple tree. She'd been doing the same thing the last time I'd visited her outside. Apple picking had been one of our few traditions in the fall, and I suspected it reminded her of Deerhaven—though what she did with all the queen's apples, I did not know.

My mother waved to me, and her eyes were as bright as her smile. Hope flickered in my heart. Perhaps today would be one of her good days. I pulled her into my arms. "You're looking well today."

"So do you," she said, looking me over. "Your skin is glowing, and you've got a bounce to your step."

Heat flushed my cheeks. "Well, yeah. I've got some good news."

"Tell me." She linked my arm with hers, and we walked slowly down the path between rows of herbs and vegetables.

"I participated in my first trial yesterday and passed."

The joy left her face, replaced by a look I knew all too well. "You put yourself in danger again, didn't you?"

It was an argument we'd had my whole life, and she could have played the part in her sleep.

"Everything is dangerous here," I said softly. "You needn't worry, Mom."

"I always worry. Ever since you were a child, you have kept throwing yourself into danger. I don't know where this compulsion to prove yourself comes from. You must've gotten it all from your father because it sure didn't come from me."

It was probably true. As much as I hated to admit it, my mother had never been one to take a stand. Not for herself, and not for me.

"I fought to prove myself because I had to. The pack is full of bullies. If I didn't stand up for myself, they would have broken me."

She stopped and turned to me, kindness in her eyes. "I know. I'm not blind. I was proud of you then, and I'm proud of the woman you've become, but you don't need to prove yourself anymore. You're exactly who you need to be."

An ache lodged deep in my throat. She didn't understand at

all. "I barely know *what* I am, let alone what I'm supposed to do in this world."

She pressed her palm to my heart. "When you forget who you are, you look right here, baby."

"I'd like to bring you home. To Magic Side," I said, glancing over at her as we continued down the path. "Is that something you'd like?"

"I'd like to be around wolves again, but I don't know about the city. Deerhaven is my home. My people."

I took a seat beside her. "They didn't take care of you. The pack in Magic Side will."

The lines of her face drew taut, and I could sense a deep sadness. "They didn't take care of you—I see that now. I went to Wyland after you disappeared, and he wouldn't help. But then the queen came for me, and..."

Her voice faltered as the memory slipped away. I opened my mouth to speak, but she shook her head. "Magic Side is fine. I guess it'd be nice to see the big city before I go."

My stomach knotted as I took her hand. "That's what I wanted to talk to you about. I think I've found a way to heal you."

She shook her head. "I've been off those medicines for a few months. I don't want any more. You have no idea how sick they made me."

"This isn't medicine, Mom. The queen grows a fruit in her garden that can cure you. You'd be healed. No more medicine, no more sickness. I can win it in the next trial."

"No. I don't want it," she said sharply. "No more medicine, no more magic. It's time to let nature take its course."

I pressed my fists into my legs, shutting out the meaning of her words. "It's not nature, it's a curse. The fae have it, too, but they've found a cure. The vines harvest magic from the land,

and it's stored in the fruit. It's what gives Ayanna and their court immortality."

She watched the fountain, determination set on her face. "I don't want immortality, Sam. Life isn't about endless summer, it's about season, and I'm in winter now. I accept that. None of us live forever. That's not the point of living."

"Please," I begged. "I can do this for you. Let me."

She dusted off her trousers, her frustration palpable. "I won't have you putting yourself at risk in another one of these *trials*. You've spent your whole life taking care of me when it should have been the other way around. It's time to stop."

Her guilt hung in the bitter air, heavy and suffocating, but I felt like I was going to choke on my own frustration and despair. "It's a cure, Mom, and I can get it for you!"

"There's no way the gods are going around giving away immortality for free. Whatever scheme you've come up with, I don't want to be a part of it." She stood and headed back to her apple picking. "There's a cost to everything, sugar, and I won't have the cost of my living a little longer be you. I've got too much pain as it is."

37

———

Samantha

Like the chill east wind driving gray clouds across Lake Michigan, what started as a perfect day turned hollow and cold. I moved through the world, listless and lost.

Daily training with my cadre had been brutal and cruel, but it had become part of my routine—an anchor in my day and within the unfamiliar kingdom. Now, the trials were over, there was no more cadre. Everyone with whom I'd formed any kind of friendship was dead or had moved on. Even Kirin was nowhere to be found in the castle.

If I wanted to train, it would have to be with Astra and the other victors. Unfortunately, they were all conniving, cutthroat bastards. It was clear how the Undying Court had become the thieving, ruthless cesspool that it was: weed out all the good people or kill them.

My wolf was desperate to run, but the queen had forbidden me to shift in public places, ostensibly for my own safety.

You cannot forget that shifters are the enemy here. There are many who have lost loved ones to the Dark Wolf God's animals, and they will be looking for an opportunity to avenge those losses.

I knew the truth: she wanted me to forget who I really was.

As the day dragged on, I felt like a tiger in a zoo, pacing relentlessly in a place that had no resemblance to its home.

I wrote to Auren and told him I'd passed the first trial. He replied, *Do you have access to the garden and the seedlings?*

I scrunched up my nose in annoyance, and responded simply, *No.*

The golden letters flowed back. *Write me when you do. -A*

That was it. How had I ever had a fucking civil conversation with the self-serving bastard?

When Sarion let the maid in with dinner, I barely acknowledged them. I wasn't hungry, and the scent of wild salmon and butter sauce meant nothing to me.

When the door shut again, I didn't turn around. I kept staring down at the lights flicking to life in the city below. Tens of thousands of souls. How many of them had ever tasted the fruit of the vines? Had any?

My mother was right.

The magic that Ayanna and her court consumed to stay beautiful and live forever was stolen. The queen was no different from Wyland, who was stealing from our pack and keeping the wealth for himself.

But how could I let my mom wither away when there was a chance that I could save her?

Everything was so fucked up. Life-giving or not, the vines were evil. They were death, and yet I desperately wanted what they offered. I wanted to steal the fruit, then destroy it for everyone else. I knew it was self-serving and contradictory, but it was what I needed.

Maybe I was a monster, no different than Astra or anyone else.

I sighed. I knew I wasn't on her level, but it felt like somewhere along the way, I'd lost sight of my purpose.

Protect. But who was I to protect? My mother? Cadean's people?

What about the people of the city below?

"I grew up down there," Sarion said.

His voice jerked me from my thoughts like a blade pulled from it sheath, and I spun around, claws out.

He stepped back, hands raised. "Easy. This isn't the trial, and I'm not a krai'tan, despite my looks."

"Sorry." I retracted my claws. I was used to Cadean sneaking up on me, but not him. Sarion never lingered.

Looking a little awkward, he clasped his hands behind his back. "Really, I thought you knew I was still here—werewolf senses and all."

I forced a smile. "Rough day. I guess I'm lucky you're not an assassin."

His face contorted with shame, and he looked away. The bitter scent of his guilt and remorse twisted my gut.

I stepped forward and laid a hand on his arm. "I'm sorry. That was a thoughtless thing for me to say—I didn't mean it like that. It was a joke, but a bad one."

He looked down at me with a sad smile. "I know. It just hits a little too close to the truth. I'm the one who should be sorry."

I shook my head. "I don't think of you that way. You're the only ally I have left here."

"You look like you could use one right now."

Letting my hand drop, I drifted back to the edge of the balcony. "I just...I thought I had things figured out. I was going to compete in the second trial, heal my mother, and...she doesn't want anything to do with it."

He joined me at the edge of the balcony. "She's right, you know—you shouldn't compete. The trials are monstrous. You've seen that now."

But I had to try, didn't I? I could still convince her to take the fruit. And I also needed access to the garden. If Cadean and I couldn't find a way in through the tunnels, the next trial would be my only option.

I shook my head, trying to clear my thoughts, or at least shake them into some form of alignment.

Sarion leaned forward, resting his forearms on the banister. "Being in the palace—it does things to your mind, and I should know. Why don't we get out of here and see that city you're always looking at?"

I glanced back at the lights below. "The queen told me not to, that it would be dangerous."

"The palace is dangerous, if you hadn't gathered that." He chuckled. "Did she explicitly forbid it? If not, you should go. You look like you could really use a drink."

It was so tempting, but I knew there would be a cost. My mother was right about that, too. There was always a cost.

I shook my head. "There's plenty of wine here."

"The wine is good, but the atmosphere is bad. There's no music or dancing, or life." The jovial smile on his lips slowly faded. "The truth is, the palace is only alive when the queen breathes life into it. The rest of the time, it's a tomb of people too afraid to die."

The thought left me with a deep sense of hollowness and unease, and I shuddered. His mask had finally slipped away, revealing a hurt and beaten man beneath. "I've never heard you speak like this."

"I shouldn't. At least not here." He straightened his back and put the smiling mask back on. "So, what do you say we go?"

Out of habit, I looked to the shadows.

Cadean wasn't there.

He was the one I needed to talk to, but then again, he was

also the only one I talked to, and almost never beyond the confines of my cell. As much as my room was a refuge, it had become an echo chamber, repeating only our voices.

"I'm not blind," Sarion prodded, "You're in no state to be drinking alone."

"Is anyone?" I asked, hardly hearing his words as I surveyed the empty corners of the room. I'd hoped Cadean would return tonight, and we'd have a chance to recreate the magic of the night before.

But the truth was, no matter how much Cadean or I wanted to or tried, it would not be the same. The magic between us had been part of the moment, part of the victory, and now that victory was gone.

There was no going back. Only forward—and I needed out.

I tapped my fist on the banister and turned back to Sarion. "Where are we headed?"

He smiled, for real this time. "I have just the place, but you'd better wear something with a hood—to hide your ears, just in case."

Throwing on a cloak, I quickly laced up my boots and slipped into the hall after him. It was quiet, and the glow of the lanterns danced off the glassy walls.

We turned down several halls I recognized, and Sarion slowed, glancing behind us before he touched a faint crack in the crystal wall. A soft yellow glow radiated under his touch, and as a hidden passageway opened before us, he ushered me inside.

Servant tunnels?

The narrow, poorly lit passage was crudely fashioned, its floors rough, unlike the polished floors of the palace's interior. I wondered how many of these transected the palace and who had access to them.

"Are we sneaking out?" I asked. "Because I was under the

impression that as long as the queen hadn't forbidden me to go, it would be fine."

"I didn't say that, precisely." He checked down a side hall. "I meant it wouldn't break the pact. The queen would be displeased if she found out, so we're going to be careful. Mainly, I want to avoid the general's men. You're under enough scrutiny as it is."

"Ah, it's good to know that grabbing a beer is close to sedition."

Sarion motioned me forward. "After tossing the head of a monster at his feet, I am sure that he's going to treat breathing like sedition. So we'll just keep our heads down and stay away from any sign of royal guards."

Voices sounded ahead, and Sarion redirected us through an adjoining passage. Narrow steps wound down into the depths of the palace, and the stagnant air carried an underlying note of death that made my stomach curl. It reminded me of the tunnels and caverns where I'd completed the trial. The scent of death. The scent of the vines.

We finally reached a door at the base of the tower that exited outside, emerging onto the cobbled street in front of the palace. A pair of guards patrolled the grounds. We hid while they passed, then slunk out of the shadows and slipped over the low wall that skirted the palace. The royal complex rose two stories above the city, and as we climbed down the network of vines that supported it, I could see how they also supported the elegant houses and streets below.

Dropping onto the roof of a mansion, I turned to Sarion. "Were the vines already here when the city was built?"

"No. They're not native to these lands." He dropped over the edge of the roof and descended a wooden lattice on the side of the building. "The court cultivated them."

"That must have taken centuries," I said, following him down an alley.

We came out of the alley and onto a busy street lined with fancy buildings. Unlike the palace, the city was constructed out of brick and stone, and their façades were adorned with ornate carvings and delicate balconies.

"Decades, according to the histories. They grow quickly, apparently fueled by the queen's magic. It's her gift to her people, but it also means that she has our entire civilization wrapped in her web."

"Now who's being seditious?" My voice faltered when I noticed the group of soldiers heading in our direction, led by the tall figure I'd recognize anywhere. "Shit." I gripped Sarion's arm, bringing him to an abrupt stop. "Slaine."

"This way." He pulled me down a narrow alley between the buildings, and we stepped out on a wide thoroughfare that was bustling with activity.

I nervously looked over my shoulder. "Do you think he suspects I'm out?"

Sarion kept his head forward, strolling casually. "Hopefully not. The general and his men frequent the taverns and brothels on a nightly basis. Just keep your hood up and try to look...not extra conspicuous."

"That's going to be a hard with a hood." I pulled it up higher anyway as we passed a street cart selling some type of hot beverage that smelled of cinnamon and cardamon. "Everyone else is dressed finely—like, the clothes are out of this world."

He ushered me down a side street lined with lampposts that cast a warm glow. "Do you recall the nobles who greeted you on your arrival? This is where they live. The crème de la crème."

How could I forget being paraded through the crowd like a strange spectacle? "Yeah, I'm not going to fit in."

He cleared his throat uncomfortably. "It's not uncommon for soldiers to appear with, ah, noblewomen who would rather not be identified...but you're right, we should probably get off the street."

"Are you part of the noble class?"

He laughed. "No. I'm lucky to have any class at all."

"Are there people who don't?"

His smile faded. "Many don't. Most of those who built this place."

"I saw a shantytown at the edges of the city when I arrived, but there's no sight of it from my window."

"It's not just at the edges, but below where we stand right now. The undercity. It's where the classless live—those who have no rank or aren't high fae. It's illegal for it to expand out to where it can be seen from the palace, but the whole kingdom depends on it."

"The caverns where they held the first trial, were those part of it?" I asked, though I didn't dare tell him about the village and the erdelfen I'd stumbled upon.

"I can't be certain, but the undercity is like a warren—some of it is built on solid ground, the rest beneath the earth. Perhaps only ten percent of the population lives above on the vines."

We turned the corner, and Sarion led me toward a short, squat building sandwiched between two others. Music and laughter filtered out of the stained glass windows, and a wooden sign out front read, *Twisted Thorn Tavern.*

"Here we are," he said, and opened the front door. A rush of noise, warmth, and the musky scent of sweat and perfume flooded out.

The tavern was filled with men and women of all walks of life, as well as a few who looked to be working girls. The clinking of glasses, laughter, and lively conversations echoed through the cozy space, and the surfaces of the wooden tables had been worn to a rich luster.

It was gods-damned wonderful.

An age had passed since I'd been in a *real* bar, let alone had the freedom to go as I pleased. This was like being home again. A sudden sadness rose in my chest as I recalled my old life bartending in Magic Side. Fates, I missed it.

Sarion led me to a small open table at the far back and flagged down a server in a long yellow gown. Her dark, curly hair was arranged in a tousled updo, the tips of her ears peeking out.

"What can I get you two?" she asked, eyeing me with curiosity.

"A carafe of early wine, a vintage that still has a little spark to it," Sarion said.

The fae woman headed toward the bar, and I wondered whether they had summer wine, Cadean's favorite. The thought of him stirred a warm flutter in my chest.

The server returned with a pair of foggy crystal glasses and a pitcher of greenish-golden wine that I was certain we'd never finish.

"I guess I should have asked if you like wine," Sarion said as he filled the glasses and handed me one. "But I couldn't resist. This place has the best imported wine from across the Dreaming Sea. I come here a few times a month for that reason alone."

I glanced at the working girls, wondering if that was the *only* reason.

I raised my glass. "I'm more of a bourbon kind of gal, but I can find a taste for wine."

The tart wine puckered my lips and tingled on my tongue, but it made me feel like I was glowing inside—like being trapped in the gray of winter and suddenly seeing crocus pushing through the ground. I sat back, savoring every detail of the place. The scents, the sounds, and being surrounded by people—I missed it all so much, it almost hurt. I refilled my glass and clinked it against Sarion's. "Here's to life outside of the court."

He drank deeply. "May we never return."

38

———————

Samantha

By the time we got to the bottom of the pitcher, I was more than a little tipsy, as were the other patrons, some of whom had begun dancing.

"Care for another?" the server asked, her eyes darting to the empty jug.

"Actually, do you serve rootwine? I'd like one of those," I asked.

Her eyes rounded before they shifted to Sarion. "Is she serious?"

Mildly intoxicated, he waved his hand through the air. "Bring the lady what she wants."

The woman left, shaking her head, and I leaned back in the hard wooden chair. "What's her problem?"

"How do you know about rootwine?" he asked, completely ignoring my question.

I shifted uncomfortably. "Astra mentioned during training. Thought I should try it."

"That you should." He chuckled and sipped the last of his drink.

The server returned with a chipped mug that she set all too harshly on the table. "This might not be the golden quarter, but we do have standards. This is not what we serve here."

I frowned at the rootwine, which looked very similar to muddy water. "What crawled up her butt?"

"What a strange phrase." Sarion looked at me inquisitively before continuing, "I think she took offense that you thought this place would actually have it. Good luck."

I eyed the mug suspiciously before taking a swig.

"Gods damn it!" I spat the mouthful back in the mug. "That's awful."

A wide grin cut Sarion's face, and his eyes glistened with amusement. "I'm sure it is. Rootwine is what the people of the undercity drink."

Heat flushed my cheeks. Astra had been implying not only that I fought like I was drunk, but that I was a casteless lowlife— someone unworthy of being treated like high fae, or even with dignity. The jibe had flown completely over my head, but of course, she knew that. The taunt wasn't for me, but to show the others what a fool I was.

I wiped my mouth as I set the glass down. "That bitch."

"Well, I wouldn't be too hasty. You essentially insulted her," Sarion said.

"No, not her. Astra." I slid the mug toward the edge of the table, so I didn't have to smell it anymore. Unfortunately, the diesel fuel was now on my breath.

Three days ago, I would have been furious. But now that Astra had actually tried to murder me, it seemed petty. Weak. A thing done by mean, insecure high school girls as they played their little hierarchy games.

It actually made me feel bad for her. She was everything that society wanted her to be—had driven her to be.

I sat back, suddenly depressed. I'd probably have to face her again.

"A few days ago, you said that you'd competed in two trials. Is the second like the first? Will I have to face off against the remainder of my cadre?" I asked.

Sarion's expression darkened, and he checked his empty glass for any more wine. "You should forget about it, Samantha. You have no business participating in it."

"I might not have a choice."

His jaw worked, and he rolled the base of his glass back and forth atop the table. "No, the second trial is not like the first. It is different for everyone, but it is always perilous and demands a demonstration of extreme devotion to the crown. They wouldn't let anyone who couldn't prove their loyalty beyond a doubt into the garden."

That might be a problem.

The happy mask had slipped from his face again, and all that was underneath was pain. Still, I had to know what I was heading into.

"I know that you didn't pass, but you survived. That's something, right?"

"It took things from me and my soul I will never get back."

"What happened?"

He clenched his jaw and looked around the room. His shoulders were taut with agony, and I thought he might crush the glass in his hands.

I opened my mouth to tell him to forget it, but he turned and fixed me with a heartbreaking stare. "My second trial was you."

My lips parted, but I was speechless.

He hung his head. "I was to infiltrate the castle and either kill or capture you. I failed. The Dark Wolf God's men tortured me. The queen tortured me. Then she took my wings. And now, if I let anything happen to you, she'll take my life."

Despair lodged in my throat, and I touched his arm. "Sarion. I'm...I'm so sorry."

"Why? It's not your fault. You're an innocent woman I was sent to kill." He slumped back in his chair. "I'm telling you this to save your life. If the queen was willing to ask that of me, what she'll ask of you will be far worse. It will be a trap."

Before I could respond, he stood and hammered back the rootwine. With a grunt of disgust, he slammed the mug on the table. "Don't attempt the trial, and for fates' sake, don't order any more rootwine."

My gut was tumbling, and I felt like I was going to be sick. She'd tortured him and taken his wings. The queen was a fucking monster.

What in the hell did she have in mind for me? Kill the Dark God himself? Or if that was too much, perhaps slay my own mother and bring the queen her head? That would prove my loyalty, beyond a doubt.

Or maybe, she'd just make me hunt down Kirin. Ayanna had seemed a little too interested when we were talking.

I shuddered.

The fact that I could imagine her asking any of those things told me all I needed to know. The trial would be evil.

Finding an alternate way into the garden was my only chance—and if I couldn't do that, then I had better figure out how to get out of this place.

A foreboding silence fell over the room, and I looked over my shoulder.

Everyone's gaze was on the imposing figure who'd just strode through the door with a small entourage of soldiers.

General Slaine.

Fuck, fuck, fuck.

My heart began pounding like a jackhammer. Once was a

coincidence. Twice—either the Fates hated me, or he'd learned I was gone and was hunting me.

His searching gaze swept over the tavern, assessing the patrons with a cold intensity. I snapped my head away and tugged the hood of my coat up a little higher.

He was definitely searching.

The soldiers began to mingle, but the vibrant energy of earlier was now dampened by their presence, and though conversations started again, they were hushed and broken by intermittent glances at the new arrivals.

My heart skipped as I spotted Sarion returning from the back. The general might not recognize me behind the hood, but he'd know Sarion when he saw him—and wherever Sarion was, I was, too.

I caught Sarion's gaze and discreetly mouthed, *Slaine.*

Sarion froze and stepped back into the shadows. He motioned for me to come, but I couldn't do that under the general's scrutiny. I didn't exactly blend in with this dark, over-sized cloak. If anything, I stood out like a sore thumb.

Whatever hopes I had left came crashing down as the general motioned the server over. She nodded as he spoke and her gaze drifted across the room. It settled on me for a long movement before continuing to the other patrons.

Okay, he was definitely looking for me. Time to make a break for it.

I flicked my eyes around the room as desperation took control. They landed on a woman with dark hair who was staring back at me.

She knew.

She gave me a subtle nod, then rose and began to idly weave through the tables. She was beautiful and captivating, with heavy black curls, a bloodred dress, and arms covered with golden bangles. She was a woman who knew how to capture a man.

Every male in the tavern was tracking her movements, some obviously, while others from behind their wine or over the shoulders of their wives. Even Slaine was entranced.

She homed in on him like a woman on a mission. "Good evening, General Slaine. It appears like you're looking for someone. Perhaps it's me."

His lips peeled back in a ravenous grin. "I am now."

Wasting no time, he possessively wrapped his arm around her waist and pulled her onto his lap. Though she blushed when he whispered something in her ear, I could see the undercurrent of tension in her body.

The woman's eyes lifted to mine, holding a momentary connection. There was a spark of recognition in her gaze, and when she dipped her head, a silent acknowledgement passed between us.

Guilt and gratitude churned within me. She had no idea who I was, she owed me nothing, but she'd seen my terror, and she'd known exactly what I needed.

And soon, the general was completely lost in her spell.

Sarion motioned to the back hallway and mouthed, *Let's go.*

Pulse racing, I stood and navigated through the occupied tables, not daring to look back again. Sarion led me past the washroom and out the back door.

The cold night air was a relief, but I couldn't shake the sickness twisting in me. "That poor woman. She threw herself on the pyre to save me."

Sarion ushered me along. "The general is a monster, but that was a monster tamer. I have no doubt that in this situation, she has complete control."

I nodded, praying he was right.

We raced down the street, keeping to the shadows whenever

possible, but the glowing orbs flooded everything in light. Suddenly, Sarion skidded to a stop and pulled me against the wall. Five royal guards were stationed a hundred yards ahead, checking everybody who passed.

Sarion turned us around and looped his arm through mine, walking casually in the other direction like lovers on a stroll. "I shouldn't have brought you here. I put you in danger."

"I was in as much danger in the palace, just less obviously," I whispered. "The question is, how do we get back?"

He glanced over his shoulder, probably to make sure no one was following. "I don't know. It appears the general has set up checkpoints at all the points of entry to the upper city and palace grounds."

"Surely you must know of a way that won't be watched. What about the undercity?"

He nodded, and we turned the corner. "As a matter of fact, that might work. Come on."

Keeping our eye out for Slaine and his cronies, we wove through the streets until we found a roofed stairwell with stairs descending.

"We'll use a service access," Sarion said.

The stench of it was foreboding—the scent of refuse, hot iron, and smog—but I followed him in. The well-trodden stairs led us beneath the great canopy of vines into an otherworldly realm.

Huge vines rose and fell around us like the arches of a cathedral, but the sight below was anything but. The buildings looked hastily constructed of whatever materials seemed to be available. It reminded me in many ways of the small village of the erdelfen, except these slums seemed far more industrial. I heard the sounds of construction and clanging iron, and could make out the orange glow of foundries, plumes of smoke rising into the air.

It was dark and dimly lit by large glowing orbs nestled in the vines above—probably the only light that the undercity ever saw.

"Who lives down here?" I asked.

"Everyone who isn't someone—who isn't high fae." Sarion said. "The original people who lived on these lands before the court moved in. Now they forge the queen's weapons and war machines and make the bricks for the paradise above, all the while staying out of sight."

"Gods."

"The gods have nothing to do with this place," Sarion said. "These people are here, hiding from the Dark Wolf God."

"Why?"

"Because when he was locked away, he abandoned them, and when the queen and her court arrived, they abandoned him to serve her. They believe that if they go above ground, the Dark Wolf God will hunt them."

"That's ridiculous. If they were once the Dark God's subjects, he would give them asylum in his lands. He'd be pleased to know that they survived all this time."

Sarion shot me a skeptical look. "You know him that well, do you?"

Shit. The wine had loosened my tongue.

"There are many fae who reside in his lands—not just shifters," I said, hoping he hadn't read too much into what I'd just said.

"And there are many villages that he ruined in ours." Sarion stopped and put his hand on my shoulder. "While you were there, you saw what he chose to let you see—the same as the queen. But you should not be blind to the fact that he is a wrathful god, and the stories that drive the fears of these people are grounded in truth."

I looked around at the squalid streets, checking the shadows for any sign of the Dark God. I was certain Cadean would never stand to see his people like this, and I wished he were here so that I might ask him.

Or maybe it was that I couldn't stand to see it, and I simply wanted to believe he felt the same.

A hot draft warmed my already overheated skin, and we continued as the clang of metal echoed through the cavern.

"I'm not blind, Samantha," said Sarion. "I know you harbor some sympathy for him and his people, even if you also harbor sympathy for ours. You're navigating a perilous path between two forces. I only hope that you'll have the wisdom to know when to get out."

I stiffened. "The Dark Wolf God is my enemy."

"I am sworn to protect you," he said, looking at me out of the corner of his eye. "I know who your real enemies are."

39

———

Samantha

Like grains of sand slipping through an hourglass, a deep sense of dread filled me as we wound through the undercity. How much did Sarion know? Had he heard? Did he suspect?

What about Slaine and the queen?

I didn't dare ask him what he'd meant or push the subject further. He'd reminded me that he was sworn to protect me, but if I broached the subject, it would drag the truth out into the open. As long as it stayed in the shadows, we would be safe.

He led me through a series of tunnels that brought supplies to the palace, dodging our way around the guards that formed the inspection teams. The under-quarters of the palace were not as guarded as I'd expected, but the spells that protected Dreamspire kept all but high fae out.

As soon as we reached my room, I locked the door and pulled off my boots. The two guards who'd been posted at my door were still absent, and for that I was grateful.

I waited for Sarion's footsteps to fade before I whispered, "Are you there?"

But the room was silent.

I focused my mind, concentrating on the silhouette of Cadean's broad shoulders and the way his shadows felt when they wrapped around me.

"Cadean," I whispered into the darkness.

Twin golden eyes appeared in the shadows. "How is it that you can call me, little wolf?"

"It was an instinct, and I really need to talk."

He strode toward me, his intense gaze burrowing into me. "Where have you been?"

"I went into the city with Sarion," I said quietly, stripping off my dirty socks and tossing them beside my boots.

The muscles in his jaw tightened. "That was risky. There are many ears in the palace."

I massaged my aching arches. "Turns out, ears aren't the problem—Slaine is. He was there, hunting me. That means, despite what the queen says, he has no intention of leaving me alone."

"Are you sure he wasn't just out whoring?"

The casual way he said that made me wonder if he'd ever passed the night in a similar fashion. I pulled my mind from the thought and met his gaze. "He got distracted by a woman, which is the only reason I got away. We went into the undercity. It was horrible. I think your heart would have broken to see it. There are all sorts of fae there, living in squalor like the erdelfen. They make her war machines and weapons, and they're all too terrified of you to flee or even go to the surface."

"They should be scared," Cadean growled.

The hatred in his expression curdled my stomach. "What? How can you say that? They were your people once! You have always protected your people."

Black shadows of fury coiled around him. "Not those who

betray me. The fae in this land welcomed the queen and her court. The erdelfen carved her fates-damned towers. Now, they're forging the weapons that kill my people. I will not shed one tear for their plight."

Fuck. Had Sarion been right?

Anger and gut-wrenching disappointment surged through me, but I fought against it. I knew who Cadean was at his core, and this wasn't it. This was the monster behind the wall speaking.

"Maybe you should give a damn," I said. "Maybe, if you weren't such a bastard, they wouldn't fear you, and they wouldn't be willing to be her slaves and servants anymore."

Cadean glared down at me. "You understand nothing, little wolf."

Wood shattered, and suddenly, there was the sound of shouting in the hall.

Heart slamming against my chest, I leapt to my feet as three thunderous bangs sounded against the door. "Open up!"

Fucking hell. *Slaine.*

Cadean vanished through the wall and was back seconds later. "They shot Sarion with something and have him at sword point!"

Dashing to my feet, I grabbed the cloak and threw it under the bed, just as the lock clicked from the outside and the door wrenched open.

The perfumed scent of lilies hit me as Slaine barged in. "Where have you been?"

"How dare you—"

He stepped close. "Tell me, now."

Nausea roiled in my belly as his sweet scent flooded my nostrils.

"I was in the lower gardens, at the base of the palace."

"The garden?" The general prowled closer, his voice as sharp as the blade that his fingers hovered over. "I don't think so. My men have searched the entirety of the palace. No. You were not here."

Cadean circled the room like a trapped beast. "Get away from him, Samantha. *Now*."

I licked my lips. "Perhaps your men are just shit at their job."

Before I could react, Slaine stepped forward and hit me with the back of his hand. My head snapped sideways, and my vision doubled. Pain spread across my lip and cheek, but it was nothing like the pain and rage in Cadean's roar.

A feral grin spread across Slaine's face as his eyes dragged over the bloody mark his signet ring had made. *That* was why the ugly thing was so large—an unsuspecting weapon for battering women.

Fuck him.

I smiled up at him, my lip stinging. "A slap is all you've got?"

I blocked his next strike, but just as quickly, his other fist rammed into my jaw. Before I knew what was happening, the general seized me by my hair and pulled my head back so that I was looking up at him.

"I know you're up to something, pet," he said in a tone dripping with derision. "And I am going to discover just what."

"My only goal here is to help the queen."

"I highly doubt that," he sneered.

I grabbed his hand and extended my claws deep into his flesh.

"You bitch!" he snarled, jerking his hand free of my hair.

Before he could recover, I swung. The crack of his nose breaking under my knuckles was the most beautiful sound I'd heard in a long while, and I grinned, despite the pain throbbing in my hand.

The general reeled back a step and touched his face. His fingers came away coated in red, and he grinned back at me through bloodstained teeth. "You have fire, little filly."

I could smell the sickening scent of his arousal, and it made me want to retch.

"Get out of there!" Cadean roared from the shadows.

But I raised my fists, and they flared to life with bluish-white moonlight. "The next time you try to touch me, I will kill you, you fucking psychopath."

He dragged his tongue along his finger, licking the blood from it. "Oh, I will touch you again, and when I do, I'll break you like a horse. And once I've ridden you to exhaustion, I'll take your pelt and send it to the Dark Wolf God himself—a token to remember you by."

The shadows exploded around Cadean like smoke billowing from a volcano. His axe leapt to his hand, and he seemed to grow, becoming one with the storm of darkness.

I could feel his rage howling through me.

The sheets of the bed rustled, and my hair flipped in the black wind. My heart skipped a beat as Slaine's eyes flicked to the sheets and then to me.

Could he see the shadows?

If he realized what they meant, the game was up.

Moonlight surged through me as I summoned my shield and released it into him. "Get out of my fucking room!"

He stumbled back into the hall, and I slammed the door shut. I grabbed the chair at the desk and wedged it beneath the knob, though I knew that it would do nothing if he truly wanted through. Hopefully, my fear was enough, and he assumed the magic stirring the room was mine.

Tremors rocked my body, and I had to force my wolf down. This was neither the time nor the place.

I looked at Cadean.

He hadn't changed—still a raging inferno of darkness and shadow. His eyes burned into me like firebrands. "I will destroy him. I will find a way."

His protectiveness thundered through the room like an earthquake, uncontrolled and relentless.

Jealousy was one thing, but seeing the fucker say those things to me was another. For him to be able to do nothing but stir the wind—I knew it was eating him alive.

As much as I wanted to weep or rage or curl up in the corner and die, I knew I needed to protect him now—from his rage, from his anger, from a helplessness that threatened to consume him.

I squared my shoulders and faced down the Dark God. "No. You will not."

His eyes blazed with golden light. "I should have protected you. His life is mine."

"It is not," I snarled. "I claim it, and I will take it when I choose. This hurt is not for you. It is my weapon, and you may not take it from me."

The shadows flared, and then they began to fade, slowly drawing back into him. I held him there with my gaze until the Dark God was gone and only Cadean remained.

A flicker of rage flashed in his eyes. "His life is yours. I will not take that from you."

I shivered under the rawness of his voice.

"Good." I headed into the bathroom and splashed my face with water. The cold calmed my nerves and mind, and I examined my face in the mirror. The corner of my lip was split, and a bright red welt was already blooming on my left jaw.

That fucker.

Cadean was still hovering in the darkness when I returned to the room, a pillar of anger carved in the form of a beautiful man.

"It's okay. I am okay," I said.

"It kills me that there is nothing I can do."

"There is," I replied, as I pulled back the covers and slipped into bed. "Stay with me until I fall asleep."

He sat on the edge of the bed. "I won't leave your side until you wake."

40

———

Cadean

Samantha stirred at dawn. She turned in the sheets, and then her eyes fluttered open. Rolling over, she smiled softly when her gaze found me in the shadows. "You're still here."

"I'm always here, little wolf."

It was barely the truth. After projecting myself day after day, I was weak. I was barely a curl of shadow.

She sat up in bed and stretched, and I sucked in a ragged breath. Her languid movements were worth an entire night's vigil.

Wearing nothing more than her tunic, she slipped out of bed and opened the window. "Can you stay?"

"No," I said, my voice as rough as gravel. "But I'll return this evening, and we will begin to train."

She crossed her arms against the chill. "We have been training, or did you have a different type of training in mind?"

At Frostfall, I'd promised, *I'll train you to use your body in ways you never thought possible.*

I gave her a sly grin. "Unfortunately, not that, but I do want to spar. It's not enough for you to simply keep summoning your powers—you need to practice using them for attack and defense. If Slaine and his soldiers decide to pay you a visit, you need to be able to handle all of them, all at once."

"Sparring?" Her eyebrows raised. "How is that even possible? You're not really here."

"The other night, I used my magic to touch you, and you used yours to touch me. Somehow, they connect. Hopefully, we can use that to fight."

She swallowed. "I don't know if I'm ready to fight a god."

"You need to be. I feel the jaws of the queen's trap closing, and you need to be ready to fight your way out, if necessary."

The playful flirtatiousness drained from her posture, replaced by determination. "I'll be ready, but not ready to run. I'm going to find a way to save my mother and free your kingdom from the queen's control. It's what I came here to do."

I wanted to beg her to flee, but I couldn't. She would never listen, and I owed it to my people to help her try.

"After last night, you know the general will be looking for a way to cross you. You need to stay sharp."

"I will. You don't need to worry."

"I always worry when it comes to you. But I must go now. Take care, little wolf, and try to stay out of trouble." I slipped away into the shadows.

Mel's tower room materialized around me, and I dropped onto my hands and knees, exhaustion overwhelming every fiber in my body.

My sorceress fetched a cup of water from the shelf and brought it to me. "You're staying longer every time. If you were a normal man, you would be dead by now."

The water was cold and sweet, and I nearly choked drinking it, my throat was so parched. "I'm not a man. I am a god, and I cannot die."

"I don't like you seeing how close you can get. You need to rest."

"Fuck that." I surged to my feet and rammed the worktable across the room. "I will not abandon her there."

"Fates, Cadean. Easy on the furniture."

"Slaine fucking hit her," I snarled, as if that were an excuse. "His appetite has been whetted, and it's only going to get worse."

"Is she all right?" Mel asked, her voice strangled with concern.

"She fucking gave as good as she got. Better. But he's stalking her everywhere she goes, and I can't protect her even when she needs me most." I turned and slammed my fist into the stone wall, leaving a massive crack. But it was useless—the agony in my heart was still there. There was nothing I could do.

I looked hopelessly at her. "What kind of god does that make me?"

"A god who is chained by bonds that cannot be broken with sheer force alone, so don't take it out on my workshop," Mel snapped. "Samantha needs your help, not your temper."

"Then give me one of your elixirs," I growled. "I need more strength."

She shook her head. "No. You need to sleep."

I glared at her, wondering how she'd managed to worm her way into my good graces when she spoke her mind so frequently.

"How can I sleep when I am helpless? I can't fucking kill Slaine because I'm little more than a ghost. I can't attack the fae because I'm trapped in this cage. And I can't even retaliate because I might fucking tip them off about Samantha."

I swung to the door and raised my hand to blast it off its hinges, but when Mel sucked in a sharp breath, I knotted my fist and let it drop. "There has never been a god more fucking powerless than I am right now."

She followed me as I stormed through the halls of Shadow-stone, my eternal prison. I found Wulfric and Kassian in the war room, poring over reports from the border. Both looked as tired as I felt. I wasn't sure whether Kassian had slept since escaping Auren's prison with the help of his own network of spies—which was fortunate, as my bastard brother had refused to sell him back to me.

Fuck Auren, and fuck Slaine.

I summoned my axe and rammed it into the wall, and they jumped back.

"Cadean, calm down," Mel said.

"I will not. I will act."

I'd chosen Mel for her wisdom, but she was too cautious, Wulfric for his valor, but he was too bold, and Kassian for his cunning, but he played too many games.

They were all weapons, but they needed to be wielded. For too long, I'd let them wield me.

"Wulfric, mobilize our forces."

He grinned, flexing his hands in anticipation.

Mel laid her hand on my arm. "Cadean, this is a bad idea. Slaine will realize this is retaliation."

I pulled away. "The whole time Samantha has been in their land, I've stayed my hand, and in doing so, I have given the queen and her generals free rein. They've had nothing better to do than to watch her like a hawk. To play with her like a toy. I shouldn't have been watching—I should've stolen their attention away."

"Now is not the time—"

"*To do nothing,*" I snarled. She flinched and stepped back, but I took her hand. "You are my wisdom, Mel, and I will never ignore your counsel. I'm not going to attack—not yet. But I will use every weapon I have."

I spread a leather map of the borderlands across the table, burying their piled reports.

"Kassian, I want you to mindfuck General Slaine. Work with Wulfric and move our forces back and forth along the border until he has no idea which way is up. Feed him information and disinformation until he is paralyzed, absolutely certain I will strike, but with no idea where."

I jammed my finger into the map and looked back at the vampire. "I want him so distracted that he doesn't have a minute to think about Samantha. Bleed his fucking mind *dry*."

Kassian grinned. "I love it when you say sexy things to me."

I turned to my general. "Whatever mad science Kassian wants to do, I want you to covertly keep people in place to get Samantha out if she has to make a run for it. Choose a few extraction points and move the main army as far away as you can. I want the queen's forces drawn off."

"I'll put my best teams in place," said Wulfric.

Mel crossed her arms. "And me? What role does wisdom have in all this?"

I stepped close to the woman who had, through the years, kept me sane. "I need you to give me strength. Find a way to help me project my power. Three times now, I've been able to touch Samantha with it. I need to be there, or as close to physically possible, to help her when she needs it."

"You ask a lot," she said, "but I will find a way."

"Whatever blood you need from me, take it. Whatever rituals we need to do, craft them." I looked from one to the other. "Over the years, I've asked much of you for the realm, but this is for me. I need her safe, and I need you to make it happen."

41

———————

Samantha

Four of Slaine's soldiers had permanently replaced Sarion as my bodyguards and brusquely escorted me to the queen. This time, she didn't walk with me but glared down from a day throne in her audience hall.

"Where is Sarion?" I asked.

"Safely guarding your mother," she said tersely.

"He's my bodyguard. He should be at my side."

Her lips drew into a thin line. "Not anymore. General Slaine informed me about your visit to the town last night. Sarion needlessly put you at risk, and I will not have that."

I gestured to my cheek and eye. "Did Slaine tell you how I got this shiner? I thought you ordered him to stay away from me."

"Clearly, you need watching. He said things got heated between you when you lied about where you'd been. I warned you that the city is a dangerous place, and you should stay away."

"But not forbidden."

"It is now." Her words bit like the early frost.

I crossed my arms. "We had a deal. I am close to taking my way out."

She leaned forward on her throne. "That's right. We had a deal. You are here to help me defeat the Dark Wolf God—or are you telling me that is no longer your objective? Because that would change the dynamic of our relationship very, very much."

The menace in her voice was palpable. Did she suspect, or was she simply used to getting her way? Would there be a difference in the end if she thought I was no longer useful?

I was deep in her clutches, and no matter how furious I was over Sarion, I had to de-escalate.

Reluctantly, I curtseyed. "I'm sorry, Your Majesty. My objective remains the same as it ever was. All I did last night was go out for a drink to celebrate my victory in the trials. If you'll recall, I was not allowed to stay at the official festivities."

"Then stick to your training, stay away from the city, and keep out of trouble." She leaned back, outwardly mollified by my submission. "And in case you're feeling like you missed out, there will be a grand ball tomorrow. All the victors are invited to join, now that they are of the second order. You may rejoice with them and be celebrated by the court."

The horror of the thought was nearly overwhelming. Being trapped in a room with Astra and the others. Being paraded about in a fancy dress and being doted on by the sick bastards of the upper court. All the nobles staring at me—and everyone asking questions—interrogating me on behalf of Slaine.

I swallowed, my throat as raw as sandpaper. "Fancy balls are really not my thing. Honestly, I think I've had enough fun for a while."

She pursed her lips in displeasure. "Skipping it is *not* an option. All the victors *will* be there, including you. This is part of the trials. You must impress these people, Samantha, if you want to advance. You must prove yourself to the court if you are to become one of them."

I desperately did not want to prove myself to the court. I would not, could not, ever be like them.

But as long as the queen believed I was still interested, still desperate for the fruit, it was my shield. Perhaps she would let her guard down, or at least keep Slaine off my back.

She raised her eyebrows. "You still do wish to attempt the second trial, do you not?"

"Yes." I nodded, trying to force determination into my voice.

She dismissed me with a wave of her hand. "Then I will see you at the ball, if not before—and please don't give me a reason to see you before. Good day."

My guards pulled me away as my stomach curdled. I was a marionette in a silly gown again, to be pranced about on strings by the queen.

The soldiers hovered over me all day, just as Auren's men once had—though at least they allowed me to see my mother, and Sarion, who was now her protector.

His face had been battered, and unlike mine, it would not heal quickly. I was sure the rest of his body looked much the same.

"I'm so sorry," I said, hand over my mouth.

I wanted to cry, and I teared up when he forced a smile. "I'm sorry that I couldn't protect you. I failed, and that is why I am here."

Shaking my head, I took his hand. "This is all my fault."

My guards motioned him back, and he released my hand. "It's my fault—my idea. But we had a very good night, didn't we?"

"We did." I smiled back at him as they led me away.

By nightfall, my anger had been boiling all day, and I was ready to unleash my rage. Cadean's mood was no better, especially after I'd told him everything that had happened.

"I want to blow something up," I whispered, terrified that the guards would now be eavesdropping on me, even in my room.

Cadean crossed his arms. "Good, because it's time you learn to kill and destroy with your power as well as defend."

"We can't practice here. The guards are on the other side of that door, and I'll incinerate the bedsheets if I call my magic right now."

Telling them I wanted to practice for the next trial, I badgered my guards into bringing me to the old training room. The vast crystalline hall felt unbearably empty without Kirin and the others. The room was soundproof, but to my dismay, the sentries weren't content to wait outside. Two took up stations on either side of the door.

"So much for talking," Cadean said sharply. "And I'll have to keep my magic toned down. Last night, Slaine looked like he saw something."

I glanced over my shoulder at my handlers. "You sure you want to be in here? My magic's unpredictable. I'm still learning."

"When you're not in your bedchamber, you're to be accompanied," the captain grunted, his tone laced with irritation. "The order hasn't changed since this morning."

I was sure they had very clear orders. This wasn't about spying or controlling my movements. It was about Slaine inserting himself into every aspect of my life. About him lording his power over me.

Well, I wasn't that easy to contain.

I shrugged at the captain. "Suit yourself."

Magic flared beneath my skin and raced down my arms to my fingertips, where it coalesced into two shimmering balls of light. My gaze flicked to Cadean, who stood at the far end of the room.

As if reading my mind, a wicked grin spread across his lips. "Light them up."

With a smile and flick of my wrists, I hurled both orbs at the far wall. They collided against the crystal points in a detonation of luminous particles that scattered in all directions. Streams of light and chips of glowing crystal ricocheted around the room like meteors, lighting up the place like the Fourth of July.

I summoned my shield around me, and it zinged with hundreds of impacts.

Cursing, the guards crouched and shielded their faces as shrapnel rained down around them. A whirling shard rebounded off the ledge above and nearly took of the captain's head.

After a few moments, the glasslike chiming of falling crystals faded, and the room was silent.

I lifted my hand to my mouth. "Oops. Are you guys okay?"

The guards scrambled to their feet. The captain narrowed his eyes, and a muscle in his jaw ticked. "We'll be waiting right outside of that door. Don't try any tricks."

"I would never dream of it."

Once the door clicked shut, I turned toward Cadean. He was leaning against the far wall, an expression of amusement and something else on his face.

I raised my eyebrows. "Impressed?"

"You're a cunning little wolf," he said, prowling toward me. "But that's not enough. You need to be stronger and faster. You weren't good enough in the first trial. Astra nearly overwhelmed you."

Frustration heated the back of my neck. "I survived, didn't I?"

"Survival isn't enough—especially after last night." Violence flashed in his eyes, and I noticed the way his hands had tightened into fists.

The thought of Slaine made my stomach twist. Though my face had nearly healed, I could still feel the sting of his hand on my cheek.

"Whether you compete in the trial or have to fight your way out of Slaine's grasp, you need to fight without mercy to win." He stalked around me. "So I'm going to push you harder than the contestants, harder than the queen herself."

I summoned my shield and met his gaze. "Give me your best shot, Wolf God."

A mischievous grin played on his lips, and then his magic lashed out at me like a storm.

42

———

Samantha

An hour later, sweat soaked my tunic, and my muscles were screaming. Cadean had knocked me on my ass more times than I could count, and I knew he was still holding back—though not as much as in the beginning.

"Again," he said.

I braced my sore palms on my thighs, breathing heavily. "Can you just give me a moment?"

Gods, he was relentless. I was regretting agreeing to it—he was going to kill me before Slaine did.

"A moment?" He crossed over to me and lifted his eyebrow. "Do you think Astra would spare you a moment because you're tired? What about the queen? Perhaps the general—he's a soft one."

Anger burned through my veins, and cool magic sparked beneath my fingers.

But before I could speak or strike, a smoky tendril shot forward and flung me into the hard crystal wall, pinning my arms and legs like chains.

Cadean strode toward me, his expression like granite. He stopped a few inches from me.

I struggled against his bonds, but they were like iron, and I couldn't make them budge. "You're a bastard!"

He dipped his head down low, close enough that his lips could graze my ear. "Then do something about it."

Memories of my childhood flooded me—being beaten up in the woods, Brent shoving me against my bedroom wall, Wyland betting against me in the ring and cheering as bigger wolves pinned me to the ground, Slaine thrusting me up against the door, his breath sickly-sweet in my face...

In that moment, my soul cracked, and a wellspring of magic poured through me, lighting up every nerve in my body. Cadean's eyes widened as his binds on me shattered in a burst of light. A primal rush pulsed through me, and my senses heightened.

Ribbons of bluish-white pressed against him, weakening his shadows like dawn cutting through night. Cadean's expression turned to surprise and awe, but then he pushed back.

Shadows snaked around my glowing shield, striking it like vipers. Each blow sent shockwaves through my bones, and I gritted my teeth.

"You've got to try harder than that," he said, his eyes taunting me.

I screamed, and a burst of radiant light shot forward, hurling Cadean back. He remained on his feet, a smug grin tugging on his lips. "There she is."

Without warning, he struck again.

A dozen coils of shadow arced through the space between us. This time, my magic came naturally, unhindered and blinding. Our light and darkness collided in a shockwave that made the air crackle and sent sparks cascading down all around us.

We were locked in a dance, our movements fluid and

synchronized as Cadean tested and I deflected. We were like oil and water, but each exchange of power between us vibrated with desire and tension that charged the air.

Heat pulsed in my core, but I refused to let it cloud my mind. I was going to win this duel.

Grinning, I said, "Is that all you've got?"

His gaze locked on me, his pupils dilating with desire. "I've always got more for you, little wolf."

His words skated over my sensitive skin, carrying an underlying promise that turned that heat at my core into an aching pulse. The air grew hot, charged with an electric energy that had nothing to do with our magic.

A tendril of smoke broke through my shield, and I stumbled.

A sly grin cut his lips. "Keep your eye on the prize."

"I was."

Every muscle in my body quivered under the strain of holding back Cadean's magic, but somehow, I pulled the power from deep within, like I was drawing it out of a hidden well.

I flung it at him, the magic burning my fingers as it poured out like a river.

Moonlight enveloped Cadean and slammed him back against the far wall, pinning him in a wall of crackling light. Arms trembling, I crossed the room to him, still holding him in place.

I stopped in front of him. "I win this one."

His gaze was filled with respect and admiration. "That you do, and in an all too familiar way."

I dropped my hands to my sides like they were leaden weights, and my magic faded to a subtle glow before disappearing.

A mischievous grin graced his lips, but his eyes were filled with hunger. "You're a worthy oppon—"

And then, in an instant, he was gone, and I felt a new presence in the room.

The queen.

"Practicing all by yourself?" she asked as she strolled into the room, hands behind her back. Six guards filed in behind her.

My heart raced, and my skin turned cold. Had she seen me dueling with Cadean's magic? Had she heard us talking?

I bowed low to hide the panic on my face. "Your Majesty, I didn't hear you come in."

"I was surprised to hear you were practicing so late. Where are the others?"

"I don't trust them, and I know the next trial is going to test me harder than before. I want to be ready."

She narrowed her eyes. "But did I not hear you speaking? Who did you *win this one* against?"

Fuck.

"Myself. I've been blasting the walls and using my shield to deflect the debris and fighting the shadows of the room." I nodded to my shrapnel-battered guards. "You can ask them about that."

"I see," Ayanna said, looking around the scorched training arena. "Sometimes, we are the only worthy opponent for ourselves...though sometimes, we're our own worst enemy." She strode to the center of the room. "Show me what you can do."

My muscles felt like jelly, but I summoned whatever remaining power I had, and a glowing shield arced around me.

She smiled wryly as delight flashed across her face—as well as something else. Covetousness?

Without warning, she whipped her hand out, and her magic swallowed me in a blaze of blinding purple light. Like the raking claws of a falcon, it tore at my shield, searching for weakness. Each strike felt like a cold blade digging into my skin, dulled only by the chilly emptiness that had started spreading through me like a sickness. Was this her doing? I fought against it, every fiber of my being resisting the queen's icy onslaught.

Sweat stung my eyes, but I pressed harder, using everything I had left. My moonlight armor flared, pushing Ayanna's magic back inch by inch. But with each passing heartbeat, the fatigue that had settled over me grew heavier.

"That's enough," I said, my voice unrecognizable.

Her lips curled in a devious grin, and the onslaught of purple magic grew stronger. My legs trembled, and I dropped to my knees. Fear clawed at my chest. Why was she looking at me like she wanted to devour me?

To hell with this. I drew on every last ounce of energy that I held, then released my shield.

As her hungry magic flooded in around me, I discharged a blast of moonlight that detonated like a bomb. A crack of blinding lavender light illuminated the training room, the shockwave shaking the walls and pushing Ayanna backward.

Her magic dissipated, and she stumbled.

Guards rushed around her, steadying her and pointing their swords at me. My vision blurred and wavered, but I could swear that Ayanna was laughing.

It was the oddest thing.

My body was shaking. I didn't know whether it was from exhaustion or fear. I'd never felt like this before, completely and utterly drained.

Ayanna strode forward and smiled down at me. "Impressive. You may be ready for the second trial after all. I could not be more delighted."

I nodded, not trusting that I had the energy or voice to speak.

"I'll have your guards escort you back to your room. You look wasted, though it's nothing a good night's rest won't fix. I expect you radiant for tomorrow's ball, so no more practicing tomorrow —one shouldn't overdo it when it comes to magic."

My head spun as the captain of the guards hoisted me to my feet and the queen strode away. My thoughts were muddled, but I swore there was a new radiance about her and a fresh glow to her cheeks.

Cadean was waiting for me when I returned, tension in his frame, his face shadowed in concern. "What happened?"

"I sparred with a god, and I sparred with the queen. Now I am going to lie down and die."

"Did she hurt you?" he asked sternly.

"No. But holding her off took every ounce of strength I had left." I looked up at him, dread in my tired eyes. "She could have killed me then and there, whether we'd been training before or not. The harder I resisted, the stronger she got."

Cadean released a savage growl and paced the room. "We're getting you out—tomorrow. Everything has unraveled, and you're in a precarious position."

I was too tired and overwhelmed to argue. "Let's discuss it tomorrow. Tonight, I can't think, let alone flee."

Sprawling into bed with my clothes still on, I rolled over to look at him. "Will you stay again?"

"Of course, little wolf."

Guilt welled up within me—even in the darkness, he had a translucent look to him. Perhaps fighting me had drained him more than I'd imagined.

He lay down beside me, and I felt a cool tingle tracing over my back, a gentle caress. I shivered as I felt a little of my strength returning. Despite the aches and my weakness, I felt warm and safe and protected.

Almost instantly, my eyes shut.

43

Samantha

When I woke the next morning, Cadean was gone, and I still felt exhausted—more drained than I ever had before. Coffee and breakfast did little to perk me up, and I wasn't sure how I was going to make it to the ball, let alone dance.

There'd been days like this when I was young—when I'd pushed too hard in a race, or later, when I'd taken on one too many fights. I'd go home, bruised and battered, and if she was there, I'd curl up beside my mother and sleep until my werewolf magic did its thing.

Like a zombie, I washed off the sweat and blood from the night before and dressed in loose clothing. Then I headed to my mother's quarters with my ever-present "bodyguards" in tow.

"You look like hell," Sarion said as he let me in. "What did they do?"

His own bruises still hadn't healed, but there was no mistaking the protectiveness and anger in his voice.

"I sparred with the queen."

His expression darkened, and he opened his mouth, but one

of my guards pulled him back. "Slaine doesn't want you two talking together. You wait outside in the hall with us."

"I can speak to whomever I want," I said.

"Not when we're around, little filly," the captain snarled. "And we're going to be around all the time."

Had he learned that term from Slaine? Was that how he talked about me to his men?

Fucking bastard.

"Careful of her vines," Sarion said as they closed the door behind me.

I looked around the room. What vines? Did he mean the plants, or something else?

Shaking my head, I headed toward my mom. She didn't have the glow of the day before, and there was an absence behind her smile.

Was it simply good and bad days, or had the queen done something to her?

"You look like hell, sugar," she said. "Another bad night at the barn?"

Hell, did she even remember where she was today?

Heartbreak hovering in my throat, I nodded. "Yeah. Bad night."

She nodded as she rose. "I told you, you have to stop. You're going to get yourself killed."

"I'm gonna stop, Mom. For real, this time."

I'd made that promise to her dozens of times, but I'd only kept it once—the day I'd left Brent and fled to Magic Side.

The dance was almost as old as we were. I'd come back beaten. She'd scold me. I'd promise to stop. But the next time the mortgage was due, I'd be back in the ring.

It was almost worth it for the times between, when we'd shift and lie together while I let the bruises heal.

"Got the strength to shift?" I asked.

She smiled. "Always, for you."

I wasn't supposed to shift here, and I'm sure she'd been told the same, but we did it anyway. The transformation drained my strength, and my bruises hurt even more, but when it was done, I felt free in a way I hadn't for ages.

I shook my fur, and then, with a smile, lay down next to the pretty brown wolf that was my mother. I closed my eyes and slept, and finally, the wounds of the queen's magic began to heal.

Pounding on the door woke me a few hours later. "Are you going to make us fucking stand here all afternoon, too?"

I sat up and growled.

"What the fuck is going on in there? We're coming in."

My spine cracked, my front legs turned back into arms, and I threw myself naked against the door. "Don't you dare, or I will kill you where you stand. I was sleeping, assholes."

I threw on my clothes as my mother shifted back as well. "Are you leaving?" she asked, pulling her nightie back on.

"Yeah. I have to be at a ball tonight, of all the gods-damned things."

"You'll be the most beautiful woman there," she said as she touched my cheek. To my surprise, it didn't hurt anymore, and I felt stronger than I had. There was something about taking my true form that always made the healing faster, but it was also being with her—being with my pack.

Sarion shook my hand as I left the room. "Good luck at the ball tonight. I know you hate gowns and looking fancy. Stay away from Astra and her friends."

"Thanks," I said palming the slip of paper in his hand. "Wish you were going to be there to keep her off me."

"Enough," the captain said, as he shoved me forward. "Get going."

Sarion leaned back against the door. "Afraid they don't let guys like me in, but I'll be right here if you need me."

I was thankful that the guards didn't have werewolf senses, or they would have heard my racing pulse and caught the nervous, agitated scent of my emotions.

What the hell was on the slip of paper?

And what had he meant by *they don't let guys like me in*? Did it mean there were no guards inside?

I was certain now that *careful of her vines* had been another clue, but what? I'd told him that I'd sparred with her and—

Fuck. I wasn't exhausted from battle. The evil bitch had drained my magic, just like the vines had stolen Cadean's. Was that her true power?

My thoughts were tumbling so quickly, I didn't even notice at first that the guards were taking me back by another route—this time, by the front of the palace. My stomach dropped as we passed the patch of vines where I'd exited the tunnels after the trial.

They'd been sealed up with stones and fresh mortar. My guards were delivering a not-so-subtle message from the general: *I will find out everything you have done and what you are doing.*

I prayed to the Moon Mother that he hadn't found out about the erdelfen who'd helped me.

When we reached my bedroom, the captain and his men barged in ahead of me.

My blood heated as they began searching the room. "What is this? Is the general really that worried for my safety? Do you think there are assassins under the bed?"

"We're not skipping any precautions *with you*," the captain snapped.

Had they heard me talking to Cadean at some point? *Triple cream fuck.*

They inspected the bathroom, closet, and—yes—under the bed, leaving no space unchecked.

"This is unnecessary," I groused. "I'm not going to do anything other than get ready for the ball."

Finally, the bastards gave up and left. I slammed the door behind them, then locked it and braced it again with my chair—not that that would do much.

My hands were shaking as I dug Sarion's note from my sleeve and unfolded it.

Something is up and we must leave tonight. The queen has closed all the portals leading out of the palace and the city. I can get you and your mother to a border post with a military recall charm. There should be an active portal there.

Fuck. The trap was closing. I still had the pact, but it didn't specify how I was allowed to leave. Technically, if I asked the queen, she could offer me a carriage and an escort of a hundred soldiers, she'd be keeping her end of the bargain. Then she could have them shoot me or drag me back the moment I crossed the border.

I rammed my fist into the table, then yanked off my necklace. It turned into a golden quill in my hand, and grabbing a sheet of paper, I wrote to Auren: *Queen has closed portals out. Do you have an alternate escape route for me?*

Fuck Auren—but at this point, if the queen was siphoning my magic and the general was allowed to control me, anywhere was better than here. I was going to use all my options.

His reply came back almost instantly: *What did you do to tip her off? The portals are essential to breaking the pact!*

Stunned, I stared at his words as the pieces fell into place. Once I'd found access to the garden, he was planning to have me sneak out through a portal and immediately return to break my pact. Then I would steal and flee—all completely unprotected.

Anger building, I scrawled back, *The plan is fucked. I need an extraction. Any ideas?*

There was a long pause.

Do you have access to the seedlings?

NO, I wrote.

Get them. I'll work on finding a way to break the pact, and I'll see if there is some way to get you out as well.

My mind reeled. *Get me out...AS WELL?* As well as the seedlings? That was all that bastard cared about?

Fuming, I drew the blinds and extinguished the lamps in the room, making it as dark as I could. Then I stormed into the bathroom and turned on the faucet of the tub.

Closing my eyes, I focused on the form of the Dark God. The rugged cut of his jaw, the piercing intensity of his eyes, his scent, his taste, the feel when he was near me. I reached through the darkness and *pulled.*

"I need you, Cadean."

Chocolate and wildfire surrounded me as his power thrummed through the room. "I am right here, my little wolf."

I opened my eyes. He was leaning against the bathroom counter, arms crossed. "I never thought I'd be one to come when called."

Opening and closing my fists to get some control, I met his gaze. "I'm fucked."

I explained everything I'd discovered: the portals were closed, Slaine had sealed off access to the tunnels, and Auren only cared for the seedlings and wasn't going to do anything to help.

Cadean grew more and more angry until the shadows whipped and danced around him like flames.

"I'll fucking kill that bastard brother of mine for getting you into this mess. Hell, for all we know, Auren may be in league with the queen."

I shook my head. "He's playing his own game. Judging by his

priorities, I think he wants to grow his own vines—destroying the queen's is simply a way to corner the market."

The black axe formed in Cadean's hands as his face became a mask of fury and betrayal. "He's trying to do what she's doing —draining my power. It's what he has always wanted. Why I thought he would ever change..."

"Auren doesn't matter. It's the queen we've got to worry about. I think she drained my power last night—Sarion hinted that she's like the vines."

A new anger flared in his eyes—this one cold and unyielding. "I will never let the queen do that to you. You are mine."

The protectiveness and gravel in his voice set my nerves alight, but I pushed the sensations away and tried to get a grip on my ragged breathing.

"I am my own," I said, meeting his possessive gaze. "There is nothing that you or I can do to stop the queen. She's more powerful than I am and can drain my magic dry, so the only option is to get away from her as quickly as possible."

A low rumble of frustration left Cadean's throat. "I will help, any way I can. Just ask it."

"It has to be tonight, during the ball," I whispered. "There will be no guards. I'll find a way to slip out—maybe climb out of a window. Then I'll grab Sarion and my mother."

"If Slain and the queen are setting a trap, they will know you will run to her first."

I met his eyes with steel. "Then I'll kill whoever stops me. Getting them is not negotiable—plus, Sarion has a way out."

Cadean stepped close. "Do you truly trust Sarion?"

"Yes. At this point, with my life."

Cadean studied my face, clearly still hesitant. Finally, he nodded. "Okay, I will trust your instincts. By the sound of it, he must have a way to get you to a military outpost on the border. You'll go with him, tonight, after the ball."

"Won't a military outpost be, oh, I don't know, full of the queen's soldiers?"

"Not when I'm done with them. I'll clear three of the outposts and give you their names, then I'll invade across the border on the opposite side of her realm. That should draw both the military and Slaine's attention while you make a break for it."

My gut twisted. He was going to war over me.

"Can you get the locations to Sarion?" Cadean asked.

"I'll convince the guards to let my mother help me choose a dress. Then I'll pass him a note back."

It was fucking risky as all hell, but the last of my time had just run out. It was leave tonight, or let the queen take my freedom, my magic, and my mother from me.

44

Samantha

Dressed in a silver gown and mask, I moved through the ballroom like a ghost—a ray of moonlight that I hoped wouldn't be noticed, that would be quickly forgotten.

My mother had helped choose my dress, and that made it feel like armor, even if it was nothing more than silk.

Diamond chandeliers and soft lights twinkled overhead, reflected in the dark crystal walls like stars in the night sky. Music filled the air as masked nobles and courtiers twirled across the dance floor, the rich hues of their clothing melding in a tapestry of color. Their laughter and conversation blended with the stringed instruments and filled the air with a relentless, inviting buzz.

It was glorious and beautiful and completely at odds with the dread that had embedded itself in my gut like the point of a spear. I'd passed Sarion my note, and hopefully, he'd come through. If not, I was a doomed woman, and my mother would be as well.

I hated the plan—there were too many variables, but there was no time to make a better one. I just had to pray and wait, pretending I was part of the happy crowd until an opportunity to slip away presented itself.

Dozens of servants moved through the room, offering refreshments, exotic fruits, and other delicacies. I plucked a goblet of wine off a tray just to have something to hold on to. A sip of the sparkling nectar did little to ease my nerves.

Everything about the ball was glamorous, from the fountain of golden wine to the bouquets of lilies and roses, to the elegant attire worn by the guests. The costumes, the happy faces, the flirtatious looks—it was all a façade. I could see that, clearer than ever.

The palace was built on the backs of the erdelfen and the people of the undercity who lived in squalor. Just as the queen fed her nobles with the fruit of the vines, she fed the lower classes lies that kept them in their subterranean prisons like slaves. And while most of her people lived in fear and poverty, Ayanna and her court danced, drunk on the life and magic stolen from Cadean's realm.

Making polite smiles and quick excuses, I drifted back to the walls, where the shadows lay.

"Stunning," Cadean murmured in my ear. His gravelly voice dragged over my skin, sending shivers along my spine. It was as cool as mountain water, a contrast with the burn of my scar every time he drew near.

I kept my gaze down, hiding my lips. "I'm surprised you like it. This ball seems far more your brother's style—glitz and glamour everywhere."

"I meant you." A flutter danced in my chest as a wisp of his magic brushed my shoulder. "Though I much prefer to see your face without a mask."

My cheeks heated, and I stared straight ahead, taking another sip of wine. "You shouldn't use your magic here."

"No one sees the magic or the shadows. They only see you, beautiful wolf."

"I do not wish to be seen," I whispered, retreating further into the shadow.

I stole a glance at him. He wore battle attire, each piece meticulously crafted to fit his broad shoulders and powerful frame.

"You look like you have interesting plans." The noise of the music and drunken guests drowned out my words, but I still spoke quietly.

"I'm preparing to wake this kingdom up—to remind them there is a wolf in the darkness, waiting to strike."

A nobleman with dark hair approached, pinning me where I stood. His pointed ears were pierced with dozens of earrings, and he wore a lapis-blue mask that covered the top half of his face and his nose. He bowed and held out his palm. "May I have this dance?"

My stomach roiled at the thought of dancing with him, but I knew it had to happen sooner or later. Someone would be brave enough to approach the wolf girl...or be ordered to.

Cadean gave a low growl, but I smiled and took his hand. "You may."

I just had to hold out until everyone was drunk and Cadean's attacks had pulled Slaine's attention to the border.

The nobleman guided me to the dance floor, one hand gripping my waist and pulling me close, as we fell into step with the other couples. "I've been watching you all night,"

"Have you, now?" I asked as the fae twirled me in a circle.

I cast a quick glance at Cadean, who I knew could hear everything. He stood where I'd left him, his jaw clenched as he watched me like a hawk, jealousy smoldering in his eyes.

"You left quite an impression on me the evening of the trial," the fae hummed.

Of course I did. I suspected any successful contestant who wasn't betrothed or married became the object of everyone's desire—fresh blood within the court.

"Well, that certainly wasn't my intention," I said.

His dark eyes narrowed as he dipped me back. "Wasn't it? You're bold, but that is a dangerous thing for a female," he continued, leading me seamlessly across the dance floor. "At least, for a female without someone watching over her."

My stomach turned. "I don't need protection or someone watching over me."

"Really?" He leaned close. "I hear you must scamper about with a pack of guards. Perhaps I could provide the protection you need—should we find a suitable arrangement."

"I'm sure that I could arrange to throw your head at the general's feet."

"You little—" His words cut off as his gaze locked on something behind me.

The sickly scent of lilies hit me, and my stomach dropped.

"Speaking of me?" Slaine asked.

Our dance stopped abruptly as the noble shoved me away, retreating before the general's approach. My mouth turned to bile at the sight of the wolf mask he wore.

Without asking, he seized my wrist with his right hand, while his left pulled me hard against him. I could feel his need, and I could almost taste his desire, it was so strong.

A dark wind stirred my hair as Cadean snarled, stalking the shadows.

I glared up at the general. "What do you want?"

"I would say a dance, but you and I have been dancing for weeks now, haven't we?" He grinned down at me, but his charm and good looks couldn't detract from the evil that lurked inside him. It couldn't hide the violence vibrating just beneath his skin.

Every word was a weapon, every look a flaying knife.

His grip on me turned to iron as his fingers dug into my waist. "There are many things I want, but right now, I want the truth." He shoved me backward into the rhythm of the dance. "How did you escape the Dark Wolf God's kingdom?"

"I told you everything already," I said, trying to keep my body as far from him as I could.

"Then tell me again," he said sharply, bending my fingers back.

Pain shot through my hand, and my fingers screamed, but I swallowed the whimper that rushed up my throat, refusing to appear weak before him. "Fucking let go, and I'll remind you."

His grip eased a fraction.

"I drugged him and escaped through the window. His brother found me in the stable and brought me across the border. That's when I stabbed him in the heart."

"So inconvenient that you missed." His tone was accusatory and biting.

"I was terrified. He's a god of death."

A sneer ghosted his lips. "Don't you find it odd that even after you stabbed him, his power somehow became stronger? Because I do."

My throat tightened. Did he know what I had done?

Slaine spun me away, then pulled me in close. "For months before you arrived, his power was waning, poisoned by the curse you supposedly placed on him. But after you were captured, he began to grow stronger again. Such a strange coincidence."

My heart was thrashing in my chest, but I tried to keep my tone even and my words steady. "I have no idea what you're talking about, Slaine. He's still locked in his realm, unable to cross the border. Nothing has changed."

"We were told that you stopped him at the border and can control the wall—a tale from the lips of his brother. Such a strange thing that an insignificant little half-breed could stop a god."

Slaine pulled me in tighter, but I stepped on his foot and created space. "I can control the wall. I did stop him."

"Then you will use your power to protect my army, or you will rot in this palace."

"I'm not doing anything for you."

The general leaned in close, his breath heating my cheek. "Because you're working for him. I think you healed him and faked your attack. I'm on to you, little snake. And once I can prove it to the queen, I will destroy you. I will pick you apart, piece by piece, until only the interesting bits remain."

The venom in his words sent a cold chill down my spine, and my magic instinctively flared to life. A faint bluish-sliver glow spilled from my palms, and when I pushed out of his arms, the air between us snapped.

He jerked back, surprise flashing on his face before it hardened.

Cadean's presence fell over me, his shadows wrapping me like armor. His anger rippled through the air like currents, and the couples closest to us slowly backed away.

"Touch me again, and it will be the last thing you do," I said, the magic in my palms burning to be released. "I've done everything the queen has asked. My loyalty hasn't changed."

With a derisive grin, the general said, "Oh, we'll see where your loyalty stands in the next trial—of that, I'm certain."

What the hell did he mean by that?

The space around us had cleared, but the air felt even more oppressive. The crowded room had become a wasp's nest full of whispers.

Had they all heard? Had they all seen?

"Breathe, little wolf," Cadean growled. "You need to remain calm."

But I couldn't breathe around these vipers.

It was like the world was dancing around me as I plummeted through the sky. The venomous looks, the scowls, the whispers. Did they suspect? Or did they just despise me for what I was?

I had to get out.

Grasping the thick skirt of my gown, I pushed through the crowd, heading for the freedom of a balcony.

I passed through an arched doorway decorated with tapestries depicting a fae hunting scene. My heart sank when I glanced up at the silk artwork—fae warriors in all states of battle surrounded the corpses of slain wolves whose blood flowed around the borders of the weavings. And everywhere, *everywhere* were the vines.

The mask of the Undying Court had fallen away, and now, only the monsters remained.

$$45$$

Cadean

Rage thundered through me as Samantha rushed onto the balcony and into the darkness of the night.

I would strip the flesh off the general. I would stake him to the walls of Shadowstone. She could kill him in the end, but I would break him first.

With every fiber of restraint I could muster, I shoved my down anger. I couldn't calm her if I couldn't calm myself.

I stepped into the shadows behind her. "Easy, little wolf. You're free of him now."

"Free? Weren't you listening? Slaine _knows_. I'm going be dead if I don't get out of here," she said, her eyes glistening under the torches with the tears she refused to shed.

"His hands are still tied. You heard him—he must prove his suspicions to the queen, and he won't find that evidence tonight."

Fury coursed through me. How did he know as much as he did? I'd have Wulfric root out the spy in our midst.

A pair of intoxicated females stumbled onto the balcony,

their laughter stopping short when they recognized Samantha. They hurried inside.

My shadows enveloped her, like they were inexplicably drawn to her. "You were brave to stand up to him like that."

Samantha tore off her silver mask and tossed it over the stone railing. Despite everything, she was a vision. I cast a tendril of magic toward her, dipping it under her chin and tilting her gaze up to mine.

"I'm going to kill him," she said.

"I know you will." I would honor my promise to the little wolf—she could have his life. But I would have his misery first, and I would take my time, ensuring that it lasted days before Samantha gave him the mercy blow.

The tension in her body eased, but the fire in her eyes shone brighter. "I'm out of time. I need that distraction you promised now."

"I will hit them like I have not in years. Is Sarion ready?"

She nodded, her gaze scanning the empty balcony. "The moment there's a call to muster to the border, Sarion will steal the teleport charm for one of the outposts and hide near my mother's cottage. As soon as Slaine and the guards are distracted, I'll slip out of here and meet him. As of this afternoon, the portals at the border posts were still active."

I tried to ignore the deep dread churning in my gut. It was a desperate plan, and I didn't have many contingencies.

"If, for some reason, Sarion cannot get the transport charm, go to the edge of the city by the southern gate. I have a squadron of eulenbjorn waiting, but it will have to fight its way in, and you'll be chased on your way out."

"Sarion will get the charm," Samantha whispered with far more confidence than I felt. "We'll get to the portal."

"I'll be there waiting. Promise me that you'll be safe, that you won't take any risks."

"I promise. Now shake things up so I'll have some cover to get out of here."

I knew I had to go, to leave her, but my feet were rooted in place. If anything happened to her, I'd raze this fucking kingdom. I'd tear apart the mists that held the lands together.

I wanted to tell her everything, but when I looked into her eyes, I couldn't find the words.

"You can do this. I believe in you." I brushed her jaw with my magic and faded into the shadows.

The scent of campfires and the hum of the army rose around me.

I opened my eyes.

The air crackled with tension, and the waning afternoon light cast a golden hue across the snow-peaked mountains and dense forests opposite the barrier. The silence across the border indicated that Ayanna's rangers hadn't been alerted to our presence. That would change very shortly.

I looked to Wulfric. "It's time. Are we ready?"

My commander nodded. "Kass reached the glade a few hours ago. We have hunters ready to clear the border forts, and I have raiders stationed along the barrier. Everything is going to light up all at once."

"We can't fuck this up, Wulfric. I need to get her back, and not just because of the oracle."

He nodded, though his face hardened. "We may lose a lot today."

The implications hung in the air, the tragic bargain I was preparing to make.

"I will never forgive myself for those losses, but she's worth everything." I gripped the haft of my axe, summoning the darkness it held. "Issue the order. It's time."

Wulfric turned and headed back toward the soldiers. Moments later, a deep, resonant howl cut across the land. It was met by another wolf's cry in the distance. A third followed, piercing the silence, then a fourth, their distant calls reverberating down the line of command.

Knowing what needed to be done, I took a breath and opened myself to the primal power.

The sky dimmed and the ground rumbled as darkness seeped into me. The cold kiss of death poured through my veins, permeating every fiber of my being, and awakening a limitless hunger that could only be sated with violence. With each passing breath, its grip tightened, my thoughts homing in on one single objective: to destroy.

I unleashed the storm, the air crackling as the torrent of magic barreled forth, bursting through the barrier with a resounding boom that shook the earth. The Moon's magic surged against mine. Waves of searing pain arced through the tendrils of my power, but I'd surrendered to the darkness, and the agony only hardened my resolve.

I knelt and sank my fingers into the ashy soil, opening myself to the vast web of mycelium that connected each and every tree and plant and fungus. I felt them all, countless zings of energy pulsing through the network, communicating. I poured my magic into them. *Destroy the vines. Ferret out the enemy.*

Trees upended, their roots tearing themselves free of the earth, snapping the cursed vines that blanketed the forest floor.

Fae soldiers filtered out of the woods, weapons readied for battle. With a low growl, I commanded the shadows to attack. They ravaged the land across the border, spreading like wildfire, cutting down everything they crossed.

I rose, severing the connection with the forest and releasing my magic. The storm faded, and the shadows retreated, revealing the broken fae corpses and splintered vines that littered the ground.

The Undying Court would remember who I was, and what it was to defy a god.

46

Samantha

Once Cadean left me, I was truly alone. There were no friendly faces in the crowd, no refuge in the storm.

The eyes of the court were on me now—judging, glaring, leering. I'd spent my adulthood behind a bar to avoid those looks. To be one step removed from the party, out of the center ring. Now, I was there, on display for all to see.

Most of the nobles had witnessed my entrance to the banquet. What did they expect from me? To throw another head at the general's feet? To turn into a wolf and howl at the moon?

I did my best to hide myself in plain sight. I danced with the noblemen, but I refused to listen to their words. I dipped my head to important ladies but refused to hear their whispers.

But the real dance was with Slaine. He was watching me relentlessly, so I watched him as well, using dancers and conversation to keep as much of the crowd as I could between us. I would not be ambushed again.

I used the dances to check the exits. Guards were stationed at most, but not on the balconies. I took air whenever I could and waited in the cold, avoiding the noise and the lights. If anyone had been tracking my movements, hopefully, they'd think I'd gone for air when I finally disappeared.

Each time I passed the banquet tables or neared a servant, I plucked morsels of roasted meats and fried breads off the silver platters and ignored the dissecting glances of the guests. I wasn't hungry, and my nerves had my stomach roiling, but I didn't know when I'd next eat.

An hour ticked by, then two, then three.

Finally, there came a sign that Cadean's distraction was working. A messenger darted through the hall, straight to Slaine. The general whispered something in the man's ear and returned to his wine. Next, a captain hurried in, and Slaine departed with him, his face crimson.

Just as I was thinking of slipping out, Slaine appeared again, but this time, I noticed several of the guards at the doors were gone.

Perhaps I'd just missed my window.

I circled the perimeter as Slaine began scanning the room. Was he searching for me?

My heart stopped as his gaze landed on me and lingered, but then it slid away, and he locked eyes with Astra. He nodded, and she began weaving her way toward him. He whispered something in her ear as soon as she reached him, and they left the ballroom.

What the hell did he want with her? I'd assumed she'd been working for him for a while, but I was suddenly intrigued.

I downed a glass of sparkling water and slipped after them. As I approached, I saw he'd sent the guards away, and I could hear their whispers echoing from the corridor. I ducked into the hallway and pressed myself into the shadows, wishing I had Cadean to help me.

Astra bowed her head. "I am honored that Her Majesty asks for me. How may I serve?"

"Our borders are being attacked, and the queen requires your assistance in the Well of Life," Slaine whispered—though with my werewolf hearing, it was easy to make out his words.

"What am I to do?" Astra asked as they strode down the hall.

"The vines must be healed, and the Dark Wolf God must be met in battle."

I could almost taste her glee. "I will prove to the queen that her faith is not misplaced."

Fuck. If I could find out what they were planning, I could warn Cadean, or even draw him close. Moreover, they were headed to the Well of Life.

They turned a corner, and I hesitated. Then I made my choice.

I took off my shoes to keep my steps silent and trailed behind the pair as they wound through the palace and into the royal wing, to his office. Everyone was either attending or serving at the ball, so the halls were quiet.

However, my luck didn't last. I turned a corner and flattened myself behind a pillar as Slaine approached two sentries still standing guard outside his office. He raised his hand, and magic wrapped around them. "You do not see the door, and you do not see who passed through the door."

They straightened. "Yes, sir."

Instead of slipping through the heavy entry to his office, however, he touched a crack in the dark crystal wall. A sharp grating echoed through the empty hall as a section of the wall shifted and opened.

A secret door.

Astra and the general slipped inside, and the door began to close. I glanced at the motionless sentries, and then at the door. *You do not see who passes through.*

Aw, shit. I was going to have to go for it, wasn't I?

I sprinted, praying my instincts were right, and slipped past the statuesque sentries just before the wall clicked shut. The seam in the crystal vanished moments later, and I found myself in total darkness.

Of all the bad decisions I'd made, this had to be at the top.

I listened as my eyes adjusted. Footsteps echoed—Astra and the general descending the spiral stone staircase at the end of the small hall. I had no choice but to follow because the stairs only led down.

As I stalked behind them, the familiar aroma of death rose— the same scent I'd noticed while passing through the undercity with Sarion.

The stairs opened onto a floor with columned arches. Vines grew throughout the space, clinging onto the stonework like ivy.

Astra and the general stood at the edge of what looked like an open space, their backs to me. A low groan sounded, and a handful of large vines appeared before them, twisting into a platform onto which they stepped.

The vines sank, and they disappeared.

I crept to the spot where they'd stood, and my breath caught.

I was in a giant well, covered in the roots of the vines. Instead of a smooth-sided hole, the well was a multi-tiered structure with rows upon rows of columns and arches. The center was open, dropping down several hundred feet.

I peeked over the edge. There was an ancient stone throne perched above a carved grillwork at the bottom as well as a stone gateway in the shape of intertwined vines—not a doorway, but a portal.

What the hell was this place?

Keeping to the shadows, I hurried down the stairs that spiraled around the well. My quarry had taken the fast way down with vines, so I had to be faster.

My lungs were burning by the time I reached the level where Slaine and Astra stood waiting near the throne. They were speaking in hushed tones about the battle, and I had to fight to keep my breathing quiet.

I was tempted to linger where I was, but I didn't want to be caught unawares by the queen or whomever else they were planning to meet. She might come through the portal, or she might descend as they had, down from above. Either way, I couldn't risk someone seeing me.

The stairs continued down, so when I was sure they weren't looking my way, I padded to the lowest level. The space was dark and crowded with roots that grew out of the muddy ground, some as wide as my torso. I wrinkled my nose at the pungent scent and carefully picked my way until I could peer through the carved stone grill overhead.

I had a perfect view.

After a few minutes, there was a burst of magic, and the portal illuminated. From my position, I couldn't see who emerged, but seconds later, the queen's signature rushed over me, the sweet and sour scent mixing with that of the vines in a nauseating perfume.

The general and Astra bowed as she strode over the grill.

"Your Majesty," Astra said. "I've heard that the bastard Dark Wolf God has infiltrated our borders. How may I serve?"

I could barely make out the profile of the queen's face from my hiding spot, but it was drawn and pale, and her eyes were heavy with exhaustion.

She stalked around Astra. "You arrogant girl. You nearly ruined everything."

Astra glanced between the general and Ayanna. "I-I'm not sure what you mean, Your Majesty."

"You tried to kill Samantha after you were given explicit instructions to stay away," the queen snapped, her tone icy.

Astra straightened her back. "I made a split-second decision, Your Majesty. I told you I saw her using shadow magic just before the cave collapsed. I did it for our kingdom. That half-breed is a traitor."

My heart stilled.

"Her magic means more to this kingdom than your life, a thousand times over," the queen said.

Before Astra could respond, the queen yanked a jeweled dagger from her dress and slashed it across Astra's throat.

Shock hit me, and I took a step back, nearly tripping over the base of a vine.

Astra's body hit the grillwork, and her blood began seeping through the holes, dripping down onto the vines.

"Don't worry, Astra. Samantha will feed the vines in the end as well," the queen said, then slammed her knife into the body, again and again.

I clapped my hands over my mouth to stop the scream that was tearing its way from my lungs.

Dozens of tiny rootlets sprang from the roots, writhing and reaching up toward the grill like sentient tendrils, summoned by the rain of blood.

A shadow loomed overhead as the general grabbed one of Astra's arms and dragged her away. Moments later, a hatch in the grillwork opened, and Astra's body fell through, landing on the muddy floor with a soft thud. Almost instantly, the larger roots shifted, wrapping around Astra's arms and legs and torso like serpents and dragging her into the earth.

Horror surged through my veins as the truth of it dawned. The vines smelled like death because they fed on flesh and blood.

I gagged and stumbled toward the stairs but froze as the queen held her bloody knife aloft. "I fed you my children, and now I will heal your wounds!"

A whirlwind of purple light raced through the well and cascaded along the surface of the vines. They seemed to squirm with pleasure.

As the storm abated, the queen dropped down on the now vine-covered throne, her body frail, and her movements slower than I'd ever seen—as if she'd been drained of life.

She dug her fingers into the stone throne. "Feed me. Drain his land! Restore my power."

The vines enmeshing the throne pulsed and throbbed in a rhythmic pattern, their skin growing supple as they became engorged. Dark, smoky wisps poured out of the vines of the throne, twisting around the queen and filling the space with the earthy scent of fire. She sucked them in like she was drinking water, her chest heaving and her color brightening with each inhalation.

Wildfires. And the taste of bitter chocolate.

I pressed back against the wall in horror. The queen wasn't just draining the life from Cadean's realm—she was draining it from him as well. His magic curled around her, drowning out her own signature.

Her mouth opened in pleasure as her cheeks flushed with color. Wrinkled skin became full again, and when she stood, her body vibrated with power. She had the same glow as she'd shown after testing me in the training room.

Ayanna turned to the general. "If anyone asks, tell them that Astra was sent on a mission, like the others. Give it a week before you tell her family that she was killed protecting the border."

Like the others.

How many others had she sacrificed to the vines? I looked closer at the mud and gore around me. It was flecked with white —thousands upon thousands of tiny white chips. Bones.

I heard the queen's footsteps cross the room, and she paused.

"Once the tenders have cleaned up the mess, find me above. I'm rather a sight and cannot appear at the ball stained in blood."

47

———

Samantha

Slaine's shadow drifted over me as he crossed the blood-stained grill.

"Fucking vines. They always get the best meat." He spat at the stone grill. "Clean this up, or those roots will be growing all over it by tomorrow morning."

For a second, I glimpsed the silhouette of an erdelfen above. Then a wave of water exploded through the grid, soaking me with the remains of Astra's blood.

I must have gasped, or even screamed, because seconds later, Slaine shouted, "What the hell was that? She can't still be alive, can she?"

Shit.

There was nowhere to go, and I was dressed in a silver gown, so even among the thick roots, there was nowhere to hide.

This pit was where I was going to make my last stand—in the bottom of a muddy well, soaked and splattered with sacrificial blood.

Slaine's boots rung on the stone steps as he descended to the bottom of the well with two erdelfen behind him.

I let my magic flare to life in my hand. The erdelfen retreated, but Slaine drew his blade and tested it as he grinned. "Samantha. Of course it's you. This was where you were always going to end up, my pretty filly."

I whipped a ball of light at him. He dodged as his magic flared, and a translucent green shield formed on his arm. He saluted me with his blade and a sickening grin. "I wasn't expecting two dances in one night. What a delight."

Slaine lunged, his blade swinging through the air.

I summoned my shield, absorbing a restless flurry of strikes as he drove me across the pit.

Breathing hard, he stepped back. "Once I gut you, I'll toss your body up there on the grate, and I think I'll sit down here just to watch you bleed. I want to catch the drops on my tongue. No reason the roots should have all the fun."

I launched another ball of light at him, but he deflected it with his shield, then dismissed it. A cruel green whip appeared in his hand, and quicker than I could react, he lashed it forward. It wrapped around my ankle and jerked me off my feet.

I slammed into the mud, and my shield disappeared.

He swung in for the kill, but I kicked his leg out from under him and scrambled away.

"Finish him!" Cadean roared, suddenly in the shadows in front of me.

I hurled a blast of magic, but Slaine was already on his feet with a shield out. My magic drove him back, and he dropped to one knee, but his magic held.

Fuck. It was time to get out of the cramped pit and get some verticality on the fight.

I battled up the stairs, and the wide-eyed erdelfen retreated to an upper gallery.

"How about a little help?" I shouted at Cadean.

"Hide in the shadows and strike from behind!" Cadean's

magic thundered through the air, but the shadows were too slow to respond. Even with our bond, his power was so weak in that pit.

Reaching the grate, I ducked into the deepening shadows along the walls of the Well and pressed myself against the tangled roots.

Slaine vaulted up the stairs and looked around. "You think you're safe in your hiding place? The shadows cannot protect you. They are where you'll die!"

He dismissed his shield and snapped his arm around. His jagged whip appeared and skimmed through the air with blinding speed. Before I could summon my magic, pain lashed across my shoulders and face. I strangled a shout as it ripped back across, leaving deep lacerations on my arms and chest.

Blood wept from the cuts, and to my horror, the tendrils from the vines grasped for me, wrapping around bleeding flesh like starving fingers. I gasped as they dug into my wounds, feeding. A chilling weakness sank into me as they syphoned my blood and magic.

No.

I summoned my shield, blasting them back from my skin. I screamed as they ripped free of my wounds, and I stumbled back.

"Got you!" Slain shouted as the whip cracked across my back. I dashed forward, Slaine's footsteps pounding on the stone behind me.

"Climb!" Cadean roared as black flames flared past me toward the general, but I knew his magic was almost powerless here. It could only truly touch me, and only I could touch it.

His magic.

A desperate thought burst through my mind, but my shout was cut short as Slaine's whip raked across my foot.

I stumbled and fell, but I kicked my other foot into the

ground and propelled myself forward in an uncontrolled leap. I thrust my hands out, and at the last second, I wrapped my fingers around the haft of Cadean's axe.

Fire ripped through my veins as his dark energy flowed into me. The universe expanded around me as time seemed to slow.

I knew in that moment what I'd begun to suspect—that it was not a weapon, but rather the embodiment of his dark power. The physical manifestation of his magic.

And I could touch it.

Cadean sucked in a sharp breath as I ripped the axe from his hands and tumbled to the ground.

Slaine was on me in a second, driving the point of his sword down toward me in a fatal lunge.

I rolled to my back and swung.

The axe cut through the air. Black flames billowed from it, fueled by the insatiable rage rising within me.

The axe crashed against Slaine's sword in a shower of sparks, sending it flying from his hand. He spun sideways with the blow and fell to the ground.

I leapt up, stronger than I had ever been but drunk with hatred.

I staggered forward under the weight of the axe's power. Every place Slaine had ever touched me burned like acid. His scent sickened me, and I knew that the only way to cleanse the air was to cut the breath from his lungs.

Slaine rolled over and managed to stand. "What the fuck do you have in your hands?"

"Death," I growled in a voice not my own.

"How do you have *his* fucking axe?" Slaine snarled. He backed away, lashing out at me with his green whip.

I summoned my shield, deflecting the blow, and continued my slow advance. "Because he is here with me, watching you cower. He will know what a coward you were in the end."

I dismissed my shield and released its power in a bolt of moonlight. Slaine took it against his own shield, but the blow drove him staggering back against the wall.

Terror sparked in his eyes for the first time, and I drank it in. The flames of the axe burned darker. I lunged forward and swung the wicked blade.

Slaine's shield exploded into a spiraling burst of magic that sent him tumbling across the floor. He scrambled up, lunging for the arched portal at the back of the room, but I unleashed a blast of moonlight that barred his way, and he staggered back. "You traitorous bitch!"

How many women had he cornered? Made to feel powerless? How many had he tortured or fed to the vines?

He lunged for his blade. Maybe the old Samantha would have let him grab it, but I wasn't her anymore. I was vengeance, I was retribution, I was death descending like a dark storm.

I dropped low and swung.

The blade lurched forward with a tidal wave of energy, cutting through the backs of his knees as if his flesh were nothing but smoke.

The general slammed down onto the grate, blood from his stumps rushing to feed the vines below.

Hatred and rage thundered through my chest, driving me forward. "You will never touch anyone again."

His dying eyes widened as I lifted the axe high and smashed his skull.

With that blow, my grip on the weapon slackened, and I staggered back from the scene of carnage. I wanted to vomit, but I seizeﾠd the rage still boiling within me and forced it down. He was dead, and the Dreamlands were better for it.

48

———

Samantha

My mind and stomach were reeling, but the sound of Cadean's voice grounded me. "Samantha, are you okay?"

"I wish I could to it all again," I said, chest heaving. "One death isn't enough for him. One moment of terror isn't enough to repay him for all he has done."

The power of the axe thrummed within me. A thousand deaths wouldn't be enough.

"It never is." Cadean's voice sounded mournful, though I couldn't understand why.

For a moment, the only sound was the roots stirring below to lap up the general's blood. My stomach twisted with disgust.

I turned, taking in the columned walls of the Well of Life. It was a sanctuary of death, a temple to the vines that fed on the blood of innocents, that drained the life from Cadean's land and spawned the monsters that murdered people.

I tightened my grip on the axe—Cadean's power made manifest. I could end it all now. I could save his people.

Smoke streamed from the axe as I lifted it into the air and swung. The magic blade sang as it sank into the roots, cutting through them like morning mist before the sun. A massive root dropped away from the wall and crashed to the ground, writhing like a headless snake. Stinking purple blood drained from the wound as the vines above began to quickly wither and crumble, powerless to bleed or devour or kill again.

"The vines regenerate, but the roots die," Cadean whispered in awe.

My breath grew ragged as I tightened my hand on the haft. Its power surged through me, strength from every kill it had ever made and the lust to bring empires crumbling to the ground.

"Do it now!" Cadean roared. "Free my land, Samantha."

My body quaked with power as I raised the axe again.

But then my dress tugged, and a pair of small hands grabbed me. "Stop! What are you doing?"

I faltered and turned to face a terror-struck erdelfen. His eyes were wide, and his face twisted in despair. *Rin.*

"I'm going to destroy the vines and end the queen's reign of terror."

He fell to his knees, grasping the folds of my gown. "You cannot. This city *is* the vines. If you kill them, we will all die, all that live above and below—it will all fall apart!"

I looked back at the withered root on the wall. It was crumbling to dust. How many tendrils had I just killed? Had his home beneath the earth come crashing down?

"Why are you hesitating?" Cadean demanded. "Destroy them, Samantha! Do it now."

I felt the axe's power leap in my chest, but it fought with another: the tug of a golden thread, and the distant whisper of voices.

Bile rose in my throat. "But the city..."

"They made their choice long ago." Cadean's words were laced with hatred, and I felt his darkness pressing in around me.

I closed my eyes and felt that golden thread tugging me

forward. A purpose I didn't fully understand, but one that vibrated through every inch of my body. One that I felt as strongly as the breath in my lungs.

Protect them.

But it wasn't just Cadean's people I was bound to protect.

I stepped back from him. "I won't condemn thousands to death. We will find another way."

"No," he growled, with a rage that took me back. "I've been trying for *centuries*. This is the way. The *only* way. This must end, now!"

My heart stopped as everything became crystal clear. Cadean and I were at odds—we'd always been at odds. How did I ever think we could work together?

The Dark God's lip curled, and his expression flashed with fury. "You're choosing to protect a merciless people that you barely know instead of your own kind? Fae over wolf, her people over mine?"

Tears of anger and hurt burned the back of my eyes. "I'm both, and I choose both. The vines are controlled by the queen —it's *her* we must stop."

Stepping away, I whirled around and hefted the axe. Black flames leapt from the blade, and a cascade of sparks exploded as I buried it into the queen's throne. The Dark God's magic surged through my arm and out of the blade with a crack of thunder.

For a moment, the only sound was the reverberation of steel upon stone.

Then the room erupted in a maelstrom of magic as the throne exploded in a hail of vines and rubble. I staggered back against the wall, my ears ringing and a wave of vertigo tilting the world around me.

I opened my hand, and the axe landed on the ground with a dull, leaden clang.

An invisible weight sloughed from my shoulders, and I

exhaled with relief as the hate and anger and boiling energy of the Dark God's magic disappeared, replaced by the cool warmth of my own power. It was far fainter, but it was mine.

"What are you doing?" The Dark God yanked the axe up off the ground and thrust it out to me. "That's not enough. This is our one chance to stop her. Finish this."

I didn't recognize him, and my heart felt like it was breaking.

"It's not the vines, but the *queen* we need to stop," I said, my voice shaking. "I've destroyed the throne that she uses to draw her power, and we'll find a way to destroy her."

"I thought you wanted to end this war." The harshness of his tone sliced through me. "Have you forgotten your purpose here? Find the strength to do what it takes."

He thrust the blade toward me—a choice to save one people by condemning another.

Standing in the darkness of the room, he was a god of death and destruction, an avalanche bearing down on me. This wasn't the man I knew. Not the man I'd kissed. This was the god I feared, the one I hated, the one who left me trembling before him.

I stepped forward anyway, summoning what little light I had to challenge his darkness. "One of us has forgotten our purpose, Cadean, but it's not me. I was brought back to protect the Dreamlands from her, and *from you.*"

"I *made* this world," he roared.

The lines of my mouth twisted in reproach. "And you've forgotten your duty to it. Fae or shifter, they're all your people. If you can't see that, then you're no longer a god. You're a petty king trapped in a glass castle. You might not have the strength to do what is right. But I do. I will find a way, with or without you."

The blade of his axe billowed with smoke, and the shadows whirled in a tempest around him. His eyes became savage diamonds, hardened with barely restrained rage and shattered with his own powerlessness.

And then, like wind blowing away a curtain of smoke, he was gone. The shadows of the room folded in on themselves, leaving only the echoes of our furious words to haunt the darkness.

I'd lost him.

~

Cadean

The Well of Life melted away, and I was once again in Melanthe's torchlit chamber.

What had I done?

Horror burned through my chest.

I dropped my axe, and it boiled away into smoke. The blinding anger drained away with it, replaced by the cold clarity of fear. I'd held the weapon too long, and it had twisted my mind.

The room reeled. I'd lost sight of everything that was important: her.

I couldn't lose the connection, not when so much was at stake. I shut my eyes and hurled my mind back through the darkness, but though I could feel the pull of our connection, I couldn't reach her. The way was blocked. I slammed my power against it, but it didn't yield.

Had she shut me out? Or was it...

I spun on Mel, who was still chanting at the edge of the circle. "I lost Samantha. We have to get her back!"

Her hands stopped the incantation, and her eyes flew open wide. "What do you mean, you lost her?"

"I don't know," I growled. "We were in the heart of the palace. She killed Slaine and destroyed the queen's throne, but she refused to take out the vines. I pushed her too hard, said words I didn't mean, and...and I lost her."

"What the hell did you say to her?"

The muscles of my neck tightened with shame. "I don't know. A thousand things I already regret, but that doesn't matter. Either she's blocking me, or the queen is near. She's in mortal danger, either way. I need to break through."

Mel's face went pale. "If it's the queen, I don't know if there is any way..."

"We can't leave her there. You can have my blood, however much you need. Just get her back!"

She rushed to her brazier, and I began pacing.

I had let her touch the axe, the worst part of me. I had let her destroy with it. Hells, I'd urged her on. That was a burden no mortal should have to bear. It should have broken her, but somehow, she'd let go.

That gave me hope, but it didn't change the truth: I was a monster, and I'd lost sight of everything.

All that mattered now was finding her.

I ripped the door open and wheeled on the surprised guard. "Send word to Kassian and Wulfric. Samantha is in trouble. She will need to be extracted from deep in fae territory. They're going over the border with everything, and I'll be there soon to clear the way."

Magic swirled around the warrior as he took the form of a sparrow and flitted through the hall.

I looked back at Mel, who was frantically preparing to strengthen the spell.

The axe had wielded me for too long, and now, I was to pay the price for losing my soul.

49

———————

Samantha

I reeled from the shock of Cadean's departure. His absence filled the towering, vine-covered chamber and pulled the breath from my lungs.

He'd abandoned me.

A million doubts played through my mind. Had he ever really cared about me? Was this his plan all along?

"What the fuck?" I whispered in disbelief. What the hell was I going to do?

"What the fuck, indeed?" the queen said.

Terror jolted me to my senses, and I spun to meet her icy glare.

She stood at the stone gateway, backlit by the fading light of the portal. Her magic swirled around her, and the roots on the wall stirred as if the entire room were coming to life.

Fear leapt into my throat, and I stumbled back. "I…"

With cold hatred in her eyes, the queen flung up her hand. "You dare to betray me?"

A billowing wave of magic swelled behind me, and reality

tore apart. I whipped around to see a glowing gash form in the air—a portal.

I bolted sideways, but one of the giant roots wrenched itself off the wall and slammed into me. My body exploded with pain as I was hurled backward through the rift. The swirling gray mists of the ether consumed me. I glimpsed the flash of tall pines against a starry sky, and then the breath burst from my lungs as I slammed into the hard earth.

I groaned and rolled over beneath a canopy of looming trees. Propping myself up on my elbows, I looked back at the shimmering hole in the sky. She'd sent me through a portal, but to where?

She stepped out of the rift like a demon striding from hell. Her dress curled around her, and her face was a mask of unrelenting fury.

I scooted backward. "Where am I?"

"In a land beyond my realm. Our pact was valid for as long as you were in my lands, so this also happens to be the place where you're going to die."

I glanced down at my wrist. The golden bracelet dissolved into smoke.

Oh, fuck.

The queen thrust out her hand, and my body was wrenched into the air.

"I vowed not to hurt you, to compel you, or to steal from you, and you repay my kindness by destroying my throne and killing my general?"

The bonds of her magic were iron around me, squeezing the breath from my lungs and the feeling from my limbs. I struggled and fought, but I could barely move. I gasped. "You were stealing my magic, and you were going to feed me to the vines."

"Because you are unworthy of it! You were given the power to stop the Dark Wolf God, and yet you're his little spy."

She slapped me across the face, then seized my jaw. Her fingers dug into my skin while her magic lanced into my brain. "You're working with the Dark Wolf God, aren't you, little wolf bitch?"

I screamed as her magic bored into my mind. I tried to remember what Cadean had taught me, but there was only the relentless agony of her power. Her energy spiked, and she forced the truth from my mouth.

"Yes," I choked.

"When I'm done with you, you won't even be able to beg for mercy." The queen dug her nails in deeper. "I'm going to tear every bit of magic from your body and use it the way it was intended: to bring the Dark Wolf God to his knees."

The queen thrust out her hand, and a deluge of silver light poured off my skin and into her open palm. It was like wildfire consuming me, a relentless agony that burned down to my bones.

"I'll tighten the barrier around him inch by inch until it becomes a glass sarcophagus. He'll spend the rest of eternity writhing and raging in a prison of your magic while he burns alive."

The horror of imagining him tortured like that cut through my own pain, and I choked back a sob. My heart broke, and in that moment, the thought of losing him was far more painful than anything else she or Slaine could ever have done to me.

The queen's eyes brightened, and she laughed. "Why, this *is* delicious. You actually care for that monster, don't you? It'll be your magic that dooms him, Samantha—don't forget that for one second as I tear it from you."

My body shook as the Moon's power poured out of me. With my thoughts clouded by agony, my head rolled to the side. "You cannot have it."

She seized my hair and yanked my head back. "What was that?"

But I barely noticed her or the trees or the world around me. There was only pain and darkness—and in that darkness, the voices of three women whispering secrets to me.

Fighting to hold on to consciousness, I met the queen's eyes. "The power wasn't meant for you. It was meant for me. And I will not let you take it."

"You don't have a choice." She laughed, then snapped her hand back, and the silver light poured out of me, flowing faster and faster.

My body jerked forward, but something in me strengthened —a truth that she couldn't restrain, knowledge that would not be silenced by her power.

"The magic is mine!" I screamed, as the truth blazed within me. Not the Moon's or a fae gift, but *mine*. My rage flared, and in an overwhelming surge of power, the magic she'd stolen snapped back to me.

The bonds of her magic shattered, and I dropped to my knees. She cursed and raised her hand, but I flung my hand forward and released a shimmering ball of magic.

Stars danced before my eyes as the light exploded around the queen, trapping her in a glowing orb. She screamed in rage and unleashed a blast of sickly green energy against the walls, but the prison of light only crackled in defiance.

I'd bound her, just as I'd once bound Cadean. But he'd broken out, and she would, too. I had to get away.

As if she could read my mind, we glanced at the rift at the same time. The queen snapped her hand up, and the portal began to dissolve.

I hurled myself through the flickering door of light as it collapsed around me. I flew through the ether, and then my shoulder slammed into hard stone, and I tumbled across the floor of her sacrificial chamber.

I glanced back as the rift sealed and breathed a sigh of relief. I was safe for a moment, but as soon as she broke through my spell, she'd make another portal back.

Time to get the fuck out of Wonderland.

Hopefully, I'd bought myself enough time to find Sarion and get my mother.

"Cadean!" I shouted.

The only response was my voice echoing in the darkness. A cruel ache strained against my chest. This was *his* war, *his* fault. And now, he'd abandoned me when I needed him most.

Fuck it. I was used to being on my own.

Still, a bitter sharp pain lanced my chest.

I shoved myself up, but my legs nearly gave out. I braced myself against the wall, breathing hard for a second as I fought off a wave of nausea. It was like she'd torn the strength from my muscles as well as all the energy I had.

Keep pushing.

I looked around. The erdelfen had fled, and I wasn't sure I had the time or strength to climb back to the upper levels. Could I use the same portal the queen had used?

There was no door. The massive stone archway framed a blank wall, but I'd seen her pass through the portal. I frantically dragged my hand over the stone, searching for a hidden latch or handle.

Finally, my fingers found a small socket, but what was it for? A seal?

I felt my bruised jaw as the memory flickered into my mind. *Slaine had a ring. Did the queen as well?*

I dashed over to his body and dropped to my knees. I grabbed his hand and yanked the golden signet ring off his finger, and after a moment's hesitation, I took the bastard's jeweled sword. There was no way I was getting out of the palace without a fight, and my claws weren't going to cut it in a swordfight.

I hurried back to the door and jammed the signet ring into the socket. *Moon Mother, please let this work.*

For several torturous seconds, nothing happened. Then with a deep, resounding boom, golden lines formed across the door. A shimmering wave of magic poured out of them and flowed over the stonework like honey.

I stepped into the golden portal and felt my body yanked through the ether.

50

———

Samantha

After a split second, I stumbled out into a dark corridor lined with vines. Where the hell was I? The transfer had been quick, so probably the tower.

I disentangled myself from the grasping vines and felt my way along the corridor until I emerged from a hidden door at the back of the queen's garden. The sky was dark, and I scanned the shadows for movement, but all was still. I sniffed the air. I was alone.

"Cadean?" I whispered as loudly as I dared.

But once again, he didn't respond. Fear fueled my rising frustration. I *needed* him.

Had he left on purpose, or had the queen's presence driven him away? She was gone, and he'd not returned.

My stomach twisted with doubts and questions. Would he be holding my defiance against me? I'd called him weak and a petty king, less than a god. I'd refused to destroy the vines when I'd had a chance.

Was that all I was to him? A tool to destroy the vines?

The bitter thought turned my stomach, but I shoved it away.

I had to escape, with or without him. The pact was broken, and all bets were off.

I crouched low and slunk through the dark shadows of the garden. I could smell the sweet fruit of the vines, and I paused mid-stride.

The pact was broken...and that meant I could steal.

Glancing around quickly, I darted toward the heavily laden vines clustered at the center of the garden. This was my chance. I found a thick cluster of fruit and sliced through the stem with the general's ungainly sword. Hope and wonder filling my thoughts, I gazed down at the glorious red cluster. I'd been on the verge of defeat, but now, suddenly, I had the solution to my mother's curse in my hands.

All I had to do was get her out.

I darted back to the shadows at the perimeter of the garden, then crept toward the ornamental gateway—the only access. Starlight glinted off armor—two of the queen's bodyguards, and I knew there would be more on the other side.

The guards, I suspected, were mostly for show. The queen's magic sealed the door and controlled access to the garden—normally, there wouldn't be any way to get through, but I was already inside. Would it be easier to get out?

I padded barefoot through the grass, sword ready and my muscles coiled. Guilt knotted my stomach. The men probably had wives and families, but I knew there was no way I was going to escape while they lived.

I waited until one of them turned, then threw myself forward and rammed the blade through his studded leather armor with the full weight of my body. His gurgling cry and the sound of rending cartilage and bone made me want to retch, but I kicked him as hard as I could, yanking my blade free.

As his body tumbled against the door, the other guard leapt forward with his saber. My magic flared along my arm like a shield, deflecting his blade. I spun and slid the tip of the keen blade across his neck. He dropped to his knees, blood rushing from the wound, and I finished them both.

A third guard burst through the door, but I met his throat with the point of my blade. "Don't say a word, or I'll open your throat, just like his."

He didn't move a muscle.

"You may recognize this sword. It belongs to Slaine. He's dead, and the queen is gone. You have no one to report to. If you want to live, you are going to do exactly what I say, and if you have a family, it might help to think about them while you do so. Drop your weapons."

With the briefest glance at my blade, he dropped his saber, slid his dagger from its sheath, and tossed it away.

I raised my hand and let the last shimmering filaments of my magic wrap around my fingers. "I'm going to lower my sword, but I can incinerate you with moonlight faster than you can scream. Got it?"

He nodded, and I thanked the Fates he couldn't smell the lie. I was absolutely drained.

"Take me to the tower residence where the queen is holding my mother."

His eyes drifted to my hovering blade, and he swallowed. "Follow me."

The guard led me through the palace, though it was largely deserted. Apparently, Cadean's distraction had worked, and everyone had scrambled to protect the border or other important assets.

I slowed as we approached the skybridge to my mother's

tower. I didn't see the sentries or Sarion, but I could smell fae blood. Someone had died here.

As soon as I was across, Sarion emerged from the shadows of the wall, and my escort started to shout. I flipped my sword around and slammed the hilt into the back of his head. The guard stumbled and collapsed to the floor with a heavy ringing of chain mail.

"Sorry about that, buddy." I plucked one of the fruits from the cluster and slipped it into his hip pack. Hopefully, he found it before someone else did.

"You took long enough," Sarion said. "The whole palace has been mobilized. I grabbed a recall charm to the northeastern outpost during the general muster. I killed the guards, but I don't know if they'll send more. We need to hurry."

I met him partway down the hall. "I know. As soon as the queen escapes, she's coming straight here."

"Escapes from—" His question broke off as his gaze landed on the bloody sword and cluster of fruit in my hands. "Gods, what have you done?"

"Enough to get us tortured for the rest of our lives. We've got to grab my mother and split, or things are going to get very, very dark." I held out the fruits to him. "Put these in your satchel. I need a free hand."

"Fucking hell," he muttered, and gently stowed the cluster of fruit in his bag.

He unlocked the door to my mother's chambers, and I shoved my way in. She bolted upright. "Sam! You're covered in blood! What happened? Are you hurt?"

"I'm fine." I wrapped my arms around her, breathing in the scent of her hair and the soft honeysuckle signature of her magic. "We're going to be fine."

"What's going on?"

Trembling, I stepped back. "I've got the fruit, so I can heal you. But we need to leave, immediately. The queen is looking for me."

Her face went ashen. "I told you I didn't want that. What have you done, my beautiful, foolish girl?"

I pulled her out the door. "I just avoided being murdered by a psychopathic woman, so think of this as a bonus."

The moment I stepped into the hall, a blistering bolt of energy tore into my side and sent me flying backward. The breath exploded from my lungs as I crashed into the wall and fell to the floor. Searing heat spread along my skin, and my vision danced, but I flipped over onto my hands and knees just in time to see Sarion unsheathe his blade.

A flash of light blinded me as a thunderclap exploded in my ears. When the patterns of light and darkness began to fade, his body was lying on the ground in front of the entrance to the skybridge.

No.

My mother screamed for me as she rose, but I could hardly hear her over the steady tone ringing in my ears, and I couldn't think of anything but the sinister form of the queen striding toward me.

An icy rage contorted Ayanna's features, and streams of dark light radiated from her hands. She was death, coming for us all.

My mother started hobbling toward me but froze the instant the queen shouted, "Stop!" The words were a distant echo above the ringing, but I felt the thrumming power of her magic in the air.

The queen held out her hand. "Return to me."

My mother turned and obediently walked toward the queen, enthralled by her glamour. My blood turned cold as the horror of it sank in. Ayanna had absolute control.

I glanced at Sarion, who was rolling to his side.

We've got one chance.

I staggered to my feet and summoned the tattered remnants of my magic, but before I could cast, the queen jammed her finger against my mother's temple. "One move, one glimmer of magic, and she dies."

Terror froze me in place. They were touching. Whatever I tried, the queen's magic would be faster and stronger.

"Let her go!" I yelled, panic pumping through my veins.

Ayanna met my gaze with a wicked smile. "You are mine."

My mind went blank as horror and failure drowned my thoughts. I'd been given the power to protect, but in the moment that I needed it most, it wasn't enough.

I wasn't enough.

The queen laughed. "You're going to submit, or I will disintegrate your mother, right here and now."

My heart hammered against my chest as despair choked my voice. I wanted to shift, to kill, to scream, but every muscle was paralyzed. Anything I did would kill my mother. My only option was to submit.

Could there still be an opening? If she would just let go of my mother, I might have a shot.

I dropped to my knees.

The light of triumph flashed across the queen's face. "Good girl."

A tear slipped down my mother's cheek as she began to shake. "I'm so sorry, my love. I was never able to protect you from the world."

I started to shake my head, but then my heart seized in horror as I realized that my mother wasn't shuddering from fear.

Her eyes flashed gold, and faster than I could draw a breath, she shifted. Fur streaked along her limbs and claws ripped from her hands as she lunged for the queen's throat with open jaws.

The queen tumbled back beneath the snarling brown wolf that was my mother.

I sprang forward, driving my bare feet into the path with each stride. "No!"

A flash pierced my vision, and the sky erupted in a firestorm of purple light. I stumbled sideways as a wave of magic cascaded over me, and I gripped the wall for support. "Mom!"

Smoke and death swirled in the air as cinders drifted toward the ground. And then the queen rose—torn and bloody, but with a savage look of triumph in her wicked eyes.

Screaming, I seized the general's blade and hurled myself forward. Purple flames flickered as the queen flung up her hands.

I swung as her magic exploded forward, but a heavy force drove me into the wall, and suddenly, I was whirling through the ether, screaming in rage and horror and defiance as I struggled in Sarion's arms.

But my cries didn't matter. My mother was gone.

51

Samantha

My stomach plunged as we spun through the ether. I could have stayed in that in-between space forever, lost in the shock and grief that had cleaved my heart apart. But moments later, the remorseless gray thrust us back out.

I stumbled barefoot in thick mud. I was in the small courtyard of a ruined keep. The stone walls had been scorched, as had the palisade of sharpened logs. The smells, the sensations of the mud, the feeling of the wind around me—all of it meant nothing.

I wanted to fall, to scream, to weep. I wanted to destroy the earth and bury my blade in the queen again and again. I felt a million things and nothing, and my body still felt like it was floating in the ether, disassociated from everything around me.

An unfamiliar voice tore me from despair. "About fucking time! We were nearly overrun by wolves, and there're only three of us left—"

The fae soldier slowed to a halt, his eyes widening as he saw me in my bloodstained gown. "Who the fuck is she, and where are the rest of the reinforcements?"

"Not coming," Sarion said. Drawing his blade, he cut the man down with a series of savage blows.

The air snapped in front of my cheek, and an arrow lodged in the mud beside me. I stared at it in disbelief.

After everything they'd taken, they were still trying to kill me.

Sarion seized my arm and dragged me to cover. The mud sucked at my feet, and I tripped. Another arrow whizzed over my head, lodging itself into the post in front of me. Sarion spun, meeting a fae warrior who attacked from the stairwell. The clang of metal reverberated through the courtyard as I pulled myself from the sticky muck.

The sniper dropped his bow and leapt from the tower on silken wings, landing just in front of me and obstructing my path. Green light flickered from his palm, and then a bolt of magic ripped toward me like lightning.

My instincts kicked in.

Summoning my shield, I blocked the blast, then charged, the overwhelming rage inside me demanding release.

He drew a short sword, but I slammed it out of the way with the general's blade. I seized his shoulder and rammed the sword into his unprotected thigh. The soldier's eyes rounded as I yanked it out, and he stumbled back into the wall. Instead of leaving him, I plunged the sword through his body over and over, each stab making my agony worse and offering no relief.

I hadn't even realized that I was screaming until Sarion gripped my shoulder and pulled me off the mutilated body. "Samantha! He's dead."

The corpses of two other fae soldiers lay nearby.

My blade and arms were coated in red, and I tasted the iron tang of the fae's blood on my tongue. I should have felt horror or some sort of relief, but all that was within me was relentless, maddening anger.

Chest heaving, I surveyed the devastation beyond the palisade. The land was a warzone. A thick layer of gray-white ash coated the ground, blanketing all signs of life, and the acrid scent of devastation hung heavy in the air. The corpses of fae and wolves littered the ground, and my stomach churned with guilt. The Dark God had gone to war for me, and this was the cost.

And I'd failed.

Sarion tugged on my arm, pulling me toward a gateway in the back wall. "The watchmen might have sent word to the palace. We must get to the portal now!"

We rushed through the door into a grove protected by the keep and a perimeter of high stone walls. It was sickening. Inside, the trees were dead, their bark was stripped, and their branches hung precariously over the littered ground—apparently not immune to the Dark God's attacks. In the heart of what was likely once a beautiful garden with grasses and flowers waited a solitary standing stone that thrummed with a powerful aura.

Sarion dashed to it and traced his fingers over the arcane sigils carved into its weathered surface. When nothing happened, he ran his hand across the stone a second and a third time, and then his shoulders tensed. He cursed beneath his breath.

"What's the matter?" I asked, my throat suddenly tight. He didn't answer, just stared at the stone. I stepped up beside him. "Sarion!"

He looked over at me, his face ashen and all hope gone from his eyes. "It's closed. The queen must have closed all the portals —even the military ones. We're stuck."

"No!" I touched the sigils, feeling every crevice, searching for an opening in the portal's magic.

"It's sealed shut. I'm sorry, Samantha."

"Then we find a way to open it!" I clutched his tunic and shoved him toward the stone. "This was your idea! Everything depends on us going through this portal." My mother—" My voice caught, and tears blurred my vision. "She gave her life so that we could escape!"

In desperation, I called what little magic I still had and cast it into the stone, but it reflected off, and the sigils remained lifeless. The world pressed in, and the barren trees around us suddenly felt like grasping hands.

We were trapped deep in the queen's lands, and I had lost everything: my mother, my chance to escape, and the chance to protect the people of Cadean's realm.

Claws ripped from my fingers, and I dug them into the earth, howling in rage as despair took control.

~

Cadean

Blinding anguish lanced through my chest, and I gasped from the pain. *Samantha.*

I hurled myself from the battle and back into the forest, my heart pounding. Slamming my eyes shut, I shadow-cast to her.

She materialized before me in an instant. The little wolf knelt near a fae gatestone, her silver gown soiled, her hands and face streaked with dried blood. Her body was quaking in grief, and her signature was overwhelmed by a torrent of emotion.

She gasped as she sensed my presence and lifted her head. "Cadean?"

I dropped down beside her. "What happened? Are you hurt? I've been trying to shadow-cast back to you, but I was blocked."

Regret and guilt pummeled me harder than any beating I'd ever taken. I'd abandoned her, let my anger blind me to what was most important.

"I failed," she said flatly, and her head drooped. "The portal has been sealed, and it's two days to the border. We're trapped, and I've failed."

There was a glaring absence in her words, a truth too painful to speak, but I felt it in my heart as if it were my own.

Her mother was dead.

"I'm so sorry," I murmured.

My soul twisted. I could see her, smell her, and yet I couldn't touch her. I wanted to sweep her into my arms and pull her away, but I was *nothing*. I was helpless to take her grief or give her comfort. "We will mourn her, and I will ensure she crosses safely into the ghost pack. But first, we must fight. You need to run."

She looked up at me, so brave and beautiful despite everything she'd survived. "I'm done running. I can't. When the queen comes, I will fight her here."

Sarion looked around, his eyes wide. "Who are you talking to? Is it *him*?"

Samantha met his gaze. "Yes, it's Cadean. He's in shadow form. I can see him even if you can't, but I'm afraid that even he cannot help us here."

Her words cut through me.

Sarion backed away. "What the fuck have I gotten myself into?"

I clenched my fists. I might not be able to touch her, but I could help. I summoned my presence and growled. "Get up." She shook her head, but I pushed my magic into her. "Your mother expects you to *fight*, but most importantly, to *live*. To do that, you must *run*."

Samantha shuddered as my strength poured into her, and finally, she rose. Her dress was torn and sodden with blood and dirt, and I sensed her deep fatigue. I clenched my fist to harness the anger that cut through me. If only I had been there for her.

But I hadn't.

Samantha shook her head. "Like I said, it's two days to the border. Even if your forces can reach me, she'll find us first."

"I will guide you through the mists. We won't follow the mistways, instead we'll run along the seam between the patches. The fae will not risk entering them."

"I thought the mists were unpassable except at crossings."

Sarion's eyes widened further. "Why are you speaking of the mists? They're perilous, Samantha. Once you stray off the mistways, they're impossible to navigate and infested with nightmares. The minds of those who make it out are shattered. I've seen it."

"Do you trust me?" I growled.

After a second of hesitation, she nodded.

"I made this realm, and I promise, I will guide you through." I glanced at her feet. "Now get some boots."

She hurried to the courtyard and took the boots off a soldier lying against the wall. His body had been sliced to pieces by a blade, though it looked like an animal attack.

I knew it had been her work.

She used the soldier's knife to cut the bottom of her dress, tearing the fabric so that her lower legs were exposed, then used it to pad the slightly oversized boots. She met my gaze and nodded. "Let's get the fuck out of here."

"Fuck me," Sarion said, hurrying after us. "You've likely lost your mind and are just babbling to shadows, but to hell with me if I'm going to let you go into the mists alone."

Closing my eyes, I sent my magic out, searching. The mists were always in flux, constantly shifting, but these were my ancestral lands. I'd shaped them when I'd forged my realm, and their magic called to me just like every living creature here. I could feel their currents like electricity over my skin and sensed their boundaries as easily as if I were looking at a map. We could follow them almost all the way to my border.

We hurried out of the ruined keep and toward the closest bank of mist. Death filled the landscape around us, and I recognized the bodies of the raiders I'd sent across the border. I would grieve for their sacrifice when the time came, but for now, all that mattered was getting her out.

We wove through the remains of the forest that surrounded the fae hillfort. When I'd been free, it had been a favorite hunting ground of mine, vibrant and full of life. Now it was just another victim of the long war.

Piercing wails resounded in the sky, and the silhouettes of deathwings appeared high above us, circling outward from the distant tower and searching the woods. The hunt was on.

Samantha cursed, and she and Sarion began to run.

I kept ahead of them, scouting and leading them on. Soon, I spotted the tendrils of mist creepingly lazily over the forest floor. The seam was close.

But not close enough.

A sudden rush of wings beat the air behind us, and a wave of arrows rained down, lodging in the trunks and branches of trees, and narrowly missing Samantha and Sarion.

Fuck. The deathwings carried mounted archers.

I called the shadows to rise and form a curtain of darkness to hide my companions from the deathwings, but my powers while shadow-casting were slow and weak. "Get to the mists!"

Had I been more than a shadow of a god, I could have ripped the deathwings from the sky with a single blast or hauled Samantha to safety. Instead, I was doomed to watch helplessly as she dodged the arrows raining down around them.

It was poison burning my heart.

Long shafts buried themselves in the dirt at their feet as they ran. Sarion glanced back, then shoved Samantha to the side as two arrows whizzed past. The third lodged into his shoulder, and he tumbled to the ground by the base of a tree.

"Sarion!" She paused to turn back.

The mists were only a hundred paces away.

"Leave him!" I growled. "He'll be fine! It's you they're after. Get to cover!"

But Samantha wheeled about and dropped beside him.

Her shield flashed as another barrage of arrows pelted the ground around them. They ricocheted off, but the glowing orb flickered out almost as soon as it had appeared.

Her signature was beyond anemic—she was almost completely drained.

"Get up and run!" I roared as I pulled the mists closer with my power.

She hauled Sarion to his feet while the deathwings circled for another strike.

Terror for her raced through me as she and Sarion fled into the endless gray of the seam. The archers kept shooting, but finally, the mists became thick enough to conceal them from the sky. When we were surrounded by the impenetrable gray at last, I stopped by a stony outcrop that would provide some cover.

The beating of wings whirred overhead, churning the mist into violent eddies, but our harriers passed by, leaving us in sudden silence.

"The queen's riders will keep searching, but I think it's safe to catch your breath," I said, still watching the skies. "In here, they're in as much danger as we are."

Samantha braced her hands on her knees and drew in ragged gasps. "That was too close."

Sarion inspected his shoulder, where the shaft of the arrow still protruded.

"I'm so sorry, Sarion. That arrow was meant for me," Samantha said.

Grunting in pain, he handed her a knife. "I got lucky—the arrows are poisoned, but at least the point went all the way through. You'll need to break it off."

She scored the shaft, then snapped it. He grimaced in pain and clutched his shoulder as his expression hardened. "Next time, leave me behind."

"Never." She shot me a reproachful look, then tended to his wound.

Although frustration tore at me, I couldn't deny the admiration that flared in my chest. She was a wolf, through and through—never one to leave a packmate.

Samantha removed the arrow and packed the wound. "You're the only reason I escaped from that place. I'm not leaving you behind."

The screech of a dying deathwing echoed through the fog, and Sarion looked around the creeping mist. "While I appreciate the gesture, I'm pretty certain we're in just as much danger in here as out there, if not more."

Samantha looked at me. "Are we?"

"You must be careful. Like blood in the water, fear and magic draw things here, not to mention sound. So speak little, and no matter what you see in the mists, keep your head about you."

She repeated my instructions to Sarion, and he adjusted his scabbard and looked around. "Wonderful. I'm going blind into the mists, led by an invisible version of the god I've spent my life fighting."

"I swear he's here. I'm not just a madwoman leading you to your death."

Sarion nodded. "I know. That makes it all the worse."

I led the two further into the fog. Normally, one crossed the mists like a river, choosing the narrow places and following well-worn paths, but we were running along the seam, following them around the entire perimeter of the patch. Our way would be far, far more dangerous.

After twenty minutes, the beating of wings returned, but with it came another sensation—low vibrations moving quickly beneath the ground.

I motioned for Samantha to stop and get down. "Deathwing. And something is tracking it. Tell Sarion not to make a sound."

Samantha crouched and put her finger to her lips.

We waited as the silhouette passed overhead. The banks of mist rolled away before it.

Hell. The fool rider was using magic to search for us.

Suddenly, the ground shook, and a dark tentacle launched upward out of the ground. Dirt rained down around us as the deathwing let out a guttural shriek and was ripped from the sky.

52

———

I clamped my hand over my mouth as a black shape dragged the deathwing's crumpled body down into the earth, just like the roots had taken Astra.

My stomach reeled at the memory.

The rumble quieted, and the chilling silence settled around us, obscuring our vision and playing wicked tricks on my mind.

"This was a mistake," Sarion whispered, and I put my finger to my lips again.

After he was certain the thing in the ground had moved on, Cadean led us forward.

The landscape changed continually as we progressed, as if someone had broken the world into pieces and poured it back out. Jagged rocks turned into slippery surfaces, and the occasional trees we came upon were twisted into gnarled forms, their branches resembling fingers reaching out toward me. And always, the gray nothingness flowed around us, creating grotesque shapes that seemed to lurk just out of sight.

"What's the matter with this place?" I whispered.

Cadean glanced back over his shoulder at me. "When I

made this realm, I brought together islands of dreams. The mists are the glue that holds them together, but many other things got caught in the cracks—nightmares, fears, fragments of memory."

I shuddered, but he smiled, and the confidence in his eyes warmed me. "Don't worry, little wolf. I created this world, and I will guide you through it unharmed."

Time seemed nonexistent, and delusion began to creep in at the corners of my thoughts. Ethereal whispers that the others couldn't hear rose and fell around me, carried by the strange currents that wound through the fog. Some were only half-mad mutterings. Others were as clear as if I'd spoken them myself.

You're a murderer. A traitor to your blood.

He does not care for you, just for the magic in your soul. He is using you.

You killed her.

Guilt and doubt tore at me, and my breaths began coming in panicked gasps.

Then, when I didn't think I was going to be able to take the muttering any longer, Cadean's magic traced over me, calming the rising torrent of emotions. "Do not heed the voices on the wind. They are echoes of your own fears, used to lure you into danger and madness. They are not real."

I stole a glance at Sarion. The haunted expression on his face told me he was battling his own demons.

"Ignore whatever you hear," I said to him.

Sarion nodded, and we continued on.

The air grew heavy with moisture and the scent of decay and stagnant water, and soon, we reached the muddy edge of a swamp. A thick layer of mist traced over the surface, lit by a sickly light filtering down from the sky that gave it an ominous glow.

Cadean guided us to a worn and broken walkway. "You

mustn't look down into the water. It doesn't reflect the sky, only the dark truths and deep fears within you."

Turning back, I repeated the warning to Sarion, then followed Cadean out onto the walkway. The first plank creaked softly, but it was solid. He paused. "Remember, I'm not really here, so choose your own path carefully. Many of the boards have rotted through."

I didn't want to imagine what would happen if we fell into the cursed swamp.

I tested each board before I placed my weight on it, and Sarion followed several paces behind. Although I kept my eyes locked on my path, my mind kept returning to the whispers.

My mother was gone, and it was my fault. I could've saved her if I'd been stronger or just a moment faster.

My foot slipped on the rotten wood, and my boot plunged into the cold, dark water. I dropped to my knees, the pain jolting me back to reality. Rippling, my reflection looked back at me from the ebony water. Then there was a burst of blinding light, and I saw my body consumed by an inferno of magic. I saw Cadean beside me on his knees, stricken with pain. I was dead, and he was mourning me.

Strong hands gripped my shoulders, pulling me upright and extinguishing the vision as quickly as it had appeared.

"Don't look into the water," Sarion said, holding me steady. "And stop shouting."

Had I been shouting?

I shuddered at the memory and rose.

"Are you okay?" Cadean asked. His hand hovered beside me, then clenched. We hadn't spoken about what had happened in the Well. Maybe there was nothing to say.

I nodded, and a cold shiver ran through me. My body no longer felt like my own, as if my soul had ripped itself free and was hovering somewhere else.

Cadean folded his magic around me like a warm coat of shadow, and the shivers eased only slightly. "What did you see?"

"Me, dying, and you weeping."

His expression hardened. "The visions are just illusions, possible paths fate could take, but I will not let anything happen to you, little wolf. Your fate has not yet been written."

I brushed away the dampness at the corner of my eyes. I didn't speak the truth that I felt rising within me. My fate *had* been written, and I'd already chosen it.

~

The causeway ended at a rocky bluff. The whitish-gray mist was denser on this side of the swamp, mingling with the faint scent of pine needles.

The rocks that comprised the bluff shouldn't have existed together. Soft sandstone melted into glassy obsidian, and limestone boulders lay scattered with basalt and jagged lava piles. Giant pine trees soared above us, their tops obscured by the mist.

Sarion stumbled as we climbed the slope. I grasped his arm to prevent him from sliding, then looked back at Cadean. "We need to rest."

"I'm fine," Sarion said. "If the poison from the arrow hasn't killed me by now, it won't."

His face was ashen, and I couldn't quite tell by his scent whether he was lying.

Cadean surveyed the landscape around us, his expression grim. "You need rest, too, little wolf. You're shivering."

Was I? I looked down at my shaking hands.

"There is a safe place not far from here," he continued.

We pressed on for what felt like hours but may have only been minutes. At the top of the bluff, we reached a place where dark stone ruins rose from the trees—the remains of an ancient cathedral. "We will rest here for the night," said Cadean. "The church is ruined, but its memory will keep the lurkers in the mist away."

Sarion collapsed by a rock, and I gathered wood to make a fire. I poured what magic I had into a stick until it glowed hot and burst into flames, then coaxed the pile of brush to light. We huddled around it, drawing what warmth we could.

I sat, staring past the fire toward the solemn banks of mist drifting in the darkness. I was unable to sleep, unable to think. Whenever I looked inward, there was no fire, no life, just infinite gray like the mist around me.

Cadean emerged from the shadows and sat across from me, saying nothing as if he understood that I didn't need or want comfort, but an anchor in the endless gloom.

For a while, we sat in silence, and then I picked up a broken stick and flicked a rock across the ground. "I can't cry. Shouldn't I be able to cry? Shouldn't I be mourning her?"

He shrugged. "No."

I flung the stick away. "You say it like nothing is wrong."

"You're at war, and you have the soul of a warrior. You know that the battle that lies ahead will require you to be focused and ready. You will grieve for your mother when the killing is done." The set of his jaw and the resolve in those piercing eyes were haunting, almost as if my sorrow were his own.

"I have no interest in killing—just in killing the queen." I dug my claws into my palms as I imagined all the ways I wanted her to pay for what she'd taken from me.

He inspected my face for a long moment, then rose. "If it's vengeance you desire, follow me, and bring that sword."

I glanced back at Sarion, who was lying against a rock with a cold sweat on his brow. "We can't leave him alone."

"Sarion is safe. Although the old sanctuary is no more, the spirits still protect the grounds—that's why we stopped here."

Mustering my strength, I rose and grabbed the general's blade. It was beautiful. The golden hilt ended in a wolf head, and a blue gem was embedded at its base between two wicked claws. Cadean began to weave through the trees, and I followed along behind. The grief that I'd buried deep began to push through the fortifications I'd built, and my chest tightened.

"It's not that I don't want to mourn her, or that I feel nothing. It's the opposite—there's so much rage and guilt and sorrow and pain inside of me that there's nowhere for them to go, no way for any of it to escape." I wrapped my arms around myself. "It hurts so damn much, I'm afraid it will destroy me if I even let a little out."

Cadean looked back at me, impossible understanding in his eyes. "Rage is a weapon, and sorrow is steel—but if you are to wield it, you must forge it. I will teach you how."

After a short distance, we stepped into a clearing nestled inside the stand of towering pines. The dense mist hung back around the edges of the clearing, and in its center stood a solitary oak, its weathered branches reaching skyward. Scars marked the ancient trunk, testaments to the tribulations it must have survived over the years. It was brutal and battered, yet small blue wildflowers pushed out from the moss that grew around the base, somehow managing to bloom amid the gloom.

Cadean gestured to the ground by the tree. "Kneel and place your sword across your lap." I did so, and he knelt across from me. "The warrior knows that they cannot grieve. That they must fight on, and the fight is their grief. I will help you swear an oath of vengeance to shape the pain you carry into a weapon."

"How?"

"Close your eyes and still your thoughts, then put your

hands on the blade and repeat the words you hear in your mind."

I pressed my palms against the flat edge of the sword and closed my eyes. Drawing in a deep breath, I let the scents and stillness of the surrounding pines ground me. "I'm ready."

Like poetry in the wind, his magic whispered in my ears, and I repeated it word for word as the echoes of his voice died away.

"I, Samantha Bennet, born of both wolf and fae, swear an oath of vengeance in the name of my mother. By the blood that binds us, I vow to hunt down the Queen of the Undying Court, and that I will not rest until she is dead, and my mother's soul is at peace. I will become the queen's unrelenting shadow, the doubt in her heart, and the terror that haunts her dreams."

Instinctively, I pressed the cold steel of the sword across my palm, and crimson warmth bloomed under the sting.

"I call upon the primal wisdom of the wolf and the ancient magic of the fae to guide my blade. My mother's memory will be my strength, and her spirit will be my courage—for I know if they are with me, I shall not fail."

"And you will not fail," Cadean whispered as he met my eyes.

His determination hardened my heart.

He placed his hands upon the blade beside mine, and I could almost feel his touch. "You've sealed the vow with blood, now seal it with your power."

The air stirred as his magic thrummed to life—the whisper of wind through the needles, the trace of wildfires, and the taste of the richest chocolate. In response, my own magic rose, filling me with a warmth and security that felt so right in contrast with the numbness. Tendrils of luminescence and shadow swirled and danced around us, sparks erupting wherever they touched.

"Always fighting me," Cadean said with a faint smile.

I'd told him once that I'd never stop fighting him, but

perhaps in this moment, I could let go of that struggle. I let his power guide mine, accepting it. The wisps of light and dark merged, and as they grew acquainted, a deep sense of harmony and unity rose in me. Like braids of rope, they wove through the blade, and the metal grew hot beneath my hands, filled with molten light. The heat seared my palms, but I held on, cherishing the pain, letting it drown the suffering in my heart. Then a surge of overwhelming power shook through me, driving the breath from my lungs. As it faded away, I was left exhausted, chest heaving.

A gentle breeze swept the clearing, and the boughs of the ancient oak creaked as if acknowledging my promise.

"The vow is made, and your enemy's sword is claimed," Cadean said, "Cherish it, for the blade knows a new purpose now—and so do you."

53

Cadean

The following night, I gazed out across the empty field that flanked my territory and the dense forest that loomed just beyond. The mists enveloped most of it, keeping Samantha safe for the moment.

The next part would be the most dangerous.

Mel left the small fire and bubbling cauldron and joined my side. "Something's out there. I can feel it in my bones."

"Ayanna," I muttered.

The silence was the tell. On any other day, the sounds of birds and other life would have filtered across the barrier.

I might not be able to see her warriors, but I knew the land.

Unfortunately, it seemed the queen had anticipated my plan—but we were out of options. She'd also secured the path where the seam crossed into my lands, as well as a bend closer to my realm twenty miles to the east. I hoped that she herself would be waiting at one of those.

"When my brother and I used to fight side by side, we called places like these killing fields. We need to make sure that it doesn't become one tonight." I glanced over at my most trusted companions. "Are you two ready?"

"To ferret out the queen's assassins and possibly die while triggering their traps?" Kassian met my gaze, and a feral grin spread across his face. "Absolutely."

Wulfric, a terrifying sight in wolf form, dipped his head and pawed the hard earth.

Whatever fae warriors were lurking out there, they were in for an unwelcome surprise.

I checked the sky. The moon was low but rising. I didn't like the light it shed, but that couldn't be helped. We needed to bring Samantha out at night, when the shadows and I were strongest, and the longer we waited, the higher the moon would climb.

"I'll shadow-cast to her as soon as you're across and into the mists. Wait at the edge with Elowyn, and I'll guide her to you. Just be careful in there."

"Have them drink these." Mel handed Kassian two silver vials. "It would be better if they could rest longer, but this should give them an extra kick and heal any small pains."

Kassian tucked the vials into the sack I'd packed for him and mounted up on Elowyn. "I'm thinking I should have stayed in Auren's dungeon."

With that, he and Wulfric slipped through the Moon's barrier and split up.

"I'll cast a protection ward over her as soon as I see them," Mel said softly from beside me. "She *will* make it, Cadean. They will all make it."

I nodded because I had no words. Failure wasn't an option.

Wulfric had made it a quarter of the way when something caught his attention. He slowed and lifted his nose.

I narrowed my eyes. "What the fuck is that?"

"I see nothing."

The air around him seemed to distort, like heat waves rising, only it was late fall, and the night air was frigid.

Wulfric jerked his head, sensing the same disturbance, and took off through the dried grass. Almost instantly, a fae male slipped into view, his arrow nocked and aimed at Wulfric. The arrow narrowly missed as the giant wolf pivoted and rounded back. He tackled the fae and tore his head off with a swift jerk.

"They're hidden in plain sight," Mel whispered as more figures appeared and converged on the two. "A concealment spell."

"Figure out how to break it," I growled, testing my blade. "I do not want to be blind out there."

Kassian cut down two warriors as he rode past, and he and Wulfric slipped into the mists.

Ayanna's forces were likely holding back, no doubt hoping to give us a false sense of security. I was certain that when Samantha exited the mist, the queen would unleash her full fury.

There was no time to lose. The concealed scouts had probably alerted the rest of the army. It was time to go. As I closed my eyes, my magic searched the ether until it locked onto Samantha's signature and threw my soul toward her.

Samantha

Cadean appeared in the shadows of the trees, and I rose from the outcrop where Sarion and I were hiding.

I joined him. "Is it time?"

"Almost."

His posture was tense, and his axe was in his hand—its presence always a bad sign. "Something's wrong. Tell me."

His eyes moved to mine, and his features softened. "Kassian

and Wulfric will be here shortly. They'll guide you out of the mist and to the border—but it's going to be a fight. The queen knows you're here, and her forces are waiting."

My hand tightened on the sword blade as my vow burned within me. "I will fucking kill her if she joins them."

"Don't be so eager to fight. This is the time to run. All that matters is that you return safely." His voice became gravel, and the intensity of his words sent a shiver down my skin. For a moment, he held my gaze, then looked away. "I never said I was sorry."

"For what?"

His chest rose and then fell with a heavy breath. "For pushing you to attack the vines in the Well of Life. I lost sight of what was important and what was right. I let my hatred for the fae and the queen consume me. I was out of line."

I glanced at the weapon in his hand. "I held the axe, and I felt its influence. I almost made the same choice."

"I cannot blame the axe. It is part of me, part of who I am." His face hardened with regret, and he dismissed it. "But I will never ask you to bear it again. And I will not hold it around you. You are too pure."

I looked down at the sword in my own hand. "I'm not pure. Not at all."

He growled. "Soon, we will both be able to lay our weapons down."

Would we? I wasn't so sure.

His gaze was mournful, almost tender, and I shifted uncomfortably. "Why are you looking at me like that?"

Cadean reached out and gently brushed his magic along my jawline. "I was thinking that very soon, I'll be able to really touch you."

I forced a smile. "You've given this quite some thought."

"I have."

The flutter rising in my belly only made the terror of what was coming next worse.

Fates, let me survive this.

Suddenly, I caught the scent of fae blood and spun, blade ready. "Someone's here."

"It's just Kassian," Cadean said. "But I'm glad you're on guard."

Moments later, the vampire stalked out of the fog with a bag slung over his shoulder. Fresh blood coated his hands and face, bringing me back to the impending shitstorm.

"Fang!" I said, embracing him. "I can't believe you escaped."

His posture was rigid, and he awkwardly patted my back. "I have a lot of spies in Auren's palace. Mainly, I was sticking around to keep an eye on you. It never occurred to me that you'd be insane enough to go into the fae realm."

"You always underestimated me," I said with a grin. My heart was aching. All these people who'd started as my enemies were now risking their lives to save me.

My throat tightened, and I looked away. I didn't deserve it.

He tossed me the small bag, casting a suspicious look at Sarion. "Clothes for you, and two potions, courtesy of Melanthe. They'll give you a boost of energy, and you're going to need it."

I passed one of the silver vials to Sarion and uncorked the other, swallowing the bitter liquid. It burned going down and curdled my empty stomach, but soon, I felt a surge of energy like I'd just had a long rest and drunk ten Monster energy drinks.

The rest of the bag contained a set of clean clothes—pants, boots, and a metal breastplate. I glanced up at Cadean. "Thank you."

He cleared his throat. "It's nothing."

But it wasn't. He knew what my ruined gown represented and whose blood stained it.

I disappeared behind a tree to change. I tore the silver dress off and left it where it lay, praying that one day, I could abandon the memories it represented just as easily.

When I rejoined the awkwardly waiting men, I was dressed in boots and pants, and for the first time in a while, feeling a little more like myself. "I'm ready."

Kassian snorted. "Hell, I'm not. But we're doing it, anyway."

We crept down the outcrop to where Wulfric was waiting with the striders. Elowyn clacked her beak when she spotted me, and my heart leapt.

"I missed you," I said, dragging my fingers through her soft feathers. She pawed the dirt and made a cooing sound.

Kassian crossed his arms. "We're going fast and hard. Sarion is on Darkwind—because he's going to be useless in his current condition—and you're on Elowyn. The queen's forces are hidden in plain sight with some kind of magic, so be prepared. It will likely be bloody."

"It's a cloaking spell," Sarion said. "It's dangerous, but the moment they move, they'll be exposed."

Kassian nodded. "Good to know. I'd never thought we'd end up fighting on the same side. Glad I didn't kill you."

"The feeling's mutual," Sarion said dryly.

Cadean moved close to me. "Today, you need to protect yourself, little wolf. Do not stop to fight unless there is no other option. Ride as hard as you can to the border. I will clear the way while the others keep the fae busy. Do not look back, just ride."

I glanced from Wulfric to Sarion, to Kassian, and then Elowyn. My chest tightened. If anything happened to one of them...

With a grunt, I slipped the general's blade—my blade—into a scabbard hanging from Elowyn's saddle. I hadn't left Sarion behind, and I wasn't going to do it to anyone else.

"Fuck the queen," I said. "Let's go."

Hatred coiled around my heart, and my palms began to glow.

Then Cadean's magic brushed across me, stirring my hair. "Fight like hell, little wolf. Make me proud."

My heart stuttered. I *did* want to make him proud.

Fates, I was fucked.

I steeled my nerve, wishing that he were going to be riding beside me. "I guess this is goodbye, then."

"Not goodbye. I'll be just on the other side, fighting for you. And I swear, I will not stop until you are safe."

He stepped back and faded into the shadows of night, and I closed my eyes. The vison from the swamp reappeared in my mind: my body broken and consumed by magic, him mourning at my side...

I shuddered.

I would not let that happen. Not today.

54

Samantha

Mounting up on Elowyn, I looked at the others. "How will we know when to go?"

Kassian chuckled. "It's Cadean. You'll know. Just ride like hell."

We moved through the trees in a tight formation, Kassian and the others taking up positions flanking me, pausing when we reached the point where the mists began to thin.

My body vibrated with adrenaline, and I dug my fingers into the feathers of Elowyn's neck to keep my arms from shaking as we waited, the torturous moments ticking by.

And then the storm erupted.

An earthquake of power swept through the forest, and the canopy above us swayed precariously. The trees bent and cracked, bowing away from us, and forming a tunnel through the forest, calling me home.

The striders bolted forward, their claws churning the rocky soil.

The mists faded away, and as we neared the tree line, a gust roared into us, flinging dried leaves and dirt through the air. I shielded my eyes with my arm. The striders pushed forward at unbelievable speed.

We burst out from our cover, and then I saw him. Not Cadean, but the Dark Wolf God.

He stood just beyond the barrier, arms outstretched. A swirling vortex of dark smoke rose around him. The storm exploded out from him like a tornado tearing across the battle-field, uprooting blades of dried grasses and whipping the trees around us.

He was the embodiment of both terror and beauty, a force of nature.

Where the storm hit, I saw fae appearing straight out of thin air in bursts of light—concealed warriors swept away by the wind.

And yet, like the eye of hurricane, the path before us was calm.

Elowyn charged into the chaos. I leaned forward in the saddle, one hand on the reins and the other gripping her feathers, as my body matched the rhythm of her powerful stride.

The air shimmered as more hidden fae soldiers on the path ahead flickered into existence, and a hail of arrows darkened the sky.

I summoned my shield, deflecting the barrage. Two arrows struck Sarion's strider in the flank to my left. The mighty beast roared but kept moving, undeterred by the wound.

Wulfric passed us and launched through the air, tackling a winged soldier who was beelining to Elowyn and me. They crashed to the ground, and Elowyn leapt over them.

I glanced over my shoulder at Wulfric, whose jaws were deep in the soldier's belly, and I felt no pity for the fae.

A fiery bolt of pain burst through my shoulder, knocking me forward in the saddle. I glanced down at the savage gash that glistened just beside the breastplate, trails of blood moving down my arm.

Deathwings dove toward us, their riders releasing another flight of arrows. Before I could switch my shield, a second arrow lodged in the saddle, pinning the edge of my pants. Elowyn veered to the right, trampling a screaming soldier as she evaded the barrage.

Fiery anger pumped through my veins, and I released a blast of moonlight. The descending arrows burst into flame as my magic consumed them, and then the sphere of crackling light wrapped around the deathwing and its rider. The winged beast screeched and flailed against the magic bonds, but with each movement, they closed more tightly. The pair spiraled from the sky and rammed into the ground with a sickening crunch.

I snapped my head forward. The barrier was right there. I bent forward in the saddle. We were so close.

The ground trembled and exploded ahead of us. Elowyn reared as the air shimmered and changed. A twisted coil of purple vines surged upward like a living throne, and atop the throne was a figure. The queen.

The overwhelming power of her signature rippled on the wind. My muscles tensed, and rage rose in me like molten lava, drowning my terror.

Her vines lashed out in all directions, crashing through Cadean's forces and clearing the space around us. "I will end you, you traitorous half-breed, just like I did your mother!"

Fury boiled my blood, and my vow of vengeance reverberated in my ears. I drew my sword, reciting each word again as a promise that I'd deliver with unwavering violence.

Kassian shouted something indiscernible, and Elowyn surged forward, veering around the queen and her writhing mass of vines.

The queen unleashed a torrent of purple flame, and I

summoned my shield. It billowed around us as I channeled my rage and hate. I would defy her power.

For a moment, my shield held, but then the consuming flames began draining my magic, and it faltered.

Cadean roared in fury, and the storm surged behind him. Smoky trails of darkness raced across the ground like ink running across a page. Ayanna's magic exploded outward, driving his shadows and storm winds back, matching his magic as if they were mirrors.

Could she truly have grown that strong? Impossible.

A brutal force slammed into my side, hurling me from the saddle. I summoned my shield at the last second, softening the impact of the ground. The breath exploded from my lungs, and the world swam.

Elowyn wheeled back toward me while Kassian charged the queen with his sword raised and his body painted in blood. Terror lanced my chest.

He couldn't take her on. Not alone.

I grasped for my fallen blade, but before I could stand, a thick vine wrapped around my chest, squeezing my ribs like a vise as I was plucked into the air.

Struggling and gasping for air, I tore into the vine with my claws as the queen slowly pulled me close to face her. "Now you will pay the price of treason."

Kassian leapt forward to cut the vines, but purple shoots sprang from the ground and flung him backward. Wulfric ripped through the base of the vine that held me, but more vines simply wound around my waist, and he was cast back just as Kassian had been.

The vines tightened, and stars began to swim through my vision.

My head rolled to the side, and I saw the shimmering wall and the Dark God fighting to get to me. Moonlight streamed off him like flames burning his skin. His feral cry shook the forest, thundering with rage and anguish, as if his very soul were being torn from his body.

Feebly, I reached out toward him. He was so *close*, yet impossibly far, trapped behind the barrier.

"I will drain you dry while he watches!" the queen screamed.

I felt the tendrils of her vines sucking the power from me, but I no longer cared. I wasn't listening to her.

He was the only thing I could see as darkness clouded the edges of my vision—the only thing that still mattered in the world, and he was killing himself trying to get to me.

"Cadean!"

A surge of power washed over me as if his very name were a spell, granting me strength. My vision cleared, and I knew what I had to do. In a moment's breath, I opened my palm and summoned the moonshard. The cool tingle of the Moon's magic entwined with my own, and I forgot everything but the sensation of her power and the glimmering beauty of the wall. It whispered to me in the wind, calling my name.

But this time, I called *it* to *me*.

Reaching out with my magic, I seized the barrier and pulled. It felt like the muscles of my arms were being torn off the bone, and I cried out at the searing pain. At first, it was like pulling a lead weight, but then, with a rumble, the dam broke.

The barrier rushed toward me in a tidal wave of light.

And in its wake, the Dark God charged, his black axe burning in one hand and the other reaching for me.

Ayanna wrenched me back from his grasp, but it was too late. Cadean seized hold of me, and in that moment, I knew that he would never let me go.

55

Samantha

The strength of Cadean's arms wrapped around me and pulled me through the barrier.

The familiar form and scent of his body flooded my senses. He wasn't a shadow. He wasn't an illusion. He was flesh and blood and holding me close. I should've been focused on the queen's magic crackling through the air, but in that instant, I let go of all my fear and horror as a single truth overwhelmed my thoughts: *I'm safe at last.*

Lightning split the air, and hellfire rained down around us. Vines whipped across the distance and twisted around Cadean's arms and legs, but he cleaved through them with his black axe as if they were nothing.

Deathwings dove from the sky, lashing out with their stingers. He hacked the wings from one, then spun to take the barb of another in his back. And through it all, he didn't let go. He was an ancient warrior god, an avatar of destruction and death. The shadows rose from him, fighting for him like nightmares brought to life.

But it wouldn't be enough—we were being overrun.

The vines parted, and the queen appeared. Her hand burned with purple flames—flames that hungered and hated and had taken my mother in a flash of light and ashes.

I squeezed my eyes shut and grasped for the radiance of the wall, drawing it in until I was bursting like the sun.

Cadean had become my shield in the darkness. Now, I had to be his.

My eyes flew open as the flames leapt from the queen's fingers, spiraling and spinning toward us, but I had no fear as my purpose thrummed through me.

Protect him.

Moonlight exploded through me, racing though my veins like geysers of steam. I claimed my power and seized control of the wall. It rippled with a wave of golden light, and in a sudden flash, it crystallized into glass.

The queen's spell crashed into it and erupted in a billowing swath of purple flames.

I felt the shuddering impact like it was my own body, but I was stronger. The tempest of the queen's magic raged beyond the wall, burning and destroying everything it touched, but on our side, all was still. A sudden quiet slipped over the battlefield.

"Fates," Cadean whispered in disbelief.

Lifeless vines lay around our feet, cut through by the wall. Deathwings and vines battered against the crystalline barrier, but they couldn't get through. Nothing could but the faint echoes of the chaos beyond.

A sudden fear lanced through my heart. Anyone trapped on the other side was as good as dead.

I pushed away from Cadean and started shouting for my friends.

Kassian shoved aside the corpse of a broodling, then slammed his blade into another of the monsters that I'd trapped on our side. "Some of us are still working, here!"

Cadean sprang forward and cut the beast down with two blows. "Find Wulfric and the others. Get everyone away from the barrier."

"Melanthe! Sarion!" I yelled. "We've got to get away from here, now!"

Mel's voice echoed from my right. "I have Sarion. He's alive—barely."

Another wave of magic hit the wall, and I staggered. Doubt and terror rooted in my gut. "I can't hold it much longer!"

"Get the striders and take the wounded away!" Cadean ordered.

I looked up and froze. The queen hovered just beyond the barrier on long, lacelike wings, her form shimmering and reflecting through the facets of the crystalline structure. Vines spiraled around her, weaving together into giant asps that loomed overhead.

Her lips curled into a wicked smile. "I know you, Samantha. I tasted your power when I tore it from you. You are weak. The wall will fall, and when it does, my legions will kill every shifter in his lands, and I will destroy everything you love."

A wall of black flames leapt into the air between us, and Cadean stepped in front of me, axe raised. "If the wall falls, you will die the moment you cross, Ayanna."

"You have such strong faith in weakness, Cadean—you are no longer the god you used to be. We are matched."

Dark shadows wrapped around her wings, and the trees bowed to her.

The truth became poison, burning my soul.

The queen had been stealing his magic for centuries. It was how she controlled and healed the vines, and the dark storm building behind her was just like Cadean's magic.

But could she really match him in power?

She slammed her hands against the barrier, and purple

lightning raced along the facets of crystal. Pain erupted through my body, and I stumbled.

She laughed. "You've already lost, you just don't realize it yet."

Cadean reached out to steady me, but I pulled away from his grasp and slammed my hands against the wall, mirroring hers. I poured all the power and resolve I had left into the barrier. *Protect us. Protect the Dreamlands. That's what you were created to do.*

The crystalline wall shuddered beneath my touch, and light built around my fingertips. It flared until the whole world was bright and silent but for my own words echoing back to me, over and over.

Protect the Dreamlands. That's what you were created to do.

This time, it wasn't my voice speaking, but a thousand whispers riding on the wind, calling to me. Cadean was gone, and the queen was gone. There was only the blinding light and the hushed voices.

"What do you mean? What am I supposed to do? How can I hold back her magic?"

We are broken like you. We cannot hold.

The voices became a whirlwind overwhelming my mind. I cried out and dropped to my knees.

Heal us. Free us.

The light faded, and Cadean grabbed my arm. "What happened. Are you okay?"

I shook my head as he helped me up. "Take me south, to the pylons. I know what I need to do."

"Grab around my neck and hold on tight. I'll carry you."

Before I could respond, his body exploded into a billowing cloud of darkness. He coalesced into the towering form of a dire wolf with fur woven of streams of shadow and smoke. When he looked at me with his savage yellow eyes, I couldn't help but shudder with uncontrollable, primal dread. I was a wolf, but he was nightmare made manifest—a beast summoned from the depths of darkness and legend. And now he was mine to ride.

He knelt before me, and swallowing my fear, I grasped the fur of his neck and swung myself up onto his back.

I pitched forward as the wall shuddered beneath another barrage of purple flame.

"Run, little wolf!" The queen laughed. "You cannot hide forever. This kingdom will be mine!"

Cadean surged forward. I flattened myself against his neck and dug my fingers into his fur. I tried syncing myself with the motion of his stride, but he was moving so quickly, it was all I could do to hold on.

The grasping limbs of dead trees flashed by as we raced through the twisted forest. I kept my face hidden. One misstep would break my neck, while a stray branch would run me through.

"You're going to get me killed!" I shouted as we cleared a ravine.

The black wolf growled, and a wave of shadow magic exploded ahead of us, devouring the forest, and sweeping the dead and dying trees away. Fragments of broken branches and bark hurtled over my head.

He accelerated, and then, with a sudden jolt, he leapt into the air. My heart thudded in my chest as his form shifted beneath me. The fur in my hands erupted into feathers, and after a few moments, when I was certain I wasn't plummeting to my death, I raised my head and looked around.

My stomach dropped, and I clung to him more tightly. The forest of dying trees raced by a thousand feet below. Cadean had become a giant phoenix—not glowing red like a fire, but black as coal. His feathers faded into streams of shadow that trailed behind us like flames.

Wind whipped at my hair as he climbed into the sky and soared southward, away from the queen and the wall and the wreckage of the battlefield beyond.

The patchwork islands of his lands flashed by below—forests and mountains, heather and marsh, all divided by lines of mist. Beyond them, a shimmering sea faded into endless fog. His realm was impossible and breathtakingly beautiful, all at once.

My soul spun in wonder. Cadean had made all of it—and now, I had to save it.

I looked back over my shoulder. How much of the barrier had I crystalized, and how much of it could the queen and her soldiers still cross?

Ahead of us, the three pillars of light that powered the walls of his prison rose into the sky. But they were broken. When I'd first seen the moonshard, Cadean had told me that he'd spent a year attacking the pylons after he'd been imprisoned. It had nearly killed him, and all he'd been able to do was break off a single fragment.

This was the wound that the voices were calling me to heal. I knew it in my heart.

I leaned low and shouted, "Take me to the pylon that you attacked—the one you took the moonshard from!"

Cadean banked slightly to the left, toward the beam of light rising from the ruins of a castle. It was the same pylon where he'd brought me once to practice, what felt like a lifetime ago.

A sudden force slammed into my back, and I lurched forward. The pain was dull and distant, but I knew what it was: the queen was attacking the barrier again. How much more could it take?

I gritted my teeth against the onslaught. "Hurry!"

Cadean sped against the wind. As soon as the castle came into view, he tucked his wings, and we began falling, faster and faster. I buried my face in his back and fought my terror. A jolt rocked my body as he extended his wings, and we spiraled down in the center of the ruin. At the last second, Cadean's form dissolved into smoke and shadow. I gasped as I dropped into the cradle of his powerful arms.

He gave me a worried look as he set me on my feet. "I've done what I can. This next part's all you."

The strained lines of his face reminded me how much it hurt him to be in the presence of the Moon's power. I squeezed his forearm. "Get back."

I ran toward the pylon, a floating white orb that emitted the pillar of light. I desperately searched the surface for the break Cadean had made. The whispers rose around me until they became like the roar of the ocean: *Heal us, Samantha. Release us.*

My heart fluttered as I found a knife-like cleft in the stone. I summoned the moonshard from the ether as Cadean had taught me and turned it over in my hand. This had better fucking work.

I jammed the moonshard in the crevice and poured my magic into the orb, trying to heal the pylon the way I'd healed Cadean of his curse. I envisioned it perfect and complete, just as the Moon had made it a thousand years ago. *Be whole.*

My magic danced over the surface, but the crack didn't seal beneath my fingers. I closed my eyes and pushed harder.

Heal. Protect this realm. Become what you were created to be.

The whispers danced through my head, echoing my own words back to me. *Become what you were created to be.*

The stone blazed with heat. My magic flowed faster and faster until I was no longer pushing, but it was being torn from me—just like the queen had done.

This time, instead of fighting, I let go, and it emptied me completely.

The stone released a thundering crack, and the fissure sealed shut. The darkness behind my eyes went white, and when I opened them and looked around, the world was gone. There was only an endless expanse of light and three stone orbs, no longer separated by miles, but by a few yards.

The Moon's magic thrummed in the air, but something about it was different. It had changed. I felt a connection I'd never had before, like it had become a part of me. Like it was flowing through me, calling to me to shape it.

Taking a deep breath, I rooted my feet and placed both hands against the orb. "I healed you. Now I need you to protect this land."

Protect this land... the whispers repeated.

"Change," I commanded.

A surge of power and sensation overwhelmed me. Suddenly, the barrier and my body were one—I could feel every point where a tree brushed against it, every stone and blade of grass. For one final moment, I was pure light. And then a limitless wave of magic ignited through me, shaping the barrier into pure crystal.

Pain erupted through me, like I was being torn apart, and the world went white as my mind plunged into infinite darkness.

56

———————

Samantha

I was warm. The searing pain of moonlight was gone, and a gentle weight rested on my shoulder.

Cadean.

His signature wove all around me, the sweet taste of chocolate and the welcoming scent of a woodfire in winter.

The world blurred as I opened my eyes, then began to take shape. The silhouette of the Dark God leaned forward. "You're awake."

"Where am I?"

His brow creased with concern. "Safe, in Shadowstone."

I pulled the blankets around me and sat up. I was wearing a white nightgown. My head swam, and Cadean steadied me as I reeled. The light press of his fingers sent a shiver down my spine.

He was real.

The pleasure of his touch made the pain coursing through my body only that much worse by contrast. My skin was sore and tender, like I'd fallen asleep sunbathing, and every single part of my body ached with exhaustion.

But none of that mattered. I grabbed his forearm. "The queen—"

"Is on the other side of the barrier. She can't get to you. You're safe."

"Mel and the others? Sarion?"

Cadean gently brushed a strand of hair from my face. "They're all a little worse for wear but fine. You don't need to worry."

I breathed a sigh of relief, but his forearm tensed beneath my fingers. "Mel says you're lucky to be alive."

By the way I felt right now, I believed it. "What happened out there?"

His face hardened with an unreadable expression. "You channeled divine magic. Mortals aren't meant to wield that kind of power. It could have killed you."

Mortals. It was a stark reminder of how differently he saw me. How fundamentally different we were—a god and a woman who was doomed to die.

I shoved the thought away. "Apparently, I'm hard to kill."

He pulled his arm back to take my hand. "Don't joke. Your clothes burst into flames, and you collapsed, screaming. You were covered head to toe with burns, and I had to heal you on the spot, or you *would* have died. You cannot channel power like that again, do you understand? If anything had happened—" His voice cut out, and he looked away for a second. "You're lucky it was only burns."

I slipped my hand out of his grasp and touched my shoulder. The skin was smooth, but it stung, like my fingers were made of ice. I reached up to my hair. It was way shorter than before. "Fuck..."

"Don't worry, I'll help you heal." He pulled my hand away and took it in his. "And you still look as beautiful as ever.

I gave him a weak smile.

His shoulders tensed, and he stood, pacing to the window and gripping the frame like he wanted to pull it from the wall. "I thought you were just trying to heal the pylon. I didn't think you were going to try to *control* the damn thing. I would have forbidden it. I should have forb—"

"I wouldn't have listened."

His jaw hardened. "I doubt that you would have, but—"

"But I lived. What happened to me doesn't matter. I need to know—*did it work*?"

For a long moment, he remained silent, looking out toward the horizon. Then he whispered, "It worked."

Relief flooded through me.

Cadean turned and locked me with his eyes. "I never imagined anything like that was possible—the whole barrier turned to crystal. The queen has been attacking it with her magic and war machines, but it hasn't cracked. Her forces can't enter my realm, and the wall cut through all the vines. She can't drain the life from my land or my power anymore."

I closed my eyes and recited a silent prayer of thanks to the Moon Mother. It was more than I'd even hoped for.

Yet the consequences began to dawn on me.

I'd sealed off his land completely. I met his gaze as my stomach tumbled. "Was your army trapped in her realm? What about your people? You once told me that you didn't want to build a wall because the shifters hunted on both sides of the border, and that animals migrate between the patches..."

"I sent raiders over the border, but they pulled back to lure her army away from you. As for me not wanting to build a wall, nothing I could have created would have kept the vines or death-wings out. But your wall does." He sat and took my hand. "You protected my people and lands from her—something I haven't been able to do for hundreds of years."

I shook my head. "I did it without asking, and now everyone is trapped inside."

"The people living in the borderlands have been trapped by fear for years. Today, they are free." He cupped my chin and rubbed his thumb across my cheekbone. "You've given me my land and magic back, Samantha. Today was the first day in centuries that I didn't wake up wondering what part of my realm she'd attack, or how many were dead. I woke stronger, and the land is stronger. I don't know how I can repay you for that."

I looked away, too overwhelmed to speak. Selene and Sigrun and their people were safe from the queen, and the fae were safe from Cadean. Somehow, I'd halted the war—at least, for now.

I looked into the limitless blue of the Dark God's eyes. "You know the queen isn't going to stop. She wants your power, Cadean. She wants to consume this land."

"Perhaps. But for the moment, the land and people have time to heal. And you can heal as well. You've done enough, more than I could have asked of you."

He traced the back of his fingers down my arm, and my skin tingled with delight. His magic wrapped around me, flowing through my limbs in cool, sensuous waves. My burns began to heal, and the lingering pain started to fade.

Every fiber of my body responded, pulling me toward him with relentless gravity, but I pressed my hand against his chest. "Stop."

His magic slowed, and he cocked his head. "I need to heal you. You wince every time you move."

"You know what your magic does to me. It's like a drug, filling me with desires that I can't resist." I leaned forward and brushed my lips against his ear. "And you can't resist, either."

He straightened his back and let his hand fall away. "I'm sorry. I wasn't trying to..."

I pressed my palm to his chest, feeling the steady thrum of

his heart. "I don't want what happens next to be because of your magic, or mine. I want you to know that I want it, that I need it, and that it's not the illusion of any spell."

His heartbeat quickened beneath my fingers, and he dipped his forehead to mine. "You're still in pain. I do not want to hurt you, little wolf."

I let the blanket fall away. "Every time you touch me, I forget my pain. Touch me, Cadean. Touch me everywhere."

57

———

Cadean

Fates, this woman was going to undo me.

The truth was, I'd accepted that fate already. She was mine, and I was hers. The hell with fate. But I needed her to be sure what she was signing up for.

"I can touch you, but I want more, Samantha. I want all of you. Once you let me have you, once I've been inside of you, there will be no going back. You will be mine, just as I will be yours. If you're not ready for that, little wolf. I can take care of you in other ways."

She crawled to her knees and looked up at me, tenderness and longing in her eyes. "I think I've always been yours, Cadean. I've tried to fight it, I've tried to deny it, but I can't any longer. I just know that you are what I want and what I need, for however long I'm on this earth."

I sensed the sadness that rose beneath her skin, and it lanced my chest. What she meant was that we didn't have long together. And she was right. Even if she lived a full life, she would still be gone in the blink of an eye.

I pushed away the darkness that crept in and gently cradled

her cheek. "I'm not going to let anything happen to you, little wolf."

I would cherish her. Protect her. And worship her for as long as I had her.

She took my hand and slowly moved it down her chest. "I need you. I want to feel you for real. I want you to take me in every way."

I undid the tie on her linen shift, the sheer fabric parting and revealing the creamy skin between her breasts. Her nipples were hard and demanding my attention. "I hope you know what you're asking."

Her skin pebbled under my gaze. "What do you mean?"

"I'm going to worship every inch of this perfect little body and find out what makes you lose control. And then I won't stop until you're weak with pleasure." I slid the hem of her shift up her thigh, my fingers grazing her heated flesh. "We're going to be in here a while."

A coy smile tugged on her lips, and her desire wrapped around me. "Then what are you waiting for?"

"I need you to tell me that this is what you want. That you understand what this means."

"Gods, yes, Cadean. Make love to me. Unlike a god, I don't have long, and I want to make every moment count." She leaned forward and took my mouth in hers.

Her lips were hungry, desperate. She tasted of forbidden fruit, ripe and tempting, demanding to be devoured.

I pulled her shift over her head and tossed it aside as I scooped her up and laid her on the bed. The sight of her naked and sprawled out before me awakened a primal heat. I'd never seen anything so beautiful in all my time. My gaze drifted over her luscious curves, each demanding to be explored. "Fates, woman. You're perfect."

I crawled over her and, with a flick of my tongue, took her

nipple in my mouth. She moaned, her back arching in pleasure. Her skin tasted like honey, sweet and intoxicating. I moved down her belly, pressing soft kisses to every dip and curve, tasting and inhaling her heady essence. My cock throbbed, but I wanted my little wolf wet and ready before I took her.

I grabbed her legs and tugged her to the edge of the bed, and kneeling before her, I met her gaze with a wolfish grin. "I've been dreaming about tasting you."

Her pulse quickened. "Then do it."

She kept her eyes on me, whimpering with pleasure, as I dragged my tongue through her soft folds. Her smooth skin felt like warm silk against my tongue, and the taste of her desire left me aching with need. I memorized each movement, remembering what she liked, what made her purr. It didn't take long before her hips were arching, and her fists were clenching the fur blanket. I sucked and licked, giving extra attention to that small bundle of nerves.

"Fates, Cadean. I'm going to—"

She grabbed hold of my hair and screamed as her climax tore through her. Her legs shook, and her body trembled. When she finally came down, she sat up on the edge of the bed and looked down at me with hooded eyes.

Her expression was unreadable.

She pulled my tunic over my head and slowly traced her fingertips over the tattoos on my chest. "You are a god."

Her touch was warm and electric, and my cock strained against my pants. Between her coming on my face and tasting her desire, I needed to be inside her.

Her brows pinched together. "Do you not like it when I touch you?"

"Gods, no. I've wanted this for months. I've never been so hard, and I don't know how long I can last."

A playful smile parted her lips. "It's a good thing we'll be here for a while, then."

With a gentle tug, she guided me so I was standing before her. She undid the buttons of my pants, and I shoved them off, freeing my length.

She blushed as she took me in, a mixture of desire and apprehension flashing in her beautiful eyes. "You haven't been the only one dreaming of things," she said, her gaze smoldering.

The scent of her rising desire was doing torturous things to me. "Your gaze alone will undo me, little wolf."

She grinned up at me as she wrapped one hand around my shaft and stroked upward. A bead of precum glistened on the tip.

"Fuck," I groaned, tilting my head back. "I was wrong. This. This will undo me."

Her touch was exquisite, but when she leaned forward and dragged her tongue along the base of my shaft, I nearly lost it.

She took all of me that would fit in her mouth, and I let out a low, guttural moan. The sight of her lips wrapped around me, desire thick in her eyes, was an image I'd never forget. I kept my gaze on hers as she moved her mouth, doing things with her warm and embracing tongue that sent a possessive heat through me.

Fates, *this woman*.

With each wet descent of her lips, my muscles tightened, and the tension built. As if sensing my impending release, she took me deeper into the soft bed of her mouth, her eyes pricking with tears. I wanted to hold on to this moment, but I couldn't last a second longer. My fingers wrapped in her hair as I exploded in her mouth, tremors of ecstasy pulsing through me as she swallowed my release like a greedy little wolf.

When I was finished, she sat back and grinned. The sight of her slowly wiping the traces of me off her bottom lip with her thumb stoked a renewed heat within me, and I nearly lost my mind as she sucked it off.

"I don't want to know how you learned to do those things." I slipped my arm around her waist and rolled her onto the bed. The thought of her mouth on any other man awoke murderous thoughts.

"I'm no virgin, Cadean," the little minx said, giggling and shifting her hips under me so my cock pressed up against her heat.

"No, you're not." I brushed my knuckles along her collarbone, dragging them down her chest under the curve of her breast. I was already hard again and ready for her. "I don't care as long as I'm the last man who gets to be inside of you."

A sinful grin tugged on her swollen lips. "You know that you have an unhealthy degree of possessiveness, right?"

I kissed her neck, licking the sweat off her heated skin as I lined up my length with her entrance. "Only with what is mine."

Her breath quickened, and she arched her hips, her taut little body opening up for me. "Then take what is yours and do it now."

I grinned down at her. She was exquisite. And her body was ready for me, begging me to fill her.

I slowly guided myself into the soft folds between her legs. "Fuck. You feel divine."

It was a mercy she'd consumed me already with her luscious mouth, because she was so hot and wet, it would have taken a miracle not to lose it right there.

She gasped, and I paused, worried that I'd hurt her. But her hands gripped my hips and pulled me closer. "Don't stop, Cadean. I want all of you."

Her words were all I needed. I slid all the way inside her, and a deep, involuntary sound escaped my throat. Her heat sent pleasure rippling up my spine, and my cock throbbed.

Needing to be deeper, I brought one of her knees up and buried myself in her again. Her head fell back, pleasure parting her lips in a soft moan. And then her body was moving under me, her hips meeting my thrusts.

It was more than sex, more than simple passion. I'd known it would be. This woman had become my everything.

She flipped us over and straddled my lap, my cock still deep inside her. I gripped her ass, guiding her hips as they drove into me. I loved that she took what she wanted.

"You feel so good, Cadean. I don't think I can last." Her words flashed against my skin. By the way her legs were trembling, I knew she was seconds away.

"That's right, little wolf. I want to feel you come apart around me."

Her eyes closed halfway, and her lips parted in pleasure as I carried her over the edge. She cried out, her hips driving home and chasing the release. The feel of her clenching around my cock was all it took. My vision went dark, and my body tensed as the most intense ecstasy I'd ever felt coursed through me.

This woman. Fuck. She had no idea the power she wielded over me. She would break me or save me, and I was utterly powerless to decide which. All I was certain of was that she was mine.

I cupped her cheek and brushed my thumb over her lip. "The oracle was right. You've brought me to my knees. I cannot resist you."

Her lips pulled into a wicked smile, and she kissed me softly. "If I'd known what it took to tame you, I would have done it sooner."

I rolled us onto the bed and claimed her mouth as I slowly pulled out of her. "That would have saved us a lot of trouble."

She laughed as she scooted up in front of me. "If only we could solve all our problems in the bedroom."

I slid my palm over her belly and pulled her back against me, burying my face in her neck. "Maybe we should."

"Fates, I wish that were possible." She settled in against me and placed her hand over mine, sobering. "I may be yours, Cadean, but I'll never stop fighting for what I think is right. If that means fighting you, I will."

Her tone was determined and calm, but I sensed the undercurrent of sadness.

So many barriers still lay between us. The fate of the fae, the vines, and my freedom. I knew she would not yield.

"I don't expect you stop." I pressed a kiss under her earlobe, delighting in the way her skin pebbled under my touch. "You promised me that a long time ago."

Her resolve never ceased to surprise me. My beautiful little wolf was loyal and fierce. Our goals weren't aligned, and they probably never would be.

But she'd claimed me, just as I had claimed her—and nothing would change that. We would find a way to keep our truce, fates be damned.

58

Soft sunlight warmed my cheeks, and my eyes fluttered open. Cadean's blurry form came into focus, lying right beside me.

Well, there's no question of whose side I'm on now.

I braced myself for the sting of terror or regret, but it didn't come. Rather, I felt more at peace than ever, just lying there, watching his chest rise and fall with steady, shallow breaths. Careful not to wake him, I gently traced my fingers over his sunlit shoulders and savored the hardness of his muscles and the subtle texture of his skin. He'd been a shadow for so long, I could still barely believe he was real.

The truth was that I cared for him. Perhaps I was even falling in love with him.

A torrent of conflicting emotions welled up inside of me, and suddenly, it became a little difficult to breathe.

The question of the other half of the oracle's prophecy hung over us like a sword. His freedom.

I knew he would ask me to release his bonds. I didn't have any idea how, but that didn't matter. No matter what I felt for him, no matter how much the thought of him trapped here hurt me, I couldn't consider it.

Millennia of beliefs have shaped who he is and what he is striving for. My brother would annihilate civilization and return the land to a feral, untamed state.

I despised Auren, but I knew his warning held a grain of truth. There was a darkness to Cadean. I'd seen it in the Well of Life, and I couldn't unleash that on the world.

Overwhelmed, I pushed back the heavy fur blanket and sat up. A wave of exhaustion washed over me, and I had to brace my hand on the mattress to offset the sudden vertigo. Apparently, raising the barrier had really taken it out of me—though the night spent making love to a god probably hadn't hurt my recovery.

The corner of my lips twitched up with a hint of satisfaction, but I couldn't so easily shake off the doubts building within me.

I stood and pulled on a fur robe.

Even if we could somehow put our differences aside, what kind of life would I make with him? I was a mortal, and he was a *god*. I would be doomed to wither away and die while he stayed eternally young.

Hell, I didn't even know if I entirely trusted him. Back in the Well of Life, he'd been ready to doom an entire people to death. That darkness was very much a part of him, and it wasn't something I could ignore—or forgive.

But he was also *Cadean*.

I looked back and traced my eyes over the hard shape of his shoulders and perfect lines of his jaw. When he was sleeping, he was no longer a terrible warlord or fearsome god of death, but a man. And when I was with him, I felt safe. He'd always been there in the darkness, watching over me. And when my mother...

My throat knotted, and I closed my eyes for a moment. That was a pain I wasn't ready to bear.

But Cadean hadn't expected any tears. He'd taken my anger and helped me forge it into something sharper that I could carry with me. No one else would have understood what I needed in that moment—and I thanked him a million times over for that.

I'd cry when I had my vengeance. And I would have my vengeance for my mother, and for all the other lives the queen and her court had destroyed.

I strode out on the wide balcony and stared out across his lands. The shimmering wall of light was gone, replaced by the faint glitter of the crystal dome arching high over his realm.

After a time, a pair of strong arms wrapped around me, and Cadean kissed my neck. "It's still standing. My people are safe."

"It's not enough." I turned in his arms and looked up into his sky blue eyes. "Beyond that wall, there are tens of thousands of fae people still suffering beneath her thumb. The erdelfen, the enslaved denizens of the undercity, even the high fae themselves. They are all victims of her rule."

There was a pregnant pause. I knew that he didn't agree with me on that, and perhaps he never would. That would be a discussion for another time.

He dipped his head and pressed a kiss to my neck. "You nearly died yesterday. You've done enough for now."

But it wasn't true. Deep in my soul, I knew that I hadn't fulfilled my purpose—that I hadn't even begun.

"What will the queen and her court do now that her vines are cut off from your realm? Will they spread into Auren's land, or will she turn them on her own?"

"If she does, it's not our concern. Auren is a traitor, and so are the people living in her realm."

I slipped out of his arms. "You made those lands, Cadean.

You may not be able to reach them, but they are still yours. And the people who live there are yours."

The line of his jaw hardened. I could sense his regret but also the scars of betrayal. "Can you not be happy with the victory you have earned?"

I shook my head. "The queen may be far stronger than I could ever hope to be, but I will find a way to stop her. I will find a way to protect those people."

Turning my back on him, I braced myself against the edge of the balcony and glared at the lands beyond the wall. "I made an oath to the gods of vengeance to destroy her, Cadean, and gods damn it, I will keep it, even if it kills me in the end."

Thank you so much for sharing this journey with us! You can anticipate a quest for vengeance, heated romance, and an epic finale in the third (and final) book of this series: *Forsaken Fate*. It will arrive in Fall 2023, but you can preorder it now (https:// mybook.to/Forsaken-Fate).

If you'd like writing updates, sneak peeks, early cover reveals, and alerts for new releases and giveaways, you can sign up for the Veronica Douglas newsletter here: https://www.veroni cadouglas.com/newsletter. We also have a Facebook Reader group (Veronica Douglas' Magic Side Insiders) where you can talk about books and interact with fellow readers: https://www. facebook.com/groups/veronicadouglas

And finally, if you would like to learn more about Samantha and the events leading up to *Wolf God*, she first appears here, in the *Wolf Bound* series: http://mybook.to/Wolf-Marked

Thanks for reading!

-Veronica

FORSAKEN FATE

RUTHLESS GODS: WOLF GOD BOOK 3

VERONICA DOUGLAS

FORSAKEN FATE
Ruthless Gods: Wolf God, Book 3

∼

Prepare for the the epic conclusion to Samantha and Cadean's story.

Expect vengeance, romance, and a dark destiny finally fulfilled.

∼

Coming Fall, 2023: mybook.to/Forsaken-Fate

ACKNOWLEDGMENTS

First off, we would like to thank all our readers for their amazing patience—this book was written during a complicated stretch of our lives and took a little longer than normal, but we hope it was worth the wait!

Thank you to Ash Fitzsimmons and Lexi George for your patience, flexibility, and amazing editing skills!

Thank you to the amazing readers on our advanced review team, with extra thanks to Penny, Sarah, Amanda, Tara, and Lynn! We love your feedback and appreciate your sharp eyes!

Many thanks to Amber Garcia for keeping us rolling, and lightening the load when we had to lock ourselves away and write. And thanks to Caethes Faron, for her insightful analysis and support. We'd be lost without you both.

Thank you to JV Arts for designing the beautiful sword and axe covers for the series. We want to also give a shoutout to JoY Author Design for creating the gorgeous character art and alternate covers that truly inspired our writing!

ABOUT VERONICA DOUGLAS

Veronica Douglas is a duo of professional archaeologists that love writing and digging together. After spending an inordinate amount of time doing painstaking research for academia, they suddenly discovered a passion for letting their imaginations go wild! A cocktail of magic, romance, and ancient mystery (shaken, not stirred), their books are inspired, in part, by their life in Chicago and their archaeological adventures from around the globe.

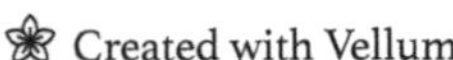 Created with Vellum